Praise for
MY IMMORTAL

"A sexy and oddly poignant tale of lust, love, and redemption."
—*Booklist*

"Well-written . . . thought-provoking, fabulous."
—*Midwest Book Review*

"Intriguing, entrancing, and enrapturing!"
—*The Romance Readers Connection*

"The writing is seamless, the story a page-turner, and the romance is one to defy all odds."
—*Romance Reviews Today* (A Perfect Ten)

"Sultry, steamy New Orleans is the perfect setting for Erin McCarthy's story of shocking sin and stunning sensuality."
—*USA Today* bestselling author Rebecca York

FALLEN

ERIN McCARTHY

JOVE BOOKS, NEW YORK

THE BERKLEY PUBLISHING GROUP
Published by the Penguin Group
Penguin Group (USA) Inc.
375 Hudson Street, New York, New York 10014, USA
Penguin Group (Canada), 90 Eglinton Avenue East, Suite 700, Toronto, Ontario M4P 2Y3, Canada
(a division of Pearson Penguin Canada Inc.)
Penguin Books Ltd., 80 Strand, London WC2R 0RL, England
Penguin Group Ireland, 25 St. Stephen's Green, Dublin 2, Ireland (a division of Penguin Books Ltd.)
Penguin Group (Australia), 250 Camberwell Road, Camberwell, Victoria 3124, Australia
(a division of Pearson Australia Group Pty. Ltd.)
Penguin Books India Pvt. Ltd., 11 Community Centre, Panchsheel Park, New Delhi—110 017, India
Penguin Group (NZ), 67 Apollo Drive, Rosedale, North Shore 0632, New Zealand
(a division of Pearson New Zealand Ltd.)
Penguin Books (South Africa) (Pty.) Ltd., 24 Sturdee Avenue, Rosebank, Johannesburg 2196,
South Africa

Penguin Books Ltd., Registered Offices: 80 Strand, London WC2R 0RL, England

This is a work of fiction. Names, characters, places, and incidents either are the product of the author's imagination or are used fictitiously, and any resemblance to actual persons, living or dead, business establishments, events, or locales is entirely coincidental. The publisher does not have any control over and does not assume any responsibility for author or third-party websites or their content.

FALLEN

A Jove Book / published by arrangement with the author

PRINTING HISTORY
Jove mass-market edition / May 2008

ISBN: 978-0-515-14462-8

JOVE®
Jove Books are published by The Berkley Publishing Group,
a division of Penguin Group (USA) Inc.,
375 Hudson Street, New York, New York 10014.
JOVE is a registered trademark of Penguin Group (USA) Inc.
The "J" design is a trademark belonging to Penguin Group (USA) Inc.

PRINTED IN THE UNITED STATES OF AMERICA

10 9 8 7 6 5 4 3 2 1

For the city of New Orleans
and all my friends there

ACKNOWLEDGMENTS

Special thanks to the following:

Christy Carlson, for helping me fill in plot points over French baguettes on Royal Street, and for reading along as I wrote. I truly appreciate your encouragement and your friendship.

Michael, for Chopin.

Kathy Love, for being the friend that's there every day, in every way. This book wouldn't exist without you.

Prologue

❦

NEW ORLEANS, 1849

Anne Donovan would do anything for John Thiroux.

She would die for him.

Sitting in front of the cracked mirror Madame had provided for her in the tiny, shabby room that was hers based on the fact that John paid to keep her available, Anne brushed her auburn hair. Embracing the familiar tingle in her body, the heaviness in her breasts, the ache between her thighs that always arose when she thought of her lover, she sighed with contentment, anticipation. John was everything to her, an absolute angel of a man, and she was completely and utterly in love with him. He had saved her from the steady stream of anonymous men she'd previously had to endure in various bawdy houses to stay off the streets, and his favor allowed her to send money to her cousin for her daughter's upkeep. It was true she'd had a private benefactor prior to John, but that one had been an oddity, and Anne had been grateful to exchange him for the beauty and passion of her current lover.

The knock on her door cut through her lazy daydreaming and had her pushing her chair back and hastily dropping the tarnished hairbrush down on the vanity table next to her rouge. She wasn't ready. She didn't have John's tray set with his drink poured, pipe out, his favorite spoon lying next to the bottle. Panicked at the thought of doing anything less than pleasing him entirely, Anne was yanking at the bodice of her gown to adjust it and rushing across the room when Madame popped her head in. Relief flooded her for a brief, glorious minute, until she heard the woman's words.

"I'm sending a gentleman in to see you."

Fear slid overtop of her relief, as Anne stared at Madame's round, fleshy, dissolute face. The phrase felt foreign, unheard for months, familiar in the sick pit it created in the depths of her stomach. "What? You can't mean . . ." Her heart pounded at the thought of pleasuring another man besides John. Touching a stranger, taking him into her mouth and body, enduring the strain of humiliation, revulsion. She had thought that behind her. "John . . ."

"Mr. Thiroux requested this," Madame said with a wink. "He's in a strange mood tonight, honey, drunk already, and asked to watch you in play with his gentleman friend."

That gave her pause. John had never made such a request before, but then again, she did recall him mentioning that he enjoyed the fact that she'd known so many men, that she had her choice of protectors, and yet preferred his body to others. He often talked at length about how she would one day tire of him and seek another, which she knew beyond a doubt she never would. Her heart, her soul, belonged to him, and she craved him, ached for his approval, burned for his body, longed for his love.

She stood indecisively. Decisions were not her strong suit. She'd made a significant number of poor ones, the succession of which had led her to the unfortunate lifestyle she had found herself in prior to meeting John. Yet none so important as this decision now, because she could not jeopardize her position with him. "I don't know . . . that doesn't seem . . ."

"Would you want to anger him?" Madame demanded. "Ruin a good thing for you and me? You don't have a choice. This man is an artist, like Mr. Thiroux. He'll be gentle, and he'll be here in two minutes. Remove your gown and save some time."

Though it still seemed as though this could be a mistake,

Anne hastened to obey as the door closed. She would do anything John wanted. Anything. She would die for him.

⚜

Gabriel St. John knew that he was fallen. From angel to demon, favorite to disdained, he embraced the change, welcomed the passion, wallowed in the ecstasy he found day after day in the bottom of the bottle, and night after night in the arms of his favorite whore. In the two years of his tenure walking the earth as a Watcher, he had absorbed the stench and pain of human misery surrounding him until he could no longer suffer the helplessness and hopelessness they brought upon him. Their sad, desperate, begging eyes were a much easier burden to bear when his over-heightened angelic senses were dulled from vast quantities of whiskey, opium, and the beautiful green fairy of absinthe he had come to adore. It was a drink he had come to worship, to crave with every ounce of his preternatural essence. His absinthe was his clarity, his respite, his one true love.

"Good evenin', Mr. Thiroux," a stout woman in full-blown scarlet silk said to him.

Gabriel stepped inside the parlor, such as it was, of the House of Rest for Weary Men. The name of the two-bit bordello never failed to amuse him, the irony even more prominent in his case, given that while he was weary, he was not a man, and in either case, rest was never what a man sought at this particular address. Escape. Fleshly pleasure. A bawdy good time. Oblivion. They were all sought at various times by various men for mere pennies passed to Madame's hand. Gabriel was never bawdy, but he longed most vigorously for escape, for a contentment that eluded him, for the respite the grandiose name promised.

"Good evening, Madame Conti, you're looking well." In fact, Madame was looking rather ill at ease, standing in front of him, blocking his way to the creaky, slanted stairs that led him up to Anne, where his glass and spoon would be waiting. Perhaps he'd forgotten to pay. He wasn't really sure when he'd last fronted Madame money for his nightly sojourns, but several months prior he had sold a painting for a significant amount, and had settled his affairs far enough into the future that he had lost awareness of the time.

"You're early tonight," she commented, fanning her heavy bosom vigorously with a faded lace fan.

"Impatient." He gave her a smile and took a step forward, assuming she would move. The dryness in his mouth was irritating, the shake in his hands increasing.

Madame Conti didn't move, which annoyed him. Moreover, she placed one fleshy hand on his chest and stopped any progress he might have made. "Anne isn't ready for you yet, Mr. Thiroux."

Gabriel despised the use of his false name. But he disliked being made to wait even more. Staying away for twelve hours of daylight was becoming more and more of a struggle for him. "I do not care. Whatever she is doing can be done in my presence."

"In all certainty. But I'm guessin' you don't want to see it."

Gabriel stared at Madame Conti, née Ginny Black, and narrowed his eyes. A former prostitute who had invested wisely, Madame was a shrewd businesswoman, with a mixed vocabulary, acute intelligence, and a devious mind. She didn't miss an opportunity to make money.

"What might I see?" Though he already had a suspicion, and it did not please him.

"Her toilette."

It was an innocuous remark, but Madame tipped her hand by shifting slightly in front of him again. Rage lit through him, clashing with the craving for his drink and pipe, and sent heat rushing into his face. "She's with another man, isn't she?"

There was no response, which was as telling as an admission. Gabriel brushed past her, pounded up the steps and down the hall, and shoved open the door to Anne's room. What he saw made his stomach twist in an unpleasant knot. Anne was beneath a man, her slim pale legs spread. A broad-shouldered man with black hair was mounting her with noisy enthusiasm. Gabriel couldn't see Anne's face, but she was giving encouraging mewling sounds. His sounds. They belonged to him.

Madame slid to a stop behind him. "It's just business," she said. "No sense letting her laze around all day."

"Dispense with him or I will," Gabriel told her. He wasn't exactly sure why he was so angry, but Anne was his. She and his opium and absinthe were all intertwined in his mind, and he loved his pipe and his drink, loved the pleasure she gave him while his mind sharpened and his body floated, while he stretched and strained to achieve an escape from mortality.

Stepping into the hall, Gabriel wiped at the cold sweat on his forehead, struggling to ignore the pervasive nausea clawing at his innards. He knew his human body was addicted to the alcohol, the opium, and the absinthe, and he felt no remorse for that, just merely resented the inconvenient symptoms of withdrawal. Leaning against the wall, he waited. It was a mere jaw-locking, bile-producing three minutes later that a man brushed past him, cursing while Madame offered him three girls in compensation for the one he'd lost.

Gabriel didn't even glance at the man, that irritated, whining voice familiar, yet not enough for him to care, to look up, to connect the pieces that floated around his agonized, sloshing brain. He was amazed that Madame had carried out his demand to get rid of Anne's unexpected client, but then again, Gabriel spent an obscene amount of money in her establishment monthly. He was a preferred client.

Anne appeared at the door, clad in a dressing gown, rich auburn hair spilling over her shoulders, green eyes wide and full of tears. "Are you angry with me?" she asked, voice trembling, anxiety palpable. "Madame said it was what you wanted, that you wished to watch, but I didn't know it was . . ."

Anger was a pale description for the depth of what he felt, but he found it wasn't directed at Anne. She was a simple woman, and she had always aspired to please him. Madame was manipulative, and Anne not bright enough to see her obvious lies. It startled him to recognize he retained such a well of compassion.

Yet he still was disgusted at what he had seen, so he cut her off by saying roughly, "Just get my drink." He pushed past her, stripping off his coat and tossing it on the chair at her vanity table.

The sight of the rumpled bedcovers increased his fury. The night was ruined, tainted, the idea of stepping in and escaping gone, replaced by the ugly and brutal reality that escape was ever elusive. He had thought perhaps tonight he'd sketch after he drank, had been feeling a pleasing tug of creativity, but it was all shattered by the sheets, soft and yellow with age, disheveled and stained.

Reaching over, he tore the sheets completely off and tossed them in the corner of the room. Mouth dry, he undid his shirt collar and sat in his chair, sighing. He felt tired all the time, his human body protesting the abuse he rendered it. His tray was next to him—pipe, glass, spoon all waiting. The bottle. Gabriel unstopped it, poured from it until the tumbler was half-full, and reached for his spoon, the sugar already carefully resting in its well. The shaking in his hands had stopped, and he focused with total clarity on the task, body tingling with anticipation, heart beating faster. When he poured water over the spoon, the liquid in the glass below kicked up a deliciously beautiful cloud, and he watched it, appreciating the swirls and ebb and flow as the absinthe turned a milky white. While it stirred and mixed and mesmerized, he struck a match and lit his pipe. The opium took him down into a relaxing languor, the absinthe pulled him back up into sparkling awareness. Together the two gave him a shade shy of bliss. Between draws on his pipe, the first glass went back smoothly, settling into his limbs and easing the ache. The second he drank just as fast, and by the time he was pouring and stirring the third, a cloud of smoke rising around him, blurring his vision and his brain, he remembered Anne, and beckoned her to him.

She went onto her knees in front of him, undid his trousers, and stroked his bare flesh as he relaxed back, eyes closed, glass in hand. He sipped and reached, seeking the sharpness of mind, the sense of confidence, of clarity, the absinthe brought. It was ironic that escape could be achieved by such pure and clear thinking. Gabriel felt more intelligent when he was in the bottle, more rational, more decisive. Perhaps the night could satisfy him after all.

Anne was caressing him with her hands, the tip of her tongue, the moist inside of her mouth, and the pleasure was acute, bright and crystallized, right. Opium, absinthe, and Anne, and he was almost out of his mortality, could almost reach the pinnacle of perfection that he had known as an angel.

Except that he was not in heaven, nor in the presence of God, but sitting in a rickety chair in a dingy room on Dauphine Street, one of the many such rooms around New Orleans, where sex was bought and hungers of all sort satisfied for a mere sixteen cents. He should have been ashamed that he had descended into such depths of depravity, but he no longer cared. All that mattered was that medicinal ecstasy rushing through his veins, that pulsing in his head, that throbbing intensity that Anne's tongue and fingers drew out from his groin as she licked and sucked on his flesh.

All that pleasure, all that shattering desire coalescing into rigidity, an acute sense of self, and the need to take, to own, to feel everything, yet nothing, to be utterly in control, yet surrender, surged up in Gabriel, and he accepted the physical release. His human body let go of its messy brand of satisfaction into Anne's mouth, and he closed his eyes, sank back, went up, then down, embracing the darkness, the incoherency, the oblivion.

When he pried his lids back open, he had no idea how much time had passed, but the candle on the nightstand had burned out, the bottle was empty, and Anne was sleeping in her bed. His mouth was dry, and he reached for his glass and tossed back whatever drops of diluted absinthe were still clinging to the bottom. There was a sour smell in the room, but Gabriel ignored it, knowing a foul odor was not out of place in the House of Rest.

He was relaxed, still floating, his vision sharp and clear, tumbling over the familiar hulks of furniture in the room despite the dark, and he enjoyed the vision of Anne lying in bed, one arm above her head, the other carelessly abandoned at her side. Most of her figure was in shadow, but the free arm was milky white, caught in a pool of moonlight bursting through the slats of the broken shutters on the window. That elegant limb beckoned to Gabriel, made him struggle to reach the paper and pencil he kept next to his chair, at the ready in case he felt the urge to sketch. He hadn't, not in months, but *Anne At Rest* spoke to him, and he moved his pencil quickly, capturing the bed, the hidden figure, the beautiful, illuminated arm.

Standing up, he stretched his stiff, weak body, ignoring that all too familiar nausea, and walked toward his lover. She was a good girl, Anne, with none of the brashness of many common whores, and she did a fine job of tolerating him. Some nights he even suspected she felt love, such as she was capable of, for him. He read it in her anxiety, her eagerness, that desperate desire to please. In return he felt something like gratitude. Now he simply wanted to capture her features, her expression, see and appreciate how her lovely, worrisome face relaxed into innocence in her sleep.

Still two feet from the bed, Gabriel's boot heel slipped on the floor and he cursed, nearly going down before grabbing the bedpost for balance. Glancing to see what had halted his progress, he saw a dark spot on the floor, raised like a puddle. Unsure what it was, he shifted forward, his hand sliding along the side of the mattress as he leaned for a better look. There was dampness beneath his fingers, and he realized the puddle appeared to be originating from the bed, a stained trail descending from the sheet to drip upon the floor.

Head snapping up, mouth hot, room spinning from the alcohol, Gabriel rushed his gaze past Anne's perfect arm and hand, to her face.

Or where her face should have been.

Unrecognizable, covered in blood, Anne was lacerated from hairline to waist with multiple stab wounds, a bowie knife placed mockingly in her other hand, her chemise and huge areas of her flesh shredded.

She was dead.

Bile rose in his throat, and he turned and spilled the contents of his stomach on the floor beside that dark circular stain of her life's blood, his heart racing, his mind registering a rapid succession of shock, horror, regret, fear. Anne had just been alive, warm and anxiously eager to please him. Now she was irrefutably and grotesquely dead.

Slashed to bloody bits while he floated in a pleasure cloud of drugs.

While he could never die, she had been viciously yanked from this mortal coil, and for him there would be no escape.

Ever.

Chapter One

❦

MICHAELS MURDER TRIAL
NEARS END OF TESTIMONY

In a case that grows more complex by the day, defendant Dr. Rafe Marino quoted the Bible, implying he was a positive influence upon her when asked about his relationship with the victim, girlfriend Jessie Michaels. "For the grace of God that brings salvation has appeared to all men. It teaches us to say no to ungodliness and worldly passions, and to live self-controlled, upright, and godly lives in this present age," Dr. Marino told reporters outside the courthouse yesterday.

Interesting. Gabriel reread the quote twice, the reference to God having leaped out at him. Curiosity had him heading to his computer, to read all recent references to the Michaels case that he could find. There was no shortage of online articles. It was a case that had captured media attention in Southwest Florida.

Two hours later, Gabriel's curiosity had coalesced into excitement. The parallels were remarkable between Jessie

Michaels's death and Anne's. This was his next project, without question.

And maybe, just maybe, it could be the way to break his curse. Of course, calling it a curse was irresponsible, implying he had done nothing to be inflicted with his present condition. The more accurate thing to say was that it was his punishment—an ignominy that ultimately punished all the women he encountered. They became a devastating collateral damage, heaping more guilt upon his already oppressive self-disgust. While he could never regain his pre-fallen stature, he wanted peace. To live in the mortal world, without hurting anyone, without the painful bonds of his past mistakes and controlling addictions.

He had to make amends, had to try to find answers.

After a little more research, Gabriel composed an e-mail and hit Send.

⚒

ACQUITTAL IN MICHAELS MURDER CASE

After nearly a year of investigation and case building by the city prosecutor, the murder of Jessie Michaels remains unsolved after the acquittal of Dr. Rafe Marino, the victim's thirty-one-year-old boyfriend. Michaels was found dead in her home on July 14 of last year, stabbed multiple times with a bowie knife in the face and chest, rendering her unrecognizable. The crime shocked Naples with its ferocity and led to an unprecedented manhunt before the prosecution turned its attention to the forty-six-year-old victim's significantly younger boyfriend.

Sara Michaels tossed the newspaper aside without finishing the article. She'd read enough. Knew this story inside and out. It was the reason she was leaving Florida. And while she had told all of her friends and her coworkers that going to New Orleans was a temporary move, in her heart she questioned if she would ever have the strength to return.

She'd sold this house, which thankfully had been bought in the eighties, before the real estate boom in Florida. So despite the sluggish current housing market, and the fact that her mother had been murdered in the master bedroom, she had still been able to sell it for a substantial profit. Money she needed, a nest egg she was grateful for, at the same time she despised that it had come to her at the expense of losing her mother. Glancing around, Sara ran her eyes over the tired beige carpet, the wicker furniture her mother had loved so much, the excessive plants and dried floral arrangements that crowded shelves and walls. She had already taken anything she personally cared about, and anything of real value. Her friend Jocelyn was going to dispose of what she'd left behind before the new owners took possession in two weeks.

Sara hadn't been able to wait. She had to get out. Now.

Sliding her purse strap back up her arm, she took a deep breath, fought the growing sense of panic and hysteria. Tried to drive back the need to run, not walk, away from Naples, her life, her mother's murder, and painful memories. She was leaving, fleeing to New Orleans really, but she could kid herself that it was logical to seek answers there. That emotion played the smaller factor in her decision.

Yet she knew she was lying to herself, and they had told her in rehab that it was a pattern she needed to break if she intended to live a clean life, free from the grip of painkillers and tranquilizers.

She wanted that fresh start. Now.

Heading toward the front door, Sara reached back and grabbed the newspaper off the sofa, folding it up into thirds. Better not leave that lying around for Jocelyn or anyone else to see. That article sitting in this house revealed too much about her and her fragile state of mind.

And the one big lie she told everyone else, but didn't actually believe herself, was that she was okay.

That she would ever be okay again.

❧

He wasn't expecting her. It was obvious by the look of appalled impatience on his face as he stood in the doorway of the gated courtyard. And then there was the fact that he said flatly, "You're not supposed to be here today."

Sara shifted, her eyes gritty, hands damp. She'd spent two

days driving, and a sleepless night in her new temporary apartment, afraid to close her eyes. It had been a hot and humid walk from where she had parked her car to Gabriel St. John's apartment in the French Quarter. She was exhausted, and she had a manila envelope full of e-mail correspondence in her handbag that reassured her she absolutely one hundred percent was supposed to be there at one o'clock on Thursday, which it was, and she refused to leave. Would not apologize or stammer or take responsibility for his error.

"This was the time we arranged to meet," she said, straining for politeness. She would not point out that he had contacted her initially. That he had suggested their collaboration on this project, at no expense or inconvenience to him. That she was the one who had traveled a thousand miles to assist him on his true crime investigation book.

No, she wouldn't point any of that out, even if she had to bite her lip until it bled.

The sun streamed into the lush courtyard behind him, but he was in the shadow of the building in a bricked passageway, and it was difficult to see his face clearly from behind her sunglasses. But what she could see surprised her. She had assumed Gabriel was older, though she couldn't pinpoint why she had come to that conclusion when they'd only been in contact through e-mail. Yet there had been something of his words that hinted at experience, a weariness.

It was startling to see in person that he wasn't much more than thirty. At first glance, he looked even younger than that, his face elegant and youthful, a rare true pretty man, with long cheekbones, rich brown eyes, and lustrous hair, streaked with multiple shades of color ranging from dirty blond to mahogany on the undersides, falling carelessly past his chin in baby-fine strands.

"We're supposed to meet tomorrow," he said, his deep voice shattering the illusion that he was innocent and young. There was an edge there that spoke of hard times, disappointment. Stubbornness.

Which almost made her laugh. God, it was like looking in a mirror. This was probably exactly what she looked like to most people right now. Haunted, remote, hovering toward bitter. She didn't want that label, to descend into a perpetual discontent, not even as she felt herself clinging to the edge of control. So she forced a smile and said lightly, "I guess we have a misunderstanding then."

Reaching into her bag, she pulled out the e-mail from him that she had printed out before leaving Florida. "August 15, one p.m. That's today." She handed it to him so he could confirm with his own eyes what he'd written. "I guess it crept up on us."

Not really. Every day had been a gaping, long, endless fight for her sanity. But it was the socially correct response. Defuse the situation. She certainly knew how to do that. She'd spent her entire life walking on proverbial eggshells with her mother, tamping down the explosions before they could start.

Gabriel didn't seem to like what he was reading. His jaw clenched and he didn't look up from the paper. "I'm not ready for you today."

Sara stifled a sigh, pulling off her sunglasses. She hadn't expected a diva. From his e-mails Gabriel St. John had seemed like an efficient, clinical crime writer. Exactly what she wanted. Zero emotion. Yet he was scowling at her for no apparent reason whatsoever other than that he couldn't look at the calendar or enter appointments into his computer correctly.

"Since I drove in from Kenner, got lost downtown after getting off on the wrong exit, and circled the block six times for a parking spot, could we just have a brief preliminary meeting to discuss the project? I can come back tomorrow, but I'd really like to talk today." Outline and clearly communicate your needs. That's what they had told her in rehab. She had to stop expecting people to satisfy her wants without ever cluing anyone in to what they were.

"Are you staying in Kenner?" He frowned. "That's going to be inconvenient. I'd thought you'd stay in the Quarter or downtown. Why Kenner?"

Because it was an innocuous suburb where the airport was, and it made her feel safer. She had been raised in Florida, in the land of the new and tidy, where the chain restaurant ruled. New Orleans scared her. Her mother had despised this city, had never returned once she'd left, and Sara herself was a little intimidated, unnerved by the shabby buildings of the Quarter, the disintegrating sidewalks, and the barrage of odors. Kenner was definitely safer to her mental health.

Gabriel watched the emotions play over Sara Michaels's face with curiosity. She was not at all what he had expected. Her contact with him had been efficient, brisk, and unemotional, like the scientist that she was. Yet the woman in front of him was a riot of emotions—they played over her face, haunted her eyes, settled into the rigidity of her shoulders. Petite and blond, wearing a billowing pale blue sundress that stopped above her knees, she looked fragile, beaten, like the only thing keeping her from collapsing on the sidewalk was the pure strength of her will.

"The rent was cheaper," she said.

And he knew she was lying. Which intrigued him. She had intrigued him from the minute he opened the gate, and that was dangerous. He showed interest, any interest, and women responded, with enthusiasm that degenerated into obsessive pitiful devotion that left him feeling guilty and horrified, them heartbroken and ashamed. It was his punishment for falling—inadvertently arousing obsession in women—and he would not, could not, show anything other than a casual business interest in Sara and subject her to that torture.

If he had known what she looked like, if he had seen the pain floating in her eyes, he would never have requested her assistance on this project, but it was too late now. She was here, and he was stuck with her. He was also being rude, which was unnecessary. Nothing was her fault, and she didn't deserve his animosity.

"Why don't you come in for a minute?" Gabriel stepped back from the gate. "I apologize for mixing up the days."

She gave him a brief smile of amusement at that, and Gabriel knew she realized how difficult admitting he was wrong was for him. Pride was yet another flaw of his. It was no secret he had many.

"Thanks."

It was also apparent to Gabriel as he walked up the curved staircase to his third-floor apartment that he had very little experience with normal one-on-one social and business interactions. He did the vast majority of his communicating online now, and he wrote in solitude. Avoided people. Which was probably why he was so uncomfortable walking ahead of Sara Michaels, why he was so hyperaware of the sound of her breathing, the scent of her perfume, the glimpse of her arm behind him, fingers stroking along the banister as they ascended.

But he was so determined, maybe even desperate, to solve Anne's murder that he would suffer social discomfort to extract the information Sara Michaels could provide.

He turned back when she gave a startled cry. "Are you okay?" She had stopped walking and was gripping the banister with white knuckles.

She nodded, taking in a deep breath. "I missed a step. It's slanted, and my foot slipped." Her hand came up and demonstrated the angle.

"Sorry. Old building. Things have shifted." Watching her visibly pull herself together, calm herself, had Gabriel feeling that spark of interest again. He didn't want to feel that. Couldn't have it. Yet Sara had dark circles under her eyes, and had traveled all the way from Florida to work with him on an obscure true crime book that attempted to solve a century-and-a-half-old case with modern forensics. She had a story, and despite his wariness, he couldn't help but want to hear it. If he was honest with himself, he'd been curious about her since discovering her mother's brutal murder in his standard trolling for intriguing cases that could be potential book material. While Sara was the daughter of the murder victim, Jessie Michaels, she was also a forensic scientist, which lent a gruesome irony to the case. Poking around on the Internet and through the newspaper articles had revealed she hadn't worked in almost a year. She also hadn't hesitated at all to leave Florida at his request. He wanted to know why.

"How long have you lived here?" she asked.

A hundred and fifty years, give or take fifty years here and there when he'd had to move to alleviate suspicion, but she wasn't likely to believe that. She started walking again, so he did too. "Ten years."

"Do you like it?"

Gabriel opened the door at the landing on the third floor and shrugged. "Sure." He hadn't thought much about whether he actually liked his apartment or not. He guessed he did. He was bound to New Orleans in exchange for shortening his punishment, and this place was as good as any other to live. He never had any particular desire to move, but whether that was from actual pleasure he took in his surroundings, or a lack of ambition, he didn't know.

"Who lives on the second floor?"

"A guy."

She gave him a funny look, staring up at him from two steps below the landing. "I mean, who is he? What does he do? How old is he?"

"I don't know. He's in his forties, I guess, but I've never really met nim." And he liked it that way. The other tenants left him alone, and he did the same. But his answer obviously bothered Sara, given her frown, and he was acutely aware of how bad he was at polite conversation designed to get to know someone better. Straightforward business, interviewing, fact-gathering, he was perfectly capable of. This type of dynamic, this innocent idle nothing sort of chatter was a challenge. In all personal honesty, he'd never been good at it, even back in the early nineteenth century before the alcohol, the drugs, had gotten the majority of his attention. He had always been more comfortable pursuing his solitary pursuits of music, painting, writing. But he had tried then. Now he almost never even needed to expend the energy to attempt to be normal.

It was hard as hell at the moment, and he was seriously regretting his initial desire to work with Sara Michaels. It had been a definite lapse in judgment, an attempted shortcut he shouldn't have taken.

"This is a beautiful color." She gestured to the walls of his living room as she followed him in. Her fingers came up and brushed over the brilliance of his green paint. "It's so alive."

It had taken him two weeks and six shades of paint, mixing yellows and greens until he had achieved the perfect eye-popping lime he had wanted. It was ironic that she would notice, because it had been the first time in a century he had allowed himself to touch a paintbrush, to explore color combinations, to bring joy and satisfaction into his life from the act of creating. It had been a celebration of sorts, of hope, that maybe if he solved Anne's murder, he could pay the debt he owed her soul. This color had appealed to him as loud and vibrant, allowing the light from the two large windows to bounce around all four walls, reflect off the floor and ceiling, and allow his furniture to bask in a warm glow.

"Thank you. I like it." He did.

"Do you work here in your apartment?" She was glancing around, casual but curious.

"Yes." The way she turned, ran her eyes over his possessions, assessing and measuring, made him uncomfortable.

No one came inside his apartment except for him. It felt invasive, disturbing. He should have offered to meet her at her hotel, or at a café. That he didn't know how to act, what to do with his hands, how to lead and direct the conversation, angered him, and he felt the unmistakable desire for a drink. The dryness in his mouth, the tightness in his chest demanded attention, and it was like an insidious whisper in his soul, the promise that everything would be easier, smoother, with a shot of whiskey sitting in his gut.

But he hadn't touched any drugs or alcohol in seventy-five years, and he wasn't about to fall for the faulty logic that tried to trip him and drag him back down into the depths of addiction yet again.

"Let me print out the projected schedule I created for this project," he said, needing to lock and focus on something to halt his wandering mind, clamp down on the craving. "You can take a look at it and we can meet tomorrow. Why don't you have a seat and I'll go grab that."

Gabriel moved into his office quickly, wanting to get away from Sara. Only she followed him. He realized it immediately, heard her sandals, the rustle of her dress, felt the air move behind him, aware of the scent of her perfume, a strange olfactory combination that he thought included cinnamon. Ignoring her, he bent over his computer and opened up his documents. He searched for his work schedule, then clicked print. While he impatiently waited for the paper to spit out of his printer, he chanced a glance at Sara.

She was spinning around on one foot, looking at his white boards, scanning over his bulletin boards jammed with newspaper clippings and timelines he'd printed out, of pivotal dates. Then she saw the sketch of Anne and she walked straight up to it, hand raised like she might touch, but stopping herself.

"Is this her? Anne Donovan?"

"Yes." Gabriel forced the admission out, the familiar and ever-present guilt rising up in his throat and squeezing. He didn't look at the sketch. He knew every line, every nuance, every smudge of charcoal.

"She's lovely. There's something . . . I don't know . . . hopeful in her eyes."

It was a cruel irony to him that Sara of all people would recognize that. Anne had been hopeful in the months before she died, and Gabriel had obviously been aware of it on some level since he had captured it in various sketches and paintings he had done of her. But he had not been consciously aware of it at the time. He had only been aware of the satisfaction and pleasure he gained from taking his opium and absinthe in her presence.

"Amazing, if you think about it, considering the life she led."

Sara glanced over at him. "As a prostitute, you mean?"

"Yes. It must have been an achievement to still feel hope." It wasn't like he had been any sort of consolation or source of hope for Anne. He often struggled to understand what the hell she had seen in him.

"God, I understand that," she said in a soft whisper, then quickly turned, her cheeks pinking, like she realized she had just revealed too much. She cleared her throat. "So where do you start with a book like this? It's a hundred-and-fifty-year-old murder mystery. Where do you even begin?"

The way he did with all his books, even if this one was personal. "You start with the murder. That's what grabs reader interest. Then when you've shocked them into attention, you go back and scene set."

"Scene set?"

"Try to set the stage for the murder. What life was like in 1849 New Orleans for a prostitute. Trace the timeline of the principle parties involved. Introduce the characters."

"I don't know if my brain works like that. I'm a forensic lab grunt. I stare at gel slides all day." She crossed her arms over her chest. "And they're not characters. They're people. Real human beings who lived and died."

"I know that." He struggled with the weight of that pressing down on him every single day. Gabriel pulled the schedule out of the printer and handed it to Sara. He wanted her gone, out of his space, away from his guilt, his raw self-hatred. "That's why I write the books I do. We both want to solve a murder, don't we? You want to solve your mother's murder, and I want to solve Anne Donovan's. And that takes logic, the kind of logic a lab grunt understands. But you also can't solve a crime without understanding the people involved and the world in which they lived."

She took the paper and gave him a slow nod. "True. I can see that. But I want your reassurance that whatever you write, you won't treat my mother's death like a juicy soap opera."

Sorry for her pain, feeling a new rush of guilt for his role in reopening her wounds of grief, Gabriel spoke softly. "I have no intention of doing that, Sara. I want to show how the use of DNA and forensic evidence can solve crime. It can solve Anne's murder, and it can solve your mother's murder, if handled correctly, and result in a conviction. But that ultimately it's the human factor that determines whether a crime will be solved, or if someone will be put behind bars for it. I don't think the police or the courts did their job, and that's not fair to you, or your mother."

Maybe he shouldn't have stated that so baldly, because she blanched. Glancing around the room at his cluttered file cabinets, stacks of papers, bookcase crammed with reference materials, she said, "I know you could have gone ahead and done this without my involvement. I know you didn't need my permission. The case is public domain, as much as that disgusts me. So I appreciate you contacting me, but at the same time I have to wonder why you did. It would have been easier for you if you had just proceeded on your own with an independent forensic consultant."

That was a legitimate question he had asked himself a multitude of times since he had contacted Sara and requested she work with him. Especially now that she was standing in his office, beautiful and wrenching in her grief, her determination. "I asked you to be a part of this project, because yes, I want your technical expertise, but I also want to respect your feelings, make sure I handle the presentation in a way you're comfortable with. And I want the tenacity of someone who is personally invested."

Now she looked like the one who wanted her gone. She even took a step back toward the door. "I am personally invested. Unfortunately."

He hadn't meant to nick at her wounds. He'd been trying to reassure her that he was in fact intending to be considerate of her feelings, of the personal nature and newness of her mother's death. Yet he had obviously upset her, and Gabriel rubbed his jaw, not sure what to say. Social skills were not his forte and he was starting to feel frustrated. So he just said what he was thinking. "I don't know what you want me to say."

"I don't know." She shook her head. "I don't know. And I agreed to do this, so I shouldn't be grilling you like this."

"It's going to be fine. I think we'll work well together. I'll see you tomorrow at one. Here." That was most likely a huge mistake, but all his materials were in his office, and if he was intimidated by one little broken blonde, then he wasn't man or fallen angel, but simply pathetic.

She nodded, clutching the schedule and her purse, backing up another step.

"Let me walk you out." His eighteenth-century manners, buried under a century of solitude, resurfaced, along with his feeling that he had control of the situation. He could deal with this.

"No, no, I'm fine." Sara moved, revealing the sketch of Anne pinned to the wall behind her. "Bye."

Then she was gone and he was staring into the pleading eyes of his long dead lover, captured by his own hands, and possibly killed by the very same.

※

Sara had only walked a half block on Royal Street when she saw a coffee shop and veered straight into it. She needed an iced tea and a minute to sit down, gather herself. She hadn't expected this would be so difficult, that she would feel so awkward in Gabriel's presence. He spoke to her with such apparent effort, like he was struggling to carry on a conversation, yet his eyes pierced her, made her feel stripped and vulnerable, weak.

That feeling of weakness was something she couldn't stand. She should just quit, give up this ridiculous quest right here and now, forget all about the past and concentrate on the present. The future, for God's sake. But she wouldn't. She knew that even before she had the cap off of her bottled iced tea. She had to have answers. Had to know who killed Anne Donovan. Had to know who killed her mother. Had to know if in some bizarre, insane, utterly unbelievable way they were connected to each other.

Her cell phone rang in her purse and she retrieved it, taking a seat in the back of the coffee shop so she wouldn't disturb anyone. It was past prime lunchtime, so the shop was quiet, only a few customers working alone on laptop computers and sipping their drinks. Her Caller ID showed a Florida phone number, but not one that she recognized.

"Hello?"

"Hi, Sara, how are you?"

Her stomach dropped. Just hearing his voice made her feel guilty. "Rafe?"

"Yeah, it's me. I'm back at my place since my release. I want to see you . . . I've been worried about you. Are you at home? I'll stop over with some dinner." His voice was filled with concern.

"Thanks, but I'm fine. You don't need to worry about me." Maybe that was an exaggeration, because God knows she could use someone to worry about her, but that wasn't his burden.

And she felt horrible that she had been such a wreck, so completely incapable of supporting him in any way during the trial. Even when she had tried to defend Rafe on the witness stand, the prosecutor had shredded her. Every word out of her mouth had been manipulated, twisted to make it look like she and Rafe were the true lovers, that his relationship with her mother was a front, a con, until she had been so afraid they were creating a case against her as well as Rafe, she had shut down entirely.

She'd abandoned him essentially. Left him hung out to dry for a crime he didn't commit, to protect herself, and now he wanted to feed her. He was definitely the better person than her.

"How are you, Rafe? Is the press leaving you alone?" Sara sipped her tea and rubbed at her temples. There was no running away. She needed to regroup, process, deal with all of her emotions, her guilt, her fear.

"Today hasn't been too bad. Nobody camped out on my front lawn. The last three weeks I could have done without though."

He spoke lightly, and while that should have made her feel better, it only drove home how much stronger a person he was than her. The last year had been hell for both of them in different ways, yet he had survived with his kindness, charm, and humor intact. He planned to move to the West Coast and revive his medical practice away from the media circus of Southwestern Florida, and didn't seem to harbor any residual bitterness that he had spent six months sitting in prison while his character was dragged through the mud.

She had collapsed under the weight of her mother's death, gotten hooked on tranquilizers, and now was sitting in New Orleans trying to feel some elusive connection to her mother's youth. That familiar guilt, self-doubt, pressed down on her, but she fought it. This was a fresh start.

"I'm sorry I wasn't there," she said. "I really am."

"I understand."

And she knew he did. "I left town."

"You left Naples? Why? Where are you?"

"I just needed to get away. I'll be back soon. You can reach me on my cell if you need to talk." She didn't want to admit to anyone what she was doing. Going to the city her mother had grown up in smacked of the need for counseling. And if she told him about the book, he'd think she had totally lost it, grasping at forensic straws to solve a murder the police considered unsolvable at this point.

"Sara . . . where are you?" He sounded worried.

Maybe he should be.

"Don't worry about it. I'm fine. I'll be back soon." Maybe. But they'd cross that bridge when she got to it. "Take care of yourself, and be sure to let me know when you're leaving Naples. I want to see you before you head west."

"Okay." He paused, then just sighed. "Be well, Sara."

"Yeah, you too."

"I'm going to take Jessie some flowers. Can I take something for you?"

That gesture hit her like a smack. Tears popped into her eyes and Sara fought for control, to not lose it in the coffee shop. "Sure. Take my mom some carnations, will you? In a crazy, wild color." It had been a source of contention between them. Sara had always told her mother carnations weren't classy, they were a cheap filler flower, but her mother had liked them. Maybe for that very reason. And she had always wanted them in bright blues, greens, and hot pinks, hues achieved through dye, not nature.

"Okay, I can do that. Promise me you'll stay in touch."

"Yep. I'll talk to you soon. Bye." Sara hung up the phone before Rafe could hear the waver in her voice.

And found herself digging in her bag and pulling out her manila folder. She flipped through the papers inside rapidly, stopping when she got to a copied newspaper article.

STABBED TO DEATH!

The headline was glaring and to the point. It was interesting to Sara that she had assumed media coverage of murder and other crimes had grown more sensationalist in the TV and Internet era, but from what she'd seen of the Anne Donovan case, nineteenth-century journalists had been just as salacious.

> October 7, 1849—Anne Donovan, age 23, a lewd and unfortunate woman, was found MURDERED in her bed at the House of Rest For Weary Men, Dauphine Street, a den of gambling, drink, and other unsavory activities. Stabbed seventeen times with a bowie knife, her facial features obliterated, and her breasts mutilated, the violent nature of the crime has shocked even the hardened Madame Conti, who sent a girl for the coroner after being alerted of the victim's state. Miss Donovan was last seen alive by Mr. Jonathon Thiroux, her LOVER, who maintains he heard or saw nothing of her death, even though he was in her room at the time. There have been no arrests, and we must ask, Ladies and Gentlemen, if this is what our fine

city has fallen to. Are murders so commonplace and the reach of wealth so deep into our city officials that our police do not even bother to investigate such a horrific death? If Miss Donovan were murdered in a better address would justice be sought in her case?

That is perhaps a question for the mayor.

So obviously the journalist had used Anne Donovan's murder as a platform for airing political grievances, but Sara figured any attention given the case was a positive. It meant more articles, more court papers, more documents, and more physical evidence had been gathered and had survived through the decades, which meant a higher probability that together with Gabriel St. John she could solve the crime. Which mattered to her, because if she would never see her mother's killer behind bars, which, despite Gabriel's opinion, seemed likely, it would give her a certain sense of satisfaction to know she had solved her great-great-grandmother's murder.

For four generations in her family, a woman had been brutally murdered, starting with Anne Donovan. Ending with her mother. It was a fear that had plagued her all her life—the bogeyman, the family curse, the toxic press of mortality clouding everything she did, every decision, every long-term goal—that she would die young, suffer a brutal death at the hands of a stranger. Her mother had laughed at it. Disregarded it.

But her mother was dead now.

And Sara was afraid that, one way or another, she would be the next to die.

Chapter Two

✦

Gabriel was in a much better mood when Sara Michaels showed up promptly at one the following day. He had gone walking the night before, to the river, down Frenchman Street, then across Rampart over to Louis Armstrong Park, grateful for the cooler night air, appreciative of the fact that as an immortal, he could walk into areas that weren't safe for the average man at night. The park was dark and desolate, the perfect place to be mugged, but Gabriel enjoyed the solitude it brought him, the joy in knowing that while everyone else stayed away, he could walk alone.

He had spent his whole life on earth walking alone. That hadn't been his job. He had been sent to Watch. Guide. Protect. But he had failed on all counts and knew there was no forgiveness, no redemption for him. He could never make amends large enough to recompense the wrongs he had committed, though he wanted to at least try in Anne's case.

It was a triumph, a goal well met that he was living a chemical-free life, and he fought hard against the temptation to slide back into bliss, the fog where he was smart and right and everything was easy and calm. That fight took everything he had and there was nothing left for sorting out a path to redemption, which was why he had never attempted to confront the truth in Anne's case, had never wanted to know if ultimately he had been the man who had taken her life.

He was ready to face that truth now. And even if he didn't and couldn't seek true redemption, an entrance back to the kingdom of God, he wanted to be released from his punishment. He wanted to be more than a Watcher. He wanted to participate in humanity, something thus far he couldn't do, because every woman he touched craved him as an opiate. They all spiraled down into desperate despair when he couldn't give them enough, was never enough, and he had chosen to isolate himself entirely rather than bring that fate on any woman. But he didn't want to be alone anymore, and he wanted to be released.

He thought maybe the answer to the future lay in the past.

Despite the rocky introduction, he felt cautiously optimistic as he let Sara into his courtyard, then up the stairs to his apartment for the second time. He had realized that this working arrangement with Sara could be mutually beneficial. They both wanted murders solved that they were personally haunted by, and it would be easier for both of them with the other acting as a buffer. They could each focus on the opposing case, and eventually compare the two, and as a result they would both be able to hold back, retain some measure of logic and control. He hadn't addressed the facts of Anne's murder since its occurrence, not wanting to find irrefutable proof that he had in fact killed her. But now it seemed the timing was providential, and there was more at stake than clearing his own name, or absolving his own guilt.

There was Sara's mother, and the intense need to fix the future of his long, mortal, flawed existence.

He didn't necessarily deserve companionship, but he was also looking forward to it. In some capacity. Without allowing Sara to get too close to him or his life. It was a fine line, and he wanted to walk it. That alone should alert him to the inherent danger, should serve as a red flag that he was seeking out the thrill again, disregarding good sense for the sake of personal interest. But Sara seemed harmless, and he was in control, in ways he hadn't been before. He was stronger now and he could handle anything.

Sara looked tired, even more so than the day before, and

her shoulders drooped, her expression pinched like she was suffering from a headache.

"Rough night's sleep?" he asked as he led her into his office.

She sank without hesitation onto the couch when he gestured for her to sit. "I couldn't sleep."

"Did you drink a lot of caffeine?" His editor complained about not being able to drink caffeine past seven, so it seemed like a safe thing to say.

"No." Sara stared back out into his living room. "Do you play?"

"What?" He looked where she was gesturing, confused for a second. Then he realized what she was referring to. His baby grand, collecting dust in the left corner.

"The piano. Do you play it?"

Never. "I used to. Not anymore. But the piano's been here since the house was built. It was brought in as they were framing the house so it would fit through the narrow doorways. There's no way to get it out now without destroying it." Much like him.

"Why don't you play anymore?" Her sad, tired eyes locked with his.

Sara Michaels wasn't losing sleep from too much caffeine. It was worry keeping her up. He felt that interest again, nagging, persistent curiosity scratching at him, and for some reason he told her the truth. Heard the words come out of his mouth before he even thought about the wisdom of speaking them. "I don't hear music anymore."

"Oh." Her eyebrows furrowed. "I'm sorry . . . That sounds sad . . . I didn't mean to. . . ." She blushed, obviously distressed.

"It's okay. You didn't know." It was true. He didn't hear music in his head, his heart, his soul anymore. Everything had gone silent. His fingers no longer ached to sketch, to capture the light and the figures around him, the notes no longer played in his mind, and words weren't clamoring to escape onto paper. "I don't miss it."

Whether that was true or not, he wasn't sure, but Sara looked like she needed reassurance. "Do you miss being in the lab?"

She propped her chin up with her hand, leaning forward so her elbows were on her knees. Wearing another flowing dress, she exuded that same sense of femininity, fragility, as she had the day before. "Not right now, I don't. Which worries me. It's been almost a year since I took a leave of absence. I should miss it more."

"Maybe it's a matter of going back. When you get there you'll realize you missed it more than you thought."

"Maybe." She didn't look any more convinced than he probably sounded. "You too, then, you know. Maybe if you play, you'll realize you miss it." When he didn't answer, Sara straightened up. "So what do you want me to do on the project? What's my first assignment?"

Business was good. They should stay there. Safe and aloof and distant. Except that this business was based on his guilt and the need to appease it, along with the desire to find justice for Anne, who hadn't deserved to die.

"First you need to familiarize yourself with the basic facts of the case. Then I want to hear your interpretation of the physical forensic evidence as we accumulate it. I'm writing the book passages myself, but I need you to assess the old evidence, determine if it's possible to use modern forensics on any of the trace evidence that still exists. We need to show the difference use of forensics makes when we compare the old case to the current case. Most of the research hasn't been processed yet. We need to follow the clues, try to unravel both cases from every possible direction."

"Why do you write true crime?" she asked. "I saw your list of credentials. You've written ten true crime books and I'm just curious how you got into this."

"I just fell into it," he told her flatly. He wasn't even sure why he studied violent crimes and wrote about them. But they were filled with negative emotion, and maybe that was why he did it. Maybe it was self-punishment. Retribution. "It's puzzle-solving. And it pays the rent."

He handed her a file folder he had put together that morning of pertinent info. "Go ahead and read this."

Sara took the folder Gabriel was handing her and tried to make eye contact with him. But his eyes darted over behind her, and she sank back on the couch and opened the folder.

Her brain felt swaddled in thick cotton, her body exhausted
from lack of sleep. She'd lain in bed for four hours, staring at
the ceiling of her stark rental, before giving up and surfing the
Internet mindlessly until dawn. She'd taken an hour nap
around ten, but besides that was running on about six hours of
sleep over the last three days.

The folder contained the police report from Anne Donovan's murder. The handwriting was hard to read, the photo-
copy a little spotty, but Sara could decipher the pertinent facts.

October 7, 1849

Second District

Name of Deceased: Anne Donovan

Residing at 25 Dauphine Street, The House of
Rest, a gaming and drinking establishment

Location of murder the same

Murder assumed to take place between the hours
of eight p.m. on October the 6th and 2 a.m. on
October the 7th according to witnesses

Victim discovered by John Thiroux, reported to
authorities by Madame Conti, owner of the
dwelling

No arrests made at this time

Witnesses: John Thiroux, Madame Conti, various
and sundry other women in residence at The
House of Rest

That was it. No description of the body, the room. No interview with John Thiroux, no mention of a weapon. Nothing
useful at all. The reports from her mother's murder had
seemed thirteen miles long, the questions endless, every hair,
every fiber, every scrap of anything out of the ordinary collected, catalogued, saved. Sara glanced up. Gabriel was at his
computer.

"Is this the only police accounting of the crime scene?"

He glanced back at her and gave a brief smile. "Not exactly stellar police work, was it?"

"No. It doesn't tell us anything at all. If you line the two crime scene reports up next to each other in your book, you've proved your point already. Forensics has essentially altered the entire face of criminal investigation. I know you want to see if we can solve the Donovan case, but how can you solve a crime based on this piece of nothing?" She felt shut down, disillusioned already.

"I can't. But better information comes from other sources. We have eyewitness accounts as told to journalists. We have the court records of the coroner's report. And the testimony of the accused murderer." He turned fully in his chair, his black T-shirt pulling taut across his chest. "Remember what I said . . . it's scene-setting. Re-creating the months, the weeks, the day leading up to the murder. Then piecing together what happened afterward. Most crimes don't have a murderer standing over the victim with the smoking gun saying, 'Well, sir, I had to do it. Nellie drove me to it.' "

Sara raised her eyebrow in disbelief, suddenly wanting to laugh. Gabriel had put on a strange fake accent, like a Southern cowboy, and it was so totally unexpected it struck her as funny. "But how do you know who was telling the truth and who wasn't?"

"You search for consistencies. And likewise, inconsistencies." He shrugged. "It's common sense. Logic. Read the rest of the folder and then tell me what you think."

So ultimately science had to work with human deduction and reasoning. It was interesting. He was interesting.

Sara watched him turn back to his computer, his hair sliding forward. She wanted to touch his hair, to stroke it and see if it felt as smooth as it looked. Which must be the result of fatigue because she didn't normally have any desire to touch a man's head. But tired and edgy, she was strangely aware of her own body, of the tactile feel of her bare legs on the soft velvet couch, of the brush of the folder over her wrist, and for the first time in a year she wanted to feel a human touch. But Gabriel didn't invite casual arm contact, let alone letting her fingers cascade through his soft hair. He had a barrier around him, a stance that said he walked the world alone, and at the

moment, he had his back fully turned to her. He was tapping a
silver spoon on the desk as he read his screen. It was a rhythmic tapping, a harmony that repeated over and over. She wondered if he even knew he was doing it, but it was definitely a
song.

MURDERED!

October 7, 1849—Even in a city where a murder
a week takes place in our less illustrious districts,
the STABBING DEATH of Anne Donovan has
captured the attention of the public due to the
severity of the crime, and the lack of an immediate arrest. While it is no secret that a vast number
of city officials frequent houses of ill repute, does
their status alone preclude them from punishment? It would seem so, given the extraordinary
circumstances explained below by Madame
Conti, owner of the house where the crime took
place, and first WITNESS on the scene.

Anne Donovan had been in the employ of
Madame Conti for approximately one year prior
to her death and was described by her employer
as "kind, gentle, a redhead, who never gave me a
day's trouble, which can't be said for a lot of
these girls." Most have been hardened by the age
of Miss Donovan, handy with a knife and inclined to steal from the clients, but by all accounts these rough qualities did not apply to the
victim. Madame Conti explained that she had let
the victim's current amour, John Thiroux, into
Donovan's room at eight p.m., and retired to her
private salon to write letters to acquaintances.
She heard nothing out of the ordinary until two
a.m., when Mr. Thiroux sought her out. There
was blood on his hands, in his hair, and on his
right leg. According to Madame Conti, he said
simply, "Anne's dead."

The sight that greeted the stout miss upon re-
pairing to the girl's room was a scene from a

nightmare. "I've seen a lot in my life—I've seen murdered people before—but this was unlike anything I've ever laid eyes on. It was unbelievable. Blood everywhere." What she saw was Anne Donovan, lying supine on her narrow bed, dressed in a simple chemise, her face and upper body mutilated by stab wounds. A knife rested in her left hand, and blood covered the bed, the floor below, the wall behind her head, and filled the room with a sickly sweet smell.

What did Madame think of Mr. Thiroux? "I never thought of him as a violent sort at all, but he was there, wasn't he? I figured he must have done it." When asked if she was afraid to be alone with him at that time, she replied, "Not at all. He had returned to his chair and was starting in on a brand-new bottle, eyes closed. I lit his pipe for him and figured I'd have a good two hours before he so much as stirred."

Yet when police arrived, they made no attempt to arrest Mr. Thiroux, whom most of our readership will recognize as a wealthy artist, who has contributed greatly to the improvement of the arts in our city. It is also widely recognized that Mr. Thiroux does not pass a day without descending into drink or opium.

MURDER OF LOCAL BAWD
HAS FELLOW STRUMPETS IN ARMS

October 8, 1849—"We're just trying to get along," maintains Sally Jackson, a resident at the House of Rest, where a fellow bawd was murdered two nights past. "A girl needs a way to survive, and it ain't safe anymore. It just ain't right." While no one appears to question the right of lewd women to hock their wares without enticing death, not everyone agrees that allowing such rowdy residences to exist legally is in the best interest of a city grown notorious for crime. Despite disgruntled area residents, official sources seem disinclined to take any action, and the police more often than not make no attempt whatsoever to seek out culprits in violent crimes. "One less to contend with," seems to be their philosophy when the life of an unfortunate is snuffed out prematurely.

Yet even the police cannot disregard such a bloody and gruesome case as the death of Anne Donovan, slashed in a frenzy so brutal even her own mother would not recognize her in death. "I heard her yell out," Molly Faye claims, from her position that night in the room next door. "But I didn't think nothing of it. Figured it was business."

Like the other girls in residence, Molly is afraid that the killer, still loose, may be wandering in and out of the house unimpeded, and in an effort to have their voices heard, the ladies of 25 Dauphine Street charged en masse into the second district police headquarters and demanded a more thorough investigation. It remains to be seen what the official response to such tactics will be.

October 9, 1849

To The Editor:

I believe I speak on behalf of the vast majority of residents in what were formerly respectable neighborhoods when I say I have concerns over the direction vice is spreading. At one time contained to the docks and the immediate vicinity of Girod Street, now there is hardly an area in the city that isn't affected by the rapid and licentious growth of entertainment establishments. On my block alone, there are at least half a dozen homes (that once housed upstanding families) that are now given over to dens of iniquity, with laughter and music pouring out at all hours of night, men in and out, and outbursts of all nature occurring on the street. Now there has been this murder at number twenty-five, only blocks from where decent hardworking citizens live. Already several neighbors have sold homes at a loss to escape the scourge creeping in our direction, and I have no doubt that by week's end another two or three will make the decision to sell their houses for less than they paid, simply to leave the rapidly declining area.

If left unchecked, the entire city will have the blight of drinking and promiscuity on every street, and there will be nowhere remaining for respectable citizens to live.

Signed,

Suffering Respectable Citizen

Chapter Three

❦

Disturbed by the tenor of the articles, Sara stopped reading for a minute and concentrated on taking slow, even breaths. She felt a panic attack creeping up on her, the kind that before would have had her reaching for the Vicodin. But she couldn't do that, wouldn't. She had to learn how to handle emotion on her own, without chemical intervention.

She sucked in another deep pull of air. She hadn't expected to feel the clawing scratch of anxiety from flipping through these papers, but there was something about the casual disregard of everyone in the articles for Anne Donovan, the woman. She almost seemed an afterthought, a happy means to air their grievances, concerns, but not worth noting beyond the gruesome, sensationalist aspects of her death. They seemed to take delight in mentioning how she'd been mutilated, but no one bothered to say where she came from, how she had found herself in the position of prostitute, or if she had left behind a grieving family.

It was so much like the media coverage of her own mother's murder that the parallels scared Sara. That had been difficult for her to learn to deal with, to let go of the hatred, disgust, annoyance, when the newspaper turned her mother's case into an opportunity to blast the prosecutor. It had never been about her mother. It was about the flaws in the police department, the stubborn prosecutor, and his determination to push through a weak case against Rafe. Everyone had their damn agenda, and no one cared that she had lost her mother.

But it bothered her that all of that baggage could resurface so easily, that she couldn't maintain distance. God, she just wanted everything to be over and done, gone. She wanted to be normal again.

"You okay?"

Sara sat up straight, mortified. Gabriel was looking at her, but she appreciated that instead of pity or horror on his face, he just looked mildly curious.

"Yeah, I'm okay." She was. She would be okay. If she just willed it enough, it would happen. It would. Because she understood something about herself. Even in the worst, horrific moments, she could still reach out and find hope. It would be better eventually. She just had to fight to get there, to not lose it along the way.

And there was something about Gabriel St. John looking at her, his dark brown eyes assuring her that he had secrets too, that he had suffered, that had her opening her mouth and saying, "There aren't just physical parallels between this case and my mother's murder, there are also media similarities. I guess I wasn't expecting that—it startled me."

Immediately she regretted speaking. Now would come the questions, the pity, the curiosity, the suspicion of her motives in working on this book with him. Talking about her mother's death always left her feeling vulnerable, exposed, and she didn't want that with Gabriel. She didn't want him thinking she was crazy.

"What kind of similarities?"

The question was so matter-of-fact, Sara realized immediately that Gabriel was different. Of course he was going to be different. He wrote true crime books. In every conversation they'd had about her mother there was no shock, no flush of pity, none of the stumbling to say something comforting that she usually got from people. He was tactful, but very matter-of-fact. That made her feel an odd sense of relief. He was used to dealing with the details of violent crimes and wouldn't pester her with uncomfortable questions. Nor had it stopped him from asking her to participate in his research, so he must not question her motives, or mental stability.

"Well, I'm not sure what I expected from nineteenth-century journalists, but just like today, every journalist seems to have an angle, a point to get across. Whether it's the lack of police attention to crimes in impoverished areas in Anne Donovan's case, or the accusation that the prosecutor was going for the big fish to win PR points in my mother's case, it's not about the victim. Which it should be."

Gabriel had one arm over the back of his standard black office chair, and he tilted his head slightly to study her. "And it is, to the people the victim mattered to. But a crime, a murder, punches a hole in the illusion that society is functioning as it should. It's a time when people look around, question what's wrong in their world, and make both accusations and suggestions for corrections. So that victim indirectly matters to everyone who touches the case in any way, who lives in the neighborhood, or reads the newspaper. They have an impact in death, and maybe in a larger way to more people than they actually had in life."

Sara stared at him, wondering why she'd never thought of it in quite that way. Noticing that her heart rate had settled down to normal, anxiety abated, she was trying to shuffle her thoughts into order and formulate a response when he suddenly stood up.

"Walk with me." He headed toward the door, his strides purposeful.

"Walk with you? Where?" Yet she found herself rising off the couch, setting the packet of papers down on the cushion, following him.

"I need to take pictures of the house where the murder took place for the book. Let's go do that now while the building won't be in a shadow." Gabriel was pulling a camera out of an end table drawer by the front door to the apartment.

Sara thought he had intriguing and eclectic furnishings. Everything looked as if it had been accumulated over a long period of time, each piece random and slightly shabby, yet overall the room harmonized, exuded a warmth. It said to her that he cared about what he surrounded himself with, appreciated objects, but not too much. Nothing was perfect or overthought. It looked like he just did what pleased him.

It was a lesson she would like to learn.

He didn't take a camera case with him, just wrapped the strap twice around his wrist and gripped the lens cap, which struck her as an accident waiting to happen. It looked like an expensive camera, and if he dropped it, she didn't think the result would be positive, but he didn't look at all concerned. Gabriel opened the door and gestured for her to walk through first.

She realized that after he followed her out he didn't lock the door behind them. She counted to three as she walked down the stairs, told herself it didn't matter, that he must have a button that he had pushed on the inside of the doorknob to lock it. But she couldn't stop herself from asking, "Did you lock your door?"

"No."

She was looking forward and down at her feet, worried about the steps, taking the curve on the narrower than normal staircase with cautious movements, afraid she'd slip and break her neck. So she couldn't see Gabriel's expression, but he didn't sound particularly worried about burglars, any more than he seemed concerned about his camera.

"It's safer to lock your door." Sara knew she sounded anal, and she was, knew she had a fear that was huge and growing irrational, but the police had told her there was no forced entry at her mother's house. That the killer had either known her mom, or the doors hadn't been locked. It seemed risky to leave a door unlocked for anyone to walk in. At any time.

"The courtyard gate locks."

"Oh, okay, good." Sara glanced back at him, and he just gave her a small, brief smile. It was hugely reassuring. She had expected he would either argue with her, or point out that she was paranoid. Suggest that she needed to let it go, get over it. She had heard all of those things, a hundred times over, from coworkers, friends, and neighbors who genuinely wanted what was best for her, but didn't understand a damn thing.

That Gabriel just told her what she needed to hear and left it at that filled her with relief. He *was* different. And it was kind of nice.

"So what was life like for a prostitute in 1849?" she asked, as they went through the gate, the sun hitting her in the face and sending her digging through her purse for her sunglasses.

"It sucked."

Something about the tone of his voice made her glance up. Was that meant to be a double entendre? It was hard to tell because he wasn't even looking at her. He had his eyes down on his camera and he was prying the lens cap off. But there had been an edge of amusement, or an awareness of the horrific irony, maybe the need to lighten the subject matter . . . she wasn't sure what exactly, because Gabriel was hard to interpret, but something told her he had just made a joke.

Which she liked.

He lifted his camera, shot a quick succession of photos from right to left, the last one of her. She wasn't prepared for it, so she was sure she was staring dumbly at him in it. "No pictures of me, please."

"But the light's good," he said, giving her another of those tiny smiles where the corner of his mouth lifted crookedly.

God, Sara really didn't want to like him.

That would be just one more way for her to trip and fall.

But she was definitely in danger of becoming a bubble girl of her own making, afraid of everything, even her own proverbial shadow.

Coming to New Orleans was an emotional risk, and maybe it hadn't been running away so much as stepping outside her comfort zone. Forcing herself to face the future without fear.

She was definitely still terrified, but suddenly reassured that this trip had been exactly what she needed to retake control of her life.

❧

VIGILANCE COMMITTEE
PRESSURES POLICE TO TAKE ACTION

October 9, 1849—While the police commissioner may not be inclined to listen to the pleas of prostitutes, it would seem he is willing to bend when the collective voices of the VIGILANCE COMMITTEE cry for action. In a city besieged by crime, it is more common than not for a murder of a fallen woman to go unnoticed, but it is just that cavalier attitude that has finally sent certain citizens beyond the edge of their tolerance. Comprised of various wealthy and influential peoples, the Vigilance Committee was formed to bring attention to the spiraling immorality and violence of certain districts. The murder of young Anne Donovan, in its fury and grotesqueness, and the lack of arrest of the gentleman who should by all accounts be a primary suspect, is a sign of the pervasive corruption and complicity in our government.

Given the dependence of Mr. John Thiroux on the well-known hallucinogenic drink absinthe, as well as his excessive consumption of whiskey and frequent opium smoking, it is not a stretch to imagine he could have carried out such an act of violence. Despite who he is, and who he may or may not have contributed funds to, if a man commits a crime, he should be held accountable for it.

It would seem the police agree, or at least fear public reaction otherwise, as they have set out to investigate Miss Donovan's murder, and by witness report are focusing their attentions on Mr. Thiroux.

The light *was* good. It hit the side of Sara's face, reflected in her blond hair, and showed the healthy rich color of her arms and legs. Gabriel lifted his camera and took another picture of her, zooming in on her face, clicking multiple times as her eyes went wide and she made a sound of distress.

"Stop!" Her hand went up in front of his lens, actually bumping it with her fingers in her vehemence.

He didn't want to make her uncomfortable, so he lowered the camera. But he wasn't sorry he'd taken the shots. Sara was a study in contrasts, like the city around her. She was strong, but fragile, had endured tragedy, yet was still beautiful. Perhaps more so now that her eyes spoke of suffering and lessons learned. He had noticed that her hands moved restlessly, always pulling at something—her dress, her hair, her purse, like she was always pondering, worrying, watching.

There was no particular logic to it, but he was attracted to her, and he recognized the danger in that. But it didn't make him any less intrigued.

"So how much do you know about the history of New Orleans?" He rewrapped the camera strap around his wrist and started walking.

"Just a vague outline."

"In 1849 New Orleans was a city that had grown quickly because of the influx of immigrants into the port and Americans who moved in for business opportunities after the Louisiana Purchase. There were also a huge number of gold rushers who stopped in that year on their way to California to make their fortune. Picture a couple of hundred thousand people living in a hot, humid city surrounded by water. A thriving port, lots of sailors and gold rushers—that all leads to drinking, gambling, and prostitution. And of course, the aftereffect of that is crime. They say there was a murder a week in New Orleans at that time."

"Which explains the attitude in some of those newspaper articles. They seemed disgusted."

"Exactly. But people get used to violence if they see enough of it. And if it's contained in an area where no so-called decent people live, then it's easy to ignore."

"I don't know how anyone gets used to violence."

Gabriel glanced back, surprised at how breathless Sara's words sounded. They were walking up Dumaine at his pace, and he realized he was striding way too fast. Sara was breathing hard, and she was still two feet behind him, her eyes trained on the precarious sidewalk.

He slowed down. "Sorry. I have long legs."

"And I have short ones." She glanced up and smiled. "These sidewalks could stand to be replaced."

"But that's part of the charm of the Quarter. And I've seen women negotiate Bourbon Street in high heels after kicking back shots, and it's amazing to me that they don't break their ankles."

"I've never been to Bourbon Street. This is my first time here."

"Maybe we can go tonight. You need to at least say you've been to Bourbon Street." Gabriel had no idea why he made the offer. Well, actually he did. It was because he was trying to make conversation with Sara, trying to make her comfortable around him, and he liked the idea of showing her around. That small, nagging attraction was driving him too, and he knew it, should stop it, but wasn't.

"Sure," she said. "That would be fun."

Though she looked like she thought it would be anything but.

"You'll see that certain things in New Orleans haven't changed in the past one hundred and fifty years. Still plenty of drinking and sex." The very things that had sucked him in, the sins he still missed. He had learned nothing, knew he should condemn the licentious, knew he should want the purity of life as he was trying to lead it now, but he didn't. He still wanted to taste a woman's flesh and to float off into the haze, removed from the indelicate rude details of mortality. Those were his vices, and he knew that.

He stopped and stared at the light blue house across Dauphine Street.

But he needed to know, needed to believe, that while he did most certainly have flaws, and deep ones, he was not capable of violence. Anger. That he could not have picked up a knife and sliced through Anne's ivory skin, drawing blood over and over.

He didn't think he could. Didn't think he'd done that.

But he needed to know. Or he would never let it go, never forgive himself, and the doubt would eat through the center of his already rotting soul.

October 9, 1849

Report taken by William Davidson, second district

The women of twenty-five Dauphine Street were cooperative in discussing the night in question, but none have any helpful insight to offer. No one saw or heard anyone entering or leaving Miss Donovan's room, other than Mr. Thiroux, and no

one heard anything out of the ordinary, aside
from a single cry from Miss Donovan overheard
by Molly Faye. Approximate time thought to be
one a.m., given that Miss Faye insists her client
was still in her room at the time, and that he left
at a quarter past the hour when he realized he
was late returning home.

Miss Donovan's room is shuttered to the street
and remained so, and there is a great hulk of a
man who watches the front door for Madame
Conti. He insists no one got past him at any time
during the hours in question. In speaking to the
six ladies who were in the house, I can conclude
with a fair amount of accuracy that there were
five men present at the time of Miss Donovan's
death, including Mr. Thiroux and the doorman.
Twelve persons total when counting the victim.
Three of the six ladies provide alibis for three of
the men, and vice versa. Two ladies provided
alibis for each other, as they were playing cards
together in their shared room. That leaves only
Madame Conti, the doorman (whose name is Jim
Fury), and Mr. John Thiroux in doubt.

While it is easy to imagine the giant of a
doorman, or the street-hard Madame Conti as
capable of violence, I cannot see where either
would benefit from the death of Miss Donovan.
Madame Conti certainly had much to lose in
terms of business from the notoriety of such a
death, and no one in the house indicated there
was ever any animosity displayed between Jim
Fury (despite his sobriquet) and Miss Donovan.

The natural conclusion, therefore, is that Mr.
Thiroux took the knife to his lover under the
influence of pharmaceuticals and stabbed her to
death.

Sara really had no interest in going to Bourbon Street.
From all accounts, it was loud and dirty, and she envisioned
drunken men spilling beer on her while women with vast

amounts of cleavage vied for attention from same-said drunken men. It made her brain hurt just thinking about it. But she had said yes immediately, because the offer came from Gabriel, and that disturbed her. She wasn't in a good place. It wasn't the time to get involved with a man.

But she didn't see herself begging off the plans either.

Gabriel had stopped walking and was taking his lens cap off again.

"Is that the house?" He was staring across the street at an innocuous light blue structure that came right up to the sidewalk like all the buildings in the French Quarter. The house had darker blue shutters closed tightly on both the bottom and top floors. Only the little third-floor dormers were open to light. While it certainly looked old, it wasn't decrepit. A little tired maybe, but not falling down. "It doesn't look very big."

"It's not. Just a parlor, which was for gambling and drinking, a private salon that served as Madame's office, and six small rooms for the girls on the second floor. Madame Conti used the third floor as her private suite."

"There were only six prostitutes working there? From that article I read I got the impression there were more."

"There were. Only not every girl was entitled to her own room. Some doubled up. And some entertained their clients in the parlor."

The image of that made Sara grimace. Sometimes she thought modern women had a glamorized vision of bordellos, but the truth didn't sound at all sensual or glamorous. It sounded cheap and dirty. A hard and dangerous way to eek out a living. "And a lot of the street was similar houses?"

"Yes."

"I wonder what led women to prostitution," she mused out loud. What had caused her great-great-grandmother, Anne Donovan, to feel such desperation? Or had she actually enjoyed it, sought it out? Likely Sara would never know.

"Drugs, alcohol, poverty, rebelliousness. Not much different than now." Gabriel squatted down on the sidewalk and lifted his camera.

"Are you a photographer too?" she asked, realizing he had said these shots were for the book.

"No. It's just easier to take my own photos."

But he did have an eye for it. Sara could see that. He shifted to the left, looked up at the sky, in and out of the lens, adjusting his shots, adjusting his zoom lens.

"It's not called number twenty-five anymore." There was an address plate above the mailbox, to the right of the door, with its single brick step leading down to the walk. It was a quiet street, with no traffic and little activity. The light blue house looked lonely, lacking in foliage or flowers. "Do the owners know a murder happened here?"

"I don't know. I've never spoken to the owner. The house is owned by a trust, and when I contacted the lawyer in charge of it, he gave me a big old no when I asked permission to take interior photos. He tried to tell me the crime happened in the house next door."

"How do you know it didn't?"

He turned and looked up at her. His dark eyes were unreadable. "Trust me. I know. I do my research."

Sara shivered. The hair on her arms had suddenly gone up, even though it was an easy eighty-five degrees. She looked past him to the house again. "What do you know about Anne Donovan? How did she end up here? Drugs, alcohol, or poverty? Or all of the above?"

"From witness accounts of her behavior, it was poverty. No one mentions drugs or alcohol at all."

"In relation to her. They said her lover used opium and alcohol."

"Yes. Absinthe in particular."

The heat and humidity were bothering Sara, which had to be caused by the lack of sleep. She was used to the air feeling like a wet towel on her head, since she had spent the majority of her life in Southern Florida. But she felt like she needed some water desperately, dizziness creeping up on her in unexpected waves. There was also a persistent ache in her right side that she thought might feel better if she wasn't standing, so she forced herself to squat down on the sidewalk next to Gabriel. Pulling her skirt over her knees, she found her balance. She didn't actually want her legs or backside to make contact with the ground.

"Is absinthe alcohol? I think I've heard of it, but I'm not sure."

"It's the famed Green Fairy, an alcoholic drink made with oil of wormwood, and served diluted with sugar water. It was thought to have hallucinogenic and addictive properties, so it was made illegal in the early twentieth century."

"Does it?" Sara turned to Gabriel, wobbling slightly. She wasn't strong enough to hold herself up without effort, though he wasn't having any problem.

Gabriel stared back, close enough to her that she could see the faint blond stubble on his chin. "It's addictive in the sense that once you've been to that place where you feel brilliant and charming, intelligent and attractive, you want to revisit it frequently. And eventually you never want to leave."

Then he stood up, abruptly, and crossed the street without looking either way. It had almost sounded like he had personal experience with addiction himself. Or maybe she was just reading that into everyone because she was so hyperaware from her own problems. With the sleeping pills, she hadn't wanted to feel intelligent and attractive, she had just wanted to sleep. Hard. To escape. And there had come a time when she hadn't wanted to wake up, to get out of bed, and that had scared her. That's when she'd gone to rehab.

Maybe Gabriel had a story. Maybe he didn't. Sara watched him take pictures of the front door, of the shutters, of the street going right and left, and the street sign. It was a strange surreal moment, the lonely, lovely little house behind him, sagging under the weight of its history, yet forging ahead, while Gabriel paced in the sunlight. He was an odd juxtaposition—fast and sporadic when he was in motion, yet completely and utterly still when he wasn't—and she liked to watch him. If anyone had told Sara two years ago she would be hunched down on the dirty cobblestones in New Orleans staring at a true crime writer she would have laughed. She hadn't expected to go anywhere, least of all this city. Yet her life had irrevocably changed and she had arrived in this moment for better or for worse.

The sky was fabulously blue behind the house, white clouds floating by, framing the roof. The third-floor windows were dusty, but the light was hitting them, enough so that when her eye roamed over the left window, she could see that a man was staring straight back at her from behind the glass.

Sara lost her balance and fell sideways onto the sidewalk, her heart racing. No one had been there before, she was sure of it. She caught herself and looked back up at the window. There was nothing there now.

"Gabriel!" she called, though she wasn't sure why. It was probably just the owner, curious to see who was out on the street. Who was staring at his house.

"Yeah?"

He turned and looked at her in question, his profile framed by the front door of the house behind him, and Sara felt the hair raise on her arms again, skin cool and clammy in the heat. She tried to stand up, but couldn't seem to figure out how to get vertical without spilling backward onto her butt or forward onto her knees. So she stayed put and nervously called, "There's someone in the house."

Gabriel was already crossing the street, his long strides eating up the steps so that he was in front of her in seconds, holding out his hand to give her much needed help. "How do you know someone's home?"

She clasped her hand in his gratefully and let his strength pull her up off the sidewalk. "Thanks." Letting go of him, she brushed the back of her skirt. "I saw someone in the third-floor window."

They both looked up. There was no one there.

"Well, I can take pictures of the exterior, whether the owner likes it or not."

That was true. And Sara wasn't sure why the man had un-nerved her so much. It was just unexpected, that face staring down on her. "Do you have any historic pictures of the house?"

"The oldest one I could find is from 1910."

"Did you grow up here?" she asked, as Gabriel gestured for them to start walking. Sara had actually been born in New Orleans, the result of her mother's brief affair with a bouncer on Bourbon Street. Her mother had been a normal, slightly rebellious but not outrageous, suburban middle-class teenager until her own mother had been murdered. Then within six months, Sara's mother had run away from her father, was drinking heavily and dancing in a nightclub, lying about her age since she was underage. By the time Sara was born, the bouncer was gone and so was her mother's job, but a new boyfriend had taken Jessie and her baby in. Two years after that, on her eighteenth birthday, her mother had run off to Florida with a retired doctor, who had brains and a lot of money, but not enough sense to know his young girlfriend was playing him for cash.

When he died, Jessie had started fresh with a house of her own, and had cut off all ties to her past until her father tracked them down when Sara won a scholarship to Tulane and had her name listed in the New Orleans paper.

Her mother had refused to speak to her father. And Sara had been too scared to take the scholarship and move to New Orleans, which would entail defying her mother, who claimed to hate her family and New Orleans, with no explanation as to why. So Sara had gone to Florida State instead, and never found the peace she'd been looking for, the connection to her mother, the need to understand what had motivated her for her entire life. Never got to hear her mother's true feelings about losing her own mother at such a young age.

Now Sara was the one who had lost her mother, and she hadn't dealt with it any better than her mother before her had.

"I did grow up here," Gabriel said, cutting across the street diagonally. "I can't live anywhere else." He glanced back. "What are you thinking about?"

"Nothing. The city. Why?" She pushed her sunglasses up on her nose.

"Because you forgot to watch your feet. So I knew you were thinking hard."

Sara stopped walking. He was right. She'd forgotten to watch for holes in the sidewalk. Yet it made her sound like such a freak. "I wasn't thinking hard. I was just thinking about the fact that I was smart not to take the scholarship I got to Tulane . . . that it was stupid at seventeen to think that I should leave home and all my friends to come here, where I was born, for no reason."

"Really? Then why did you want to come here in the first place?"

That was the goddamn rub, wasn't it? "I don't know. It doesn't matter." And how completely annoying that Gabriel had homed straight in on the crux of her dilemma. She wanted answers, wanted to know why her mother had made the choices she had. And the truth Sara needed to come to terms with was that there probably were no answers to her questions.

Side hurting again, Sara rubbed it with the palm of her hand, and looked around her. "Where are we, anyway? This isn't the way we got here, is it?"

"No. We're going in the opposite direction. To the cemetery."

Chapter Four

❦

Gabriel had expected Sara to protest. It was clearly on her lips to say no, but she surprised him, just like she had with his suggestion to head to Bourbon Street. She had agreed to the cemetery trip simply by following him. Only now they were at the gates of St. Louis #1, having crossed North Rampart to the shortest "Walk" sign ever created, and the cemetery was locked.

"Damn. They close the gate at three o'clock. We must have just missed it." But he wanted pictures of the cemetery, of Anne's tomb. The light was still good, the sky a crisp cerulean, and he was here. He didn't want to come back. He didn't like the cemetery any more than Sara did, given the way she was rubbing her arms like she was cold, and crossing her ankles, eyes wary.

To Gabriel, the cemetery symbolized the fact that he could never die, that much better people than him left this mortal realm, some far too soon, and he was condemned, by his own misconduct, to walk the earth forever without purpose. The cemetery made him angry, and it frustrated him that he was denied entrance, figuratively and literally. He didn't often use his strength, chose largely to ignore what he was and what he was capable of, but he wanted in, so he reached out, picked up the lock, and yanked it down.

It broke, separating so that he could easily detach it from the gate. "Look at that," he said, showing Sara the busted pieces, before shoving the gate open. "Guess we can go in after all."

Sara made a sound of protest. "Gabriel! It was locked for a reason. They don't want us in there."

He was already moving inside, knowing she would follow him. Her fear of the cemetery, of breaking the rules, wasn't nearly as great as her fear of being left alone. The shells crunched under his feet as he walked, and pausing at the first tomb on the right, he turned back to her. "Come on, Sara. It's not a big deal."

"The gate was locked." She had inched forward, just inside the gate, but she was peeking around like she expected to get arrested for trespassing, or maybe to encounter either a mugger or a ghost.

"I'll replace the broken lock. But since it's open, we might as well take some pictures. I'll show you Anne's tomb." He wasn't sure why he didn't just let the whole thing drop. Why he didn't just turn around and take Sara back to his apartment. But he thought she needed to be pushed. Or maybe he wanted to be pushed, and if he pushed her, she'd push back.

They had a lot in common. Both living in a precarious little isolation tent, struggling to survive, to be normal. Kidding themselves. Lying and ignoring the blatant truth—that they were clinging to the edge, one stumble short of going over the side.

"Come on," he said again, and this time he reached out, took Sara's hand in his, and pulled her forward into the cemetery.

She sucked in a quick breath and looked up at him with luminous blue eyes. Her head went back and forth, a protest, but at the same time, she walked forward, settling in beside him, her hand light and warm in his. It had been a long time since he had touched anyone, and the sensation of warmth, of her hand lightly shifting in his, their skin caressing, felt so acutely good, so intense and real, that painful longing rose up in him. The desperate need for someone to share pleasure, conversation, time with. Futile, ridiculous wants that he had no business entertaining.

So he let go of her hand and moved forward at a pace he knew she couldn't match.

He was standing in front of the tomb he had paid for, that held the remains of Anne Donovan, when Sara stopped next to him and said, "It's very peaceful in here."

"Yes." It was. The cemetery was quiet, the sun silently beating down on the many white tombs, casting a shadow over the front of Anne's tomb. "This is where Anne Donovan is buried."

"How do you know? There's no nameplate."

"It fell off. Marble tends to crack from the moist climate, and then it just drops off without warning." And he hadn't replaced it. Wasn't exactly sure why not, but he hadn't. "But church records indicate this is the correct tomb. She's interred in it alone." Another point about which he felt some guilt. It made no logical sense, given that he knew her soul didn't reside in the brick structure, but in New Orleans tombs were crowded, families buried together, the bones of three, eight, twenty people, all together in one tomb. It seemed a comfort, an appropriate display of connectedness to other mortal beings. Anne lay alone. In death as she had in life.

"I read that John Thiroux paid for the burial."

"Yes. She was cremated first."

"I wonder why."

Because he hadn't been able to handle the image of her body, once so young and beautiful, decaying beneath its brutal wounds.

"I don't know." It was an attractive tomb, with a wrought iron gate around it, tidy and recently painted, a weeping angel statue resting pensively on top. Gabriel hadn't wanted that damn angel statue, had been appalled when he'd first seen it a hundred and fifty years ago, but he had given his lawyer at the time the funds for the tomb and had him handle all the details. He'd been too grief- and guilt-stricken, too chronically drunk to make the arrangements on his own, and it was of course the ultimate irony that the lawyer had chosen the symbol of an angel weeping to decorate the top of the tomb.

Lifting his camera, he took shots of the tomb, of the angel.

"It must have been a sad, lonely funeral."

Gabriel shook his head, wondering if that would have

been better or worse than the spectacle he could still see and hear and feel as clearly as if it were the day before. "Quite the contrary. People have an intense fascination for murder. Anne Donovan's funeral was a crowded, throbbing mob of morbid curiosity seekers. It rained that day, a torrent of steaming, warm water, and the street, the sidewalks, the cemetery, were a sliding, muddy mess. The temperature had dropped twenty degrees with the storm, and there was a fog, so that all you could see was the black hat in front of you, and the tombs rising suddenly out of the mist. A fitting ending to a gruesome death." And Gabriel had also seen a woman who had approached him, a child's hand clasped tightly in her own, her face pinched with anxiety, cheeks streaked with tears. She had slapped him soundly, straight across the cheek, penetrating the fog of the air, his brain, the ever-present guilt. It had been Anne's cousin, or so she had said, and she urged him passage to hell, before retreating, never to be seen or heard from again.

But the irony was that Gabriel had already been condemned to a personal hell long before receiving her vehement request. He was still in it.

Sara leaned against the wrought iron gate surrounding the tomb and stared at the blank spot left by the crumbled nameplate. "No one deserves to die like that. It's obvious, isn't it? Yet so true."

Her arm brushed his, the top of her head only coming up to his chin. Gabriel was surprised again at how petite she was, at how fragile she could look, yet how determined her voice was. "This must be hard for you, because of your mother."

A sigh slid out of her mouth. "It is." Fingers gripped the fleur-de-lis spikes of the fence. "Her funeral was similar to Anne's in that there was tons of media coverage. Spectators. It was noisy and obnoxious, and disrespectful. And everything was happening so fast in those first few days, the police questions changing, always shifting, always looking for something, the media searching for the angle, trying to figure out which way to take the story. I really wasn't aware of it at the time, I was just numb, trying to help the investigation, trying to deal with the details, and the shock. The police were at the funeral, a good ten strong, in full patrolmen uniform. It was to ensure crowd control, they said, but it was so invasive. And the paper made a big deal out of me showing up with Rafe . . . but the thing is, he cared more about my mom than anyone else. He and I were friends. Of course I would go with him."

"You went with Rafe?" Gabriel knew that actually from reading the articles online about Sara's mother's death, but he wanted to hear what Sara would say about him.

"It was completely normal to go with my mom's boyfriend given that I don't have any other family." A finger slipped under her sunglasses and wiped at her eye, but he didn't think she was crying. "At the time I didn't realize he was the primary suspect. It only took the police five days to decide he was guilty and arrest him for murder, but it took nearly a year to acquit him in court."

"Like John Thiroux." Him. "Is that why you're interested in this case? Or is it strictly your mother's case that you want to solve?"

"No. I want to solve both. Though I don't think my mother's murder is solvable at this point. I came more to see if forensics could shed light on Anne's case, and yes, because there are strange similarities. The weapon used, the method of the murderer—killing them in bed. Boyfriends accused. Boyfriends who discovered them." And something else that Sara suspected no one else knew, not even Gabriel. That Anne Donovan was the great-grandmother of Jessie Michaels. That before her mother had died, she had received a copy of the original newspaper article announcing Anne Donovan's murder.

Sara hadn't told the police, or Rafe, or Gabriel what her mother had gotten anonymously in the mail thirty-six hours before her death, because Sara had the horrible feeling that only one man could have known about the connection, and confirmation of that would shatter her. Some answers were far worse than never knowing at all. She shouldn't even be talking to Gabriel about her feelings, emotions over her mother's case, but he was easy to talk to. He stood and listened, and there was never any judgment written on his face. It was like he understood he had no right to cast stones, but at the same time he was capable of compassion, rational discourse.

"I would guess there have been a lot of boyfriends accused

of killing their lovers. And I'm sure a large percentage actually did it."

"Do you think he did it? John Thiroux?" Sara stared hard at the tomb, at the crumbling square where a name and date should have been, but was gone, obliterated, like the woman behind the stone. The surface blurred and crossed in front of her eyes, the heat enveloping Sara and closing up her throat.

"I haven't read all the documents yet. We don't have the DNA results from the knife back yet. I don't know if he did it or not."

It shouldn't even matter. But it did. Sara felt that if she could figure out what had happened to Anne Donovan, she could figure out the pieces of her own life. She could triumph over death, let the past go, face the future with hope. Go back to work. Be normal.

The grieving process was different for everyone. Sara found that hers included striving desperately to find ways in which she could exert control, rebel against a universe that dictated her fate.

"We're going to pick this apart until we have an answer," she said. "For Anne. For my mother."

Gabriel made a sound. "It's for you and me, too, Sara, as much as it is for them. We need to know, don't we? But the thing is, there may be no answer."

She believed him, even though she hated it, even though she wondered why it mattered to him. What did he care, really? This was her family, her past, her present, her future. Not his.

The dizziness wasn't abating, and the cemetery suddenly felt stifling, claustrophobic. "Can we leave? I need a drink of water."

And without waiting for him, she turned and headed toward the gate, sliding in the gravel in her terry-cloth flip-flops. When she burst out onto the front sidewalk, she felt like she could breathe again. But the anxiety didn't go away.

She wondered if it ever would.

❧

After stopping for water from a street vendor, Sara had decided to go back to her apartment and try to sleep, and Gabriel figured that was probably the best thing for her. She had looked pasty and clammy in the cemetery, actually swaying on her feet slightly as she turned to leave.

The water seemed to help, restoring color to her face, and she had bought a granola bar and eaten it before getting in her car to head back. Gabriel had accepted her plea to postpone their trip to Bourbon Street until the following night, and he walked back to his apartment, feet comfortable on the uneven sidewalks. He had lived in the French Quarter for a hundred and fifty years, had never lived anywhere else on earth, and he appreciated its familiarity. He knew every crack, every building, every nuance, every odd local, and every change that occurred, however slight. Intentionally, he chose to cut down Bourbon, to pass the bars that were already gearing up for Friday night. To force himself to walk past signs that advertised beer as three for the price of one. Hand grenades. Mojitos. Jager bombs. To smell the unique odor of beer, bleach, and fried food.

It gave him a feeling of power, of control, an encouragement that he was still his own master, when he could stroll past temptation to drink every three feet and not succumb. In his human body it was easier to fall prey to weakness and sin, to struggle the way mortals did. It had been meant to serve as a source of understanding for him as he had watched and protected those around him, but it had only accelerated his fall. Illuminated his own flaws and stoked his craving for escape from the overwhelming reality of human pain and suffering.

Whenever Gabriel started down Bourbon Street, he always wondered what would happen if one day he could no longer traverse the hot coals, and picked up a drink. But so far he had always resisted, and he did again.

Only to arrive home and find Alex waiting just inside his courtyard gate, lounging in Gabriel's wrought iron chair reading the newspaper.

The gate was still locked, of course. Alex was fond of the dramatic.

Gabriel sighed, not feeling up to dealing with Alex and his manipulations, but at the same time grateful Sara had gone home. He didn't want Alex encountering her. "What are you doing here?"

Alex smiled, a charming smile full of straight white teeth. "Is that any way to greet an old friend?"

"I wasn't aware we were ever friends." Gabriel walked straight past him, and headed for the stairs.

Following him, Alex said, "I think technically our relationship is more like that of brothers. We were angels once together. Now we're demons. Grigori demon brothers." Alex laughed. "I like that. It sounds like we're a circus act. The Amazing Grigori Demon Brothers will dazzle you with their scintillating feats of sin."

Gabriel rolled his eyes as he jogged up the stairs.

"Hey, you're not laughing. That was funny. I'm funny."

"Whatever." He opened his front door and went in, dropping the camera on his end table. Ignoring Alex, he headed for the kitchen. Lunch was long gone, and he was hungry.

"Since you have no manners whatsoever, I'll just invite myself in and make myself comfortable," Alex called from the living room.

"I knew you would." Gabriel couldn't even bring himself to ask Alex why he was paying him a visit, even if he was curious. He didn't want to show any interest at all, because Alex—like all the other Grigori demons—was not a man Gabriel wanted to spend time with. The Grigori demons were a reminder of what he had been, what he was, what he thought in his heart and soul he was better than, but time showed over and over he wasn't.

As Gabriel pulled out a frozen burrito and tore off the wrapper, Alex said, "I'm looking for Marguerite. Have you seen her?"

Gabriel paused in shoving the burrito into the microwave and glanced back. He couldn't see Alex, who was probably sitting on the couch. "I haven't seen Marguerite in years." Didn't want to. Marguerite had betrayed him during his trial and he trusted her even less than the rest of the Grigori.

"No? I hadn't realized that. But if you do see her, please let me know. I need to speak to her about something and she's been gone for months, and I can't seem to find her."

"Maybe she doesn't want to be found. At least not by you." When the bell dinged, Gabriel removed the burrito from the microwave and dropped it on a paper towel.

Alex sounded offended. "I'm her father. We have a good relationship."

Gabriel didn't know what constituted a quality relationship between a demon and his half-demon daughter, but Alex and Marguerite did seem to get along. But it had nothing to do with him. "I'll let her know if I see her, but I can't imagine I will."

"You don't get out much, do you?"

"No." That was intentional. Gabriel walked into the living room, taking a bite out of his snack, and found Alex sitting on the couch looking at his camera.

"Who's the blonde?" Alex turned the camera around and Gabriel saw Sara on the viewing screen, standing on the street, in profile.

Damn. The idea that Alex would even know of Sara's existence made him uncomfortable. Striving to sound casual, not wanting to alert Alex in any way, he just shrugged. "Just a girl who does some research for me."

"She could be hot if she didn't look like she's just come off a three-day bender only to find out her cat died." Alex made a face at Sara's image, his lip curling up. "You could do better than this if you're looking for a little fun."

Gabriel didn't agree with Alex's assessment of Sara at all, but that wasn't the point. "I'm not looking for fun. It's a business relationship." Not that he wouldn't like to explore other, more intimate possibilities, but it couldn't happen. He wouldn't allow it to happen.

Alex set down the camera and gave him a wry look. "I don't doubt it. You're not exactly known for being a fun guy. What I have never been able to figure out is why you don't just embrace what you are. You're fallen. You're a demon. Live it up a little, Gabe. Enjoy it."

Yet Gabriel still had a conscience, where Alex had none. Or at least Alex could rationalize his way through anything. "Your concern is touching, but I'm fine."

"What you are is in a purgatory of your own making. You don't seek redemption, but you don't embrace sin either." Alex stood up, frowning at him. "It's like you have no purpose—you exist just to exist." He clapped him on the shoulder. "Take care. I'll see you around."

And he was gone, leaving Gabriel with a half-chewed bite of burrito in his mouth and the knowledge that Alex was right. Until he knew if he had killed Anne or not, he could never move on.

To what he didn't know, but that was a step for another day.

First he had to get to the truth before the doubt consumed him and the loneliness eventually drove him back to the comfort of the bottle.

❧

Sara was struggling to stay awake, knowing it would be a disaster to take a nap at five in the afternoon when she was already having trouble sleeping at night. She paced back and forth in her apartment, hating the dingy gray carpet, the purple and gray tweed sofa. It was cheap furniture, but that wasn't what bothered her—she didn't need labels or expensive fabrics. What she didn't like was that it had no character. Nothing in the room reflected her—her likes, dislikes, interests. She loved houseplants and artwork, soft, aging quilts, and flat-screen TVs with TiVo so she could watch all the reality shows she couldn't get enough of.

It had only been two days, and she was already realizing that she was no transient. It wasn't her personality. She needed her possessions, her life, surrounding her with familiarity and a sense of comfort, of sturdiness. But her life was all boxed up in a storage unit in Naples.

When the phone rang, she dove for it, grateful for the distraction from her sleepiness. She was afraid if she sat down, she'd be out for the count, and then all possibility of actual REM that night would disappear.

"Hello?"

"Is this Sara Michaels?"

"Yes." Wishing she had checked the number on the screen, Sara answered cautiously.

"This is Robert Blackman with the *Naples Daily News*, and I wanted to speak to you about Dr. Marino's acquittal."

Shit. Sara sighed. "No comment."

"Is it true you've moved to New Orleans?"

"Who told you that?" she asked, shocked. It sent shivers up her spine to realize they were watching her, tracking her in essence. Then in an attempt at recovery, hoping he would drop the issue, she added, "No, it's not true."

"No? But I know you've sold your condo and your mother's house and quit your job. So when Dr. Marino moves to the West Coast, you'll be going with him then?"

A shudder of disgust rolled over Sara. "No." She hung up, shaking. It wasn't over. It had followed her.

But she had known that all along. She could run, but she couldn't hide.

And the whole truth she had been trying so damn hard to accept and act on was that it was time to turn and face it.

Conquer it.

She picked up the phone with shaking fingers and dialed Gabriel.

"Hi, it's Sara."

Gabriel sounded surprised, but maybe, she hoped, pleasantly so. "Hi. How are you feeling?"

"Much better." Sort of. Sara took a deep breath. "Is the invitation to hit Bourbon Street still open? I think it could be fun after all."

If she had been worried about his reaction, he gave her a good one. He was definitely surprised. Definitely pleased. He answered without hesitation. "Of course it's still open. And maybe we can grab some dinner first. The street doesn't get really interesting until after ten."

"Great. I'll be over in about an hour." Just enough time to get ready. The idea of a drink on Bourbon Street suddenly held a hell of a lot of appeal.

October 9, 1849

Interview with Mr. Thiroux, conducted by William Davidson

Mr. Thiroux willingly agreed to questioning, and refused the right to contact his attorney. Interview was conducted in his suite on Royal Street, at the corner of Orleans. Mr. Thiroux expressed what appeared to me to be sincere remorse and regret over the death of Miss

Donovan, and indicated he would be paying for
her burial, as there is no family to take care of
arrangements and expenses.

When asked to explain what happened on the
night in question, Mr. Thiroux gave this account:

"I had several glasses of absinthe and smoked
a small amount of opium. I fell asleep shortly
after arriving at eight p.m. When I awoke it was
dark and I thought Anne was sleeping, since I
could see she was on the bed, her arm lying by
her side. I decided to sketch her and began to do
so, after a few moments moving closer to see the
expression on her face. I slipped in her blood on
the floor and, glancing up, saw what had been
done to her. She was obviously dead, horrifically
so, so I went for Madame Conti. First though, I
disgraced myself by vomiting on the floor, so
shocked I was by the sight before me of what had
been done to a woman I cared a great deal for."

If no one else entered the house, if there was
no struggle or resistance from Miss Donovan,
which witnesses verify, the sad conclusion I must
draw is that Mr. Thiroux, under the influence of
inebriants, entered into a violent rage and
murdered his lover, with no premeditation, or
memory of the incident. It is a horrific testament
to the rage drink can bring out in a man, and
Miss Donovan paid the ultimate price of liquor.

Chapter Five

❧

ARREST IMMINENT!

October 10, 1849—The police in three days have gone from being prepared to dismiss the murder of Miss Donovan as unsolvable, to having Mr. John Thiroux virtually TRIED and CONVICTED of the crime even prior to his arrest. No attempts have been made to investigate alternative suspects, and official police reports read by this reporter indicate sights are firmly set on the prosecution of the artist, philanthropist, and quiet scholar.

Temperance advocates, gather your arguments, as this case will prove to be a testing ground for the tolerance of the citizens of New Orleans to excessive drinking and pharmaceutical use. Choose your side and line up accordingly, as the impact on our local businesses, residences, and the very tenor of our city could be drastically altered by conclusions drawn regarding the crime of murder and its correlation to alcohol consumption.

"So just like that, they arrested John Thiroux?" Sara asked Gabriel, seated across the table from her at Brennan's restaurant on Royal Street. "With no evidence?" She ran her finger around the rim of her wineglass and turned the facts around in her head. It was interesting to sit and talk through the case logically, detached, removed by more than a century from the grim reality. For the first time, she could see the appeal of what Gabriel did for a living. Playing Hercule Poirot, but with no one to let down if you couldn't actually reach any conclusions. Much easier than thinking about her mom.

The sudden change of tenor in the original Anne Donovan investigation struck her as odd. Was Thiroux's arrest really media driven? The police were afraid of negative press? It seemed too broad a leap to make so early in her reading and research, but there had been a clear shift in the four days from murder to arrest.

"Well, there was evidence. He was in the room, he had blood on his hands. No one heard a struggle. No sign of any forced entry. Circumstantially, it would appear that John Thiroux was the logical suspect. As for motive, well, that's dicier, but he certainly had the opportunity." Gabriel spread a thick glob of butter on a piece of crusty French bread and bit it.

He'd already had three equally burdened slices and Sara was eyeing the butter with longing. It wasn't fair that Gabriel was tall and lean, yet he could eat half a stick of butter without batting an eye or seeming to gain a pound. If she ate that, she would sprout love handles spontaneously by the time the check for dinner arrived.

"If you think about it, under the exact same circumstances today, they would definitely take the person present at the scene in for questioning. You have to admit, he looks guilty." Gabriel bit the second half of the slice of bread, finishing it off.

"But you don't think he is, do you?" Otherwise she didn't think he would be investigating and writing about the case.

"I think it's all oddly inconsistent. We have a man, with no history of violence, under the influence of opium, which is a passive drug, and intoxicated from absinthe, which is non-hallucinogenic."

"You think. You said at the time they thought absinthe was

a hallucinogenic. And can you really know what it was he took that night?"

"No, I guess not. We just have his words. And I'm sure quality of the product varied." After sipping his water, Gabriel added, "But he stayed in the room. He sketched her. Why would he do that?"

"Because he had no clue what he was doing, what he had just done, out of it on drugs. Or because he took a sick pleasure in it? So he wouldn't get caught leaving the house with blood on him?" Sara shrugged. "I don't know. Why do criminals do anything? Crimes are random and weird." She glanced over at the restaurant's courtyard, its lush trees swaying in the night breeze, the fountain lit with a soft spotlight. There were tables out there, but none were being used, and it looked lonely, hidden, secretive.

"Not as random as you think. The reasons for murder are usually fairly simple. Greed. Rage. Curiosity. Greed is calculating, rage is messy, and curiosity kills are staged. It's the psychopath who curiosity kills, and psychopaths all have two things in common—they feel no remorse and they don't want to be caught."

"Was John Thiroux a psychopath?"

Gabriel's dark eyes stared steadily at her. "I don't think in this case anyone at the time ever considered it could be a premeditated crime. They seemed to assume it was a crime of passion, and I would have to agree, given the frenzy of the kill. Mutilating the face is considered a personal crime by modern profilers. If he did it, he probably wasn't a psychopath, because it would be odd for him to stay at the scene of the crime. Psychopaths don't want to be caught, and you would think he would have planned an escape if he had intended to kill her. But the police and the prosecutor never approached the murder as intentional. The entire court case revolved around Thiroux's culpability, his state of mind at the time of murder . . . Was he conscious of his actions? Strong enough in his stupor to kill violently? The coroner thought only a person of great strength could have committed the crime. The prosecutor contended that in a drunken rage, anyone can wield a knife to that fatal effect."

Unfortunately, Sara figured the prosecutor probably had

the right of it. Adrenaline and rage could allow almost anyone to kill when the victim was in a vulnerable position like Anne had been—in bed, possibly asleep already. "But if it wasn't him, who was it? Could someone have come in and murdered her while he was just sitting there drugged out?" Sara had a hard time picturing that. It seemed like he would have heard something. Had a sense of danger. But then again, she knew what two sedatives at bedtime could do. Her house could have burned down around her some nights and she wouldn't have known. That had been the point.

"Someone she knew? A stranger? I don't know. But I imagine it wasn't all that hard for someone to come and go undetected. The neighbors were used to seeing various men in and out of the house. No one would have paid attention."

"But none of the women in the house said they saw anyone."

He gave her a rueful smile. "Didn't most of them also claim to be occupied at the time?"

Sara felt an inexplicable blush creep up her face, which irritated her. They were prostitutes, of course they had been having sex. That wasn't news, nor was it anything to be embarrassed about, since it wasn't like she was talking about sex in relation to herself. Yet for some reason, there was heat in her cheeks as Gabriel smiled at her. "Yes, I think all but two of them were supposed to be occupied with men."

"And people living in that kind of area, in that hand-to-mouth, vicious lifestyle tend to keep their nose to the ground and mind their own business. They don't want to be involved in anything that might negatively impact them. We see that today too. You can have a gang shooting with seventy-five witnesses and they'll all claim they didn't see a thing."

"I'm sure." Sara shifted back to let the server set her salad down on the table in front of her. When he retreated, she asked Gabriel, "So what is the ultimate question here?"

"Did John Thiroux kill Anne Donovan? That's the ultimate question. How intoxicated was he and could a man in that state of inebriation kill with that kind of fury? If he didn't do it, who could have? If he did do it, how was it possible that he got away with it? And if forensic science had existed in the nineteenth century, could they have solved the crime? Or is the human factor of the jury always the deciding factor in a criminal case in court regardless of the forensic evidence?"

"Can we really answer any of those?" The task seemed daunting. The records were sparse. The evidence, for the most part, was unavailable to them. Sara considered herself a lab technician, not an investigator. She conducted serological and DNA analysis of unknown substances and evidentiary material from crime scenes and then wrote a report about it. Even though she was determining questions like whether a dried rust-colored liquid was blood or not, and if blood, whether or not it was human, she wasn't involved in actually connecting that information to the criminal investigation. Wasn't sure she knew where to start.

But Gabriel raised his water glass to her in a cocky toast. "We're going to try." Then he glanced over at her salad as she stabbed a cranberry, and his mouth curved up. "The Degas Salad, huh?"

"It's very good," she said, not sure how to read the expression on his face. He looked like something had amused him, a private joke. "Have you ever had it?"

Gabriel didn't answer, his fork sitting unused next to his own chopped salad. "I haven't been here in a long time." He glanced around the restaurant. "It hasn't changed much."

"It's very nice." It was. A quiet, elegant restaurant with well-trained staff. She had been surprised that it had been his choice for a spontaneous dinner, having for some reason expected him to suggest sandwiches or burgers. "I guess the salad is named for the artist Degas. Didn't he live here for awhile?"

"For about a year. So he gets a salad named after him."

"Maybe it's not named after him. Maybe it's a coincidence."

"I don't believe in coincidences."

Sara swallowed her mouthful of lettuce and pecans and stared across the table, past the candlelight dancing off the votive, at Gabriel. He was an attractive man, his skin flawless, his cheekbones graceful, chin proud, hair unexplainably long, yet perfect for him. Overall it was a pleasant package of a man. Worth glancing twice at it, but nothing so extraordinary you should remember five minutes after walking past. Just another reasonably good-looking male. It seemed that should be the case. Until she met his gaze, and was reminded every time of how she couldn't dismiss him, couldn't push him from her thoughts. When she met those brown eyes, whether by intention or accident, they arrested her. Just absolutely stopped her, drew her in, held her. And she could see depth there, sorrow, a silent, desperate plea.

It had to be her. She was seeing what she wanted to see. Reflecting her own emotions onto him. Wanting to not be alone in her confusion, her grief, her search for a future that she could understand, embrace.

"What *do* you believe in?" she asked.

That sent his gaze skittering over her left shoulder. Then he picked up his fork. "I don't know. I've forgotten."

Definite secrets there. A story. "Like you don't hear music anymore?"

"Yeah, something like that." He stabbed his salad. "So how long have you been a forensic scientist?"

Not very subtle, but she'd let him change the subject if he needed to. "Seven years. I got my degree eight years ago, but since I haven't been working this year I guess I can't call it being a forensic scientist for eight years."

"Don't beat yourself up for taking some time off."

Easier said than done. "I can't help it. It makes me feel useless."

He shrugged. "So be useless for awhile. Who cares? You're entitled to be useless in your grief for a bit."

Sara was so shocked by his response that she actually let out a brief laugh. She had expected a pep talk, a variation of the same one she'd heard from friends repeatedly over the past year about how she needed to forge ahead, work through it. No one had ever given her permission to be useless before.

"Who the hell said you had to spend every minute doing something meaningful? You can't busywork your emotions away."

God, that was the truth. She had tried to do that for two months after her mother's death, and had discovered that when she ignored her feelings, they just reared up and bit her in the ass when she was least expecting it. "You're absolutely right."

Finishing her wine, she stared at him in wonderment. It

was odd, surreal, weird, yet so completely right that she was sitting across from him, at that particular moment. And with one casual sentence, he had banished a year's worth of guilt she had been carrying around. She had been through something brutal and debilitating, and while some people could brazen their way through, she couldn't. And that was okay.

"So you're a writer, a pianist, a photographer, and a philosopher. What other hidden talents do you have? Tell me about yourself."

Tell me your story, she really wanted to say. *Share that pain in your eyes with me*. It was a palpable need, the urge to hear his sorrow, to comfort him the way he had her, just by his company. His silent acceptance of her oddities.

"What do you want to hear?"

Everything. "Why the Degas Salad bothers you."

Gabriel laughed. "It just does. No other painter gets a salad. What makes him so special?"

Sara dropped her fork, suddenly getting it. "You paint too, don't you?"

"No. Not anymore."

Of course. Not anymore. "What do you still do?"

"I write true crime books." He lifted his fork, his smile charming. "And I have dinner with beautiful blond women."

"One at a time, or in groups?" Sara couldn't believe those words came out of her mouth. She was flirting. She actually remembered how, and she was enjoying it.

"Always one-on-one. I prefer no distractions."

She had the feeling that she would really enjoy being the sole focus of Gabriel's romantic intentions. "Are you distracted easily?" Sara picked up her glass of chardonnay, swishing the liquid around and around before taking a sip.

His eyes dropped to her glass before immediately returning to her face. "No. I'm not distracted easily. I'm tenacious in my pursuit of what I want, whether it's wise or not."

If that was a warning, Sara was fairly sure her hormones weren't heeding it. She felt the smooth caress of his words all the way down her body, and the warmth between her thighs wasn't the result of wine.

"What is it that you want?" she asked him, knowing she was being reckless, flirting both with Gabriel and danger.

If a certain small part of her wanted the excitement of hearing him say "you," she should have expected that didn't mesh with what she knew of Gabriel's personality. He wasn't a charmer, nor was he always obvious.

"I want to solve a murder. Then do it again."

Of course he did. So did she. But it still felt deflating to hear him say it so baldly. Which was ridiculous. She had no intention of engaging in any sort of affair with him.

"Then I'll be free to pursue other things I want."

And that was all it took to reignite her desire.

Sara had envisioned Bourbon Street as a sort of really long pub crawl, and while that was accurate, nothing had prepared her for the assault of sound, smell, and sights. There were people everywhere, walking in and out of bars and clubs, talking, laughing, spilling drinks, grabbing beads thrown off of balconies, and groping each other companionably. Music poured from every direction, spun by DJs and played by live cover bands. Lights blinked and flashed, splashing across the dark, humid night, bright and raucous, yet somehow never entirely penetrating the corners and side-street shadows.

"Hey, how about a lap dance for your lady?" a doorman said to Gabriel with a wink.

Gabriel shook his head. "No, thanks." But then he turned to her. "Unless you want one."

"Uh, no." Definitely not her thing. Though looking around, she was starting to wonder what was her thing. She'd been pelted on the head by a set of Mardi Gras beads, which hadn't really been all that fun. She was wearing them now over her T-shirt to blend in a little. To try to embrace the experience. *What* experience remained to be seen. Gyrating to hip-hop wasn't her thing any more than a lap dance was, though she did like to dance to classic party music. She had an odd fondness for eighties music, probably because her mother had enjoyed blaring Journey, Boston, and Whitesnake her entire childhood. Somehow though she didn't see herself jumping out on the dance floor in her denim skirt, T-shirt, and ballet flats with Gabriel.

It was too loud to have a real conversation. Which left

drinking and people watching. Gabriel gestured they should go into a bar, so Sara forged ahead of him at his urging, picking her way through the crowd until she reached a bar stool. The bartender asked her what she wanted and she ordered another glass of chardonnay. Before she could even open her purse, Gabriel had paid for it, brushing aside her protests.

"Thanks. Aren't you getting a drink too?" she asked him. Sara realized that while she'd had several glasses of wine throughout the night, he had only been drinking water.

He shook his head, putting his wallet back in his pocket and lifting the glass of wine to hand to her. "No, I don't drink. I'm an alcoholic."

Sara almost fell off the stool, her shoes slipping on the rung they were resting on. "Oh, God. I had no idea. I'm sorry." She instinctively snatched the wineglass out of his hand, horrified that she'd been flaunting temptation under his nose all night long.

But Gabriel laughed. "I wasn't going to chug it or anything, I promise. I haven't had a drink in years."

"That's good." God, what was she supposed to say? They practically had to yell to be heard over the music anyway. "But we didn't have to come here if it's uncomfortable for you."

"I'm fine. I'm in control, Sara. It's not even uncomfortable for me." Strangely enough, Gabriel found there was truth to that. It wasn't the alcohol that was tempting him. Even though he could smell beer, could see plastic cups filled with wine, tubes of shots, and containers filled with the infamous New Orleans hand grenade in the hands of people all around him, he didn't have the urge to drink. What he had the urge to do was to touch Sara. To sweep his fingers across her soft skin, to move his body in closer to hers, to press his lips along the corners of her ripe mouth, and close his eyes while they brushed, connected, and reached for a tactile solace, a reminder that they weren't alone.

They were both lonely. It was obvious. He had known that about himself, fought the sense that he existed removed from the world around him every day, and Sara wore the same fear in her eyes. She had a naked vulnerability, hidden behind her strength and determination, but when she looked at him, it was there. She liked him. Desired him. Was afraid of her feelings.

So was he.

And yet they were in a crowded bar and it felt like it was just the two of them. He leaned on the bar next to her stool, indulging himself by letting his knee brush against hers. She sat up straighter, moving her leg away. Then shifted it back, as if she had decided to defy her initial instinct.

"If you want to leave, just let me know," she said.

"Not until I see you dance."

Sara rolled her eyes. "Then you'll be standing there awhile. I'm not going to dance."

"Why not? You obviously want to. Your foot has been tapping to the music since you sat down, and you're practically bouncing on the stool."

It was a Bon Jovi song playing, which was not music that particularly moved his soul, but Sara seemed to like it.

But she shook her head. "No. I'm not going to dance by myself."

"There's other women out there already." At least a half dozen women, and one random guy, were flailing around in front of the small stage.

"No. Quit it." She tucked her blond wavy hair behind her ear and straightened her spine.

But then the band starting playing AC/DC and Sara made a sound, her shoulders wiggling rhythmically to the beat. Gabriel felt her struggle, her desire to stay reserved, to hold herself in control, and it bothered him. He was wondering what she would do if he just pushed her out onto the floor, when the problem was solved by a woman wearing a purple and gold feather Mardi Gras wig. She shimmied over, grabbed Sara's hand, and gave her a big, friendly "get out here" nod as she tugged her off the stool.

Sara protested, but the woman was determined, and thirty seconds later, she had Sara next to her out on the dance floor. For a second, Gabriel thought Sara would bolt and head back to her stool, but her shoulders relaxed and she swayed to the music, laughing with her new companion.

Then she was dancing, hair sliding forward, hips moving in her short denim skirt, arms out at her sides. Gabriel stared, his mouth dry, as the lights from the stage turned and reflected over Sara, as she gave herself up to the rhythm of the music. Her smile was full, genuine, and she glanced back at him, shrugging in amusement.

It was arousing to watch her come alive, to shrug off her reticence and embrace the entertainment. To put herself on display and not worry what everyone was thinking. Gabriel suspected she was never like this, not anymore. Not since her mother's death.

She was beautiful, tantalizing.

He hadn't had sex in seventy-five years, and his body wanted her aggressively, painfully.

He couldn't have her.

❦

"John, where are you going?"

Gabriel glanced back at Molly, who had sat up in her bed, her hair disheveled, her face anxious. She was pretty and enthusiastic, and he'd had her twice that night, a desperate attempt to soak his senses with pleasure and forget. Eradicate the horrific memory of Anne, mutilated and still, from his mind.

But Molly was getting clingy. "I'm going home."

"No!" She leaped off the mattress with a dexterity that was impressive given she was naked and tangled in bedsheets.

Gabriel hastened to pull his trousers on, head pounding, hands shaking. He needed a drink. His own bed. Now that he had sated his physical needs, the sound of Molly's voice grated on his nerves, and he wanted to be alone with his absinthe, wanted to climb to a higher place, then crash down into his bed and sleep until he could find the strength to open his eyes and start this all over again.

"Spend the night, Johnny. I'll make it so worth your while." Her fingers slid across his chest and her mouth came toward his.

Turning his head to avoid her lips, he reached for his shirt. It was smothering, this kind of attention, devotion. She hadn't seemed such an emotional sort when he'd taken up with her, more out of convenience and opportunity than any real interest.

"No, I'm going home."

She burst into tears, loud and wet, and he was appalled. Molly stood there, stark naked, her rosy breasts heaving up and down, her hands reaching for him, eyes pleading. "Say you're coming back tomorrow."

"I don't know." He shoved his arms into his wrinkled shirt-sleeves. "I don't know."

This had clearly been a mistake. He had only been seeing Molly for a week, and sporadically at that. He hadn't expected her to get the wrong idea. He was not interested in dramatics, in a permanent sort of arrangement. It had only been two months since Anne's death, and he wasn't ready to attach himself to another woman.

He suspected he had loved Anne.

Her hand grappled with his arm. "Promise me you'll be back tomorrow. I can't go a whole day without you, I just can't."

The vehement statement was so odd, Gabriel found himself pausing to glance down at her tear-streaked face, her dark brown hair tousled and sticking to her cheek in disarray. "Why on earth not?"

"Because I'm in love with you," she said passionately, leaning her lower body flush against his. "I have to have you."

Gabriel reared back in horror. There was nothing about him worth loving. Not one thing.

He had done nothing to encourage, to deserve, such exalted emotion.

"You're not in love with me. The very idea is ridiculous." Gabriel stepped into his shoes, dodging her fingers, as she got a grip on his waistband.

"I am! You can't say that I'm not. I will die if you don't come back tomorrow."

That overwrought and childish proclamation, that mockery of life and death, disgusted Gabriel. Breaking free, he moved forward, not wanting to touch Molly, not wanting to use force to hold her back, but needing to get away. "You're not going to die, and it's offensive to me that you would suggest such a thing in light of what we have all endured in grief for Anne."

But the chastisement had no effect on Molly. She threw her head back in defiance, pulling her hair off her cheek, chin *thrusting up. "I'm glad Anne is gone. If she hadn't died, you never would have come to me. And all I want is you."*

Gabriel grabbed his coat and fled, slamming the door behind him on her tears, his heart pounding. The encounter had been illogical, but he was too raw to decipher it.

He'd go home and have a drink.

Everything always made more sense after a drink.

Mrs. Jane Gallier
117 Esplanade Avenue
New Orleans, Louisiana

Mr. Jonathon Thiroux
34 Royal Street
New Orleans, Louisiana

17 December, 1849

My Dearest John,

I know it is somewhat improper for me to be writing you in such a forward manner, but I have not been able to prevent myself from contacting you. I am entitled to some leeway given my status as a widow, but I know it is still not the thing to engage in correspondence with you. However, it has been three days since I have seen you, and I cannot bear your absence any longer.

I was compelled to write, to express my extreme disappointment in your sudden eviction from my presence, and to ask you most sincerely, most ardently, to allocate time in your busy schedule to pay your addresses to me today.

Perhaps you are painting. I admire and respect your artistry and do not wish to interrupt. However, it was my understanding that since we embarked on a new, more intimate relationship, that we would be spending time together. I feel sorely used, I must say, and neglected now that I have given myself to you. I had thought you better than that, better than so many selfish

*and insensitive men who charm and flatter a woman
merely to gain her bed, than discard her carelessly. If
that is what you have done, I admit I was fully duped,
and may you feel a sickening and painful shame, along
with the sting of my hatred, for such illicit behavior.*

*But, dearest John, I mustn't chastise you. That is not
you, I know that. You are different, I am convinced of it.
I do not mean to scold, to put such unkind motives and
character flaws upon you, even though I am hurt and
quite lonely. You no doubt have extensive and important
demands that must come before me. I am not a young
girl, and I harbor no illusions about romance or promises a man makes. Yet, I must tell you that I have never
felt the way that I feel about you. It is humiliating, but I
find that if necessary I will beg you—yes, beg—that you
pay your respects in person as soon as is humanly possible. I cannot bear the thought of even one more day
without your touch upon me, without your lips coaxing
me to such exquisite pleasure.*

*I cannot get enough of you, John, and I will go mad
with want if you do not return to me immediately. I wait
most desperately for return word, or better still, to see
your face outside my door.*

*With love and longing,
Your Jane*

Gabriel's back hit the wall in the alley, and he glanced
right and left, the view spinning from drink. Holding on to the
bricks for balance, he tipped his head back, closing his eyes,
as the street whore he'd visited the last three nights went down
on her knees in front of him.

There was a sharp chill in the air, but it just added to the
sting, to the over-heightened sense of his legs struggling to
hold him upright, the cloud of confusion that swirled around
in his brain.

This one would be different. This was a hardened, angry
woman, with filthy fingers and missing teeth. She wouldn't
want anything more from him than his money so she could buy

herself whiskey, or a bit of bread to eat. There would be no communication, no expectations, no professions.

And he could ease his panicked mind.

Swallowing hard, his mouth dry, missing the bottle he'd emptied a full thirty minutes earlier, he tried to enjoy her ministrations, tried to pretend that his stomach wasn't rebelling in disgust at what he was doing.

But it was, and he wanted to turn and toss its entire contents onto the fetid, sewage-soaked cobblestones. Taking deep breaths, he focused on his cock, on the warmth that surrounded it, on the base human throb that rose from deep inside it, and grew to a feverish pitch with the strokes of a hot tongue. It had nothing to do with his head, his heart, but sought only guttural release, and he forced himself to distance, to focus, to let his body take what it wanted.

He was grateful the event was quick and to the point, absolutely relieved that his body cooperated, and she was rearranging his trousers in less than two minutes. He wanted to go home. Prying his eyes open, he held his hand out to her, so she could rise off the street.

The sudden coy smile on her face startled him. "You're an odd one, ain't ya?"

It was only the second time he'd heard her speak, and her voice was high in pitch, but rough. Gabriel shrugged, fumbling around for a coin to give her, his fingers ineffectual, shaking.

"Same place tomorrow?" she asked, straightening his coat in an oddly tender gesture.

Gabriel felt his alarm returning. He was about to say no, he wouldn't be seeing her the next day, when the streethardened whore, who had probably lost her place in a bordello due to bad temper or excessive alcohol consumption, brushed his hair back off his face with her filthy fingers.

"A body could fall for a strange one like you. Please say you'll be back tomorrow. I'll do it for nothin'."

"No, that's not necessary." He didn't even want her physical attentions. It had been to prove a point to himself, to show that what he suspected to be his punishment was merely a figment of his fanciful imagination.

But her fingers gripped the front of his shirt. "Please say you will. I like the way you taste. I been thinkin' 'bout you all day."

Oh, God. Gabriel felt the automatic plea rear up in his mind, though he knew he was not going to receive any help from that quarter. He was fallen, so deep and dark down in the pit that he had been given the ultimate punishment beyond banishment from heaven. He had been given the curse of having his flaws emulated by the women he encountered.

"I'll do whatever you want, just let me be with you, love you," she said, eyes red-rimmed and desperate, greasy hair tumbling over her shoulders, callused hands running along his chest.

And he knew it was true. This was his punishment. Every woman he had an intimate physical relationship with grew to crave him, to desire him the way he longed for his absinthe.

He was addicted to alcohol and opium, and they were addicted to him.

It was overwhelming in its horror, and Gabriel shifted left, moved out from under those smothering, clinging hands, and stumbled down the street, ignoring her pleas, the pounding of her shoes as she followed him, chased after him.

There would be no more women, ever.

Chapter Six

❧

"Are you sure you don't want to stop in anywhere else?" Gabriel asked, as they walked down Bourbon toward Dumaine.

"No, I definitely need to call it a night." Sara couldn't believe she'd danced as long as she had. Gabriel must have been bored out of his mind sitting there with his ice water while she danced through an entire band set.

But it had been so much fun, so liberating to just move to the music. To not think, to not worry, to just feel. To interact with people in such a casual, anonymous way.

She sighed, fingering the strand of beads around her neck. Lack of sleep and the wine were catching up with her, making her weary, but in a pleasant, content way. "Thanks for taking me out. I had a good time, and I appreciate you suffering through a boring night to show me Bourbon Street."

"It wasn't boring at all," he said. "I enjoy your company, and I like to people watch."

Sara told herself to accept that, take it at face value. Enjoy walking beside Gabriel. "There were definitely some people worth watching." She laughed, picturing the older guy who had suddenly decided to break-dance. It had been worthy of an A for effort, but not much else.

"You have to hit Bourbon with the expectation that you can see pretty much anything at any given moment." Gabriel gestured to the street to the right. "This is our turn."

Sara glanced over and lost all her good humor. The street looked pitch black and empty, the few storefronts on it closed up and locked for the night. "This doesn't look safe."

"It's fine. I walk here all the time."

It went against every dictate of common sense to stroll down what amounted to a wide alley at one-thirty in the morning. "I don't think this is a good idea."

"There's no other way to get home," Gabriel told her. "We have to walk down one of these streets, and it makes sense to walk down the street we actually need to be on. We stayed on Bourbon as long as we could." He gave her a reassuring smile and started down the sidewalk, shadows covering him. "Come on. It's just a block and a half. We'll be there in three minutes."

Sara rushed after him, not because she was convinced they weren't going to die, but because she sure in the hell didn't want to be left alone.

"Nothing has ever happened to me," he added.

As far as she was concerned, that meant he was statistically due to get attacked. But she wasn't sure how much of her concern was based on good, solid common sense, and how much on the fear she grappled with from her mother's murder. Maybe it was both, but the end result was she had clammy skin and a sick churning in the pit of her stomach. Shoving her hands in the pockets of her denim skirt, Sara glanced back and forth, back and forth. Checking every doorway, every dark nook and cranny, and ensuring she was close enough to Gabriel to grab him for assistance if necessary. His shirt was in touching distance in front of her, and she found that immensely reassuring.

Especially when she heard a shuffling sound to her right.

Reaching out, she wrapped her fingers around Gabriel's forearm to halt his progress and whispered, "Did you hear that?"

"What?" He stopped walking and glanced back at her, looking only mildly curious. Not at all concerned.

Sara's fear was so solid and palpable she could have served

it on a platter and eaten it. And she could hear the sound again.

"To the right. I hear a shuffling. Someone's in that doorway two feet in front of you." She was trying to pull him backward, but Gabriel was resisting. He was actually trying to move *forward* to see where the noise was generating from.

Which was ridiculous. Suicidal. There was probably some guy with a gun just waiting to rob and murder them. The logical thing to do was to turn tail and run. They could hail a cab on Bourbon Street to take them back to Gabriel's.

Obviously Gabriel had a different plan. His involved pulling away from her and just strolling straight up to the doorway. What kind of stupid idea was that? Sara opened her mouth to scream, just in case she was going to need to alert the masses that they needed help, as he peered around the storefront window.

She held her breath as his head tipped downward and his shoulders relaxed. "It's just a cat, Sara."

Oh, shit, thank God. Sara grabbed her chest and expelled a huge burst of breath. "Are you sure?" she asked.

"Sure that it's a cat? Uh, yeah." He sounded amused as he went down on his haunches and held his fingers out.

Okay, so that was a stupid question. Sara forced herself to move forward and see for herself that this was absolutely nothing to worry about. It was a cat, just as Gabriel had claimed. It was a kitten really, a small gray ball of fur, thin and scrawny and blinking up at them with brilliant green eyes.

It gave a small, pitiful meow as it locked gazes with her, and Sara forgot her fear. "Oh, look how sweet." She squatted down beside Gabriel to get a better look. The kitten was emaciated, its fur dirty and matted. "Oh, my gosh, this poor thing."

When the cat refused to sniff his fingers, Gabriel pulled his hand back. "It's obviously a stray. No collar. Probably just a few months old, and from the looks of her ribs, she's been on the street awhile."

Sara reached out and stroked the top of the kitten's head. The cat didn't balk at the touch, and actually tilted her head and rubbed against Sara's wrist. "I'm going to take her. I can't leave her here like this." The doorway was filthy, covered with cigarette butts and blobs of old chewing gum. Reaching forward, she scooped up the kitten, who didn't squirm or try to slip away at all.

Sara expected Gabriel to protest, to make a comment about the cat's lack of cleanliness, possible state of disease, or question where she was going to keep a cat, but Gabriel didn't say anything. He just put his hand on the small of her back, urging her to continue walking down the street.

"She weighs nothing at all," Sara commented as she snuggled the kitten closer in her arms, not wanting the cat to make a leap for freedom. Not that the kitten seemed inclined to go anywhere. She was collapsed against Sara's chest and purring loud enough to be heard.

"We can feed her at my place." Gabriel moved his hand from Sara's back to her elbow, pausing her so he could glance past the parked cars and make sure no cars were driving down Royal Street before they crossed it.

It was a nice protective gesture, one Sara liked. One that surprised her, frankly. Gabriel seemed so internal, so focused on his own thoughts, that she wasn't expecting that level of solicitude. But then again, he had been that way all night. Maybe when he turned off work, when he focused on the world around him, she saw his true character. It was strange that she thought of him as an introvert, even though he talked to her, sometimes quite a bit, like he had at dinner. Yet it always seemed like there was a barrier between him and everything around him, a distance. A reserve.

She didn't feel that as he pushed open his courtyard gate. She just felt safe and protected in the dark and gloom of the poorly lit street, and she was grateful when he shut the gate behind her and clicked the lock shut. The dark, the looming buildings, the corners and shadows, had terrified her. Gabriel didn't, even though she knew she had no concrete reason to trust him.

After all, maybe his preoccupation with murder was to quiet his own murderous intentions. Maybe he enjoyed writing true crime books the same way Ted Bundy had gotten a sick thrill from working at a crisis hotline center. He could be a killer. Anyone could. Yet, with nothing more to go on than her gut instinct and the look of sorrow, of longing, in Gabriel's eyes, she didn't believe that he was capable of violence. He was as damaged as she was, and it drew her to him.

"Do you have a box or something I can put the kitten in? I don't want her getting under my car seats or the gas or brake pedals."

"I'm sure I have something." Gabriel jogged up the stairs and opened his apartment.

Sara followed more slowly, and by the time she got upstairs he already had a bowl of milk in his hand. He brought it to the floor in front of the couch, so Sara sat down on the hardwood floor, the kitten in her lap. It didn't take long for the cat to smell food and venture forward, her back legs still on Sara, her front straining to reach the bowl. She lapped out tentatively, then more enthusiastically, drinking quickly. Once she glanced back, milk dripping off her nose and whiskers, and blinked at Sara before sticking her face back in the bowl.

Sara was so keeping the kitten. She was too adorable to give up, practical or not.

"Here's a towel to use as a blanket," Gabriel said, handing her a white towel smelling of fabric softener and so sharp in color that it looked bleached.

Gabriel had laundry skills.

"Thanks." Sara took it, but added, "It's probably going to get ruined. She needs a bath, and she's going to get this towel filthy."

"Why don't you just give her a bath now? You don't want to be carrying her around like that. And her fur's all matted. It's probably really uncomfortable for her, tugging her skin."

Sara looked back at Gabriel as she ran her fingers lightly across the kitten's fur. She had the sense that the room around her had gotten clear, the objects in it sharply focused, more real than they were earlier. It made no sense, but it seemed that she and Gabriel themselves were in sharper focus, and she ached again with the need to touch and be touched, to lay her head down on a man's shoulder, and rest. The night was dark and silent, and her body weary from lack of sleep, but her mind skittered back and forth, manic and excited, the fear held completely at bay for once. She'd had a fun night. Hadn't realized she still knew how.

Now she was sitting in Gabriel's apartment with him, and he was offering up his shower for her to bathe the kitten. It seemed like it should be odd, that they were there together. That their paths in life had crossed.

And he was an alcoholic. Which meant they were potentially poison for each other. They both had addictive propensities.

But it was a working relationship, and a strange, budding friendship that she desperately needed, and she wasn't going to walk away because of the slim, off chance that it would go too far.

"That's a great idea, if you don't mind."

"Not at all. You can do it in the bathroom sink so it won't be as scary for her."

Sara smiled. "Thanks." Any man who was considerate of a mangy kitten was a good man. She felt so damn safe with him, and normal. God, it felt normal, even as her head swam from lack of sleep when she stood up quickly. Or maybe it wasn't that she felt normal. That wasn't the right word. Normalcy was still elusive. Maybe it was that she felt alive.

For the first time in a year.

❧

Gabriel watched Sara trying to soap up the squirming and desperate cat in his small bathroom. There was water all over the front of her tank top, dripping from the top of her hair, and splashing all over the mirror. Filthy or not, the cat didn't want a bath, but Sara was determined. Kind and gentle, but determined.

After a chaotic five minutes, she had the cat bundled up in a towel and snuggled against her. She shook her damp hair out of her eyes, and laughed as she glanced over at him. "There. Not so bad." She kissed the top of the cat's gray and damp head. "You survived, Angel. From here on out, life will be a piece of cake, I promise."

Surely he had heard her name for the cat wrong. Or she had just spoken it as a term of endearment. "Angel?" he asked cautiously.

"That's her name." Sara smiled and kissed the cat again. "It suits her."

It took all his effort not to roll his eyes or to turn and just leave the bathroom. She wouldn't understand that sort of reaction. She didn't know, couldn't know, wouldn't know the truth. So he just said, "Nice. Why don't you take her to the couch and try to dry her off a little better? I'll get you a fresh T-shirt. You're soaking wet."

Alarm skittered across her face for a second before she masked it. "Great. Thanks."

On the way to his bedroom, Gabriel paused, glancing into his office. His eye was drawn to his absinthe spoon collection. He was wandering into dangerous territory again. He was condemned to be alone, by his own sins. He couldn't involve Sara, regardless of how tempting a simple friendship with her was. He'd get her a T-shirt and send her home, and maybe tell her she needed to work from her apartment. They didn't need to be sitting together to sort through research.

But when he came back with a shirt, after digging through three drawers trying to find one that wasn't too old and torn up, didn't have a strange phrase on it, and wouldn't swallow Sara whole like the whale did Jonah, Sara was asleep on his couch. She was stretched out fully, and the kitten was still snuggled in the towel on her chest, out cold like her owner. He couldn't wake Sara up. That would be cruel, given that she'd been having so much trouble sleeping. He also suspected she was afraid to go outside, that the streets at night had truly terrified her.

So he found a blanket in his closet and put it over her bottom half, below the cat. Then he paced around his apartment, refusing to acknowledge that she looked battered, yet so at peace in her deep sleep. Refusing to see the way the lamplight filtered over her cheek and hid the dark shadows that offended the beauty of her face. Refusing to see the way her delicate fingers dug into the cat's fur, clinging and cleaving, a desperate need to hold on.

He would not sketch her. He had not picked up a pencil in a hundred and fifty years, hadn't felt the urge to do so. He did now. His fingers itched, the artist inside him wanting to reemerge and capture the view, the light, the woman, in front of him. He wouldn't do it.

There was no beauty to be found through the skewed lenses of his sinful eyes.

Police Description of the Crime Scene (Undated),
written by William Davidson

The room in which Miss Donovan resided and
was murdered was approximately six by ten feet,
street facing, single window shuttered. Miss
Donovan's bed was on the south-facing wall, next
to the doorway leading to the interior hallway.
Bed was an inexpensive wood frame with a thin
mattress. Dressing table and chair on opposite
wall, covered with various female toiletries. Chair
and small table in center of room, facing bed. An
opium pipe, one empty bottle of absinthe, second
bottle of absinthe one-third empty, empty glass,
and spoon on tray on table.

Miss Donovan's trunk contained five dresses,
two pairs of shoes, three dollars, and various
personal effects, including a diamond necklace
that is undoubtedly a fake. Trunk was closed,
though not locked. Victim was wearing an under-
dress and nothing else. There was a pool of blood
on the floor next to the bed, blood on the back
wall behind the victim's head, and splattered on
nearly every inch of the mattress. For
description of the victim, refer to coroner's
report.

Madame Conti and Mr. Thiroux agree nothing
was missing from the room or was out of the
ordinary.

The following items were collected from the
room:

—One bowie knife, found placed in victim's left
   hand. Assumed to be murder weapon, given the
   size of the six inches in length, one half inch wide
   straight blade, which matched the approximate
   size of victim's wounds.

—Bottle of absinthe and opium pipe (to be disposed
   of properly).

—Two absinthe spoons, one with blunt edge (on tray on table), the other in the shape of a fleur-de-lis (which was found on floor in blood).

—Personal effects, to be given to deceased's family, if any family can be located.

—Drawing in pencil of a woman's arm, found on the floor next to the bed. Blood streaked on it.

Sara shot out of sleep, stiff and disoriented, instinctively sitting halfway up. She didn't think she'd been dreaming, but something had ripped her out of sleep, and she realized immediately she was still in Gabriel's apartment on his couch, and the kitten was no longer on her chest. Panic didn't even have time to take hold before Sara saw that Angel had just scooted down and was sleeping on the couch at her feet.

Rubbing her eyes, her heart racing from the sudden interruption of REM, she wondered how long she had been dozing. The room was dark, and Gabriel was nowhere around. There was a lamp still on in the far corner, but all the other lights had been turned off. A clock ticked somewhere in the silence of the apartment, and she realized it was still the middle of the night, and there was a blanket over her legs. Gabriel must have left her sleeping and gone to bed.

That was sort of embarrassing. She'd been so sleep-deprived it had actually caught up with her and she'd passed out on his couch. That was actually more than embarrassing when she thought about it. That was scary. Or at least it should be. She should be freaked out that she had fallen asleep on a man's couch and slept like a rock. Instead, it just seemed to her like maybe there was a reason she'd been able to successfully sleep at Gabriel's when she couldn't anywhere else.

What that implied was what was truly scary, not that she'd been asleep and vulnerable.

Spotting her purse on the end table, she pulled out her cell phone. 4:46 a.m. She'd slept for almost three hours. That was impressive for her lately. And she felt pretty good, despite a stiff neck and a dry mouth from the wine she'd had. Going back to sleep would be impossible though. She was wide

awake and needed to use the bathroom. Making sure she
didn't disturb the cat, she got up.

She picked her way carefully across the living room, went
down the hall, and used the bathroom, wincing at the loud
flush of the toilet. She had to pass Gabriel's bedroom on her
return trip to the living room, and his door wasn't shut. It was
too much temptation to not at least glance inside. Between the
lamp on in the front room and the moonlight from his window,
she could see him, a dark shadow lying on his side on the bed,
back to her. The sheet came up to his waist, and his hair fell
over his bare shoulders.

Sara recognized that feeling in her chest, in her body, when
she looked at him. She was interested in him, not just intellectually, but sexually. There was no obvious reason why it was
him as opposed to someone else, but he was the first man in
well over a year who had coaxed desire from her. And he
wasn't even trying. He didn't flirt, had never come on to her.
Yet the sight of him in bed, his shoulders taut, moonlight on
his lean yet muscular body, had her mouth dry, nipples tingling, inner thighs throbbing.

It wasn't like her to have such an obvious physical response
to a man she barely knew, and she didn't know what to do with
it. She'd never thought of herself as a highly sexual person, but
now she wanted sex. Absolutely wanted it. With Gabriel.
Wanted his weight pressing down on her, wanted his lips taking
hers, wanted his body filling hers, hard heat thrusting inside her
while she spread her legs for him. She could practically feel it,
craved that moment when he would push against her and her
body would give, accept him, and they would be joined together
in the blissful escapism of sexual pleasure.

Disturbed at her thoughts, Sara crossed her arms tightly on
her chest and commanded herself to stop.

His room was small, and sparse compared to the rest of his
apartment, with only the bed and a dresser in it. He hadn't bothered to pull down the shade on his window, which she found
interesting. He either slept through the sun rising, or he used it
as an alarm clock. It also fascinated her that she couldn't hear
him breathing. He made no sound at all, and given his angle,
she couldn't even see the rise and fall of his chest. It was utterly
silent, and he wasn't moving.

Maybe he was dead. Not that there was cause for death, since he had been alive and well a mere three hours earlier, but once the idea took root, Sara couldn't shake it. It was possible. Anything was possible. And he wasn't making any sound at all. What if she moved around the front of him, and found that he had been stabbed? Throat slit. Blood could be all over the bed, and she wouldn't be able to see it from where she was. He could be dead, cold, his eyes wide open, glassy and empty.

She knew she had to be overreacting, knew he couldn't possibly have been murdered while she was sleeping on the couch. But then again, he didn't lock his doors, and she had been down for the count, sleeping hard and deep. If his throat had been slit, he wouldn't have made any noise.

Bile rising into her mouth, Sara knew she couldn't leave the room until she saw for herself that Gabriel was alive and well and fast asleep. Heart pounding, she moved forward, her palms sweaty, her sandals outrageously loud in the silence of the dark. She felt like she was going to throw up as she moved around the foot of his bed, not wanting to touch him, or lean over his back. Touch was too intimate, and she needed to *see* first, to process if the unspeakable had happened. Closing her eyes briefly, she moved between his bed and the window, shuffling so she didn't trip on anything he had on the floor.

Then bracing herself, she turned and forced herself to look at the front of Gabriel, terrified of finding the worst. Almost sick with relief, she saw that his throat hadn't been slit. There was no blood anywhere. And he was very much alive, his hand shifting slightly on his pillow.

"Thank God," she whispered, holding her chest with her right hand. He was fine. Everything was fine. She needed to get a grip, stop seeing danger and death around every corner. And most of all, she needed to get out of his bedroom before he realized she was standing there staring at him.

Stepping back, Sara bumped the radiator. It didn't make much of a sound, but a glance back at the bed showed Gabriel's eyes open, blinking at her.

"Sara? What's the matter?"

"I . . ." She stood there, not sure what to say, how to explain.

"Are you cold? I got out a dry shirt for you. I left it next to your purse. I'll go get it for you." He was starting to pull himself to a sitting position, exposing his boxer shorts.

"No, I'm not cold, don't get up." Sara was embarrassed by her behavior, by his solicitude. "I was just going to the bathroom and I saw you, and I thought . . . you looked . . ." She felt herself blushing. "I thought you were dead. I was just checking to make sure you were okay."

"Oh." His brow furrowed.

Sara stood there, feeling like an idiot.

"Well, I'm okay. Not dead, I promise." He smiled at her, propped up on his elbow.

"I can see that." And she was mortified. Yet still afraid. It had been so easy to picture the blood, picture the cuts and lacerations, his still gaze. What did that say about her? "I'm sorry I fell asleep on your couch. I'm not sure what happened. I should go home."

"Right now?" Gabriel frowned. "Absolutely not. You're not walking to your car and driving all the way to Kenner. Just sleep here." He patted the bed next to him. "Come on. Just lay down and we'll go back to sleep."

In his bed? That seemed like such a bad idea. Yet so damn tempting. She stood there, indecisive. "I left the kitten on the couch."

"She'll be fine there. Come on." He pulled the sheet back so she could get in. "I can see your fear, Sara. It's okay to be afraid of the dark after what you've been through."

That kicked her in the gut, made her want to burst into tears. How could he see so clearly what she tried so hard to hide? She was afraid of the dark. Afraid of the unknown, the shadow around every corner, the future. So she kicked off her sandals and climbed onto the bed with Gabriel. She didn't want to be alone all the time. Her head sank back onto the pillow as he pulled the sheet up over her. The bed was warm from his body heat, and soft. The pillow felt like down. And Gabriel was very masculine next to her, his body close, but not touching.

She stared at the ceiling, not wanting to look at him. Normally she slept on her side, but she wasn't comfortable with the idea of facing him on the bed. That would be too intimate. But alternatively, turning her back on him seemed rude. So she lay there, eyes wide open, trying to slow her breathing, trying to reach for sleep, knowing it wouldn't come.

"Relax, Sara," Gabriel murmured to her. His hand slid into hers and squeezed before letting go. "It's okay."

It was. She knew that. Everything was okay. She was okay. Kicked, torn apart, nearly destroyed, but still alive. Still her. And she slept on her side, normally, and she wanted to be normal, so Sara turned up on her left side, facing the window. When Gabriel moved in closer, his fingers stroking the back of her hair, she closed her eyes, sighing softly. It felt so good to be touched, even if it wasn't sexual. Maybe because it wasn't sexual. His body, warm and relaxed, brushed against hers, and he yawned right next to her ear, the rush of his breath tickling her skin.

He had taken over half of her pillow, and his hand rested on her hip, heavy and comforting on her denim skirt.

Opening her eyes, she stared out into the courtyard, watching a tree sway back and forth in the moonlight. For the first time in a long time, she didn't feel the need to yank down the blinds and shut out the night. It was a beautiful view, leaves dancing, shadows shifting and changing, and she was safe inside.

Eyes drifting back shut, Sara fell asleep.

Chapter Seven

❦

Summary of autopsy of Anne Donovan conducted by Dr. Maxwell Raphael on October 7, 1849, at 2 p.m. in the presence of Dr. William Gregory.

Female victim, dead approximately twelve hours, Caucasian, twenty-three years old, with a post-birth cervix, indicating she had given birth to at least one child. Victim had only a small amount of liquid and no food in her stomach at the time of death, indicating she was not intoxicated. Slightly malnourished, but no sign of disease.

Cause of death a seven-inch cut across the neck running from right to left, which severed the larynx, cartilage, surrounding tissue, and carotid artery, resulting in victim hemorrhaging until death. No bruises or signs of restraint anywhere on body, expect for a thumbprint-size bruise to the right of the mouth, above the lip, and two inches from the nose. In addition to neck injury, victim was cut seventeen times in the chest, abdomen, and genital area, most wounds ½ inch in width, with a significant amount of depth. All organs

intact and accounted for, though the uterus,
bladder, stomach, and left lung all had puncture
wounds from injuries. Given the uniformity of the
wounds, the single weapon appears to be a straight
knife. Death was immediate from the initial neck
wound, and other stabs were postmortem.

There are no signs of sexual intercourse.

꧁ꗞ꧂

Death Certificate of Anne Donovan

Be it Remembered, THAT ON THIS DAY, to-wit:
the eighth of October in the year of our Lord One
Thousand Eight Hundred and Forty-nine and the
seventy-sixth year of the Independence of the
United States of America. Before me, John
Richard Thomas, duly commissioned and Sworn,
RECORDER OF BIRTHS AND DEATHS, in and for
the PARISH OF ORLEANS, STATE OF LOUISIANA,
Personally Appeared, Jonathon Thiroux, a
competent witness, residing in this Parish, and
doth declared that Anne Donovan, departed this
life on the yesterday at approximately one-thirty
a.m., aged about twenty-three years.

"What makes sense about this?"

Gabriel turned away from his computer, where he'd been studying the effects of wormwood in absinthe on users, and turned to Sara, sitting on the couch in his office, her legs crossed and tucked under her long skirt. He could see the palpable frustration on her face.

"Why the hell would John Thiroux be the person submitting the info on Anne's death? If I'm reading this right, he essentially filed her death with the recorder's office, and the police had nothing to do with it."

"He was the person to discover her death." And would never forget it. Gabriel only wished he could remember what the hell had happened before her death. But it was a blank, just a hazy memory of Anne, and pleasure, then floating off into the abyss. Then blood. Death. "That was normal for the time period."

"He might have killed her! Why was he filing her death certificate? That's just weird."

"Do you think he killed her?" Gabriel asked. He was curious. He wanted, needed, to see that he was innocent. But Sara had no such stake. Maybe she would come to a different conclusion than him, and who was to say who was right? Without DNA confirmation, they could only rationalize. They couldn't know conclusively. But he wanted to come as close as possible.

"I don't know," Sara admitted. "I don't know enough yet. But I want to investigate John Thiroux a little better. There doesn't seem to be a lot of information on him in these papers."

She wouldn't find much either. John Thiroux had suddenly appeared in New Orleans in 1847, and had just as suddenly disappeared in 1851. Gabriel had reassumed his true name when it had become apparent he wouldn't be leaving. That he had been locked out forever, bound to New Orleans for an indefinite amount of time.

"So that's your mission?" He felt a strange guilt that she was determined to research and ferret out facts about him, the man sitting straight across from her, the man she had slept in the same bed with the night before. He had offered her comfort then, and he had enjoyed that. The closeness, the sense of just *being* with another person. It was wrong to let her traverse down a path that would result in a dead end, wasting her time. He knew all the answers she wanted. Yet he couldn't give them. She would never believe he was immortal, never understand his punishment.

"I think it is. That feels like the logical place to start to me, since there are no other suspects. What about you? How do you piece this book together? You said you start with the crime, then scene set. Then what?"

"The principal players. Which are John Thiroux, who you are handling, Anne Donovan, and absinthe. The autopsy suggested she'd had a child . . . did it survive? What happened to it? Did Anne have enemies? A husband or boyfriend she'd left before becoming a prostitute? And I want to know if absinthe is psychoactive. I can't explain exactly the process of how I lay out a book . . . it's logical to me, but I can't really explain it." He followed the story, wrote it like a story, albeit with facts. But that was normally, when he wasn't personally involved. Anne's story was different, and he wasn't unbiased. He had a desperate stake in the outcome, an intense need, or maybe hope, to solve it, to give Anne justice and to right the wrong. He also wanted closure for Sara, in some way, with her own mother's case.

Sara tapped her finger on her bottom lip. She had gone home after they'd woken up, and Gabriel had doubted whether she would actually come back that day or not. She had looked embarrassed, had acted uncomfortable when the morning arrived and they were sharing a bed. But after breakfast and a shower, she had come back with her cat, and had attacked his stacks of research documents tenaciously.

"I guess I'm just going to have to trust you to write it." She smiled at him. "Since it is your book, after all. But you know what's bugging me? If Anne was a prostitute, don't you think it's odd that there was no evidence of sexual intercourse? I mean, wouldn't they have had sex when Thiroux got there? I don't think he was paying her to chat with him."

No, Gabriel hadn't paid her to chat with him, though Anne had been companionship. He wondered now what Anne had thought of their relationship. It hadn't seemed crass or dominating to him at the time, but maybe she had felt that way. Maybe she had despised him, only saw him as a means to an end. He would never know. "If he'd consumed enough alcohol and opium I doubt sex was first and foremost on his mind."

The bigger question in Gabriel's mind was why there was no evidence of intercourse when he himself had walked in on Anne with another man. He hadn't been drunk yet, though he had been distracted by withdrawal symptoms. But he had seen a man overtop of Anne, thrusting in perfect parody of sex. He was absolutely 100 percent certain of that. So why hadn't the coroner found evidence of that?

He also wanted to know who the man was, because aside from himself, the stranger was probably the most likely suspect. But in all witness statements, there was no mention of him. On the witness stand, Madame Conti had denied Anne had seen a client before him, even when Gabriel's attorney had asked her point-blank. Which meant she had been lying. But why?

"It's hard for me to believe that sex is ever far from a man's mind."

Gabriel gave a laugh. "Yeah, well, when you're making love to the bottle, a woman isn't always necessary."

Her face fell. "I'm sorry. I didn't mean to make light of alcohol addiction."

"It's fine, Sara. You don't need to walk on eggshells with me. I'm not overly sensitive." Maybe that was true, maybe it wasn't. Sometimes he did feel hypersensitive, but not with her. Maybe because she didn't seem like the type to insult him intentionally, nor was she a know-it-all. She had too many of her own issues to pass judgment on his.

"Can I ask how long you've been sober? You seem like you're handling it really well."

He couldn't tell her it had been seventy-five years without her doubting his sanity, so he said, "Seven and a half years."

She looked impressed. "Wow. That's fabulous." She bit her lip and glanced down at the stack of papers in her lap. Then she met his eye. "Can I tell you something?"

"Sure." Even as he said yes, he knew he shouldn't encourage intimacy with Sara, but he wanted it. He knew he did, and he *was* encouraging it, fostering it. Which made him wonder if he had learned a damn thing in the last century.

"I was addicted to sleeping pills. After my mom died. I couldn't sleep, and I started taking sedatives, then more and more, then suddenly I realized that I had a serious problem. I just got out of rehab six weeks ago."

She drew back slightly, like she expected a backlash from him. A verbal blow, maybe. But Gabriel wasn't surprised, nor was he disappointed in her. He understood what it was like to feel the crushing pressure of reality weighing down on you, how appealing and easy it was to escape it artificially, to seek answers where there were none. What impressed him about Sara was how quickly she had fought back. Her mother had only been dead a year, so he figured she'd really only struggled with the sedatives for six months or so. That was commendable, that she had reached out for help so quickly. And watching the determination on her face, and from what he'd seen of her personality since they'd met, he had no doubt that she would conquer her dependency. Even if she couldn't conquer her demons, given that she had no idea one was sitting four feet away from her.

He didn't want to be her demon.

And he needed to back off emotionally.

But not before reassuring her that he thought she was amazing.

"I think that's great that you addressed the issue so quickly. It took me a long time to admit I had a problem, and even longer to actually do something about it. You should be proud of yourself for facing it head-on, and fixing it. I totally respect that."

"Thanks. I feel better. I do. I'm kind of a control freak, and I didn't like being out of control in my life."

Gabriel knew that control was a fine line between screwing the lid so tight on your emotions you couldn't breathe inside, and reckless, scattered explosion. "Do you have any idea as to who killed your mom? Or what went wrong in the investigation?" It was rude to ask, but lack of answers drove her, that was obvious. It had driven her right into the grip of sedatives, and right out of the state of Florida.

Sara pulled her skirt tighter over her legs, but she didn't balk at the question. "I don't know who could have done it, I really don't. If it wasn't Rafe, which I truly believe it wasn't because, first of all, he loved my mom. And second of all, I saw him drive off in the opposite direction that night. We were at dinner, and we all parted ways. She was killed only an hour later. And I think the investigation stalled because from day one they thought they had it solved by turning to the obvious. They didn't even look into any other possibilities as far as I'm concerned. So any other leads they might have had are dried up by now, I'm sure."

That was probably true. Which showed a failing on the part of the justice system, but then again, there had probably been no other direction for them to investigate. "They had a lot of trace evidence. Did they test everything?"

"There's the irritating part—they would never tell me exactly what they had and didn't have. They couldn't disclose that information . . . She was my mother and they wouldn't give me any details. All I know is that hair and clothing fibers on her matched Rafe, which made sense since they were just together at dinner and he was in her house frequently. In her bed frequently, I'm sure. They had been dating for a year."

"That must have been frustrating to you . . . being a forensic scientist yourself and not allowed access to the data."

She nodded. "Oh, yeah. Very frustrating."

Gabriel made a mental note to see if he could get the court records now that the trial was over. He was curious about that trace evidence, as well as a few other things. "Did Rafe frequently spout Bible quotes during the trial?"

"Bible quotes?" Sara looked confused. "Rafe? I don't think so. Though I wasn't there for the majority of the trial. Why?"

That was interesting. Too random to ultimately be random, given the complexity of the quote from Rafe Marino that Gabriel had read in the paper. "I just read an article where he was quoting the Bible, referring to living a righteous life."

"Really?" She looked skeptical. "I never thought of Rafe as a religious kind of guy."

Gabriel shrugged. "Maybe it was the stress of the trial. But Sara, I'm sorry, I really am, that the case has gone cold. But maybe there will be some new evidence, maybe they'll solve it still. You never know."

Her head tilted. "Come on. Do you really believe that?"

If they had taken a man to trial and he'd been acquitted, then no, he didn't believe they would ever locate the killer. Maybe the man they'd tried really had done it. Maybe he hadn't. But the odds were very much against the police and the prosecutor ever accumulating enough evidence to actually try someone else for the crime at that point. So he told Sara the truth. "No, I don't really believe that. I think it's done, and you're left trying to figure out how to deal with the fact that there will never be justice for your mother."

Sara stroked her cat's head steadily, looking out the window behind him. "Yeah. That pretty much sums it up. And I appreciate your honesty. I get tired of people giving me 'look on the bright side' speeches. There is no fucking bright side. Even if they convicted someone, what does it matter? My mother is dead, and her last minutes on earth were torture.

And yes, I have to figure out how to live with that, how to go forward."

The curse from Sara surprised him, but he actually took it as a positive sign. She was venting, in a controlled way. She was letting it out, without losing it. That was a good thing. "Yes, you do."

"Do you know that there's no such thing as instant death? That if a person's throat is slit, they are still conscious, unable to make a sound, as their arterial artery bleeds out enough volume of blood to cause death. So they're aware, on some level, as the killer stabs them in the chest, the stomach, the face, and they can't do anything about it. They're helpless."

"I know." It was another layer of his guilt, that he could not die, but mortals did and could, painfully and slowly. That Anne had suffered that way while he had slept in a pleasure fog. "I know a lot about murder."

Suddenly she laughed, rubbing her face with the palms of her hands. "God, we're a pair, aren't we? Call us Gloom and Doom."

"Okay. I'll be Doom, you can be Gloom. Though you're going to have to ditch the kitten if you want people to believe you're macabre."

Her eyebrow went up. "What's wrong with Angel?"

"That. You can't be depressed and sour with a kitten named Angel. It's an oxymoron. And I refuse to wear leather pants, by the way, so I think we're going to have to give up our plan."

"We'll have to be happy?" Her mouth tilted up in the corner.

"I'm afraid so."

"I guess there are worse fates."

Indeed there were.

Sara's cell phone rang. "Do you mind if I answer that?"

"Go right ahead." He put his headphones on, classic rock blaring, so he wouldn't hear her private conversation, and turned back to study the breakdown of the ingredients in absinthe. Ethanol—definitely psychoactive. Wormwood—arguably, though it was virtually impossible to determine how much might have built up in an absinthe abuser. Especially since it could be toxic at high levels, yet Gabriel had been immortal. So there was no telling how much had been in his bloodstream at the time of the murder. Nor had he been drinking quality absinthe at that point. He hadn't cared enough to spend top dollar when a cheap substitute would get him drunk just as fast. It probably had been filled with lead and other filler metals.

It was disgusting to consider what he had put inside his body.

Gabriel reached for a spoon from his collection and tapped it on his desk.

Yet part of him would always crave the comfort, would always remember fondly the beauty of pouring water over the sugar-laden spoon and that moment of erotic anticipation as the absinthe turned from brilliant emerald to cloudy lime.

Part of him was still an addict, and until he conquered that once and for all, he was still cursed.

To be addicted to the addict. It was a terrible fate, and he would have to be careful he didn't ensnare Sara into such a horrific ending.

❧

Rafe's name was on her cell phone screen, so Sara answered it. "Hello?"

"Hey, it's me. How are you?"

His ears must have been burning. And for some reason, Sara felt guilty having discussed him with Gabriel, however vaguely. It still felt like she hadn't been staunch enough in her support of Rafe during the latter part of the trial. It felt like she needed to make that up to him, over and over, by reminding people of his innocence.

"I'm doing good," she said. "You haven't left Florida yet, have you?" She really did want to see Rafe before he went to California.

"No. It will be at least two weeks. I have to tie up some loose ends." He paused, than asked, "Are you really in New Orleans, Sara?"

She closed her eyes briefly. She hadn't wanted him to know, hadn't wanted him to worry. "Who told you that?"

"It's in the friggin' paper. But I know how capable they are of printing lies, so I wanted to check with you. Warn you that if you are there, they know."

They. The mythical *they* who had followed her, photographed her, called her, asked rude and insensitive questions. Disrupted her mother's funeral. Uncovered her brief stint in rehab and splashed it all over gleefully. The media.

"Yeah, I'm in New Orleans. Thanks for letting me know."

"Can I ask what you're doing there?"

That was a loaded question, and one she couldn't really answer in its entirety. "I just needed to get away. I'm sightseeing. I took a three-month lease on an apartment."

"An apartment? In the French Quarter? The Garden District?"

"No. Kenner."

"Never heard of it. So sightseeing, huh? Okay." He didn't sound like he believed her, but neither did he pry. "Make sure you check out the cemeteries. Everyone says you have to see them."

Not that she would normally seek out a jaunt through the cemetery, but in this case she could answer in all honesty. "I've already been there. Very interesting."

"Eat some gumbo for me, and come home safely, alright?"

"I will. Thanks. And if you need any help with the move, let me know."

"Thanks, but I'm fine. That's what moving companies are for. Call me next week, okay?"

She could do that. He sounded worried about her, and that was a nice thing to have. "I will."

"Good. Love you."

"Love you, too."

Sara hung up and glanced over at Gabriel. He didn't seem to be listening, but would he think it was odd for her to say she loved her mother's boyfriend? But she did, in a truly platonic sense, because Rafe had made her mother happy. He had loved her mother, calmly and consistently, and that wasn't an easy feat for anyone. Her mother had been volatile and difficult to live with. But Rafe had been a calming influence on her.

No one would even think twice about it if Rafe had been sixty to her mother's forty-six. But because he had only been thirty-one, everyone had doubted the legitimacy of their relationship. Doubted that any man could love an older woman without an ulterior motive.

Gabriel was spoon tapping again. He seemed to have a spoon collection, though they weren't souvenir spoons. She wasn't sure what they were exactly, but he had at least twelve of them, lined up on the wall, hanging from nails that he hooked through the holes in the bowl part of the utensil. He had a different one in his hand than he'd had the other day, and he flicked it on the desk to the rhythm he was obviously hearing through his headphones. He was musically talented, judging by the ease with which he held the rhythm, while reading his computer screen. Which wasn't surprising, given that he played the piano. Or had played the piano.

She wondered if he associated the piano with alcohol.

That would be a good reason to distance himself from music. If not, she thought it was terribly tragic that he didn't hear music anymore.

Adjusting her laptop computer on her legs on the couch, Sara checked her e-mail. She'd been surprised that Gabriel had wireless access in his apartment since his building was so old and lacking in other amenities, but he really did need it to do his job. It wasn't vital in her field, and she'd been off of work anyway, but she did like to check her mail occasionally. She had a lot of spam, and some forwarded jokes from her friend Jocelyn, as well as a personal e-mail from her inquiring how her sightseeing trip was going. Sara felt a little guilty for misleading Jocelyn as well, but she hadn't been able to tell her why she was coming to New Orleans. It had just seemed too odd, too desperate, for anyone else to understand.

Sara dashed off a brief reply that said a whole lot of nothing. Clicking through the rest of messages in her inbox, she paused at one.

The subject header was "Questions Remain In Michaels Case," and the sender was not an address she recognized.

A chill ran over her arms and she clicked to open the e-mail reluctantly. It was a link to the *Naples Daily News* online articles. She scanned it quickly.

> The murder of Jessie Michaels is not a closed case, according to the Naples police. Despite the fact that Dr. Rafe Marino was acquitted of the July 2007 murder of his girlfriend just last week,

prosecutor Daniel Smithton has indicated there is a new lead in the year-old murder. Despite accusations in the media that the indictment of Dr. Marino was botched, the prosecutor maintains the case against him was strong. The drawn-out and highly publicized trial has been devastating to Smithton's reputation and former conviction rate of 100 percent for homicide cases.

Smithton theorized during the trial that Marino and the victim's daughter, Sara Michaels, had been engaged in an affair, and together plotted the murder of mother and girlfriend. Given that Dr. Marino cannot be tried for the same crime twice, Smithton's dogged pursuit of a closure to this case would suggest that attention may be turned to securing a conviction of Sara Michaels for complicity to commit murder.

Shit. Taking deep breaths, Sara willed herself not to be sick, not to read the rest of the article, which was just a recap of everything she already knew. Arresting her was all just speculation, the media trying to draw out a trial that had garnered them a great deal of attention. There was no evidence to prosecute her. Rafe's attorney had assured her of that over and over again. There was no evidence at all of a relationship between her and Rafe, and the evidence against him presented in court had been purely circumstantial. It had hurt him that he hadn't had an alibi, but she herself had been at work that night. But despite a lack of alibi, no one had seen him at her mother's that night either. No one had seen anyone entering the house, or seen his car parked in the driveway, or on the street.

The basis of their prosecution had been the hair and clothing fibers, and a single fingerprint on the window in her mother's bedroom that matched Rafe's left index finger. But he and her mother had spent virtually all non-working hours together, mostly at her house, so that meant nothing as far as Sara was concerned. In the end, the jury had agreed. It hadn't been enough to convict him.

And there wasn't anything to convict her on. She had to

remember that. She had never spent time with Rafe without
her mother present, and there had been no phone conversa-
tions between them other than when he was at her mother's
house. No one had any reason to believe, or any proof, that
they had been involved with each other and could have done
something as heinous as plot her mother's murder.

Besides, why would they have needed to kill her mother to
be together? It was completely illogical. Rafe was a doctor.
He didn't need her mother's tiny insurance policy or house.

Sara was tempted to delete the e-mail, just to get rid of it,
but she knew she really should keep it. She should pursue who
had sent it to her, try to determine if it was a random person or
if it was the newspaper trying to coax a response from her. But
she wasn't up for an investigation at the moment. She wanted
Florida to stay in Florida. And the only murder she wanted to
think about was Anne Donovan's, leaving her mother's for
Gabriel to deal with for the book, so she moved the e-mail to
a folder labeled "Misc." and closed her browser.

Then she opened up a Word document and started typing.
There were questions she wanted to answer about the Donovan case, whether or not they could ever reach a conclusion as
to what happened. There were things she just wanted to know,
so she typed them to organize her thoughts:

Where did John Thiroux come from?

Where did he go after his acquittal?

Who was keeping Anne Donovan's child?

And there was the ultimate question, which she found difficult to even type in black-and-white, that tied present to past,
Florida to Louisiana. She had never spoken it out loud, never
told anyone. They would think she was either insane or making it up, or look at her like she was a complete and utter
freak. Because there was no way around the truth, the question
to which she had no answer:

Why were my great-great-great-grandmother, great-
great-grandmother, grandmother, and mother all murdered? Was it a coincidence? A curse? Why was Anne

Donovan's granddaughter, Mary Conway, not killed?
Does someone know about the first two murders and
have they decided to perpetuate them with the last two?
Could it have been my grandfather?

Am I next?

The last was a small question, but one which held all her
fears, encompassed the very drive behind everything she had
done in the last year. The very real terror that it would be her
turn at any given moment.

"Want to go to lunch?"

Sara jumped at the sound of Gabriel's voice. Not wanting
him to read what she'd written, to know what she'd been
thinking, she slapped the computer lid down hard and blinked
at him. He had turned around in his chair and was looking at
her curiously. She knew immediately she had overreacted,
though he didn't call her on it.

"Uh, sure. Lunch would be good." It was a little late for
nonchalance, but she faked it anyway.

"Cool. Let me know when you're ready." He started shut-
ting down his computer, and hung the unusual spoon back up
on its hook next to its brethren.

It was really very nice that whatever Gabriel thought of
her, he didn't seem to think she was a freak, which was frequently how she felt. He didn't so much as blink at any of her
odd behaviors, including the utterly random act of staring
wide-eyed at him at four in the morning as he tried to sleep.
Nor had he made her feel uncomfortable for doing that, or
anything else.

"Does it bother you that I'm in your space?" she asked him
as she stood up and stretched. "I realize I could probably do
all of this at my place if that works better for you." She did
feel guilty for invading his apartment, his life. She hadn't realized how much time she would actually spend reading documents and sorting them. It wasn't something he really needed
her to be on-site for, at least not on a daily basis. She wanted
to give him the opportunity to lose her if he really preferred to
be alone.

"This works for me."

That's all he said, and all he needed to. Sara accepted everything Gabriel said at face value, because for whatever reason, she trusted that he spoke the truth, and didn't waste words where they weren't necessary.

And she was oddly relieved he wanted her to stick around. Or maybe it wasn't so odd, really. She liked him. She was attracted to him, even though he had given her no encouragement, no real flirtation, no sexual innuendos. Yet she still enjoyed his company, and in a small, quiet way, knew she was hoping that at some point they would cross the line and explore a physical relationship. She didn't want anything permanent, not a real relationship, but sex she really could use.

But it was probably a good thing that he wasn't hitting on her. The complication was something she really didn't need, even if her body disagreed.

"Will the cat be okay here?"

"Sure. Let's just close her in one room so she doesn't get into anything. We can put her in my bedroom. She can't get into trouble there."

Gabriel scooped Angel up off the couch and held her with one hand against his chest. His fingers scratched behind her ears. Sara followed them, wanting to make sure Angel was settled.

Then was sorry she had. When she walked into Gabriel's bedroom, the first thing she saw was an oblong red streak of blood on the outside of his window. "Oh my God! What is that?"

He moved toward it, dropping Angel onto his unmade bed. "A bird must have hit the window. It's probably down in the courtyard."

Sara shuddered. She worked with, or had until the past year, blood samples in the lab on nearly a daily basis. Her entire adult life had been spent knee-deep in blood, by choice.

But now she was starting to wonder why it seemed to follow her everywhere.

Chapter Eight

※❦※

Gabriel opened the results of the fingerprint analysis on Monday, before Sara was due to arrive. The e-mail was long and convoluted, but the conclusion was that the fingerprint, preserved in blood, on the sketch of Anne's hand that he had drawn the night of her murder, was not a match to the right thumbprint of the set of fingerprints he had submitted for comparison.

His fingerprints.

So that wasn't his finger in blood, which surprised him, because he remembered picking the sketch back up after he had thrown up. After his fingers had been wet and sticky from touching the blood on the mattress. So it should have been his fingerprint. But it wasn't. Which meant his memory of events was unreliable.

Which did not make him happy.

What else did he remember inaccurately?

There was only one other person still walking the earth who had any knowledge of the events of that night, and the months that followed, but Gabriel refused to contact Raphael. Didn't even know where he was at this point.

Gabriel had spent the last century cutting off all ties with the Grigori, denying the truth of his status, pretending that he was in fact just another mortal. But he wasn't. He had been an angel. Sent to watch, guide, and protect mortals. And like Alex and the other Watchers before him, he had succumbed to human vice, to one of the seven deadly sins. For Alex, it had been lust. He had copulated with human women, and had fathered two demonic daughters. For Raphael, it had been wrath, his anger simmering under a passive exterior, boiling over in his obsession with violent sports, both as spectator and participant. But for Gabriel, it was gluttony, the overconsumption of drugs and alcohol. Addiction was the ultimate form of gluttony, the inability to stop consuming even after it was dangerous, detrimental, destructive.

Alex had accepted his sin, embraced his title of Demon, but Gabriel tried to deny his. He didn't feel evil, and he didn't enjoy perpetuating sin in others, or hurting humans. He had a loud conscience, and he appreciated it, wanted to nurture it. His flaws, and sins, were his own, and to his core, he felt he was truly not Demon or Angel. He was human.

Yet irrefutably immortal.

He had to let Anne go. Had to know he hadn't destroyed her life, so he could move on, to a future that wasn't stagnant, a purgatory of his own making, as Alex had pointed out.

But he wasn't sure how to get to the truth. Had no idea who the fingerprint could belong to.

If he had Anne's DNA, he would have an answer of sorts, because if the blood flakes still preserved on the bowie knife didn't match Gabriel's or Anne's, then there had been a third person in the room. One who had nicked and cut himself as he slashed Anne in a frenzy. It wouldn't tell Gabriel who that person was, because there was no one alive to do a DNA comparison with, and no other suspects besides the mysterious man in the room prior to him, but it would be enough for Gabriel to know it hadn't been him who had taken life.

He needed to know that in his weakness he hadn't violated his own nature and the laws of morality so deeply as to kill a defenseless woman.

Through the open windows Gabriel heard someone come into the courtyard. It was probably Sara, since she had said she'd be there at ten. She had been a little nervous with him on Saturday, jumpy almost. He had figured it was because she was embarrassed that they had slept in his bed together, but for whatever reason, after lunch she'd gone back to her apartment and he hadn't seen her since.

He was perfectly content with his own company, but he hadn't realized how lonely he was until he'd met Sara. Or more accurately, he had known it, but been able to ignore it. Now that he had access to Sara, it was different. He enjoyed talking to her, sharing ideas, hearing her soft laugh. Smelling her feminine perfume and touching the small of her back. There was no denying the pleasure he took from her presence, and he was pleased to hear her pushing the gate open.

He'd given her a key to the gate, so she could come and go without having to stand there waiting for him to open it. Normally, he didn't even remember to lock it on a regular basis, and neither did his neighbor, but Sara needed it locked. It was a crutch, an illusion of safety that she needed to have right now, and he respected that. She had been through a hell of a lot, and unlike him, she wasn't immortal. She could die.

It took him a minute to realize that she wasn't coming up the staircase to his apartment. He listened, allowing himself to utilize his heightened senses, and after deciphering movement, he knew she had actually stopped in the courtyard. She was walking around on the old bricks, pulling out a chair at the wrought iron table that had been in the same spot for a decade.

Gabriel stood up and went into his bedroom. He had washed the streak of blood off the glass, and the window was closed again against the August heat. But he could see her through the pane, sitting at the table, reading something from a manila envelope in her lap. She had propped her feet up on another chair, tucking her yellow skirt neatly around her legs. Her blond hair spilled back over her shoulders, and she reached up and buried her hands in it, tousling and piling it up on top of her head, before letting it drop again.

The sun shone across her legs, but the building shadowed her cheek and nose.

Without giving any thought to it, Gabriel went and got his camera and, as quietly as possible, lifted the window. Angling the lens down, to capture the feeling of watching her from above, he tested the light with several shots. Then he shifted to the left and zoomed in on her face, wanting her profile, want-

ing to capture the curve of her sensuous lip, the strength of her
jaw, the delicacy of her petite nose, which struggled to hold
her sunglasses in place. He clicked, over and over, moving in
and out, shifting from her face to the whole image of *Sara at
Study*, shoulders tense as she bent over, in contrast to the relaxed posture of her lower body.

As he grabbed shot after shot, Gabriel's frustration grew.
He didn't want to preserve with the click of the button. He
wanted to capture through creation. He wanted to see if his
fingers could copy the curves of her body, the expression on
her face, the duality of light, and the angle of descent. Setting
the camera down on the bed, he went into his closet, yanking
boxes out of his way and tearing into a case he had shoved to
the back. It held a brand-new, never used sketchbook. With
one single pencil, sharpened and ready to use. Bought in a
moment of weakness, of longing for the feel of the slender
pencil between his fingers, stroking and sliding across paper,
generating thought and emotion on the page.

The materials felt good in his hands, and he flipped not to
the first page, but to the middle of the book. At the window, he
only needed a minute to shift from photographer to artist, and
then his lines appeared, swift and sure, outlining Sara's body,
the scratch of pencil to paper urging him on. As he worked,
glancing up and down, manic in his need to emulate her juxtaposition of tension and relaxation, she shifted in her chair, and
released her skirt from its prison under her legs.

She must have been getting hot in the sun, because she
took the hem from where it hit at her knees and shook it up
and down to fan her legs. Then, still reading, she hitched the
skirt up toward her thighs and dropped her knees apart, one
foot moving off the chair to the ground.

Gabriel's mouth went dry.

It was sexual, but unintentionally so. She was concentrating on the papers in her hand, the relaxing of her legs a signal
of her absorption. But that was part of what was so sexy,
knowing she wasn't trying to seduce. She just was.

Flipping to a clean page, Gabriel started over, wanting this
new frame captured, this sense of abandonment from Sara.
Her sensuality. The length of her neck, her slender legs. It was
stunning, and he raced to draw her, wanting it down before she

moved, before she became aware of him, before the sun shifted. His fingers remembered, even though it had been a hundred and fifty years, and he embraced the memory, the moment, the gift he had been given.

Sketching standing up had never been natural for him, and in impatience, he gripped his pad and climbed onto the window ledge, the sill providing a narrow seat for him. He dangled his feet over the side of the brick house and spread his legs to make a surface for his sketchbook. And went back to work, satisfied with the progress he was making, entranced by the quiet of the courtyard, no sound but the rustle of leaves in the trees and bushes and the sound of Sara flipping through the pages in her lap.

She tugged her skirt up higher, exposing a delicious expanse of thigh on the leg that was still stretched across the chair.

He wanted to touch her, to slid his hand up that warm, firm limb and move underneath her skirt and stroke her intimately, watching her face to see her relax, capitulate, accept pleasure at his hand. He wanted to hear her sigh for him. See the full extent of her beauty.

Outline of her form down on his pad, he studied his raw sketch in comparison to the living, breathing woman below him. It was good, and he was pleased with it.

It had been worth the risk, worth breaking a personal rule. This was his, to keep.

He was smoothing out the line of her shoulder with his thumb when he heard her scream.

❧

Sara was soaking up the sun, enjoying the feel of it on her face, her arms, even as it heated up her skin and made her start to perspire. The courtyard was peaceful and it had beckoned to her. The table and chairs were a little rickety, or maybe it was that the ground was uneven, mossy bricks that had settled and crumbled. But it felt good to sit enclosed by the vine-covered brick walls and read the remaining stack of police reports from the Donovan investigation in solitude.

She was nervous about seeing Gabriel again. She had been weird on Saturday and she knew it. But sleeping in the same bed with him, overreacting both on the street and then again in his apartment when she'd thought he might be dead, plus getting that random e-mail suggesting her guilt—it had all been too much. Embarrassing. So after lunch she had ditched out, and now she was a little nervous about seeing him.

Not that Gabriel was exempt from eccentricities himself. He was a little more abstract than the average person. So she knew intellectually she shouldn't worry about his reaction, knew he probably thought nothing at all about her behavior, but she was still grateful for the few minutes in the sun to collect her thoughts before she saw him. Maybe if she was lucky, he would look out his window and see her, and come down to say hi. Then she could greet him sitting down wearing sunglasses instead of standing there shuffling her feet as he opened his front door, her eyes darting all over the place.

It wasn't a very solid plan, and was in fact highly wimpy of her, but she couldn't face everything straight on all the time. She was allowed to avoid once in awhile, and she hadn't even considered not showing up at all. She wasn't that big of a wimp.

Something out of the corner of her eye moved and she glanced up.

And screamed, leaping out of her chair. "Jesus Christ, what are you doing?"

Gabriel was sitting in the open window and half of his flippin' body was actually out of the frame and dangling into the ether. Her first thought was that he was trying to jump, but he was just sitting there, with a big pad of paper in his hand.

"Hey," he called down, waving.

Very casual. Like sitting in the goddamn window forty feet above brain-smashing bricks was normal.

"What are you doing?" Sara clutched her papers and eyed him, waiting for him to lose his balance and come pitching forward. She honestly didn't think she could catch him, given he had a foot in height and forty pounds on her.

"I was inspired," he said, showing no signs of retreating inside. In fact, he swung his legs back and forth and held up the pad of paper for her to see.

"Inspired to do what? Fall to your death? For God's sake, get back inside! Carefully."

"I'm not going to fall. And I was inspired to sketch. Come up and see."

Sara was intrigued and pleased that he had felt the urge to sketch, but at the same time she couldn't fully appreciate the implication because fear was choking her. "I'm not leaving until I see that you're safely inside."

His head tilted slightly and he smiled. Then he just nodded and said, "Okay."

She clutched her papers to her chest as he turned and pulled his legs back into the bedroom. But she didn't really start breathing again until he was standing up inside and pulling the window closed.

Good grief. What the hell had that been all about? She didn't think his sense of survival was well honed. He didn't lock doors, he strolled into dark doorways at two in the morning, and dangled out of third-floor windows.

Yet another good reason why she shouldn't get involved with him. She would constantly be worrying about him, and frankly, she had enough to worry about without adding him to the mix.

Not that he was trying to get involved with her. She had to remember that, too.

Prepared to reprimand him yet again, Sara went up the stairs and through the wide open door of his apartment. She sincerely hoped he had just pulled it open in anticipation of her entrance and that he hadn't been home all day with the front door gaping open. Though she would bite her tongue before she said something to him about the door and sounded like a nag. Driving the point home about dangling in the window was one thing, but add the locked door issue on top of that and she'd sound like a freak.

Which maybe she was.

But all thoughts of stern consternation fled her mind when Gabriel held up his sketchbook in front of her.

She felt her mouth drop. Actually was aware of her jaw descending and her mouth flapping open.

It was *her*. He had drawn her, beautifully. With clean lines and a raw sort of honesty, and appreciation.

She saw how he had seen her from the window, relaxed, but still pensive. Warm in the sun. Legs spread.

Good God.

"It's . . . lovely. You're very, very talented." And she was going to have to revise her opinion of his lack of interest in her. The drawing was alive, and the artist was attracted to the subject. She could *see* that. Feel it. Unless he had done that just for effect. But she didn't believe it. He had perceived her pose as sensual, her posture as making love to the sunshine, accepting it, wanting it.

"Thanks." He glanced at the sketch, a satisfied smile on his face, pencil tucked behind his ear. "Like I said, I was inspired."

"Why did you ever stop drawing?" Sara reached out and tipped the book back to her, so they could both see it. It was highly flattering, very gratifying to see herself on paper. "If you did this in just a few minutes, I can't imagine what you could do with paint and a week."

Gabriel glanced down at her, his arm, leg, body close to her. She could smell his aftershave, and the oddly innocent odor of baby shampoo, and she realized that individually there were pieces of Gabriel that she really liked, appreciated, was attracted to. Sometimes, put all together, she wasn't entirely sure what she was looking at, but studied in sections, she saw nothing but aspects that pleased her.

"There's a reason I gave it up, Sara. Drawing, painting, playing the piano . . . they all require emotion. Vulnerability. Exposing a piece of me." His thumb slid over the page, rushing over the top of her hair in pencil.

She shivered, feeling again that flood of desire he inspired.

"When you're an alcoholic, and trying to get sober, that sort of free-flowing emotion and total abandonment is a really bad thing. You need control, or at least I did, to stay away from the alcohol. I had to clamp down on all my creativity. Does that make sense?"

"Yes." She understood. Completely. "I told you I'm a control freak. I know exactly what you mean." Glancing up at him, she asked the obvious. "So why now? What makes it okay now?"

He shrugged. "I don't know. It just felt right. I'm in control. And I enjoyed doing this."

"It shows." She felt her cheeks pinken as she saw how truly far apart her legs had been. "I thought I was alone."

"I know. That's what made it so enticing. You were completely unaware of me."

"How long were you dangling out of that window? You just about gave me a heart attack."

He laughed. "Not long. And I have very good balance."

"So do cats and they fall sometimes too." She rolled her eyes to finish off her point.

Gabriel startled her by running his fingertip along her cheek, softly, slowly. "Don't worry. I have nine lives."

The touch felt good, and she struggled against the urge to close her eyes, to lean into it. "Nobody lives forever, Gabriel. Don't take unnecessary risks."

"Maybe every day feels like I am going to live forever. Maybe it feels endless." His dark brown eyes bored into her as his finger fell away.

He had a deep voice, at odds with his delicate bone structure, and it washed over her, his face closer to hers than she had realized. Their bodies were brushing casually, no sense of personal space between them, and she gave in to the urge to touch his hair. Just the end. Lightly. Smoothing it. It was as silken and soft as she had imagined. "Maybe it's time to rediscover some of the things that brought you joy before."

She meant painting, the piano. But he got a licentious look in his eye. "Oh, yeah? Like what?"

"Whatever you like. Sketching, for one."

"Maybe. If you'll model for me."

Sara stood still. He was so close to her his breath danced across her face. His eyes studied her, challenging her. He was going to kiss her. She was sure of it. And every inch of her welcomed it, wanted to feel his body against hers, wanted to taste his mouth, dip her tongue inside him, and have permission to plunge her fingers into his hair and tug.

"I'll think about it," she whispered. "But I'm a very self-conscious person, so if I model, it will be stilted."

"I don't believe you," he said. "I think if you decide to do something, you do it, without hesitation."

She wasn't entirely sure he was right. Nor was she sure if that was all he meant, or if he was asking her something. All she knew was that if he wanted her to initiate a kiss, it wasn't going to happen. She wasn't going to risk ruining their work-

ing relationship, the budding friendship sort of thing they had
happening.

"Like dancing," he added. "Once you decided to go out
there, you went for it."

That embarrassed her. Maybe because dancing, putting it
out there, reminded her of the flaws in her mother, that lack of
control she had frequently displayed. Sara backed up, broke
away, both physically and emotionally. He wasn't going to
touch her, she could sense that. And she was too raw to make
a move, wasn't sure it was a good idea at all. "Yeah, and when
you decide to sketch, you climb out of a window to do it."

Gabriel didn't answer, just watched her with eyes that
spoke volumes, yet not in a way she could understand. "Is
there somewhere I can get some coffee?" she asked. She
needed to get away from him.

"Turn right on Royal and go down a block."

It never seemed to jar him that she switched subjects clear
out of the blue, and he never missed a beat. Maybe it was because he was as random as she was.

"Thanks. Want anything?"

He shook his head no. But he gave a soft laugh, a sort of
scoff of disbelief.

"What?"

"Nothing."

It was possibly the most irritating word in the English language.

So without bothering to pursue that any further, Sara dug
into her purse for her sunglasses and headed for the door.

Chapter Nine

❦

Gabriel wanted to find the child. If the coroner claimed Anne had given birth, then it was possible the child had been stillborn. Or died shortly thereafter. But if the child had died at birth, or some point after, there would be birth records. Assuming that Anne hadn't given birth before the age of fifteen, Gabriel had ordered the birth records for children with the surname Donovan for all of New Orleans for the years 1841–1849. He didn't think it was possible that Anne had given birth the year she had died, because he had known her most of that year, but it wouldn't hurt to scan the results.

While Sara was off getting coffee, he sorted through the data, which had been e-mailed to him. Since he didn't need to see the actual physical birth certificates until he found a viable name, he could just search and scroll through the list of names.

It was possible that if Anne had actually had a child, it had been left behind in Ireland, but Gabriel doubted that. Anne had told him she was thirteen when she'd made the trip across the Atlantic, and he had no reason to doubt that. Though he supposed his next search should be passenger lists to verify her arrival, along with her name and age. He had no birth certificate for Anne, only her word at the time that she was twenty-three.

Donovan also was her unmarried name, and Gabriel wondered if she had given birth to an illegitimate child what name it would have been given. Most likely Donovan, but it was also possible that the child had been adopted, or given to friends to raise.

It was a long shot, but something told him it mattered. Or maybe he just wanted there to be a child. Maybe he wanted to know that a piece of Anne had continued, that she hadn't died before really living, before leaving a legacy.

There were fifty-five children born with the last name of Donovan in New Orleans Parish during the eight years in question, some listed solo, others with birth parents. Those who were listed alongside their parents' names had their mother listed by maiden name and married name, then the father next to her. Three had mothers named Anne, though one was spelled without an "e" on the end. Then one was listed simply as A. Donovan, with no married name and no mention of a father.

Gabriel flagged those four and sent an e-mail ordering copies of the actual birth certificates for them.

Then he changed his mind. He didn't want to wait. If he went to the library himself, he could view them on microfilm, then order copies as needed.

He would just leave a note for Sara and leave the door unlocked.

The idea of waiting for her and walking over to the library together was appealing, but he had felt her withdrawal from him earlier. He had done or said something wrong, obviously, though he had no idea what. But she had definitely bolted. Which was just as well. He had been severely tempted to touch her, and that was an extremely bad idea.

So he would stick with the note and give her some space. They'd known each other less than a week, yet their relationship felt intense, advanced, for the time span. It made sense to back off, to limit the time they were together.

Even if he didn't want to.

❧

Sara went in to the same coffee shop she had a few days earlier and ordered an iced coffee to go. She was too restless to sit and drink it. Gabriel had nicked at her calm, and she felt the need to walk, to burn off the nervous energy.

She had wanted him to kiss her. Badly. She had wanted him to talk her into modeling, then she had wanted him to put down his sketch pad and make love to her, touching her everywhere intimately, his lips on her body. It wasn't why she had come to New Orleans, and while part of her felt like it would only end in utter disaster, another part of her kept whispering, *Why not?* Why couldn't she have a hot affair that reminded her of the pleasure of being alive?

It wasn't why she'd made the trek from Florida, but it could be a serious fringe benefit.

Of course, she had also come to New Orleans to try to discover bits of her mother, the way she had been in life, as opposed to death. To try to understand the girl she'd been, the careless woman she'd become. As Sara walked back down Royal Street, she realized it was a futile effort. Her mother had been emotionally distant, and in death she wasn't going to give what she hadn't in life.

But Sara knew that her grandmother's death had altered the course of her mother's life. She had been only sixteen when her mother was murdered. And Jessie Michaels had been the one to find her mother, stabbed to death in their suburban home. It was only six months later that she had run away from her father and taken up dancing on Bourbon Street.

None of those radical choices had ever been explained by her mother. She had never elaborated any more than her standard "I didn't like rules."

On impulse, Sara cut up Orleans Street toward Bourbon. The sun was relentless on her bare shoulders, and she pushed her sunglasses up, checking for sidewalk holes. It amazed her that every street in the Quarter shared the same basic characteristics—the narrow thoroughfare, the buildings flush to the sidewalk, the wooden shutters and doors, and the wrought iron railings. Yet each street took on its own personality, its own tone. Some were seedy, others elegant, some quiet, some boisterous. Orleans was calm and reserved, with a hotel that extended for most of the block to Bourbon, which suited her. This was truly her first stroll around the Quarter on her own, and while she wanted to like it, enjoy herself, she could never seem to shake the sensation that she didn't belong. That she was vulnerable. A target.

It was important to confront those feelings, to recognize that she was just outside of her comfort zone, and nothing more. There was no danger, and no one was out to get her.

She debated which way to go on Bourbon, but opted for left, figuring there was more in that direction. The club her mother had danced at no longer went by the same name, but the night she'd died, her mother had been drinking a steady stream of margaritas at dinner with Sara and Rafe and she had suddenly started reminiscing about her days dancing. She had mentioned that the club was in the four hundred block of Bourbon where there were several gentleman's clubs. Then she had told Rafe it was a shame he hadn't seen her table dancing, because, to quote her mother, she had been hot shit.

Sara had been appalled, but Rafe just smiled and told her she still was. Then he mildly suggested maybe another margarita wasn't wise if she wanted to be able to walk to the car. If Sara had said that, her mother would have torn into her, and defiantly kept drinking, but she hadn't been offended by Rafe's comment. She just laughed and said maybe he was right, but that it was still a shame that he had been in diapers when she'd been dancing.

And just four hours later, her mother was dead.

Sara was walking right past strip clubs, posters plastered all over their exterior walls, advertising barely legal girls and world famous sex acts. None of the pictures looked very appealing to her, and the one with a woman sitting aggressively on a bike seat looked downright painful. The pictures went on and on—smiling women, naked and airbrushed. Sara had never been inside a strip club, and for some reason, she paused in front of the door of one after spending a few minutes perusing their posters, wondering how the dancers themselves compared to the cheerful images on the wall. Were strippers really that happy and perky? She wanted to see inside, wanted to know, wanted to picture how her mother had been bold and sassy enough at sixteen to lie about her age and dance partly naked in front of men.

"Are you looking for work?"

Glancing over at the doorman, Sara willed herself not to blush. "No."

"Are you sure?" He smiled at her, a man in his mid-thirties, attractive and wearing a suit. "The money's good, and we could use a blonde. One of our best customers already saw you and asked about you. You're guaranteed fifty a night in tips from him alone if he likes you."

"What do you mean he saw me? I just walked up." Sara hadn't seen anyone on the sidewalk but her and the doorman. Though admittedly she had been busy studying the pictures with morbid fascination.

"A minute ago. He saw you when he was going inside." He tipped his head to the door, giving another charming smile. "Come on in and watch a few of the girls, see what you think."

It amazed her that dancers were on stage at noon on a Monday, but it was Bourbon Street, after all. Bars were advertising three for one, and karaoke was going. "No, thanks." Though she couldn't prevent herself from glancing in the open door. All she could see was a dark hallway, and a woman's legs on the stage.

And she suddenly had the feeling that someone was watching her. From inside the club.

Sara shivered, rubbing her hands over her arms. Maybe the customer the doorman had referred to was still checking her out. Which she didn't like at all.

"Well, have a good afternoon then, and if you change your mind, stop on back." The guy waved and diverted his attention to two men passing by on the street.

Giving one last backward glance into the club and seeing nothing noteworthy, Sara started down the street, returning the way she had come. She wanted to go back to Gabriel's apartment, to the security of his courtyard. Finding pieces of her mother's motivation on Bourbon Street wasn't going to happen. She had to accept she was never going to have answers to those questions. Hell, maybe she wouldn't want them if she did have them. Ultimately, she and her mother had been diametrically opposed to each other in the core of who they were.

Funny that she had never given much thought to her biological father. It would seem logical that if she were nothing like her mother, she must be like her father, yet she had never been interested in finding him. Only once had she asked for his name, and her mother had told her she didn't remember his last name, only his first, which had been Brian. The last name "started with an S" but beyond that her mother couldn't recall. Sara had never asked again. Who Brian S. had been and why he had been a bouncer and what he had seen in her sixteen-year-old mother had never really mattered to her.

Maybe because it was her mother who had driven her life, not him. It was her mother who had raised her, her mother who hugged her and yelled at her, who had vacillated between effusive affection and stone-cold remoteness. Her mother had influenced her psyche on every level, and now she was left alone to deal with the mess of her life.

It made her angry. At her mother. At the world.

Sara walked faster, dodging sidewalk holes and avoiding further doormen and one aggressive bartender already hocking shots in plastic tubes in the open doorway. She needed to let it go. Let it all go. Start over right here, right now. Yet it was so damn hard to start over when she physically felt the past following her. It was there in the Anne Donovan case, it was there in the e-mail she'd gotten suggesting her guilt, it was there in the book Gabriel was writing, it was in the disturbing sensation that even as she walked someone was watching her, following her.

For a minute, she panicked, forgetting which cross street she wanted to turn down, and certain she'd gone too far, but then she saw the sign for Dumaine and realized that was the street Gabriel's apartment was on. Glancing behind her as she turned onto Dumaine, she scanned the street for a clear indication of someone following her, but she only saw several women together in a cluster wearing summer business skirts, and a man hosing the street down.

God, she was totally paranoid. Yet she couldn't shake the feeling, and she walked faster and faster until she got to Gabriel's gate, which was open. Then she jogged down the enclosure and up the stairs to his apartment, looking forward to seeing him, hearing his reassurances. There was a note on the door.

Went to library. Back soon, go on in. G

Sara ripped it off the door and turned the knob. He'd left
the door open. And the gate. Plus a note indicating to anyone
who happened by that he wasn't home and everything was unlocked. He was afraid of nothing, and she was paranoid
enough for the both of them, and one extra person besides.
Sara went in and locked the door behind her, heart pounding
from her aggressive walking.

Then she pulled out her cell phone in case she needed to call
911, and walked through his apartment, checking to make sure
she was actually alone with the door locked behind her. She
went through every room, even throwing open his bedroom
closet and peeking behind the shower curtain. She ended in his
office, and collapsed on the sofa, feeling on the verge of tears.

She fought them, hating to cry, knowing it meant she
wasn't better, despising that she was not totally and completely in control. Popping back up to distract herself, she
went over to study the spoons that hung on the wall by
Gabriel's computer. She thought they were vintage, but she
couldn't be sure. She wasn't even sure if they were technically
spoons since they had holes in them, and oblong ends, more
like a pie server than a spoon.

Agitated and restless, Sara knew she should just go back to
the file folder of research documents she had with her. She
hadn't brought her laptop, and she didn't feel comfortable using Gabriel's computer without asking him first, but she could
write out longhand all the questions she had. She wanted to
find out more about John Thiroux—where he had come from
and where he had gone after his acquittal. Newspaper articles
at the time hadn't seemed to delve into his past at all. Everything she had read concentrated on his artistic endeavors and
his drug problem. No one mentioned his family, his education,
where his wealth had originated from, and how he might have
strayed down the path of alcohol and opium.

But instead of working, she found herself looking at the
various objects lying around his desk. Never a nosy person,
she wasn't sure why she was standing there filled with rabid
curiosity, eyes roving over an old loving cup used as a pen
holder. The abandoned water bottle turned on its side,
crushed, and stuck with paper clips that had been twisted open
and straightened out to reveal their ends. Stacks of books with

criminology titles. Gabriel was messy, but not dirty. There
was no dust, no food wrappers, no indiscriminant sticky spots.

A file folder was open next to the computer, and it was impossible not to see the copy of the sketch sitting on top. It was
a woman in profile, sitting on the edge of a bed. She thought it
was Anne Donovan, but it was hard to tell from the side. But it
was signed in the corner JT. Sara stood there staring at the
sketch, telling herself not to do it, but she couldn't stop herself. Sliding the first copy over, she revealed a second one behind it. This was Anne on her stomach on the bed, nude, head
lying on her arms, looking more sleepy than sexual. Like
she'd woken to discover her lover had been sketching her for
quite some time.

It was an intimate image, and Sara felt a profound sense of
sadness for Anne, for the life she had led, and the brutal, un-
timely end to her existence.

But at the same time, going on pure instinct, Sara felt as
though the man who had drawn that picture had respected the
woman before him. There was a tenderness to what he had
captured. The artist didn't seem interested in her nudity for
titillation, but as a display of her total beauty, her curves and
soft feminine form.

There were three more sketches in the pile. The first
showed Anne at her dressing table fussing with a pot of pow-
der. Another was of Anne smiling, an intense devotion to the
artist on her face, revealing, in Sara's opinion, that she had
loved John Thiroux. Or at least desired him, admired him,
been grateful to him. There was intensity in her eyes, not disgust or boredom or tolerance. The third sketch was one of her
neck, curls tumbling over her shoulders, the graceful lines of
her muscles and bones delineated. A pearl necklace was resting above her décolleté, and her fingers played with the beads.
Her face wasn't visible, but she had slender fingers and neatly
manicured nails.

The final two sketches had Sara pulling back in shock. "Jesus." Both were copies like the others, the first a rendering of
the crime scene. It was appalling, brutal. Sara's stomach
roiled at the image of a woman, on her back in bed, her face
and upper body mutilated, the bedsheets darkened to depict
pools of blood, the stain descending to the floor and collecting

in a puddle. It was only a pencil sketch, with lines blurring and details of the wounds hard to decipher, yet it conjured up memories of her mother's death, of the crime scene photos they had briefly showed in court, and the utter violation of what had been done to her.

The final sketch was a close-up of Anne's arm, graceful and delicate in the moonlight, her fingers dangling over the side of the bed. It was a Xerox copy, but there were dark streaks across the paper, slashing through Anne's wrist, and smattering across the right-hand side of the sketch. When Sara saw the faint outline of a fingerprint, she realized that the dark spots made from the copier were originally blood, Anne's blood, and that whoever had picked up the drawing before the blood had dried had embedded a fingerprint in it.

John Thiroux maybe. One of the police. Or another, unknown killer. That fingerprint belonged to someone who had been there, seen the body soon after Anne's death. Sara dropped it back onto the desk, tossing the sketch on top of the other one of the crime scene, not really wanting to see either anymore. Though the second she dropped them, she found herself picking them both right back up. Whether she wanted to or not, she had to search for answers. She had to know who had killed Anne Donovan.

And who had killed Anne's daughter.

And Sara's mother and grandmother.

From the Court Records of
the Willful Murder Trial of Anne Donovan,
State of Louisiana vs. Jonathon Thiroux
Statement of one Marguerite Charles,
January 7, 1850

PROSECUTOR: Before me, James R. Jackson,
    prosecutor for the Parish of Orleans, sits
    Marguerite Charles, who is acquainted with
    the defendant, Jonathon Thiroux, and has
    been duly sworn and charged to answer all
    the questions the court presents before her
    in this case. Mrs. Charles, how long have you
    known the defendant?

CHARLES: For one year.

PROSECUTOR: In what capacity did your
relationship originate?

CHARLES: We met at a ball through mutual
friends. I believe it was at the Huntsworths'
house, but I cannot remember for certain.
Anyway, in the course of polite conversation,
it was made known to me that Mr. Thiroux is
an artist. I expressed interest in his art, and
we fostered a social relationship.

PROSECUTOR: Did you see one another outside of
large social gatherings?

CHARLES: Yes. I began to model for Mr. Thiroux
for his sketches. He sketches in pencil, then
paints in oils.

PROSECUTOR: Were you alone with him during
these artistic sessions? Where did they occur?

CHARLES: Yes, we were alone. They were in his
studio on Royal Street, where he currently
resides.

PROSECUTOR: Did you pose in costumes, or gowns?

CHARLES: Sometimes in costumes or gowns.
Other times they were natural poses.

PROSECUTOR: On those "other times," are you
implying, forgive me if I am making an
incorrect assumption, but are you saying that
by natural poses you mean you disrobed
during these drawing sessions?

CHARLES: Yes. John did at least three nudes of
me. He was interested in capturing the
physical form of a more voluptuous woman
and I was flattered to do so.

PROSECUTOR: Indeed. Why did you stop posing in
this illustrious manner for Mr. Thiroux?

CHARLES: Because during our final session,
which was last June, he threatened me with
a knife when I complained that I was stiff
and required a break.

PROSECUTOR: Threatened you with a knife?
Where did he get this knife from? Tell us

exactly what happened during this shocking encounter.

CHARLES: I was sitting on the divan, not reclining, but sitting upright, front facing, legs crossed, palms pressed on the sofa.

PROSECUTOR: What were you wearing?

CHARLES: Nothing. And my shoulders were sore from the extensive session and I asked permission to take a turn about the room. But John said no without even looking at me. He was completely absorbed in his sketch. However, I was truly uncomfortable and feeling a jabbing headache beginning behind my eyes, so I requested for the second time some relief, explaining my discomfort. Before I was even aware what he was about, he was in front of me, a knife in his hand, which he waved wildly in my face. I don't know where he got the knife from as I never saw him draw it. But he told me to shut up, to sit still, or he would stick me.

PROSECUTOR: Were those his exact words? "Sit still or I'll stick you"?

CHARLES: Yes.

PROSECUTOR: Had Mr. Thiroux been drinking?

CHARLES: Yes. I saw him drink two full glasses of absinthe in the hour preceding the incident.

PROSECUTOR: No further questions. Thank you, Mrs. Charles.

CONGRESSMAN'S WIFE POSED NUDE FOR POTENTIAL MURDERER!

January 8, 1850—Yesterday saw the further attempt by the prosecution to malign the character of defendant John Thiroux and show that he has a history of violence. For those in attendance at the courtroom, it was a scene setting worthy of the theater. The attractive and artistic defendant, the charming attorneys for both sides, the gruff judge, and the pretty and bountiful wife of two-time Congressman Pierre Charles were all present playing their respective parts.

The trial commenced again at ten a.m., and every eye turned when Mrs. Charles swept into the room in her modish gold paisley print silk day dress, raven curls spilling over her curvy shoulders. She took the stand with confidence and alacrity, speaking her oath in clear, melodic tones, hand delicately placed on the Bible.

Only the defense knew at that point why Mrs. Charles had been called to witness, though many, this reporter included, correctly concluded that Mrs. Charles and Mr. Thiroux were acquainted from residing in the same social circles. It should have been anticipated that a gentleman as charming and innocuous as the defendant would have no difficulty in securing women, even those gently bred, to serve as inspiration for his art. Such a revelation raised a murmur in the courtroom, but no more than was required to express the acknowledgment of the sense of Mrs. Charles's statement. Bored ladies with absent husbands will accept compliments where they are received, and no greater flattery exists than the request to preserve a woman's face and figure in oil.

I think it is safe to assume, however, given the collective gasp from those present, that nary a soul anticipated that Mrs. Charles would confess, without so much as a blink or a blush, that she had, in fact, posed for Mr. Thiroux's artistic renderings as nature had presented her.

Even more stunning was the revelation that Mr. Thiroux lost his temper with the charming and vulnerable Mrs. Charles in such an offensive manner. It is not surprising to discover the defendant was enjoying an open bottle for this encounter, nor does it present him as in control, respectful of women, and thoroughly misunderstood as the defense would have you believe.

A great number of questions arise from this
testimony, not the least of which is whether or not
Congressman Charles was aware of his wife's
very liberal and forthcoming support of the arts.

Naples Daily News, July 17, 2007—As testimony
continues in the trial of Dr. Rafe Marino for the
murder of his girlfriend, Jessie Michaels, the defense shifted tactics slightly yesterday in the
courtroom. Up until this point, the defense has
focused on the lack of evidence being presented,
and insisted that what forensic trace evidence
was present at the scene was the result of the victim having a relationship with the accused. But
now the defense has taken a more aggressive
stance, suggesting that a woman such as Jessie
Michaels, a former stripper and drug user, and an
alcoholic at the time of her death, led a double
life. One in which she was the middle-class suburban girlfriend of the upstanding and charming
young doctor, another in which she frequented
strip clubs and mixed alcohol and recreational
drugs. The defense suggested that such behavior
could have brought her into contact with her murderer.

Throughout the course of the trial, Dr. Marino
has adamantly declared his love and affection for
the victim.

Chapter Ten

❧❧❧

Sara left Gabriel's and drove back to her apartment, having scratched a return message on the bottom of his note to her. She couldn't stay, not without access to her computer, and no idea how long it would be before he returned. It had been a mistake to leave her laptop and Angel at her place. She missed her kitten, was worried about her.

And those sketches had shaken her. Had shown her that this was real, no matter how distant in the past. This had happened and it wasn't a puzzle or a murder mystery weekend to solve. It was a woman and her life. Just as real as her mother had been.

Growing up in the congested traffic of Naples and the surrounding areas, with laborious commutes on inadequate infrastructure, Sara hadn't thought twice about getting an apartment twenty minutes from the French Quarter. But she was starting to see why Gabriel had expressed surprise. The convenience of the Quarter, with walking distance to food and shopping, was appealing, and the drive to Kenner was getting annoying. Or she should say the drive *from* Kenner. What kind of Freudian slip was that?

She had already pulled into her assigned parking spot when she realized there was someone at the door of her apart-

ment. Instinctively, she reversed and pulled into the spot opposite hers and sat with the engine idling, watching the man
knock repeatedly and actually peek into the window right next
to her front door. He looked very normal, average height and
weight, short brown hair barely visible under a baseball cap,
dressed in tan khakis and a green golf shirt. There was a package or thick envelope in his hand, and a cell phone balanced
on top.

The rational, reasonable thing to do would be to get out of
the car, approach him, and inquire what he wanted. But Sara
wasn't about to do that. Observing from her car felt safer,
even if it was highly likely the man was selling magazines or
offering religious flyers. Or he was a reporter.

That was likely her paranoia rearing its ugly head, but she
didn't want to risk it. She had nothing to say to the press.
Other than an expletive that involved four letters followed by
the word *off*.

Her cell phone ringing caused her to jump. "Shit." Sara let
out a breath and yanked the phone out of her purse, eyes still
on the guy. He was pressing the doorbell again, lingering
longer than was appropriate for a salesman.

Caller ID showed it was Gabriel. "Hello?"

"Hi. Where did you go?"

"Back to my place. Didn't you get my note?" Gabriel
sounded irritated with her, but she was too distracted by the
man in front of her to bother to try and appease him.

"Yeah, but why? You just came over and then you left
again."

"You left too." So there. "I went for coffee and you left."

"But I came back."

"So did I."

"But then you left again."

If she hadn't been so distracted by her tenacious doorman,
she would have laughed. "We've established that. We both left
and came back and I left a second time and didn't come back,
because I didn't know when you were coming back."

"I wasn't long," he said, a little petulantly.

"Okay." Now Mr. Nice Guy was actually trying the knob to
her apartment, giving it a turn and a shove. It didn't open, obviously, since she was neurotic when it came to locking her

door. Maybe she should call the police. Though a guy aggressively knocking on her door wasn't exactly threatening even if he had tried the knob. They would think she was a loon, and all it would do was call attention to her.

"Sara? Is everything okay?"

"Yeah . . ." Sara turned her car off, frustrated with herself and her fear. "Stay on the phone with me, okay? I'm in the parking lot and there's a guy at my apartment door, and he won't go away. I think I need to see what he wants."

"Does he look dangerous?"

"No. He looks like a Little League coach actually. But he's been hovering for a good five minutes so I think I need to just see what he wants and get rid of him."

"Okay, I'll be right here."

It was ridiculous to think that having Gabriel on the phone with her, fifteen miles away, was going to prevent her from bodily harm, but for some reason it was extremely comforting.

"I think I found a birth certificate for Anne Donovan's daughter," he said.

Sara was getting out of the car and crossing the parking lot. "Are you serious?" Sara briefly wondered if she should confess she knew who Anne's daughter was—that she had all along. But if she did, Gabriel would want the whole truth, and she wasn't prepared to tell that yet.

"Yes. Her name was Margaret Donovan, and she was six years old at the time of Anne's death. I have no idea what happened to her though, but it's a starting point. If we could find descendents of Anne, we could actually do something with the blood flakes that have been preserved from the knife found at the scene."

"How? We don't have John Thiroux's DNA. If we found blood that didn't belong to Anne, based on a comp to a descendent, it doesn't tell us anything except that someone else was in the room, which of course we knew, since someone killed her."

"Well—"

"Hang on, Gabriel." Sara was behind the guy, and he had turned around curiously. She kept the phone at her ear but moved the mouthpiece down toward her chin. "Can I help you?"

Giving her a friendly smile, the man raised the envelope in his hand and waved it back and forth. "Are you Sara Michaels? I have a delivery for you."

"Thanks." She held out her hand, still weirded out by his behavior. He wasn't a mailman, and he wasn't wearing a delivery uniform. No truck with FedEx or UPS on it in the parking lot either.

"Can you sign here? I'm glad you showed up. I can't leave this kind of thing on a doorstep. I don't get paid until I can say I put it directly in your hand."

That made the hair on the back of her neck stand up. "What kind of thing?" She propped her cell phone on her shoulder and signed the paper he held out for her, using what amounted to an S followed by a slash. It seemed like a bad idea to use her official signature, but she wasn't going to argue either. She wanted him off of her sidewalk.

"Usually court documents. Subpoenas, stuff like that." He shrugged and gave her an apologetic smile. "Sorry."

"Well, who sent it?" Sara glanced down at the envelope. It had a return address, but no name.

"All I can tell you is what it says right there." He tapped the return address.

It told her nothing, other than a Naples address. Heart pounding, she said, "Okay, thanks." It had to be from her lawyer. He was the only one who knew her current address. Just paperwork from the house sale, or something regarding Rafe's trial. He was just trying to keep her informed and up-to-date.

It wasn't a warrant for her arrest or anything like that. They didn't mail something like that to you. They just showed up and slapped cuffs on you.

"Have a great day." He waved and jogged down the path to the parking lot.

"Yeah. You too," she murmured absently, fixing her phone so she could talk. "Hey, it's just a delivery guy. He gave me a package."

"Oh, okay. Good. So what were we talking about?"

Sara turned, saw that the guy had gotten into his car and was pulling away, and then opened her apartment door. Locking it behind her, she told Gabriel honestly, "I have no idea.

And I think I should go. I think this package is from my lawyer and I should probably check it out."

Glancing around her apartment, she spotted Angel reclining on the sofa arm, sound asleep. Tossing her purse down, she tore open the envelope, not even wanting to wait until she was off the phone. She needed to see it was just house or banking documents. Something to do with probate court. Boring. Nothing more, nothing less.

"Your lawyer? What do you have a lawyer for?"

"For settling my mom's estate and stuff . . ." Sara frowned. The papers she was pulling out didn't feel like forms or documents. They felt glossy, like . . .

Pictures. She gasped as she saw the image of her mother, dead, blood everywhere—on the wall, the bed, her mother's neck, shoulders, chest, stomach, arms.

"Oh, God," she said, flipping through the stack in her hand. "Jesus Christ."

"What?"

Sara struggled to take deep breaths, to not throw up. To not give in to the fear and shock that were crawling up her throat and cutting off her air.

"Sara. What is in the package?" Gabriel's voice was calm and commanding.

"Pictures. Of my mother. Dead." She got to the last one, taken at a downward trajectory through her mother's bedroom window. It showed the wounds on her mother's chest in brutal, gory detail, her naked flesh ravaged by the knife and her killer.

Sara rammed it back into the envelope. "I'm going to be sick."

Her stomach heaved and she choked on the heels of a gag. She had seen the crime scene photos in court, but that had been brief, a quick flashing in front of her as the prosecutor had tried to unnerve her. She'd never had time to study them, to take in their full glossy gore.

"Sara, listen to me. Put the pictures back in the envelope and close it. Do you understand?"

"I already did," she said, voice trembling, tears in her eyes, as she swallowed hard, the urge to vomit thankfully dissipating. "Did you request these pictures for the book?"

"No, of course not. I would never do that without asking

your permission. But I wouldn't use crime scene photos anyway. And if I did want documents from your mother's case I would have them sent to me, not you."

That was true, that all made sense. "So who would send these to me?"

Even before the words were completely out, Sara felt fear creeping up. Someone knew where she was, her address. No one had access to those photos except the police and those involved in Rafe's court case. She pulled the pile of photos back out of the envelope and found the one taken at a downward angle. Were these truly police shots of the scene or were they taken before the police arrived? By the killer.

"Oh, God, what if the murderer sent these to me?" Skin clammy, she looked around her apartment again. She hadn't even checked the windows or the other rooms. Angel leaped off the couch, the movement startling her. "He knows where I am."

"Sara, I'm coming over. What's your address?"

"Uh . . ." She couldn't think. Couldn't remember her address. Maybe she'd never known it. The blood spatters in the picture she was clutching blurred, her head swimming, and she had the horrific realization that she was going to faint. She fought and clung to reality, forcing her eyes open and air into her lungs, groping for the wall. The black spots and the ringing in her ears retreated and she managed to stay standing.

Cramming the pictures back into the envelope again and closing the metal tabs, she dropped it onto the coffee table and shifted a magazine over top of it. "Sorry, I can't remember my address. I just moved here."

Like he didn't know that. God, she was losing it. Yet she forced herself to pick up the envelope yet again and read off her address from the front to Gabriel. How ironic. The person who had sent her the photos knew where she was more than she did.

⁂

Gabriel could actually fly. He could manipulate air and space and the laws of physics with his immortal body and his demonic, bastardized angel powers. He was tempted to use his talents to reach Sara quicker, but he wasn't sure how he would explain arriving without a car. He could also project his voice, his thoughts, into a mortal's mind, and he could soothe Sara, offer words or comfort or reassurance, but the risk was that she would think the voices in her head were signs of insanity, and he certainly didn't want that.

So he would have to be patient, and mortal, and he would have to drive his car on I-10 west like anyone else would under the circumstances.

Which didn't make him at all happy.

It was twenty minutes before he pulled into Sara's apartment complex, and if he had used any sort of common sense, he would have called her back on his cell phone. He should have used the drive to talk to her, to calm her down. Though she hadn't sounded hysterical. She had sounded almost numb, which worried him just as much, if not more so.

But she answered right away when he knocked loudly and impatiently on her door, checking the metal numbers a third time, making sure it was the right unit.

"Hi," she said, trying to smile, but the effort only resulted in a wobbling lip.

"Hey," he said, softly. He wasn't good at comforting anyone, and had very little experience at it. He'd never been social, never chatty or quick to respond. He had always been an observer, a people watcher, an artist, a creator. Yet he knew instinctively that Sara needed physical comfort. He just felt it from her, like he had when he'd woken up and she'd been standing by his bed.

Sara liked, wanted, needed, to be touched.

So he did, knowing it wasn't wise, but unwilling to pretend he couldn't see what she was suffering. Wrapping his arms around her, he pulled her against him, kicking the door shut behind him with his foot.

"Lock it," she said, voice muffled against his chest.

"Okay." Gabriel loosened his grip and turned, clicking the dead bolt in place.

"Where's the cat?" she asked, eyes darted around. "She didn't run outside, did she?"

"No, she's lying on the coffee table."

Only then did Sara sigh and relax into his embrace, snaking her arms around his waist. He held her, rubbing his hands over her back, enjoying the softness, the warmth of her body against his. The scent of her hair filled his nostrils and he breathed deeply. "It's going to be okay," he murmured.

"I want to believe that. But I'm scared." She peeled her head off his chest and looked up at him. The plaintive look in her eyes, laced with fear, jabbed him in the heart. "Who would send me those pictures? Who knows where I am? And you should see them. I almost think . . . I almost think they were actually taken by the killer before the police arrived."

"Let's go back to my place and we'll look at them. We'll figure this out." He squeezed her a little tighter to him. "Now pack your stuff and Angel and let's go."

"Pack my stuff?" She frowned.

"I don't think you're comfortable staying here alone, are you?" If he had to guess, he'd bet she'd spent the past twenty minutes pacing back and forth, biting her fingernails and checking and rechecking her door and window locks.

Sara blanched. "No. I guess I'll have to break my lease. Or maybe I can just stay in a hotel for a few days and see how I feel." She shuddered. "But you're right, I don't think I can stay here tonight. And I don't want those pictures anywhere near me."

"You can stay with me." There was no way he was depositing her in a hotel and walking away. She was pale and shaky, her skin clammy. He pictured her bolted into a hotel room, chair pushed against the door, awake all night long, worrying. Afraid. The desire for a pill, just a little something to help it go away, ease her mind, let her sleep and rest, growing stronger and stronger.

He didn't want her to have to fight that, to be afraid. And it was possible that she actually was in danger, though he didn't really believe that. More likely the photos had been sent by some incredibly insensitive reporter.

Either way, he wanted her safe, with him.

"Gabriel, I don't know . . . That's generous of you to offer, but is it really such a good idea?"

She looked worried, but she was still leaning against him. "Why wouldn't it be a good idea?" he asked.

"Because . . . I don't know."

Because they were attracted to each other. That's what she

was silently saying. He could almost hear it, read it in the plea in her blue eyes as she volleyed the decision over to him.

Hold her or push her away. Irrational or rational. Cruel or compassionate. Both choices were potentially devastating. To both of them.

"There's no logical reason we can't go to my place. Where's the cat food? I'll get Angel's stuff together while you pack a bag." He brushed her hair off of her forehead, just because. Just to feel it, just to touch her. Just to reassure himself that he wasn't going to regret his decision. To remind himself that casual touching led to caresses which led to kisses which led to sensual pleasure, which led to women clinging to him, begging and pleading and crying for more. Desperate for him, all of him, his mind, his body, his heart, his soul, as they tried to swallow him whole and replace themselves with him.

One step at a time, that's how it happened, one touch, then another, a gradual, unsuspecting immersion, just like one drink led to another, an occasional glass led to a bottle, once a week led to every day, to every two hours until you never left the stupor and you cared for nothing but the fuzzy abyss and wet slosh of more liquid in your mouth.

Maybe Sara was different.

Maybe he shouldn't test that irrational theory based on nothing but hope.

Yet when she went to pack her bag and he went to collect the cat accoutrements, he felt only a defiant satisfaction and anticipation for more time with Sara.

LADY KILLER!

January 10, 1850—There was more entertainment in the courtroom today in the case of accused murderer Jonathon Thiroux, as one Molly Faye took the stand. A working girl in the House of Rest for Weary Men, where Anne Donovan was murdered in her sleep, Molly Faye confessed to the room at large that she, like Miss Donovan before her, had entered into an illicit business understanding with the defendant after the death of Miss Donovan.

While this was arguably in poor taste on the part of Mr. Thiroux, it was not a CRIME to move so quickly from one lewd woman to another, but the prosecutor maintains that this illuminates unpleasant aspects of Mr. Thiroux's character. But before one could even truly form an opinion as to any implications of Miss Faye's ardent testimony, yet another unfortunate, Sally Swanson, took the stand. Miss Swanson likewise described HER relationship with Mr. Thiroux in such salacious detail that Judge Henry stopped the proceedings and ordered all women and children under the age of eighteen from the courtroom before allowing Miss Swanson to continue.

A dance hall enthusiast, and fond of the sound of her own voice, Miss Swanson spun a tale of devotion and tawdry pleasures of the flesh worthy of the infamous Marquess de Sade, and unfit for description in this newspaper. Yet while most in attendance were either shocked into silence, or simply silent in the raucous, immoral hope of hearing more spill forth from the cherry red lips of Miss Swanson, there was one who could not maintain quiet. Miss Faye, outraged at Miss Swanson's timeline of her affair with Mr. Thiroux (which invariably overlapped Miss Faye's own), interrupted most vehemently in protest of Miss Swanson's "no-good pack o'lies!"

What followed was scarcely to be believed. Miss Swanson calmly stated that Miss Faye was in no uncertain terms a word unprintable in this paper and, frankly, one which is best left on the docks. To which Miss Faye rushed the witness stand and soundly slapped the pretty cheek of her romantic opponent. Such tussling, such pulling and slapping and tearing of hair and cheek and dress, as I have never seen in Judge Henry's courtroom erupted, and it took three bailiffs a solid two minutes to separate the bawdy hellcats. As the women were being escorted from the bench, Miss Faye wrenched free of her captor and flung herself at the feet of Mr. Thiroux, wrapping arms around his legs and appealing for him to tell the truth, to tell everyone "that he loved her and only her!"

Mr. Jackson has maintained throughout the course of the trial that Mr. Thiroux took knife to flesh and killed Miss Donovan after the "intemperate use of spirits."

This reporter has to admit that if Mr. Thiroux is constantly subjected to such disgusting displays as what we saw in the courtroom yesterday from both women, then it is not at all shocking the man has descended into the bottle. In fact, if he has such an effect on women as to find them wrapped around his kneecaps on a regular basis, it is simply astonishing that he hasn't yet taken a knife to his own flesh to remove himself from such ludicrous feminine hysterics.

Mrs. Jane Gallier
117 Esplanade Avenue
New Orleans, Louisiana

Mr. Jonathon Thiroux
34 Royal Street
New Orleans, Louisiana

10 January, 1850

Mr. Thiroux,

After reading, with much dismay and disgust, of the events in the courtroom yesterday at your rather unfortunate trial, I must confess myself horrified and betrayed. Yes, betrayed. I had thought, sir, that while you are of a passionate nature (as is true with all men of your artistic ilk), those inclinations were contained to your canvases and myself. Imagine the distress, the hu-

miliation, the devastation, I felt upon reading in print for all to see the company with which you have been consorting.

If you have such little respect and regard for me, then I think it is best if we no longer see one another. To that purpose, I will have my butler deny you entrance when I am at home, and I am also returning the lock of hair that I snipped from your head as you slept. I cannot bear the sight of its angelic strands one minute longer, as it only amplifies my weeping, and contributes to the shattering of my generous heart.

One day I hope you will live to regret that which you have lost.

Sincerely,
Mrs. Jane Gallier

Mrs. Jane Gallier
117 Esplanade Avenue
New Orleans, Louisiana

Mr. Jonathon Thiroux
34 Royal Street
New Orleans, Louisiana

11 January, 1850

My Dearest John,

Please disregard my irrational letter you received yesterday. I do not know what came over me, and I have regretted my action every minute since the vile missive left my possession. Pray tell me you'll forgive me, and visit me today, as I am devastatingly lonely for you. As an olive branch, I have procured your favorite vintage for your enjoyment.

Please say you'll be over, and that you forgive me. I cannot bear the thought of never seeing you again, and I wait most anxiously for your arrival, and hope that when you are back in my presence, allowing me to make

amends for my harsh words, you will return the lock of
hair to me that I so impudently returned.

Please, John, dearest, please make haste and come
to me today.

Your ever loving and most ardently devoted,
Jane

Sara was looking better. There was color in her cheeks and
her back was straight, head high. In fact, Gabriel would almost
argue it was the best he'd ever seen her look, calm and ani-
mated. As if after seeing the photos, hitting the bottom of the
barrel and almost drowning in the dregs of her fear, she had
climbed out with a whole new determination to not live her
life that way.

Gabriel had thought she would want to be distracted, to ignore the two murder cases for awhile. He had been prepared to
suggest a walk to the river, a late lunch, maybe even a movie.
But when they'd arrived back at his apartment, Sara had
dropped her bag in the living room, put Angel's cat food away
in his pantry, and then sat down on the couch in his office and
asked him to outline the physical evidence they had from the
Donovan case that had the potential to be tested for DNA.

"Are you sure you want to do this right now?" he asked. He
had taken a peek at the crime scene photos she'd received
when she was packing. They were gruesome, and it was her
mother. She had to be devastated.

But she just nodded firmly. "Yes. I want to do this. I want us
to write this book, do everything in our power to either solve the
crimes, or at the very least to show the advances in criminal investigation." She adjusted the straps of her tank top, her hair
smoothed back and contained in a twisted ponytail of some
kind. "I believe in forensics. I've always enjoyed the satisfaction in my job of taking an unknown substance and identifying
it. Giving the investigators the facts they need to connect the
pieces of the puzzle and convict a criminal. Maybe you and I
can't achieve that here, but we can try, and regardless of the outcome, when we write 'The End' and you turn the manuscript in
to your editor, I'm going to have gained some sort of personal
closure. That's what I want. To be done. To move forward."

If it were only that simple. Gabriel had often wondered if

closure was a psychological myth. Nothing ended, ever. Things simply faded, hurt less, but stuck to the side of your subconscious forever, altering your thoughts, your essence, your future.

But all he said to Sara was "Okay. Here's what we have. A lock of John Thiroux's hair, courtesy of Mrs. Jane Gallier. One fingerprint in the sketch of Anne Donovan's arm. Blood flakes from the knife found at the crime scene, as well as blood found on the absinthe spoon lying on the floor. That's it. That's all we've got. And maybe, if we're incredibly lucky, we can trace Anne Donovan's child on down to a descendent, though that's probably wishful thinking. And even if we could find a descendent, who is to say they'll agree to give us a sample?"

Sara made a face. "I suppose a lot of people would find it disturbing to be approached with something like this."

It was possible he might offend someone, but Gabriel thought it was time he set aside irrational feelings and aggressively pursued every angle he could. "Dealing with the dead is disturbing to the living."

He was leaning against his desk, feet crossed, arms over his chest, and he watched Sara, took great pleasure in seeing her fingers pull her ponytail over her shoulder and absently stroke the ends of her hair. Her orange tank top clung to her breasts and Gabriel remembered the way she had felt, pressed against him, every curve of her body clinging to his. It was a good thing the timing had been so incredibly inappropriate, because he was becoming more and more tempted.

"It almost seems as if everything is disturbing to the living." Sara's eyes went a little wider and she asked him, voice low, "What do you think is out there? Where do you think the dead go?"

"To heaven." He could say that without hesitation. He had seen it, lived it, felt it. He had never wanted to leave, had wanted to spend eternity in his palace of light, where visitors found answers, where he felt generous and wise. Then he had come down to earth and had been overwhelmed by suffering and despaired of his ineffectiveness, until he had found his palace again in the bottom of a bottle.

"I hope so," Sara said quietly. "I hope so."

But before he could respond, she straightened. "So. Anyway. So we have John Thiroux's DNA and possibly Anne

Donovan's. We have blood from the weapon and blood that was on the absinthe spoon, which was found on the floor. Presumably both will be Anne's blood, but possibly the murderer's. The fingerprint is useless unless we can find prints for John or Anne, and for the same finger that touched the sketch, which is highly unlikely."

They had John's fingerprints since they were his own, and he now knew they didn't match, but Gabriel couldn't exactly reveal that little fact to her.

"Where are the samples? Have you submitted them to the lab? How did you get them anyway?"

"Everything is already at the lab. I should hear something soon actually. I'm hoping early next week." He ignored the question about how the items had been acquired. He couldn't tell her that he had the lock of hair because he was John Thiroux and Jane Gallier had mailed it to him. That it was his hair. Or that he couldn't really explain why he had kept Jane's letters, including the hair that had accompanied the one, stuffed in his desk for all these years. Nor could he tell her that he had never engaged in an affair with Jane beyond a few dinner dates and one kiss, despite her words to the contrary. That his demonic appeal altered women's behavior drastically, made them see and feel what wasn't there, what wasn't real.

"It's a shame the coroner's report is so inadequate. A lot could have been determined from the blood spatters, a better description of the injuries, a more accurate time of death."

"That's the point. To show precisely that." He wanted to compare Anne's case to her mother's, to illuminate the progress forensics had made in criminal investigation, but show that ultimately, the human factor couldn't be removed from the justice system. It was people who solved crimes, who convicted or acquitted, not physical evidence.

She pursed her lips before saying, "You want to show the autopsy report from my mother's case, don't you?"

"It would be the best way to illuminate the difference forensic science has made in criminal investigation. But only if you're comfortable with that."

"It's okay. It's not like it's a secret how she died. The papers and the news trotted out every gory detail."

And she had gotten the pictures to prove it.

Chapter Eleven

❧❧❧

"So we need to list the similarities between the two cases." Gabriel was frustrated by the limitations on what he could tell Sara, but he had to be realistic in how he could write the book anyway. His personal knowledge of a lot of facts couldn't be explained.

"Boyfriends that were the last one to see them alive. Facial and upper body mutilation. Use of a bowie knife. Attacked while in bed. No sign of forced entry. No sign of sexual intercourse." Sara typed into her laptop computer as she spoke. "Anything else you can think of?"

"Does Rafe have a drinking problem?" He had wondered about that since the very first article he'd read.

Sara looked at him like he had completely lost his mind. "No. Not even close."

"Is he religious?"

"No. You asked me that before and I told you no. Honestly, I've never known him to go to church or to even mention God."

That struck Gabriel as completely odd, given the quote he'd read in the online article. He was tempted to open it in the folder he'd stored it in on his computer and read it to Sara, but he resisted. "So, in your opinion, where did the investigation into your mother's death go wrong?"

Sara hesitated. "I don't know. I understand it wasn't an easy case. There was no trace evidence really . . . no semen, no blood that didn't belong to my mother, no fingerprints other than the one print of Rafe's. There were no witnesses, no unusual cars, no noise, no strange activity around the house in the days leading up to the murder. The blinds were closed, the window closed. No one saw or heard anything."

Gabriel had to ask, just like she had asked about John Thiroux. "Why don't you doubt Rafe? What makes you so sure he didn't do it?"

"Because he loved my mother. He's a doctor. He's a very charming, protective, healer type of personality." Sara glanced down at her computer, shoving it off her lap. Then she met his gaze. "I can't be wrong. He just couldn't have done it. Because if I am wrong, that means I have no ability to judge a killer from a nice guy."

So that was the real root of her stubbornness. No one wanted to think that someone they had cared about, spent time with, championed, could have been lying to them, conning them, their smile hiding a heart filled with evil intentions. "Sara, if he is guilty, then it's not your fault for not recognizing it. It isn't. Remember when we talked about psychopaths? They're charming, attractive, and they fool everyone. That's how they're able to kill and get away with it."

"That doesn't make me feel any better. Don't you see how if it was Rafe, which I really, truly don't think it was, that I would feel like I should have known? Should have done something to prevent it?"

"I know. But you can't do that to yourself. You couldn't have known. You couldn't have prevented it."

"That's very easy for you to say. You don't have any guilt to live with."

That was a ridiculous, sick understatement. "You think I don't have any guilt?" Gabriel dropped his arms and scoffed. "My guilt could fill the Superdome. You asked me why I write true crime books? It's retribution. My lame, half-ass attempt to make up for the fact that my girlfriend was killed and I didn't, couldn't stop it."

It was reckless, dangerous, to tell her that, but he was too angry to care. She thought she was the only one who had suffered, the only one who staggered under the burden of guilt that she was alive while a loved one was dead. He had felt the weight of that so oppressively for a hundred and fifty years it was amazing that he was still mobile.

"What?" She looked slapped. Her cheeks drained of color. "Oh my God," she murmured. "Oh, God. That's why you started drinking, isn't it? That's why you don't paint, why you don't hear music . . . Oh, Gabriel, I'm sorry. I'm so sorry."

It wasn't right to accept her pity. He didn't want it, hadn't earned it, wasn't entitled to it. So he said, aware of how harsh his voice sounded, "Don't. It's not your problem. It's mine."

"I know it's not my problem. But Gabriel, you have the same problem I do. And I've been sitting here acting like the victim, like I'm the only one who has suffered, when you obviously have too. I'm sorry for that."

She looked so plaintive, so concerned, that he was exasperated. He wanted to be angry, and she prevented him from having that release. She sucked all the anger right out of him with her soft features and luminous eyes. Which irritated the hell out of him. "Don't be sorry for anything. You have your shit to deal with and I have my shit to deal with. It's all even."

"I wasn't suggesting a tally sheet. What I'm saying is that I've been so wrapped up in my own grief, I couldn't see yours."

"I don't have any grief." It was guilt. Disgust. Self-recrimination and a desire to find some kind of meaning in a long, endless existence.

"No. You have a determination to ignore your grief."

Gabriel didn't know when the conversation had turned into her trying to enlighten him, and he moved away from her, determined to end the ridiculous dissection of his psyche.

"You deny yourself pleasure—physical and emotional pleasure—as a punishment for yourself. God, I should have guessed about your girlfriend. It's so obvious to me now."

That sparked his anger again. He wasn't obvious. He was a demon, for hell's sake. She didn't know any fucking thing about him. "Well, congratulations." He knew she was coming up behind him, with the purpose of touching him, so he shifted, avoiding her touch, but turned back and locked gazes with her. "You think you've figured me all out. And while I know you're wrong on a lot of levels, you got one thing right.

I do deny myself physical pleasure. I can't handle it. Alcohol, sex. I can't handle it. I don't want to handle it."

"Maybe I can't either," she said, her voice soft, sad. "I'm sorry."

"Stop apologizing!" She had nothing to be sorry for.

But she winced at his vehemence and he felt like a complete asshole. "Sara, *I'm* sorry. Damn it, how did we wind up here?"

She just looked at him and said matter-of-factly, "Murder. That's how we wound up here."

It was so bold, so obvious, so harsh, that all his anger deflated. "That's certainly true, isn't it? And it sucks."

She didn't answer him. Instead she moved around him to his desk. "What are these?" She touched one of his spoons.

"Absinthe spoons." Rather a disturbing little habit he had—to buy them whenever he ran across one in an antique or vintage shop—but it actually helped him. It kept his present life in perspective to have a constant reminder in front of him of his past.

"That's what an absinthe spoon looks like? I had no idea . . ." She touched one, running her finger along the tip, frowning. "I was reading about them in the police reports, but I didn't really know what one looked like. Why do you think John Thiroux had two spoons in the room with him? Why would he need two?"

"I don't think he would, unless he was double-fisting drinks." That had always perplexed Gabriel, but he had attributed it to the fact that Anne kept his spoons at the time. Maybe she had gotten one out, then forgotten and gotten another. Or maybe he had brought one with him for no apparent reason other than that the fleur-de-lis spoon had been his favorite, because it was wide in the middle due to the pattern and he didn't spill any precious drops over the side when he poured.

"And why did one end up on the floor and not the other?"

"I'm sure he knocked it to the floor when he stood up to look at Anne."

Sara was touching each spoon, making them swing back and forth. She was clearly thinking, their disagreement or burst of anger or whatever it had been clearly passed, forgotten. Suddenly she grabbed the one she'd been swinging and whirled around. "Wait a minute."

"What?"

"If the crime was a crime of passion, not planned on the part of John Thiroux, why would he be carrying a bowie knife? Who carries a bowie knife in their pocket for no reason? Did John Thiroux hunt or fish?"

Gabriel almost snorted. Hardly. The extent of his sportsmanship had been driving, riding, and boxing. He had never had an interest in wildlife. "I don't think so. He was an artist. Records indicate that drinking was his hobby, not gutting his catch of the day."

"Then seriously, why would he be carrying a knife?"

"He said in court it wasn't his knife. That he never carried a weapon. But the prosecutor maintained that he could be lying, since it was a dangerous part of town. It would have made sense to carry a weapon."

"But a bowie knife?"

"I agree, it's illogical. A bowie is meant to gut or kill and it's big, cumbersome."

Sara shook her head. "He wouldn't have carried that unless he had intended to murder her. And I don't think he would have drunk himself into a stupor or stuck around after the fact if he had intended to kill her. If it was a spontaneous crime, you would think he would pick up the nearest weapon—the absinthe bottle, a glass, the absinthe spoon, or even his bare hands—and kill her. Hell, he could have strangled her with her hair ribbons or smothered her with the bedsheets or beaten her to death with his fists. Do you think the knife could have belonged to her?"

"It's possible." Actually, Gabriel was almost certain it hadn't been Anne's, but damn it, he couldn't share what he truly knew with Sara. He couldn't tell her that he knew the knife didn't belong to John Thiroux, knew Anne wasn't streetwise or hard enough to carry a weapon of that power. That it would have scared her. "What about in your mother's case? Who would have had access to that type of knife?"

"I don't know," she said, biting her lip and leaning back against his desk. "Rafe isn't the outdoors type. And he wasn't carrying a knife in his shorts and golf shirt when I saw him at dinner." She gave a short, disbelieving laugh. "God, the idea of Rafe with a knife like that is just insane. He wouldn't hurt a fly."

"We should see if we can find out who sent those pictures to you. There's got to be a tracking number or something." That bothered him. There didn't seem to be a logical reason for those pictures to be sent to her, especially without any explanation or instructions. And it had taken effort to locate her temporary address in Louisiana.

Sara shuddered. "I know. But I'm almost afraid to find out who sent them. Or to find out we can't find out who sent them, you know what I mean?"

"I know."

She threw her hands up in the air. "Arrgh. I just want to solve all of this. I want it to go away. I want murder to go away. I'm so goddamn afraid and I hate it, I hate this."

And Gabriel wasn't afraid at all. Not of what Sara feared, which was death. Gabriel would embrace death, would welcome a return to the other world, but that was not his choice, not an option open to a sinner like himself, and he wasn't stupid enough to wish for Hell. He had to stay on earth, mortal, alive, until he paid for his sins. It made him weary, exhausted from the strain of living day in, day out, with no goal, no meaningful friendships, no sense of purpose other than making it through, one step at a time. He was worn out, fucking tired, and he wanted it to either end or he wanted to find a future.

What he feared was that neither one would ever happen, and he was destined to stagnate, to fester indefinitely in his own personal hell.

❧

The more Sara thought about it, the more she was convinced that John Thiroux was a psychopath, an attractive, charming killer, who may have murdered other women before Anne Donovan, and possibly after. In the twenty-four hours since she'd packed her bag and battened down in Gabriel's apartment—determined to find something, anything, that smacked of an answer to any of her thousands of questions— she had tried to find information on John Thiroux before and after his murder trial and had drawn a complete blank.

Gabriel had dropped her off at the library for several hours while he went to track down where the pictures of her mother had been sent from. As Sara sat at the computer, stiff from immobility and cold from the overzealous air-conditioning, she suspected he wasn't having any more luck than she was. John Thiroux appeared in the society pages of the *New Orleans Bee* for the first time in 1847, at a large party hosted by a congressman, then disappeared without a trace after early 1851, when she'd found record of his selling his property on Royal Street.

A search of Ellis Island and Port of Orleans records showed no evidence of his arrival in the United States, though she did discover that one Anne Donovan, age thirteen, had arrived in New Orleans in 1839 in the company of her mother, Mary Donovan, age thirty-four. Sara wasn't sure if it was the same Mary Donovan, but she did find a death certificate for the same name, same age, a mere three years later. Which might explain how Anne Donovan had wound up a prostitute, if she had no family and no income at the age of sixteen.

But John Thiroux was a mystery, and Sara's research skills weren't up to the task of ferreting him out. Maybe he was innocent, maybe he had just moved a lot, and historical records were spotty, but it still seemed more and more likely to her that John Thiroux had killed Anne, and that it had been planned. He had brought his bowie knife and slashed Anne to death intentionally, counting on his position in society and his remaining in the room to guarantee he wouldn't be charged with the crime.

Nothing else made sense to her.

Unless he really had been passed out and someone else had come in and murdered Anne. But why?

No answers, only questions.

Hungry and tired, Sara left the archives room with her notebook crammed with harried notes, and went outside. The sun felt warm on her chilled arms and she sat on the steps, pulling out her cell phone. It was hard to feel afraid when there were people rushing around downtown in every direction, the sun was shining, and she had the comfort of knowing she didn't have to go home to an empty apartment. Gabriel would be there, and God, she liked that.

It was a dangerous feeling, an emotional crutch, a kick in the teeth of her independence, a mockery of her strength, but she liked the rhythm of being around another human being. Liked the ability to say a thought out loud and have someone there to hear it. Liked the sound of movement, his feet echoing across the hardwood, his throat clearing, the crack of his knuckles when he was thinking, and the growing familiarity of his smile, the toss of his head to rid his eyes of dangling hair, his always clean smell. Liked knowing that it didn't have to be difficult with him, that silence was okay. And she liked waking up with the solid presence of a man beside her, since he'd insisted she sleep, platonically, in his bed with him. It should have felt uncomfortable, overly intimate, but it didn't. The fear stayed small, contained, in its locked box when she was around Gabriel, and sharing an apartment, her thoughts, her life with him seemed altogether so easy that she was afraid to think about it too much and what that might mean.

She had never lived with a man other than the occasional weekend or vacation spent with a boyfriend. She'd never experienced true cohabitation with a man, just being together, moving in and out of the day's routine, each other's space, living and working and coexisting. At twenty-nine, staying with Gabriel, she realized she was ready for that.

Of course, she couldn't have that with him. It was an illusion, a fantasy. They were both barely hanging on. They'd just fall over the edge faster if they were hanging on to each other.

But that didn't stop her from desiring him. From wanting to pretend, for now, that they were friends, together.

Digging out her sunglasses, she popped them on her head, stretched out her legs, and called Gabriel on her cell phone. "Hey."

"Hey, are you done?"

"Yeah. Can you pick me up or should I take a cab?"

"Did you find anything?"

"No, not really. John Thiroux disappeared after his trial."

"That's what I figured you'd find, but it was worth checking out." There was rustling as Gabriel obviously shifted his phone. "I have one more thing to do. Do you want to wait for me or take a cab back?"

"I can take a cab. Are you at the apartment?"

"No. I'm downtown. I'll pick us up some dinner and I'll meet you at home."

That use of the word *home* sent a little shiver through Sara, which annoyed her. She couldn't do that, couldn't go there.

There wasn't a future with Gabriel, and home was what and where she made it herself. She was on her own. Just like she'd always been.

She must have paused long enough to concern Gabriel, because he said, "Are you okay going in the apartment by yourself?"

And he actually sounded worried about her, as opposed to impatient or irritated at her overreactions. For some reason, his concern made tears pop into her eyes. Blinking hard, she said, "I'm fine. Thanks. If I freak out, trust me, I'll be calling you." She forced out a laugh, though it probably sounded completely fake.

"Absolutely. Call me. I'll be home in like an hour, tops, okay?"

"Okay." Sara said good-bye and hung up. Let the tears roll down her face and her chest heave with her silent sobs.

Maybe she didn't cry enough. Maybe she needed to let it out. Let it go. Allow herself to feel.

Gabriel had ensconced himself in the corner of a busy coffee shop to talk on the phone to the reporter, Dan Fieldhouse, from the Florida paper who had covered the bulk of the Michaels investigation and trial. He had arranged the interview on the pretext of clarification for his book, which was true. But Gabriel now had a personal investment in discovering the truth about the case. He wanted closure for Sara. He wanted to protect her from incidents like getting those horrific pictures sent to her.

After they went through the basics of the case, Gabriel asked him, off the record, "Going on your experience, Dan, and your gut, did you think Dr. Marino was guilty?"

"Off the record? Hell, yeah, I think he did it. Though unlike our esteemed prosecutor, I think he did it all on his own. I saw the victim's daughter several times, in court and at the funeral. No way was that chick involved in having her mother killed. She was grieving for real. But Marino's grief, it's that glossy, paint-by-numbers grief. It's calculated. I've seen a lot of murder cases, seen a lot of petty criminals and violent criminals. They all lie. Some are just better at it than others. Marino's a good liar, but he's still a liar, in my opinion."

That was the same vibe Gabriel had been getting. The charm, the poise, the perfect grieving boyfriend, the care and concern he showed Sara—it had all set off alarms for him. He had thought maybe it was just jealousy on his part, or the fact that he didn't know Rafe so it was easy enough to judge him, but Dan Fieldhouse was confirming his own gut reaction.

"So you think it was premeditated?"

"No, I think something set him off on that particular day. But I suspect she's not the first woman he killed. But I have no facts to back that up. Just a feeling."

"Did he ever say anything incriminating in your interviews with him?"

"Well, his lawyer was always there, so he was pretty much giving me the party line every time I talked to him, you know what I mean? But one day I dropped by the prison without advance warning figuring he'd say no without his lawyer around, but he actually agreed to talk to me. And he was chatty that day. Full of himself. Talked about his plans to go west and start over as soon as he was acquitted, which he was sure he would be. Then he dropped a quote on me, which was weird as hell."

Gabriel sat up straighter in his booth, phone propped on his shoulder, laptop open, and fingers ready to type. "Was it a Bible quote?"

"No. Hang on, let me look it up." There was a pause, then Dan came back on. "He said to me, 'My soul can find no staircase to Heaven unless it be through Earth's loveliness.' It's a quote by—"

"Michelangelo," Gabriel said before Dan could finish. He knew the quote. Knew it well because the artist had seen angels in his work. He had found heaven through his painting, sculpting. Through earth's loveliness . . .

"Yeah. Michelangelo. The artist. There was no lead up, no reason for it, he just rips that off in the middle of a conversation where I'm digging at him, trying to get a motive for the crime, trying to ask if they had problems, if he hated women, you know, and he just drops this line on me. What the hell is that supposed to mean?"

Gabriel was just about certain it meant Rafe Marino was a killer.

Sara was trying to hang tough and not put in a panicked call to Gabriel as she got out of the cab, walked the two steps across the sidewalk, and unlocked the gate to the courtyard. It wasn't a big deal. It was no big deal. No one was in the courtyard, no one was in the apartment.

Only there *was* someone sitting on the steps. It was a young woman in her early twenties, her hair dyed dark black, her bare shoulders and arms tattooed with a swarm of butterflies. She was sitting with her satchel purse in her lap, biting her black fingernails.

Sara smiled at her, prepared to walk right past her, assuming she was waiting for the guy who lived on the second floor, who Sara had yet to encounter.

But the girl jumped up when Sara started walking up the stairs. "Hey, wait, is that your apartment?" She pointed up to Gabriel's front door.

"Yes." No point in getting into lengthy descriptions of the truth.

"What happened to Gabriel? Did he move?" She was nibbling her nails again, even as she spoke, her eyes anxious.

"No, he still lives here," Sara said cautiously, not sure where this was headed.

"You live with him?" The nail-bitten finger came out and pointed at Sara.

The rudeness irritated Sara. "Yes. Can I help you?"

"I'm Rochelle," the girl said.

Okay. That told her a whole lot of nothing. "Would you like me to tell Gabriel you stopped by?"

Rochelle seemed to think about that for a second. "When will he be home?"

"Later."

"And you really live with him?"

Sara could have told the truth, that she was just staying with him temporarily, but she didn't feel inclined to point that out. She just held up her apartment key. "Yes."

To which Rochelle burst into tears. "How could he do this to me? I'm . . . I'm in love with him . . . and he stopped coming in to the shop, and now you're here, and I . . . God, I just want to die!"

Rochelle turned and ran down the stairs, her sandals pounding on the courtyard bricks.

"Wait!" Sara called, running down the stairs after her. She needed to be honest and tell Rochelle that she wasn't really living with Gabriel, not in the truest sense. What if Rochelle really was his girlfriend and she'd just screwed up their relationship? Part of her couldn't help but think, *Oh, well,* but the better part of her knew it was wrong to mislead Rochelle.

But the girl was gone, almost to Royal Street already, running faster than Sara was capable of. Great. Wonderful. How the hell was she supposed to explain to Gabriel that she had potentially ruined his love life? Not that she'd known he had a love life. He had never indicated to her in any way that he was involved with anyone. There had been no phone calls when she'd been around, and he spent the majority of his time with her, so how was she supposed to know he had a Rochelle on the side?

And why was he inviting her to sleep in his bed if he had a girlfriend? That was just wrong on so many levels.

Irritated, jealous, and yet somehow fairly certain he didn't have a girlfriend, Sara was still standing in the doorway five minutes later when she saw Gabriel come around the corner carrying a brown bag.

"Hey," he said as he approached her. "What are you doing?"

"Your girlfriend stopped by," she said, trying desperately not to grimace at the words.

"My girlfriend?" He looked legitimately puzzled. "I don't have a girlfriend."

"Rochelle."

His face was still blank. "Who's Rochelle?"

That was interesting. "About five foot three, long, black hair—bad dye job, by the way—fair skin, wearing an ankle-length burgundy skirt and an olive green tank top." Gabriel still didn't look like he was making a connection, so she added, "Tattoos of butterflies all over her arms. She said you stopped coming into the shop, but she never said what the shop was. Just that she was your girlfriend."

Which she obviously wasn't, which gave Sara no small amount of satisfaction.

The butterfly tattoos appeared to have jogged his memory. "*Oh*. I know who you're talking about. She's not my girlfriend, she never was. We never even went out. I'm not even sure I knew her name was Rochelle." Gabriel looked totally perplexed. "She works in the sandwich shop on Decatur. For awhile I was going there a couple of times a week. But I got burned out on po'boys."

That almost made Sara laugh. "You just got burned out on po'boys? She acted like you were seriously hot and heavy. Wow. That's weird."

"How did she know where I live? Or hell, my name, for that matter." Gabriel held out his arm for her to move into the courtyard ahead of him.

Sara turned back to look at him as she walked. "Do they ask for your name when you order your food?"

"Yeah." He made a face. "But just my first name. I wonder if she followed me home or something."

"She looked like the stalker type. Though now that I think about it, she didn't actually say she was your girlfriend, just that she was in love with you."

"In love with me?" Gabriel's eyebrows shot up. "I just ordered a few shrimp po'boys from her."

"She said 'in love with' you, I swear. And she was really upset when I told her that we live together." In retrospect, it was probably a good thing that Sara hadn't caught up to Rochelle on the street. It was better for the girl to think Gabriel had a girlfriend so she could move on past her oddly delusional crush.

Gabriel was fighting a grin as he stopped in front of the stairs. "You told her we live together?"

Sara wrinkled her nose. "Yes. It's true. I am staying here, for now."

"Were you jealous?" he asked in a low, teasing voice.

She scoffed. "Of course not."

"You shouldn't be, since I obviously don't have any sort of relationship with her. But I'd like it if you were."

God, he was flirting with her. There was no denying the tone of his voice, the way he was leaning toward her. "Oh, yeah? Why?"

He was so close to her, the only thing that separated them was the bag of take-out food in his hand. She smelled spicy oriental chicken as he touched the end of her hair with his free hand, twirling a strand around his finger. "Because that would mean you're okay with me doing this."

"Touching my hair?" she asked stupidly. He was so close she found herself staring at the stubble on his chin. There was no rhyme or reason to his hair growth. It was sporadic and random, the hairs soft, darker than the hair on his head. Yet even though he hadn't shaved, if you were a foot away from him, you'd never be able to tell there was stubble. He had no imperfections on his face anywhere, no scars or blemishes or discolorations. Up close, he was even lovelier to look at than when she was standing across the room. Up close she could see the strength of his jaw, the sharpness of his cheekbones, and the deep, rich desire in his compelling eyes.

Up close, she had no hope, no intention, of resisting him. His fingers in her hair made her shiver with anticipation.

"Yes. And this."

Then he leaned forward and kissed her. She closed her eyes immediately, wanting to enjoy it, savor. He came at her with a short, testing-the-waters press first, then without hesitation he went for broke, taking her mouth with his, hand buried in her hair, holding her head.

It was sexy and skilled and Sara felt it everywhere. Gabriel was giving her the kind of kiss that reverberated throughout her entire body, awakening her breasts and inner thighs, stirring up both an appreciation and a restless want for more. He tasted, felt, so damn good, and she gave it back, opening up for him, burning with want for him.

Gabriel was aware with half his brain that he shouldn't be doing what he was doing, but he ignored the voice of reason and continued feeling, touching, tasting Sara's mouth. She was delicious, warm and soft, and small, yet strong, confident, kissing him back with passion and fervor, and when he slid his tongue inside her, she opened for him without hesitation. Their tongues intertwined and her fingers dug into his forearm, and it was a damn good thing he was holding a bag of Chinese food or he would have pushed her against the wall, ground his aching erection against her, yanked down her T-shirt and sucked her breasts.

It would be very, very easy to lose control with her, to go from kissing to touching to their bodies naked and sweaty as he thrust inside her. He wanted that. Wanted to take it. Knew he could.

But a kiss would have to be enough, so Gabriel ravaged her mouth, pressed and licked and sucked, plunging his tongue deeper inside her until Sara stumbled backward, losing her balance under his urgent pursuit and breaking their connection. She blinked up at him, lips shiny and wet, as they both panted. Her fists opened and closed at her sides, and her nipples were clearly visible, taut against her shirt. There was a piece of hair stuck to her bottom lip and she didn't bother to pull it away. He could read the capitulation on her face, could see that one word and they could be upstairs in his bed, yanking off denim and cotton and enjoying each other's flesh, and he wanted it. Bad.

The only thing he wanted more was freedom. Because he couldn't make love to Sara. Rochelle was a reminder of that. He didn't want to see Sara grow desperate with the illogical and demon-driven urge to be possessed by him, over and over. He couldn't live with himself if he took Sara, then had to watch her lose herself in a debilitating addiction to him, who wasn't worthy of any sort of devotion.

He had only touched Rochelle once, brushing an ant off her arm when she had handed him his change, and look what that had done, what that had created in Rochelle.

There was no choice to be made. Gabriel had to stay strong, so he wiped his mouth, regretting his actions. It was going to be harder to resist what he had already tasted. But he would. Especially knowing that he was keeping truths from her. Knowing that she was going to hate him if she ever learned any of those truths, especially if Rafe really was her mother's killer.

"Are you hungry?" he asked, readjusting the bag of food into both hands.

"What?" she said, blinking like a baby owl. Then she took a deep breath, tugging at the hem of her T-shirt. "Right. Dinner. Great. Thanks."

Chapter Twelve

From the Court Records of the
Willful Murder Trial of Anne Donovan,
State of Louisiana v. Jonathon Thiroux
January 13, 1850
Attorney for the defense, Mr. Swift, questioning
Dr. Stephens.

MR. SWIFT: Dr. Stephens, can you explain to us
    what absinthism is?
DR. STEPHENS: Certainly. Absinthism is a
    syndrome that chronic ingestors of absinthe
    eventually incur. It is characterized by
    addiction, seizures, delirium, and
    hallucinations.
MR. SWIFT: What precisely do you mean by
    addiction?
DR. STEPHENS: Addiction is a physical dependence
    on the intoxicant itself. In this case, absinthe.
MR. SWIFT: And you say this absinthism results
    in seizures, delirium, and hallucinations?
DR. STEPHENS: That is correct.
MR. SWIFT: Could a person suffering from this

unfortunate syndrome lose their faculties
during one of these seizures, states of
delirium, or hallucinations?

DR. STEPHENS: Absolutely. That's the nature of
the beast.

MR. SWIFT: So they could come to after one of
these episodes and have no memory of what
had occurred in the interim?

DR. STEPHENS: Certainly. They very easily could
have memory gaps as a result of these brain
traumas.

MR. SWIFT: Would you say that someone who has
consumed absinthe every day for a period of
at least eighteen months is at risk for
absinthism, resulting in these seizures, states
of delirium, and hallucinations?

DR. STEPHENS: Absinthe every day for eighteen
months? Good God, I would say most
assuredly a person ingesting that level of
drink would be suffering from absinthism.
Without a doubt, in my mind.

MR. SWIFT: Thank you, Dr. Stephens. I have no
further questions.

From the Court Records of
the Willful Murder Trial of Anne Donovan,
State of Louisiana v. Jonathon Thiroux
January 14, 1850

PROSECUTOR: Dr. Raphael, in your medical
opinion, would the wounds inflicted upon
Anne Donovan be easy to create using a
bowie knife?

DR. RAPHAEL: I am not certain what you're
asking.

PROSECUTOR: I apologize. Let me rephrase the
question. We have heard testimony as to the
severe damage a bowie knife can do to an
individual. It is inarguably a most vicious
weapon. Would you say that anyone, whether

they are of great strength or not, could have
inflicted these wounds upon Anne Donovan?

DR. RAPHAEL: I wouldn't say that. The depth of
the wounds, the violence of the attack, and
the damage to both organs and bone indicate
to me that the killer was a man of size and
strength.

PROSECUTOR: Even though the bowie knife is
used by sportsmen to easily gut fish and skin
animals?

DR. RAPHAEL: I am not an expert in knives. I can
merely tell you that bone was penetrated in a
multitude of places, and as a medical expert,
I do not believe that a person who was
intoxicated to the point of unconsciousness
could have inflicted wounds with this type of
severity. I don't believe a woman could have
done this. I believe only a very strong man,
in full command of his faculties, could have
done this kind of damage.

PROSECUTOR: Have you ever acted as coroner in
a prior murder case where a bowie knife was
used?

DR. RAPHAEL: No. I have only taken the position
six months past.

PROSECUTOR: Is it true, Dr. Raphael, that you are
a prior acquaintance of the defendant?

DR. RAPHAEL: Yes. I had met the defendant on
several occasions, always in a large social
setting.

PROSECUTOR: Were you friends?

DR. RAPHAEL: I wouldn't say that, no. We barely
exchanged a dozen words.

PROSECUTOR: Yet you were seen dining alone in the
company of the defendant twice last year by at
least seven witnesses. No further questions.

Gabriel had kissed her and pulled back immediately. Then
fed her Chinese food. What did that mean? She had no idea,
and she wasn't in the mood to guess.

There was no energy left for prevaricating. She had used it up on grief, sleep deprivation, and fear. So as they ate, she swallowed a noodle, then just said, "You didn't have to stop, you know."

"Stop what?" he asked, but she could tell he knew what she was referring to, because he got a wary look in his eyes.

"Kissing me. I was enjoying it." Immensely. And she wanted to enjoy it again, all over her body. She wanted him to take her to his bed, peel off her clothes and kiss her between her thighs, stroking his tongue over her until she came, then push his hard body inside hers. The idea thrilled, just from thinking about it, and she found that intriguing. It wasn't like her to respond so sexually to a man, and while she didn't entirely understand it, she was too aroused to even consider waiting to decipher what it meant. She just wanted him, wanted to feel alive, whole again.

"I know. I was too." He fiddled with his chopsticks.

It amazed her that he could actually use the utensils. She always wound up flinging chicken chunks onto the carpet when she tried to use them.

"But?"

"But . . . Sara, I can't. I'm not capable of giving you what you need." He shot her a beseeching look.

She wasn't having any of that, because she wasn't asking for anything. "Why, are you impotent?"

Gabriel let out a startled laugh. "No." He gave a small smile. "I'm pretty certain of that."

"Then we don't have a problem, because I'm not looking for promises or forever or anything other than sex. We're attracted to each other, so what's the big deal?" Even as she spoke, she knew she was simplifying things, but she suddenly felt there was a really important reason she needed to win the argument. That she needed to have sex, with Gabriel. That she needed to *know*.

"It's not that easy. When is sex ever really just sex? Emotion always creeps in." He dropped down his chopsticks onto his plate. "I have all this guilt over my girlfriend, and sex, it's like the ultimate letdown of all your guards, you know? I think it's dangerous for me to lose control."

"Why? Because if you lose control, you might have to admit that it's okay to live, to have a good time, without your girlfriend?"

He looked defiantly at her. "Yes. You should recognize me in yourself."

That was why she understood him so well. That was why she was certain they were both damaging themselves further by letting the guilt eat at them. "So if I push it, and you eventually give in, I'm the bad guy, aren't I?"

He shook his head. "No. I won't give in. And eventually we'll both lose interest."

"Oh, really?" She had to admit, that infuriated her. "You have it all figured out, don't you?"

"Absolutely." He nodded with confidence.

"Then why the hell did you kiss me?" She wasn't sure whether she regretted it or not. It had been a fabulous kiss, and she had been curious what it would be like, but on the other hand, now she knew their chemistry was real, yet he was telling her they couldn't do a damn thing about it.

"Because I'm an idiot."

Which was the male answer to everything. They seemed to think if they just admitted their stupidity, somehow it exempted them from responsibility for it.

"I can't really argue with that." It was snarky of her, but she didn't want to play those games. Not with him. Not now.

He just smiled. "You shouldn't."

Sara stabbed a carrot, still feeling irritated. "You didn't find out who sent those pictures, did you?"

"No. But I think we should inform the police, both here and in Naples."

That was the last thing she felt like doing. "They'll just make me fill out a bunch of paperwork, then they'll never do anything with it."

"You're not just some random person showing up with gruesome pictures. This might have some bearing on their investigation."

"What investigation? They think they found their man. They're done, and whether he was convicted or not, as far as they're concerned the case is closed." Sara had tried to tell herself she wasn't bitter about that, but hell, she sounded bitter. She was.

Gabriel didn't call her on it. He just said, "It's up to you. We can say something or we don't have to."

"I don't want to. Not right now. Maybe later." And what would change later to make her suddenly take the pictures to the police, she didn't know, but she was having trouble being definitive. Changing the subject before he could reply, she said, "What do you think of that whole absinthism argument? Do you think that was a real syndrome? And could it have debilitated John Thiroux to the point where he wouldn't have been able to use that bowie knife on Anne?"

Gabriel said, "I think absinthism was just a term given to alcohol addiction. I'm sure drinking excessively would result in blackouts with absinthe, like any other form of alcohol. As for hallucinations and delirium? I doubt they were true hallucinations. I think alone, absinthe acts mostly like a heightened alcohol drunk."

Sara was sitting next to Gabriel on his couch, the food on the coffee table in front of them. Angel was perched on the window ledge, looking out at the courtyard. It was weird to her how comfortable she felt with him, in his apartment, in his life. Now that she knew about his girlfriend, saw clearly how he punished himself for her death, she knew it was a major concession for him to allow her in his space. And she wanted to help him move forward as much as she wanted that for herself. "I wish I knew exactly what that kind of drunk felt like. Can you still buy absinthe?"

"Yes. Mostly online." Gabriel was no longer eating, but just shoving rice back and forth on his plate. "I have a bottle of it."

"Why?" she asked him in surprise.

"Because I thought the same thing you did. That if I could know exactly what it felt like, I could determine for myself who was right. Thiroux maintained he was out cold and didn't hear a thing. The prosecutor said that in a violent rage he sliced Anne Donovan to pieces. The coroner said a man under the influence couldn't have exhibited the force necessary. I want to know. So I bought a bottle of absinthe."

Sara stared at his profile. He was speaking with nonchalance, but she knew exactly what he was saying. "You can't drink it and you know you can't. It wouldn't be worth it."

"I know." He dropped his chopsticks and pushed the plate away from him. "That's why it's sitting in my kitchen cabinet unopened."

"I'm glad you didn't." Sara touched his knee, stroking the denim with her thumb, her heart aching for his pain, for hers. "But I can. I'll drink it." If he wanted to know badly enough that he had risked that kind of temptation, she could answer the question for him. Alcohol was not her demon.

"You don't have to do that." Gabriel looked at her in that way he did sometimes, where he just watched, and his brown eyes bored into her, unreadable, like he had a thousand thoughts that he wanted to share, but couldn't, wouldn't.

"I know I don't have to. I want to." Now that she had decided, she was determined. Sara stood up and headed for the kitchen. "Which cabinet is it in?"

Gabriel got up and followed Sara, torn between letting her drink his absinthe and forbidding her. He suspected if he told her flat-out no, that she couldn't have it, she wouldn't pursue it, and that was what his first instinct was. To just haul her out of his kitchen, put himself between her and the cabinets, break the bottle, and dump the drink down the drain. He had a slight panic in his gut at the thought of her going into his bottle, taking herself to that place he had loved so much and still craved. But Sara wasn't him, and she wasn't doing it to escape, she was doing it to understand. And he also suspected she was still shaken from the packet of pictures she had seen. Drinking the absinthe was a grasp at control, ironically enough, a way for her to express defiance in the face of death and two murder cases that appeared to be unsolvable.

He wanted to tell her no. Even said, "Sara, this isn't a good idea."

But when she found the bottle by opening all his cabinets, and pulled it down, he didn't yank it away from her.

"It *is* a good idea. I need to know, Gabriel. Don't you understand that? I can't do anything else . . . I can't bring my mother back and I can't . . . with you, but this I can do. I can do whatever it takes to solve Anne Donovan's case, at least to our personal satisfaction."

The defiant and desperate edge to her voice forced him to realize that she did absolutely need to do this. She needed to let go of her fear, move herself out of the corner she had backed into, and allow herself to be bold, angry. The feral expression on her face had him contemplating the other way she could let go. They could have hot and sweaty sex. He could lift her onto the kitchen counter and hike up her skirt and plunge into her the way he ached to.

She wanted him to. It was on her face, in her words, in her body language as she held the bottle up against her breasts. She licked her bottom lip, and he had a painful, throbbing erection that demanded release. There was no doubt in his mind it would be passionate, intense, fast, with grinding and pushing and gripping, a hot, hard slapping of their bodies together.

He wanted that.

He couldn't take it. God help him, literally, but there was less danger from the absinthe than from sex.

"I'll get you a glass." He turned, away from that offer, away from that pleading, and opened his cabinet, pulling out a tumbler. They were supposed to be for juice, since he didn't keep any glasses for alcohol, and no corkscrews, no ice buckets. No implements at all for alcohol. Except for his absinthe spoons.

"Thanks." She was inspecting the bottle. "Do I just drink it straight? Is it like a shot?"

"You don't want to drink it straight. It's going to taste awful to you." Gabriel set the glass down on the counter, right where he had pictured spreading Sara's thighs. "We'll dilute it with water and sugar, the traditional way. You can even pick one of my spoons to use if you want. Might as well have the full experience." And if he sounded less than thrilled, it was because he was holding on to the edge of his own control. Not to drink. That wasn't the temptation. He was struggling to prevent himself from touching Sara. He wanted to run his fingers down her shoulder, her arm, and grasp her hand in his. He wanted to lace their fingers together, draw her to him, and kiss her, better and longer than he had downstairs.

Instead, he unscrewed the cap and splashed two inches of absinthe into the bottom of the juice glass.

Sara leaned over and sniffed. She instantly recoiled. "Ugh. It smells like NyQuil."

That almost made him laugh. "It has anise in it. That's why I suggested diluting it."

"I'll go get a spoon." She had her nose curled up and her arms tightly over her chest. "Though doesn't diluting it just mean I'll have to drink more of it?"

"You can try it both ways." Gabriel went for the sugar and a glass of water.

Sara returned almost immediately, the most ornate of his spoons in her hand. It was carved with extensive curlicues on the handle, and it was elegant, had been expensive. She rinsed it off and dried it, then handed it to him. "I've always liked this one."

Gabriel rested the spoon across the glass. A warm feeling of euphoric anticipation stole over him, an associative memory that this preparation was followed by a beautiful, impenetrable clarity. A confidence that he was brilliant and in control, achieving all his goals and all that had been asked of him.

It was all an illusion of course, and he was tempted to smack the spoon back down on to the table. Hurl the glass. Exercise his own mastery over life, destiny, emotion.

But the better way to express that control would be to pour for Sara and hand her the glass. To give it up, move it from his hand to hers, after seeing the water slide through the sugar and drag it down into the absinthe via the holes in the spoon. To watch water and absinthe blend in a beautiful cloud, to lift away the spoon, and hold the heavy glass in his hand, feel its weight, its promise.

Gabriel handed it to Sara, meeting her eyes head-on. She took it from him, wide-eyed, a question clearly in her expression. But all she said was "Thanks," in a gravelly whisper.

"I recommend sipping it like wine or a beer. Don't toss it all back at once. Why don't we go sit down and watch TV or play cards or something. Do you play gin rummy?" He actually despised playing cards, because while he appreciated the logic of the games, he didn't enjoy being subjected to chance, which was what pulling cards always was. But he would play cards with Sara if she wanted to. They couldn't just sit there while she drank. *He* couldn't just sit there while she drank.

"Cards would be fun. I was a card shark in my dorm in college." She took a very tentative sip from her glass. Her face screwed up. "Well, it's no margarita."

He wouldn't know. He'd never had a margarita. They

hadn't been on the menu in the nineteenth century and Gabriel hadn't had a drink since Prohibition. "Lick some sugar if it's that bad."

She did, sticking the tip of her tongue onto the absinthe spoon and tasting the sugar that had remained behind, clumped from the water. Gabriel turned away, retreating to the living room in search of a deck of cards. He couldn't watch her, couldn't stare at the pink, wet tip of her tongue and not imagine touching it with his own, feeling it on his body, thrusting his own inside her mouth, her inner thighs.

It had been too long for him. He had stayed away from women entirely in the last eighty years. It had been easier in the early part of the twentieth century to visit a woman anonymously in Storyville and know she had no ability to track him down. He had made sure to have sex with women whose senses were dulled from drugs and alcohol, so they wouldn't remember, wouldn't respond to the interaction, wouldn't want him irrationally and unnaturally. He could appease his physical urges and get the hell out before there were consequences.

But it wasn't that easy anymore. There was no anonymity. Anyone could find another person if they really wanted to. And the thought of going to the lowest of the desperate low, the women who were strung out on crack and littered with disease, living on the streets, offended his aesthetics, not to mention his sense of right and wrong. He couldn't, wouldn't, use a woman like that for his base, physical satisfaction, and he wasn't attracted to sex for the simple sake of release anymore. He could do that on his own.

And there was no way, absolutely no way, he would engage in a sexual relationship with a woman he knew, someone who would potentially fall for him, become addicted to him. He couldn't subject any woman—like Sara—to that, not even for the most desperate sexual want. It was also true what he had told Sara, that sex was lifting the lid off of his control, and he wasn't sure he could handle the consequences. So he had been celibate for nearly eight decades, and was feeling the effect of that acutely and painfully.

His hand could take the edge off, but it could never replace the feeling of burying himself inside a woman.

So he moved away from Sara, out of touching distance. After digging cards out of a drawer, he sat in a chair across from the couch, dragging it up to the coffee table. He busied himself packing up their Chinese food while Sara wandered in, sipping the absinthe.

"It gets better with each sip," she said. "Maybe that's because I'm actually killing my taste buds or something."

"Maybe. Do you want to deal?"

"No, you go ahead." She took another sip.

Gabriel found himself getting tenser as her glass emptied, while Sara got chattier, looser. With each sip, she relaxed her shoulders a little more, allowed her knees to gape apart another inch. While he gripped his playing cards, bending them in the tight fan he held, she waved hers carelessly around as she spoke.

And she talked about everything. Work. Housing. Him. On and on as he watched her get quickly and giddily intoxicated.

"I like my job," she said. "I really should go back. Don't you think? Except I'm afraid of screwing up. I don't sleep at all anymore. Did I tell you that? Of course I told you that."

He couldn't even get a word in and she was onto her apartment. "My couch is purple. I hate purple. It's a rich, syrupy color. It's medicinal. And I would never wear purple. It's like a cure for coughs on your clothes. The only time I like purple is when it's a flower. Irises are beautiful."

Gabriel discarded, not sure what the hell he was supposed to say to that.

But it didn't matter because Sara was plowing through her second glass and speaking her thoughts out loud with confidence and clarity.

"Play the piano for me, Gabriel."

"No." The idea wasn't even remotely appealing.

"Please. Pretty please?" She stuck out her bottom lip and pouted, her blue eyes glassy and bright from the alcohol. "I want to hear you play."

"No. I told you I don't hear music anymore."

"You're just being stubborn." She tossed back the remainder of her glass. "How much am I supposed to drink? I don't feel drunk at all. Just sort of relaxed, like everything is sharp and focused. I feel very logical, like all my thoughts are better organized. Am I acting different?"

"Yes." She wasn't a sloppy drunk—that wasn't what the absinthe did. But it gave the illusion of intelligence to the drinker, like every thought one had was utterly brilliant. "You're very chatty."

"Oh." She fanned herself with her five-card spread. "Am I bugging you?"

"No." What she was doing was turning him on. Her legs were wide apart, her skirt hitching up past her knees. Her tank-top strap had fallen off her shoulder and she hadn't bothered to pull it back up. "I like to hear you talk."

Because if she stopped talking and decided to touch him, they were going to have a serious problem.

"You don't talk enough." Her finger came up and shook at him in reprimand. "You're like Mystery Man."

That made him smile. "Maybe I'm not worth listening to."

"Or maybe you're meant to express yourself through painting and music, not spoken words."

That ripped the smile off his face. She might as well have kicked him in the groin. "Sara . . ." He meant it as a warning, to let it go, that she was too close, crossing a boundary, treading into something that was none of her business.

But either she was too drunk to realize his intent, or she was choosing to ignore it, because she said, "Play the piano for me. Right now."

"No, damn it," he said in frustration.

"You have a choice. You can play the piano or you can kiss me."

Oh, yeah. She was drunk. He knew she would have never said that otherwise. Yet, it was clear she meant it. She was tossing down her cards and leaning across the coffee table, palms on the flat surface. She was going to kiss him, and he wasn't going to be able to resist.

"Fine. I'll play the fucking piano," he said angrily, dropping his own cards onto the table and standing up, quickly, before she could touch him. Anything to keep her away from him.

"It wouldn't hurt, you know," she said. "You might even like it. A kiss, that is."

Was she even serious? Gabriel stood with his feet apart, erection throbbing. "That's not the problem. I know I would like it. But there are *issues*. I can't."

Before she could respond, argue, breathe on him, he moved across the room and flipped the piano lid open. The instrument was probably grossly out of tune and he was completely out of practice, but if she wanted to hear sour off-key notes, more power to her.

"What do you want me to play?" he asked, sitting down in total irritation. He didn't want to do this, but he was already cracking his knuckles, relaxing his shoulders, giving in, feeling the pull of the keys.

"Whatever you want to play. Whatever you have music for."

What he wanted to play was something dark, something frustrated, to express his feelings. Something yearning and intense. "I don't need sheet music." Once he learned a song, he always played from memory. It was all still there, he was sure of it. His fingers remembered, even if he no longer heard it. So he tested the scales, getting the feel of the instrument. He closed his eyes, letting his fingers guide him, sighing at the unexpected pleasure the first strains of Chopin's Ballade in G Minor gave him.

Maybe he had missed it after all.

The music swelled in his soul, and he let it flow from his fingers, the rhythm of 6/4 suggesting an underlying waltz, a tender poignancy that was perfect for his mood, for the unexpected longing that arose from the feel of the keys beneath his fingers. For music, for beauty, for Sara.

Gabriel found his confidence as the ballade increased in musical intensity, swelling into one of Chopin's spectacular embellishments of eighteenth notes against solid quarter-note chords, a flourish that pleased him. With two-note slurs, the music pushed forward, yearning, a keening cry that was perfect for his mood, echoing the frustration he felt, the anguish, the growing hope and desire that was being ground into the dirt by the unrelenting reality of murder. Crushed by his sins, his demon status, the bounds of his punishment.

In the music he could allow himself freedom, an abandonment, and he swept into the breathless speed of arpeggios fearlessly and without hesitation, understanding the ballade's intent, feeling it. He was lonely, and there was a lovely woman who desired him, both physically and intellectually, and he couldn't have her. He couldn't touch her. Even when he craved her body, her mind, her heart, he couldn't have her.

So instead of pouring himself into her, he poured himself into the music, the passion increasing, the notes feverish and frightening, unexpected outbursts of emotion before it slowed down again, shifting from fast and angry to melancholy, resignation. Gabriel was resigned.

And he suspected so was Sara.

He glanced over at her, realizing that she had been quiet since he had started playing.

Gabriel's fingers paused when he saw her. Bloody hell. She had reclined onto the sofa on her back, knees up in the air, eyes closed, and her chest was rising and falling rapidly, her thumb brushing over the taut nipple beneath her tank top. Her lips were open in sensual abandonment, like a woman being stroked and aroused and loved by a man's hand.

"Don't stop," she whispered, a tiny moan of disappointment that lacerated his control and sent his fingers tripping sensually over the keys the way he wanted to touch Sara.

God, he wanted to touch her.

He stroked the piano instead and hoped his control would hold.

Sara lay back on the couch and let her eyes flutter closed. She didn't feel drunk, not in the way she was used to. Wine made her giggly, mixed drinks made her stumbling, shit-faced drunk, and beer made everything seem extra loud. This wasn't like any of those. She felt alert, wide awake, completely in control. Everything felt sharp and focused and real, and everything seemed so much more logical than it had before. She was feeling prosaic about her mother's death, dissecting the path of her mother's life, and seeing how like Anne Donovan, when a woman flirted with danger, drugs, alcohol, stripping, prostitution, her risk of harm increased. It didn't mean she deserved it, but it meant simply that her odds of tragedy were greater. Sara could see that. She thought it sucked, but she could see it.

And she could see that coming to New Orleans had been a brilliant idea. It truly had. She was facing the past, the present, the future. She actually felt confident that when the book was finished, she could go back to work. Move forward.

Gabriel's piano playing was beautiful, the strains of the music flowing around her, over her, in her. It rose and fell, a desperate, frustrated piece that reminded her of the man himself. He was locked inside himself, an introvert. Yet what was in there was passionate, creative, demanding, sexual. He wanted her, she was sure of that. She could see that in his eyes, hear it in his music.

Never in her entire life had she wanted a man to fill her body as rabidly as she did right at that moment. Lying there, her body ached for him, every inch tingling and aware and raw, wanting that touch, that brush, that push, that possession.

It didn't occur to her that she wasn't alone and maybe it wasn't the time or place to touch her nipples. She just accidentally brushed one, and it felt good, right, so she did it again. If he wouldn't, she could. There was no harm in that, and maybe it would ease the ache.

When he paused for a moment, she asked him not to stop, and he continued, the notes harder again, louder. Sara looked over at Gabriel, watched his profile from her angle, studied his fingers moving. He had elegant, gorgeous fingers, long and tapered, strong and masculine, commanding in their control of the music, but artistic. Fingers that brought beauty and pleasure.

Fingers that she wanted on her. As she stared at him, watched in awe the quickness of his playing, the confidence, the grace of those long fingers, she imagined what it would feel like to take one into her mouth, to suck it to the tip, pull the entire length into her mouth. To have it pluck at the tightness of her nipple, slide smoothly down her abdomen. To slip into the heat of her body, his length giving her the satisfaction of depth, his elegance the pleasure of skilled stroking.

His lips were pursed, a scowl on his face—of concentration, irritation, frustration—she wasn't sure. It didn't seem like he was struggling with the music. There was no hesitation, no trips or pauses or bad notes that her uneducated ear could detect. Sara let her knees fall apart, onto the couch, because it seemed like they needed to be open. Everything ached and desired and she inched her skirt up past her knees, feeling hot and aroused. Gabriel wasn't going to touch her, she knew that. He was playing the piano, and he needed to do that. She really knew he needed to do that, for his sake.

But she couldn't just lie there, alone, wanting him so desperately that she could feel the dampness in her panties, feel the tug and pull for sexual fulfillment in her womb. It was just impossible. And while her fingers weren't his, she could touch, so he could play, and they could both have what they wanted.

It made perfect sense to her in his dark apartment, the absinthe convincing her that all her ideas were amazing ones, while Gabriel's music danced around her, an expression of his giving in, his freedom, his creative joy. His sensuality. Sara slid her hands along her inner thighs, sighing. Not the same at all, but it still felt good, especially when she brushed the back of her thumb over her panties.

Gabriel made a sound, and she glanced over at him. He still played, but his eyes weren't on the keys. They were on her, and they were burning. He had seen her touch herself, could see her white panties, that was obvious. He looked a little shocked, but mostly, he looked like he liked it. Sara moistened her lips and his eyes narrowed. Oh, yeah. He liked it.

So she turned away, looking up at the ceiling, and touched her chest with one hand, squeezing and rubbing her nipple, while she stroked across the front of her panties with her other hand. It felt so good that she sat half up and yanked off her tank top, dropping it to the floor so she could feel her skin, reach inside her bra and free her breasts, cupping with both hands. Maybe she was drunk, because it seemed perfectly natural, and she didn't hesitate. It felt amazingly good, heady and voyeuristic, to know he was watching her, wanting her. Instead of being angry that he wouldn't take, she felt the power of that tease, the heightened titillation of knowing that everything she did could both bring pleasure to herself and acute arousal to him.

She pulled her skirt up all the way to the waist and slipped her hand inside her panties. The warmth heated her skin and she lay still for a second, just feeling the anticipation, feeling the heat of Gabriel's eyes on her, feeling the cool breeze from the air conditioner propped in the window a few feet away tickling over her bare stomach and thighs. Even though she knew nothing about music at all, particularly classical music, she could hear and feel what the piece Gabriel was playing was intended to convey. It was passionate, wild, no longer anger, but not melancholy either. It was a song of seduction, a challenge to continue, to ignore convention and propriety and embrace pleasure.

Closing her eyes, she stroked inside her panties, rushing along her clitoris and into the moistness of her body. The first touch tripped off intense need, and she moved more urgently, stroking in and out, her breathing turning into a low pant, her back arching, her heels digging into the couch cushion. She wanted to ask him to help her, to come over, to replace her finger with his, but she couldn't speak, couldn't make the words come out loud and be heard over the music. Couldn't spoil the moment, the pleasure, the feeling that in a way, he was the one touching her. It was his finger, his music, his creation, the swirling rise of ecstasy in her body the result of him, all him.

And when she came, when her inner muscles convulsed around her finger, it was him she came for, and the image of his fingers deep inside her. That way, he could play, fill the room with the sound of his music, at the same time she could shatter in pleasure, her hips lifting up in the air, body tensing everywhere as she rode it out.

She wasn't sure if she made any sound, but she felt the moans, heard them echoing in her head, the tight pulses settling down as she relaxed her legs, her back. Prying her eyes open, she swallowed hard. Wow. She had never been so aggressive before, so frantic in pushing herself to completion. That had been hot and exciting and unexpected, and she wanted more. She was sitting up, ready to strip completely, yank off her bra, ditch her skirt, go in for a second time, longer and deeper, up on her knees, when she saw Gabriel.

He was watching her, and she couldn't read his expression. It was tight and he had stopped playing.

Then he said, "Get over here."

"What?" Sara reached for her glass, emptying the last few drops, her mouth dry, throat sore and hoarse. She wasn't sure what he was saying exactly, if he intended to yank her bra back over her nipples, lecture her, or fuck her.

"I said, get over here. Right now."

Hoping it was the latter, Sara stood up and walked over to him, letting her skirt fall down over her thighs on its own, her body still moist and slick with want, her breasts still spilling over the top of her bra. She pushed her hair back off her head and went to him, enjoying that walk, enjoying the way his eyes watched her, the way his fingers stayed tight, poised over the keys, but not playing. His hair fell over one eye and he shook it off by jerking his head.

She went up to him, right to the bench, and slid in front of him until she touched his arm with her thigh. "Yes?"

Gabriel moved his arm until he was surrounding her, holding her, enclosing her. Then he shocked her, literally yanked the air right out of her, by gripping her waist and lifting her up, clear off the floor, and slamming her ass down onto the keys. Her back collided with the top of the piano, and she teetered, unbalanced, startled by the angry vibration of a dozen keys hitting at the same time, and by his unexpected action, her toes struggling to touch the floor and keep her from falling over in a tangled heap. "What are you . . ."

Then she lost her thought, her words careening into a cry of shock and ecstasy as he yanked her skirt up, shoved her panties to the side, and bent over, plunging his tongue inside her. "Oh, holy shit." Reaching left and right, slapping her hands around for something to hold on to, anything, Sara felt the force of his tongue in every inch of her body. She instantly had a mini-orgasm, an aftershock of the one before, and a reaction to his aggressive behavior.

It was so intense, so sensitive, her clitoris tight and hard, the pleasure almost painful, that she tried to retreat, tried to back up. But the piano ground into her, held her in place, held his tongue deep inside her, and she glanced down, finally dropping her hands to his shoulders for help in keeping her upright. His hair fell forward, covering his face from her view, and those silken strands, in their curious variety of colors, caught the light, looking ethereal, preternatural, surreal like the moment itself, the sensation of his moist tongue sliding along her hot flesh too real, too intense, for anything else to feel normal. It all seemed glossy and shiny, strange and crisp, like she was inside a painting, like the wall behind him was a canvas that could shift at any moment, like the only thing that she could trust in as being real was the feel of his shoulders beneath her fingers, the smell of his cologne, the hard press of the piano in her back, and the touch of his mouth on her desperate, overstimulated, agonized body.

She wanted to say something but she couldn't think, grab on to any words. It was all just sensation, sound, want, reaching for a release, which came suddenly in a tumultuous wave that had her gripping his T-shirt, her head snapping back as it took her under. Sara bit her lip so hard she tasted blood, rocking forward, vaginal muscles vibrating and straining, her mind empty, breath held. The intensity overwhelmed her, the pleasure all-consuming. As the last spasms subsided, she had to force herself to relax—fingers, legs, shoulders, abdomen—to suck in air and remind herself to breathe, to remember who and where she even was. "Jesus Christ," she said, loosening her death hold on his shirt.

Mouth thick and in desperate need of water, she took another deep breath, swallowing hard, suddenly aware that the hair on her forehead was damp and that her legs were trembling from the position. She wanted to say something, needed to say something, but she just looked at him, waiting for him to either flip her entirely onto the top of the piano, which struck her as a bad idea, or yank her down to the floor or the couch to finish what they had started. To fill her with him, to take both of them into that ecstasy, that completion, together.

But one glance at his face had her amending what was going to happen next. Gabriel wasn't going to have sex with her. It was obvious in the tightness of his shoulders, his face, the frustration she saw etched in every muscle, in all of his body language. He was already pulling away, literally and figuratively. As he retreated, he pulled her skirt down, covering her, his hand wiping his mouth dry.

She refused to feel ridiculous, slighted, annoyed. She had known why he was resisting, known it was too soon. She hadn't intended to force him into action. He had done that. She would have been content with what she had done on the couch. Knowing he was watching, getting aroused, had been enough for her, and this was his choice.

So she decided to take the upper hand, instead of waiting for him to embarrass her by reminding her he wouldn't have sex with her. "I'm going to take a shower," she said, peeling herself off the piano. She trailed her fingers across his cheek, through his hair, as she moved past him. "Thanks for playing. I really enjoyed it."

He opened his mouth. Then shut it. Then opened it again. "No problem. My pleasure."

The irony of that nonchalant statement made her laugh.

And Sara headed for the bathroom, stopping to scoop up her shirt on the way, feeling more relaxed than she had in a year.

⁂

Gabriel watched Sara head down the hall, her tank top swinging back and forth in her hand, her light laughter carrying as she gave him one last glance over her bare shoulder. The look was saucy, pleased. She had gotten what she wanted and didn't seemed offended that he wouldn't take it to the next step.

He wasn't feeling at all pleased. He was sick with self-disgust, at his complete lack of control. The taste of her was lingering on his mouth, and he could still feel the warmth of her thighs as he gripped her, keeping her legs spread, her panties pushed to the side, as he had moved his tongue in and out of her receptive body. She had been wet, eager, easy to orgasm, and he had known when he'd seen her sit up on the couch and reach for her skirt that she was going to peel off her clothes and pleasure herself some more, and that he was going to take her himself instead.

It had been stupid. She was drunk, dancing with the green fairy, and had let down all of her inhibitions. She was going to regret touching herself in front of him the next day. He should have left it alone, just concentrated on the notes and not even watched. He should have stepped out of the room to give her privacy. He should have resisted the urge to touch her.

But he felt a kinship to Sara, an intense longing and lust that superseded any and all common sense, and he suspected that he was succumbing to the very angelic emotion of love. He had thought that since his fall, since his plunge into self-ishness, he was incapable of stepping outside of himself and caring about another person, but maybe he had been wrong, because his desire for Sara was complex. It wasn't just lust, but a need to connect, to feel her, to touch, to please, to protect, to make her happy.

Gabriel pushed D above middle C with his thumb. The note rang out, then faded. It had felt good to play again. He had heard the music once he had touched the instrument. But it had made him lose control.

Or maybe he had never been in control.

He didn't know what he was doing. Who he was. Why it mattered to solve Anne's murder.

He didn't know how to prevent Sara from falling victim to his sins.

And he didn't know how to move beyond his purgatory into a better life, one where he could have a positive impact on the world, humanity. One where he didn't stand around motionless in the muck of his sins, but took action.

Gabriel played Bach idly. He didn't know any contemporary music, or anything twentieth-century, for that matter, since he hadn't played in a hundred years. But he liked the traditional intricacy of eighteenth- and nineteenth-century composers.

He needed to stay away from Sara.

But he knew he wasn't going to.

"Gabriel?" she called from down the hall. "I forgot a towel. Can you bring me one?"

Without hesitation, he got up and went down the hall.

He was fallen, after all.

No one expected him to have a halo anymore.

Chapter Thirteen

❦

DONOVAN WITNESS DEAD!

January 11, 1850—In a shocking twist to the willful murder trial of Anne Donovan that has the city riveted, witness Molly Faye, former lover of elusive and charming defendant Jonathon Thiroux, is dead, by her own hand.

After engaging in a heated and illustrious argument with another witness, also a lewd and unfortunate woman, just two days past, in which Miss Faye learned she was not the only object of the defendant's affection, Miss Faye took her life in the decisive manner of slicing open her own throat.

Found by the proprietress of the House of Rest for Weary Men, Madame Conti, in the victim's own bed, the vision first conjured up images of the scene last October when poor Anne Donovan was found in a similar state just two rooms down the hall. But whereas Anne had been sliced repeatedly, with such brutality and force as to render her unrecognizable, Molly Faye suffered merely one wound, from the left side of her throat to the right, approximately six inches in length and of a shallow depth. Dr. Raphael, the coroner, has concluded her death a suicide, as the weapon was in her hand and the slice tentative, as is often the case when a person hesitates on the threshold of death. The deceased's personal effects were tidy and in order, and though no note was left, that can be explained by the simple fact that Miss Faye was not literate. Next to her bed, on the nightstand, was a torn-out clipping of the newspaper article written by this reporter detailing the courtroom scuffle involving Miss Faye and Miss Swanson. There was no money in the room, no evidence of next of kin, and possessions only enough to fill a small satchel.

A sad ending indeed to a sad life.

One questions how many women like Miss Faye wander our city, at the mercy of fate and fortune, weary from the fight to subsist.

It would seem the murder of Anne Donovan provides no answers, only questions.

Gabriel was reaching in the hall closet for a towel when he heard a knock on the door. For a flash of a second, he thought it was another demon. A female. Then he dismissed the idea, not sure why he had even thought it was. He couldn't feel any energy, only the warmth of a human being outside his door. Definitely a woman though.

Rapping on the bathroom door, Gabriel waited for Sara's "come in" impatiently. He wanted to dispense with whoever was standing outside the door so he could go back to Sara. Finish what they had started. What Sara had started. What he wanted to finish, regardless of the consequences.

He quickly opened the door and tossed the towel on the floor, unable to prevent himself from glancing inside. She was still behind the shower curtain and he couldn't see her at all, which was probably a good thing. "There's someone at the front door. I'm going to answer it. I'll be right back. Don't go anywhere."

She laughed. "Where would I go? I'm naked and wet."

Just what he didn't need to hear. And he decided not to mention that he had brought her a towel. "Be right back."

The minute he opened the door, he regretted it. It was the girl from the po'boy shop. The girl who Sara said had stopped by earlier. He'd already forgotten her name, yet she was standing on his doorstep, big, wet tears in her eyes and her arms crossed tightly on her chest. She had a giant army green purse over her shoulder, diagonally so that she didn't have to hold it, yet she was still clutching it in front of her.

This was going to take tact. Something he wasn't all that great at. "Hey, this is a, uh, surprise. How are you?" he asked, hoping to feel out exactly why she was there.

"How do you think I am?" she asked, her voice high and shrill. "I'm awful. I'm sucky. You're just standing there looking at me all politely and you have a woman living with you. I'm in love with you and you have a woman living with you."

Not knowing where to go with that, Gabriel shook his head, keeping his voice even and, he hoped, soothing. "I'm not sure why that would matter to you. You and I . . . we said hello a few times. We didn't have a relationship beyond that."

"Yes, we did." Her voice was trembling now. "It was there, in the way you looked at me, in the way you touched me. And I felt it. When I met you, I knew that you were it for me. I met you and that was *it*, do you know what I mean?"

Gabriel felt absolutely awful. He couldn't even remember her name, and she was declaring that her life had altered when meeting him. It was a burden he despised, one that he resented, loathed, felt the injustice of over and over. Why should someone else be punished for his sins?

There was no answer, only the echo of the question in his head, and the feeling that there was something he was missing, something he was supposed to know, to learn, to solve. An end.

"I do know what you mean, and that's really flattering, but I'm not worth it, honestly. I don't deserve these feelings you have for me." Gabriel wanted to touch her, to reassure her, but that would be a mistake. That would only encourage her.

She was weeping now, her nose red and dripping, tears

streaming down her face. Swiping at her cheeks with the canvas of her purse, she said, "Don't do that. Please, God, don't do that."

"Do what?" he asked, wishing he knew how to free her, how to just make it all go away.

Of course, he knew how to create the illusion of making it go away. That was what absinthe and opium could achieve. The modern version of heroin would work just as well if not better. But that would only accomplish oblivion for him, not her. It wouldn't fix anything. And he would hate himself even more than he did standing there watching her sob, pathetic and irrational.

"Look at me like that. With pity. I don't want your pity. I want your love."

He didn't know how to erase the pity from his eyes, from his face, from his soul, when he did feel it. Pity for her that she had fallen victim, that she was suffering. "I don't have any love to give."

Maybe that was true. Maybe that was why he stayed this way, year after year. Maybe that was why he could never return. He hadn't loved, enough or well. Hadn't loved God, himself, Anne. Maybe he didn't even know what love was.

But he did know he wanted to reach out to this girl, wrap her in his arms and tell her he was sorry for her pain, sorry he had stumbled across her path, ripped her out of normalcy and into agony.

"Gabriel, is everything okay?"

Damn. He turned and saw Sara standing in the living room in her tank top and skirt, no bra, toweling her wet hair dry.

Before he could respond, she glanced around him and saw the girl in the door.

"Rochelle? What are you doing here?"

Rochelle. That was her name. How ironic that Sara remembered when he didn't. "Sara, just give Rochelle and me a minute." He didn't think it was a good idea for Sara to be involved, for Rochelle to be further humiliated.

But when he turned back to face the girl, he caught a glimpse of shock and horror on her face before she sobbed and ran, her pace so fast Gabriel was afraid she was going to trip and fall down the narrow stairs.

"Damn." He said to Sara over his shoulder, "Stay here. I need to talk to her. I can't let her leave like that."

"Gabriel, I don't think that's a good idea."

But he was already heading down the stairs. This was his fault. He needed to fix it. He didn't know how, but he had to try.

When he got to the bottom of the stairs, he saw that Rochelle had stopped in the passage to the street, bent over her purse.

"Rochelle, I'm really sorry if I've hurt you, but I had no idea you felt this way about—"

Gabriel forgot what he had been trying to say when Rochelle turned, her big dark eyes wide and glazed with shock, pain, misery. Something fell out of her hand, clattering on the bricks, and he realized it was metal, long and narrow, with a straight edge. A switchblade. Her wrists and palms were covered in blood as she held them out to him, eyes beseeching, purse falling slack against her thigh.

It was almost impossible to process, to believe what he was seeing. Her pale fingers raised up, the vivid red of the blood streaming across them, back down her wrists, the jagged wounds brutal and desperate, the crimson stain pouring over the swarm of butterfly tattoos on her young, delicate skin.

He had done this. His weakness, his addiction, his gluttonous lust for escape, the need to boost his faltering confidence, his inability to cope with his responsibilities and the job he had been entrusted with.

Watch. Guide. Protect.

"Sara!" he yelled as loud as he could. "Call 911."

Yanking off his T-shirt, he reached out and pulled Rochelle's hands and wrists together, swaddling the shirt around them tightly, so her fingers entwined. Pulling to create pressure, hoping to staunch the flow as much as possible, he looked into her eyes. She was losing focus, her legs starting to crumple, and he slid his free arm around her back, holding her up against his chest so she wouldn't fall.

"Stay with me, Rochelle."

"I . . ." Her eyes started to roll back into her head.

Gabriel shook her a little. "Look at me."

She did, sad, confused, scared.

And Gabriel did what he never did. He locked gazes with her and let her see into his eyes, his soul, his true nature. He let her see the light and full force of his power, the hope and beauty and promise and future. Projecting into her mind, he showed her what she could have—a man who truly loved her, a house in the Quarter with a lush courtyard, her every heart's desire. He found her love of art and passion for sculpture in her racing thoughts, and so he showed her a successful career, where her work showed in national galleries and the art community knew her name. It was wonderful and it could all be hers if she held on, clung to it, chose it.

Her eyes widened, in wonder, awe, joy.

And then she lost consciousness, slack in his arms.

Sara drove back from the hospital, eyes scratchy and throat dry. Gabriel had insisted on staying with Rochelle, who was thankfully okay, but had been admitted. Sara was exhausted, with a clinging headache and a ravenous cotton mouth, which had to be from the absinthe drinking. She hadn't wanted to leave Gabriel, who was taking Rochelle's suicide attempt hard, but she had realized her presence was only distressing Rochelle, and distracting Gabriel.

So she had decided to come back to the apartment and leave him to wait for Rochelle's parents to arrive from Baton Rouge.

She had no idea how they had become embroiled in this girl's problems, or why Gabriel seemed to think he had any reason to feel guilty about anything, but she completely understood wanting to stay with her, to try to help her.

It had been heartbreaking when Sara had seen the girl in a faint, blood all over her hands and arms. When Sara had first grabbed the phone, dialing 911, and run down the stairs, she had almost fainted herself. The sight was so shocking, so unexpected, the blood jarring and vivid and a horrible reminder of her mother's death, that Sara had almost thrown up. She had still been drunk, which she hadn't realized until that moment, when her mind had rolled slowly and laboriously to process what she was seeing, to take action, to separate fear from reality and understand that Rochelle had tried to kill herself.

She hadn't seen that coming, hadn't understood how truly desperate Rochelle had been, and she had actually told Gabriel he shouldn't follow after the girl. Now she knew that they would have probably found Rochelle dead in the passageway in the morning if Gabriel hadn't had the compassion to go after her.

His face had been so intense, so rigid, so filled with self-condemnation when he had looked up at her, Rochelle slack against his chest, her blood smeared on his bare chest and forearms, that Sara had actually been frightened. It had made her realize she didn't know exactly what had happened to Gabriel's girlfriend, only that he clearly still lived with the damage from the tragedy every day, just like she did.

Interesting, though, that neither of them had chosen the out that Rochelle had. Sara had never wanted to die.

But maybe she and Gabriel had been slowly killing themselves with sleeping pills, alcohol, guilt, anguish.

She didn't want that for herself or for him. She wanted to live, to breathe in at the start of a new day and look forward to what was ahead.

Finding a spot on Dumaine, which she was starting to realize was a miracle in the French Quarter, she pulled in and then readjusted her car to be aligned better. The day was already hot, even though it was barely eight in the morning. It was quiet, the sound of water dripping down from the recently watered potted plants on the balcony above creating a rhythmic and soothing pattern. Sara stepped out and tipped her head left and right, trying to release the tension in her neck. Eventually when Gabriel got home, they were going to have to talk about Rochelle. Try to process what the hell had happened. And acknowledge what Rochelle had interrupted.

What had seemed so logical and reasonable when she'd been drunk now had her blushing in the daylight. She would have sworn on a stack of Bibles at the time that she wasn't drunk, and her thoughts had been so clear, her actions so natural, that she hadn't hesitated to touch herself in front of him. It had been right, good, sexy as hell. Last night.

Today she was feeling a bit like she wanted to run away and never be seen by Gabriel again, clothed or unclothed. God, what had she been thinking? He had told her straight-out he couldn't get involved with her, couldn't have sex with her. So her solution was to masturbate in front of him? Nothing about that made sense.

But it had been sexy. And he had liked it. She felt warm just remembering the look in his eye, the sound of his music swelling around her, the way he had grabbed her and tossed her on the piano. His tongue inside her.

Sara pushed open the gate and stepped inside, unable to prevent herself from glancing at the spot where she had found Gabriel with Rochelle. She was expecting to see dried blood splashed on the ground, but it wasn't there. Which made sense. Most of Rochelle's blood had been caught by her shirt and Gabriel's, and it wasn't the kind of wound that sprayed and dripped all the way down to the ground anyway. But Sara still looked before heading up the stairs.

And stopped in shock when she saw what was sitting in front of Gabriel's apartment door.

It was an unopened bottle of absinthe.

What the hell was that doing there?

Sara went up and studied the green bottle sitting there. It was the same brand that Gabriel had opened the night before. Maybe he'd had a second bottle. Maybe he'd bought another one to replace the one she had put a serious dent in. But she knew immediately that made no sense because he wouldn't have had time to do that and he wouldn't have left it sitting on the landing.

A cold chill raced down her spine. She darted her eyes back down the staircase, then tested the doorknob to the apartment, leaning around the bottle. It was locked. She'd locked it after the ambulance had left with Rochelle, before she and Gabriel had headed to the hospital.

Picking the bottle up, she saw there was a decorative tag attached to the neck with a ribbon. It was a quote.

In Him we have redemption through His blood, the forgiveness of sins.

Sara didn't know what it meant, or what the point was supposed to be, but it kicked the fear up another notch. It didn't look like something the liquor manufacturer had intended to be there. And someone had intentionally set the bottle out for her. Fumbling with the key and the bottle, she managed to get the door open, herself inside, and the door locked behind her.

Only to scream when she saw a man sitting on the couch typing on his BlackBerry, legs crossed casually.

"Whoa," he said, glancing over at her. "You have bigger pipes than I would have given you credit for given that you look like you have TB. In person you're even more waifish than the pictures Gabriel had of you."

Sara gripped her purse, trying to dig inside it for her cell phone. "Who are you?"

"I'm Alex, Gabriel's friend. We go way back. I'm surprised he hasn't mentioned me."

She shook her head, not sure if she should turn and run, or if she should believe him. He must have used a key to get into the apartment, which had to indicate he was Gabriel's friend, whether Gabriel had ever mentioned him to her or not. She and Gabriel didn't know each other that well, frankly. He probably had lots of friends she knew nothing about.

"You must be Sara."

Not sure what to say, she just nodded. "Yes." The assumption would be then that Gabriel had mentioned her to Alex, which further legitimized his claim of being a friend. But she was still suspicious and a little freaked out.

He stood up, tucking his BlackBerry into the pocket of his dress pants. He was dressed like he was headed into the office, his blue button-up shirt crisp and ironed. Alex had short, dark hair and the kind of smile that, while perfectly charming, almost looked condescending. Walking toward her, he stuck his hand out. "Gabriel told me about you. Nice to meet you."

"You, too." She shook his hand automatically.

"Where is Gabriel, by the way? I was hoping to talk to him."

"Uh, he's at the hospital. There was an incident outside our apartment last night." Sara suddenly realized she had referred to Gabriel's apartment as belonging to her as well, and felt heat start to creep up her cheeks. This was Gabriel's friend and she didn't want to sound presumptuous. She also didn't want to explain Rochelle's weird obsession with Gabriel.

"An incident?"

"A girl tried to kill herself and Gabriel is visiting her."

Alex rolled his eyes. "He's at it again, is he?"

"What do you mean?" Sara wanted a drink of water and some aspirin desperately. She felt like she was having a hard time processing information, like her brain had slowed to a snail's pace, and her head was throbbing.

"Gabriel. He gets too emotionally involved with these girls."

Sara raised an eyebrow. "Well, she did try to kill herself. He's just being compassionate."

Alex gave her a wry look. "I call it being stupid. You don't know how many times I've seen him do this."

"Do what?"

"Take in a broken woman thinking he's going to nurse her back to good mental health. Like a bird with a damaged wing."

Like Sara, maybe? Not a flattering thought.

"It's a big waste of his time. You can't fix another person."

That was very true. She could vouch for that with her own mother.

"I don't think he's trying to fix this girl. He just felt bad for her. It was a very random thing." She didn't know what else to say. She really wanted Alex to leave so she could take off her shoes and curl up on the bed with her kitten. Go to sleep finally.

"Well, I'll take off then, since he's not home. I need to go see my daughter. She's having boy trouble, as usual. But if you could tell Gabriel I stopped by, I'd appreciate it."

"Sure. It was nice meeting you. Sorry, I'm a little out of it from lack of sleep." Sara wondered how old Alex was that he had a daughter dabbling with dating already. She would have put him at no older than thirty-five, but then again, she herself had been nineteen when her own mother was thirty-five.

"I understand. It was nice meeting you, too." He smiled.

Sara remembered the bottle of absinthe in her hand. Alex must have brought it as a gift. "Oh, did you want me to give this to Gabriel?"

But Alex just shook his head and studied the bottle. "I didn't bring that. It was sitting on the doorstep when I got here."

"Oh." She wished he had. The alternative was too disturbing.

"And Sara, just a little warning. There will be others."

"Other what?" Gripping the green bottle and her purse, she just blinked at him, her mouth and face hot, palms sweaty. She really needed to lie down.

"Other girls. Women. They can't resist Gabriel. They all want to coax a smile from him, and they all want to be the one who is special, who manages to get a reaction from him. None of them can though, and they become obsessed with him."

There had been others, besides Rochelle? With that kind of intense reaction? That was a disturbing thought. Yet she could understand it. She herself had been drawn to Gabriel from the beginning, intrigued by his solitary life, his lonely eyes, his physical beauty. Didn't she want to think she was special, that he let her in, and her alone?

Alex added, "Don't let that happen to you, because it really is pathetic."

She felt a stab of humiliation. Of course it was. As was what she had done on the couch in front of him the night before.

Alex reached out and flicked the label of the absinthe bottle. "I didn't know Gabriel was back on this shit. Interesting." He pulled the attached card out to read it. " 'In Him we have redemption through His blood, the forgiveness of sins.' That's not a very sexy label for alcohol. It doesn't make me want to drink a drop. And it's wrong. Sins are never forgiven, and never forgotten."

Giving her a smile and a wave, he headed toward the door. "Have a good one, Sara."

Then he was gone and Sara was left wondering what the hell had just happened.

And with the knowledge that she knew much less about Gabriel than she had thought she did.

Chapter Fourteen

❦

From the Court Records of
the Willful Murder Trial of Anne Donovan,
State of Louisiana v. Jonathon Thiroux
January 14, 1850

ATTORNEY FOR THE DEFENSE, MR. SWIFT: Mr.
   Thiroux, describe to us what the room
   surrounding Miss Donovan looked like when
   you regained consciousness and discovered
   her dead.
MR. THIROUX: It was hot in the room and there
   was a sweet, sickly odor. It was dark, except
   for moonlight. Anne was lying on the sheet.
   She must have remade the bed with the
   intention of going to sleep because I had
   actually taken the sheet off earlier.
MR. SWIFT: Why did you do that?
MR. THIROUX: It was tattered.
MR. SWIFT: Tattered?
MR. THIROUX: Yes. She had hosted a visitor in
   her room prior to my arrival and I was
   offended by the evidence of that.

MR. SWIFT: So there was another man specifically in Anne Donovan's room before you arrived?

MR. THIROUX: Actually, he was still there when I arrived. I informed Madame Conti that he needed to vacate Miss Donovan's room as I had an understanding with her that Anne would always be available to me.

MR. SWIFT: So you were paying a retainer for her services?

MR. THIROUX: Yes.

MR. SWIFT: So it was unusual to see another man in her room?

MR. THIROUX: Yes, very. In the nine months I had been seeing Anne, I had never encountered another man in her room.

MR. SWIFT: Can you describe this man?

MR. THIROUX: I did not get a very good look at him, as his back was to me, and I left the room immediately. But he was dark-haired, with what appeared to be an olive complexion. I can get no more specific than that.

MR. SWIFT: But Madame Conti saw him in Miss Donovan's room?

MR. THIROUX: Yes. As stated, I demanded she force him to leave, which she did. I heard her offering him three girls for the price of one as compensation for his inconvenience.

MR. SWIFT: Did she refer to him by name?

MR. THIROUX: No, she did not.

MR. SWIFT: Were you inebriated at that point?

MR. THIROUX: Not in the slightest.

Gabriel was shaking the hand of the young, personable physician in the ER who had treated Rochelle, ready to leave now that her parents had arrived, when he suddenly realized what he had never bothered to investigate. He had read all the online articles in reference to Jessie Michaels's murder case. But he had never seen any pictures. The articles had all been text.

He wanted to see Dr. Rafe Marino, who Sara seemed to think was attractive and charming, with a heart of gold.

Gabriel had his doubts about the good doctor's true character, especially after his conversation with the Florida journalist.

It was the biblical and Michelangelo references. They had been rolling around in his head, bothering him, nagging that something was not right.

So instead of going home, he headed straight over to the library, ignoring the fact that he'd been up all night and hadn't eaten. He did a general search on Dr. Rafe Marino. He got what he wanted immediately. A staff picture from the hospital in Naples where Dr. Marino had worked prior to his arrest.

"Holy shit." Gabriel sat back in his chair, heart pounding. It couldn't be.

It was Raphael.

A fallen angel.

Once a healer.

And now, obviously, a killer.

The face smiled back at him, familiar and open. Raphael wasn't suave yet disdainful like Alex, or quiet and intense like Gabriel. Raphael had always been the one who could put people at ease, could draw out a smile, a laugh, even from the most devastated.

How could he take that trust and destroy mortal lives?

Unbelievable, just insane. Gabriel couldn't believe that Raphael was capable of such heinous acts. It wasn't possible to understand how anyone could do what had been done to those women, but Raphael, a man he had known, spoken to, shared meals with. That he had committed such evil, it was incomprehensible.

But true. And he was a demon, after all. Raphael had sinned like all the rest of them. He had succumbed to the pleasure of flesh and food and wine and turned his back on his duty. In the nineteenth century he had cared more for the cut of his coat than his position as coroner. But murder? Gabriel would have never guessed. It sickened him.

Tapping quickly, Gabriel did another search. This one yielded an e-mail address and phone number. Raphael hadn't tried very hard to cover his tracks. Working for twenty minutes, digging up everything Gabriel could—history, education, professional associations—on Rafe Marino, he hit the jackpot when he found that one Dr. Rafe Marino was the sole benefactor of a trust. The very trust that had purchased a house in New Orleans two years prior. On Dauphine Street.

It was the House of Rest for Weary Men.

Owned by Raphael.

Which unlocked the memory of the man, angry and swearing at Madame, leaving Anne's room. The voice that had sounded familiar to Gabriel, but which he'd spent a hundred and fifty years trying to place without success. It had been Raphael. He was absolutely certain of it, so obvious to him now he couldn't imagine why he had never realized it before.

Raphael had killed Anne.

Gabriel hadn't.

Relief and horror mingled together and left him staring blankly at the screen, the words blurring together.

"Are you okay?" the lady sitting next to him asked. "You look like you're going to be sick."

And then some.

"I'm fine, thanks," he said automatically, glancing over at her. She was in her eighties, her skin loose and peppered with age spots and veins. Her navy sweater enveloped her as she hunched over the computer keyboard, her glasses perched on her nose.

She patted his knee with her soft and delicate hand. "Whatever it is, this too shall pass."

"Sure." Wherever there was evil, there was always good, and this woman was his reminder of that. A memory of duties long ignored. So he smiled at her, and for the second time that day, he let someone see the depths of his power, the beauty, the promise, the vision of his palace in the sky.

Her hand gripped his knee tightly, the strength in her astonishing, as her eyes went wide. "Have you come to take me?" she asked.

"No. It's not your time yet." He could feel that in her. She had years of vitality still.

"Are you my guardian angel?"

The longing rose in his soul, aching and heavy, painful, dripping sorrow for what he had done, for what he had lost, for what he had betrayed and could never be again.

Gabriel stroked the top of her withered hand. "No. Just a friend."

From the Court Records of
the Willful Murder Trial of Anne Donovan,
State of Louisiana v. Jonathon Thiroux
January 16, 1850

ATTORNEY FOR THE DEFENSE: So, Dr. Raphael,
   what you're saying is that in your expert
   medical opinion, Jonathon Thiroux could not
   have killed Anne Donovan?
DR. RAPHAEL: That is what I'm saying. I do not
   believe Jonathon Thiroux had the strength to
   kill Anne Donovan.

From the Court Records of
the State of Florida v. Dr. Rafe Marino
July 26, 2007

PROSECUTOR: So, Detective Manson, what you're
   saying is that in your expert opinion, given
   the lack of forced entry, and the victim's
   daughter's assertion that her mother locked
   her doors and windows, the victim knew her
   assailant?
MANSON: That is what I'm saying. I can say
   there was no evidence anyone came into the
   house who wasn't let in by the victim.
ATTORNEY FOR THE DEFENSE: Objection! How can
   he know that the doors weren't left
   unlocked?
JUDGE: Sustained.
PROSECUTOR: Can you explain how you have
   reached the conclusion the victim knew her
   assailant?
MANSON: Well, how do you explain that the front
   and side doors were dead-bolted and chained
   yet the back door was wide open? What
   makes sense is that the victim came into the
   house with her assailant or she let him in,
   then locked the door behind him. Then after
   he killed her, he unlocked the back door and

> left, leaving the door a foot open so he
> wouldn't make any more noise than was
> necessary. That's the most logical scenario.

Gabriel was climbing the stairs to his apartment, wondering what exactly he should tell Sara—or not tell her—when the door was flung open and she stared down at him.

"Thank God you're home."

"Why, what's wrong?" Concern kicked in and he jogged up the remaining steps. Sara looked pale and shaken.

"Who's Alex?" she asked.

Great. Just what he needed, Alex sniffing around Sara. There was no telling what the demon would say to her. "I've known him a long time. Why? Was he here?"

"Yes. He was sitting on the couch when I got home. He said you gave him a key because you're old friends. I thought he brought this—"

She reached behind her and pulled a bottle off the table in his entryway. "But he said he didn't. It was just sitting outside the front door. Who would do that?"

It was a bottle of absinthe. Gabriel's mouth went dry. Alex was either lying and had in fact brought it as a way to mock him, or it had been another demon. Possibly Raphael. Only demons knew who Gabriel was, and what he had been. There wouldn't be any reason for anyone else to associate him with absinthe.

Whoever it had been, they were pushing him into a confrontation. He wasn't going to tolerate anyone interfering in his life, his problems. With his Sara.

But his first priority was reassuring her.

"I don't know who would do that." He took her elbow and gently urged her inside. "Come on, let's go in."

"Do you think . . ." She swallowed hard. "Do you think someone could have seen me last night? Drinking the absinthe and . . . everything?"

By everything, she meant touching herself. Lifting her skirt and stroking herself to a beautiful, shuddering orgasm. Then leaning against his piano while he tasted between her thighs with his tongue and lips. It was an everything he would love to repeat.

He wouldn't. Not after Rochelle.

But then again, Sara didn't seem obsessed with him in the aftermath, and he had poured all of his passion, feeling, intensity into her. It had been a touching with intimacy and emotion, frustration and lust, and yet while she had responded as a woman, she didn't seem to have altered her attitude toward him. Maybe she was immune to his punishment.

It was a dangerous path of rationalization.

It would happen. She would become obsessed, addicted to him.

It always did.

He couldn't live with himself if she became Rochelle.

"No, I don't think anyone saw you. How could they? This is the third floor and the only window in the room faces the courtyard and the roof of the carriage house."

She bit her fingernails. "You're right. But why the hell was there a bottle of absinthe sitting outside the door?" Running her fingers across her bottom lip, she paced, Angel darting out of her way and leaping onto the couch. "First the pictures, now absinthe. Someone is toying with me, and it's starting to really piss me off."

Gabriel could see that. She had pink cheeks, tousled hair, and an exasperated look on her face. While there was definitely fear in her eyes, there was also anger. She was mad that someone was interfering in her life.

"I want to be left alone."

"Me, too," he said with all sincerity. The question was, how much did he tell her about Raphael, who was known to her as Rafe? She liked the guy. Thought he was innocent. And Gabriel had no proof of anything other than the fact that Raphael had known both women, which of course he couldn't share with her. Nor could he tell Sara that he was concerned about Rafe's actions because he had in fact known him in the nineteenth century when he had been Jonathon Thiroux. "I can't explain what is going on here, but I want you to know that you're safe here with me, Sara. I'll protect you."

To the demon death, if necessary.

She didn't deserve that, had done nothing to bring this kind of fear, suffering, on herself. Gabriel couldn't undo the past, but he could prevent any more harm from befalling Sara. It felt like his fault, like he had somehow been responsible for introducing Raphael into Sara's world, which was totally irrational. He hadn't known that Raphael could have killed Anne, and had never thought of him as a threat to anyone. He had lost track of him years ago and had been perfectly content to not know anything about him.

Back in the nineteenth century, Raphael was actually the one who had introduced him to Anne. She had been Raphael's mistress first, but Gabriel had bought her away from him, attracted to her auburn hair and sweet smile. Raphael hadn't cared. He had said he was tired of her, had indicated she had a level of prudery he had no patience for.

But if Gabriel hadn't killed Anne, then Raphael had, which meant he had very much cared, hated. The relief that it hadn't been him, the very thing he had longed to believe for so many years, his innocence, didn't bring the comfort Gabriel had thought it would. It was a relief, yes, but with it came a fresh wave of guilt that if it was Raphael, he should have known. Should have prevented it.

Gabriel reached for Sara, needing to feel her in his arms, wanting her hands likewise on him. She came into his embrace from the side, wrapping one arm around his front, the other around his back, burying her face in his shoulder. Her body was soft, warm, petite alongside his, and he felt it again, that unmistakable swelling of emotion in his chest.

He was in love with her.

Yet she deserved so much more than him, a damaged burned-out shell of a man, with guilt that clawed and ate at him, and a control that vacillated depending on the day.

"How's Rochelle?" she asked, head still in his shirt.

It was that concern, that compassion, that intensity of heart and soul and feeling that he admired, adored, in Sara, and it was the very thing that would crush her if he let their relationship go any further. There was no future for them. He had to acknowledge that. Even more so now that he knew about Raphael.

"She was doing okay. She was awake when her parents got there. She seemed confused and embarrassed more than anything else." Gabriel stroked Sara's hip. "I feel so damn bad about what happened."

"It wasn't your fault."

Indirectly, it was. He knew that. Accepted responsibility.

Hated it, and wanted to fix it. But didn't know how. If he thought for one minute he could get a straight answer, he would go to a demon, like Alex, and ask if they knew how he could end his punishment. But he suspected Alex would either mock him or give him false answers for his own personal amusement. He had distanced himself from all the other demons, including Marguerite, who he had once considered a friend. He hadn't spoken to her since she'd betrayed him and lied during his trial.

"You need to stop doing that," she said.

"Doing what?"

"Your silence is your denial. You don't say anything when you disagree with me. It's something I've noticed. Obviously you don't like conflict any more than I do. But in this case, you are wrong. You're not responsible for whatever is wrong with Rochelle. She imagined a relationship, and she obviously has some serious issues that have nothing to do with you."

Or Rochelle had fallen victim to his demon lure. But Sara was right. He wasn't going to argue with her. There was no way to argue his point. And while it bothered him that Sara didn't know all of him, didn't understand the true depth of who he was and what he had seen, done, there was no option to tell her the truth. She would think he was insane and leave.

And he couldn't let her go.

"I guess this is where I stay silent again."

She gave a muffled laugh. "You're a good man, Gabriel St. John."

He wished he could claim that. "I haven't tried hard enough. I'm going to try harder from here on out." He needed to fight for redemption, for the right to live among mortals without the danger of causing them harm. He wanted the opportunity to use his gifts again, for the pleasure of people, and to inspire, to allow them to see beauty around and within themselves.

Escape no longer appealed.

He was ready to change, to make it all right.

"Gabriel, I have something to tell you." Sara took a deep breath, not at all sure how Gabriel was going to respond to the fact that she had lied to him. But she needed to tell him, now, before they went any further. He had let her into his life, into his work and his apartment. Into his sketching and his music.

He had offered her comfort, security, passion, and understanding. He had looked at her and let her know that he knew what it was like, how she felt, what grief and fear and addiction could do.

She owed him the truth.

"What's up?" he asked, squeezing her upper arm.

It was hard as hell to peel herself off of him and meet his eye, but she did it, because she was tired of being afraid, exhausted from the cowering and the worrying and the looking over her shoulder all the time. "There's something I didn't tell you about myself. I agreed to help you on this book because I wanted to solve my mother's murder, that's true. But I thought that was really a long shot . . . that if the police couldn't solve it and the court couldn't get a conviction, then there was nothing I could do. But I thought maybe in going through the case, comparing it to Anne Donovan's, I could find some closure."

She wrapped herself tighter around him, knowing he would pull away, not wanting him to. "Because what I haven't told you is that I'm interested in Anne Donovan's case because she was my great-great-grandmother. And I want to know why the women in my family are murdered the same way, generation after generation."

Gabriel's eyebrow went up as he stared at her. "Excuse me?"

"I'm Anne Donovan's descendent." She could feel it—he was moving away, trying to disengage himself from her arms—but she hung on. "And the coincidences between her murder and my mother's scared me. That's why I came here."

"Why the hell didn't you tell me? We have your DNA—we could have done a comp to see if our blood samples were Anne's or John Thiroux's or someone else's entirely." His hands were on her elbows now, trying to gently push her away. "You let me waste an entire afternoon looking to see if Anne Donovan had a child, when you knew she did. You knew the kid's name. You knew I was trying to track a descendent."

"I know and I'm sorry." She had felt guilty about that. "But the thing is, I didn't want you to think I was a nutjob. That I had ulterior motives or a bias." Maybe she hadn't really had a good reason, but she had been protecting herself. Plain and simple. "Everyone for the past year has been looking at me with pity, Gabriel, waiting for me to crack. They think I'm insane, and maybe I am. But the one secret I managed to keep during this whole ugly investigation and trial is that in every generation of my family, a woman has been murdered. Can you imagine the kind of story the media would make out of that? I'd be a freak show, looked at with pity, fascination, horror. I would have no chance at a normal life." Just the thought of the headlines, the media camped out on her lawn again, the flash photography going off in her face, filled her with panic. "I swear, some loon would probably even murder me just to be the one who sealed the 'curse.'"

Why wasn't he saying anything? He was just looking at her, eyes narrowed, frowning, head shaking slightly. "So you're saying that every generation has had a murder? What kind of murder? Domestic violence, robbery shooting, or random unsolved murder?"

"All of them were random unsolved murders." A chill went up her spine just saying it out loud. "My mother never seemed to think it was a big deal. She used to joke about it. I personally find it scary as hell. But I'm trying to tell myself it's a horrible coincidence, that the women in my family who were murdered all lived edgy, dangerous lives. With the exception of my grandmother. As far as I can tell, she was just a suburban housewife."

Gabriel had at least stopped trying to tug away from her, but now he looked puzzled. He wasn't actually looking at her, but over her shoulder. "I find that really disturbing," he said.

Somehow it was the right thing to say, yet the completely wrong thing she needed to hear. At the same time she wanted him to admit and acknowledge that it was weird, beyond coincidence, scary, she didn't want him to. Because Gabriel had his own baggage. Adding hers to his created a set too heavy to haul around. It might be the very thing that would make him definitively pull away from her. Literally and figuratively.

"I know. And I can't bear the thought of anyone knowing, of dealing with the fallout from that. Do you understand that?"

He nodded. "Yeah. I get that. But this changes everything."

"What does it change?" she asked, a sick churning in her gut kicking into overdrive. She relaxed her hold on him. She couldn't bind him to her by pure desperation and want. That would make her no different than Rochelle. Seeing, forcing what wasn't there. If he wanted to pull back, she had to let him.

Even if she had fallen in love with him, which she suspected she had.

That knowledge hit her harder than she would have expected. Hadn't she known she was in love with him? Maybe she had, and she'd chosen to ignore it, pretend that it was lust, attraction, interest brought about from their circumstances, their close proximity. Because maybe it wasn't love. Maybe she was like Rochelle, having feelings that were false, spinning fantasies about loving him and being loved in return.

But she didn't believe that. She knew what she felt, knew it was real, knew that she loved him clearly and poignantly for the man he was, whether he would ever return those feelings or not.

It wasn't wise to love him, not at all self-protective, fraught with the danger of getting her heart trampled, her feelings lacerated, but God knew she couldn't control it. That was what the last year of her life had taught her—control was elusive. She couldn't manipulate or change certain events in her life, but she could choose to accept and live the best she possibly could. The search for control, for answers, had landed her in rehab. Sometimes there were no answers.

She had to live with that.

And if Gabriel wanted to walk, she would gather herself and move on. If anything, she had learned she was a survivor.

"This changes the respect I had for you. I thought you were lovely before, Sara, but now I think you're truly the most amazing woman I've ever known."

It almost made her cry. Suddenly and without warning, they were there, tears in her eyes, from relief and gratitude and modesty. God, she didn't feel amazing, but she wanted Gabriel to think she was. It felt so freeing to have someone look at her and think that she had it together, that she wasn't a wreck, a mess, a woman on the verge of a breakdown. She didn't think she was. She had skirted the edge a few times, but never entirely fallen off, and she was tired of everyone assuming a crash was inevitable.

"Thank you," she said, blinking hard. "I appreciate you saying that. And we can do whatever you want with my DNA for comparison."

"We can do whatever *you* want, Sara. Only whatever you're comfortable with." He pulled away, but only to turn fully to her and take her cheeks in his hands. His eyes searched her, for what she wasn't sure. "I've been selfish. I know how difficult all of this must be for you, and I haven't been sensitive enough to that."

Ironically, she felt the same way about him. "I don't think you've been selfish at all. We're just trying to wade through ugly stuff . . . It's hard. It's emotional. I actually think we're doing a pretty damn good job of holding it together. Especially since we had the incident with poor Rochelle."

He looked away and sighed, his hands falling away from her face. "I want you to take everything Alex says with a grain of salt, okay? Alex is charming, but he's also a liar."

Sara raised an eyebrow, not sure how he'd jumped back to Alex. "Okay. But why would he want to lie to me? I don't even know him."

"He lies just for the fun of hurting people."

"So why are you friends with him?"

"I'm not. We've just known each other a long time."

"So he probably brought the absinthe then?" That actually reassured her in a weird way. It was better to know how it had gotten there than to imagine something worse. That someone had been watching them, mocking her.

"Probably."

"You drank absinthe, didn't you? When you were having your drinking problem." She was positive that's what Alex had meant by his comments.

Gabriel nodded briefly, leaning down and scooping up Angel with one hand as the kitten walked past him. He settled her against his chest and scratched behind her ears. "Yeah. It was appealing because you don't feel drunk. You feel very in control, very intelligent."

"I understand." And had the burning cheeks to prove it. She had felt utterly in control peeling her clothes off and touching herself in front of him. Which they had yet to discuss or even mention.

"But that's all in the past. I don't drink anymore at all."

"I know." Why did it seem like he was telling her something else? Reassuring her, yes, but himself also. And there was something lingering, waiting, hovering between them . . . like everything had been said and yet nothing.

Or maybe she was just tired and needed sleep. It had been almost two days since she'd slept, and she had gotten drunk in the interim. That wasn't good for her body, or her state of mind. She was exhausted and hypersensitive.

Which might explain why she said randomly, "Your mistakes shouldn't supersede your gifts."

He brought Angel up to his face and nuzzled the fur on the back of her neck with his chin. "What is that supposed to mean?"

"I mean that your drinking problem shouldn't prevent you from drawing and playing the piano. You have extreme talent . . . those are gifts that you can't deny. They need to be shared."

She wasn't sure what she expected him to say, but he didn't say anything. He didn't protest, didn't agree, didn't scoff, just put Angel down on the couch and looked at Sara. His poignant looks destroyed her, because they said everything, yet nothing. They were cries for help, tosses of defiance, pleas for understanding, hints at love, yet a barrier that warned the world off. He broke her heart with those looks, made her yearn for solidarity, togetherness, for the comfort of leaning on another person, for the pleasure of being that shoulder in return. To take care of and be cared for. To love and be loved.

"Come lie down with me," he said, reaching for her hand. "I need some sleep."

Apparently that was all Gabriel could offer her.

He had warned her, and she had harbored no illusions that it could be more, really, when she had thought that she could have an affair with him, some hot sex to feel good, to forget. But Gabriel didn't do casual sex, that was obvious, and maybe she didn't either. If she never had before, why the hell would now be different, when she was actually emotionally engaged, intrigued, longing for Gabriel in ways she couldn't have him? Sex would be disastrous, would shatter her resistance, strip away her barriers, show him the truth about what she was feeling.

She suspected neither one of them was ready for that.

But Gabriel could and was offering her companionship, a quiet and safe place to stay, to rest.

She took his hand and walked to his bedroom with him.

Chapter Fifteen

He disappointed her.

He could sense that. Sara wanted more. She wanted him to touch her, to make love to her.

Gabriel wanted to do that. Both his body and his soul yearned for that connection with her. But he couldn't. He wouldn't be able to live with himself if he stripped away Sara's strength, if he made her miserable and desperate and clinging.

He wanted to give her everything, to let her know how he felt, but he didn't know how, and his mind was distracted, swirling with the implications of what she had told him about her connection to Anne Donovan.

"What time is it?" she asked as she climbed onto the bed, peeling the comforter back.

"I don't know. It doesn't matter. We're just going to lie down." He knew that Sara would worry about the time, would mentally tick away the minutes as she lay there and couldn't find sleep, so he didn't want her to think about it. In the past ten days she had probably slept two or three hours a night, and none the night before. He wanted her to relax, to fall deep into sleep.

Because when she woke up he was going to have to tell her about Rafe. Or at least the portion he could tell her.

Sara sighed when her head hit the pillow. "I feel like I've run a marathon. My joints ache."

"Tension and alcohol. Not a good combination. I shouldn't have let you drink last night." He debated taking his jeans off, but figured that was an incredibly bad idea. He settled for kicking off his shoes and peeling his T-shirt off before getting in bed. Flicking his hair out of his eyes, he realized he could probably use a haircut. But he could never be bothered. Though he wondered what Sara thought of his hair, if she thought it was too long.

"Apparently there were a lot of things I shouldn't have done last night."

Sara was lying on her side, facing away from him so he couldn't see her face, but her tone was wry, slightly embarrassed, and Gabriel didn't like it. "Hey." He was going to touch her hip, but stopped himself. "Don't regret anything else. I don't. You're a beautiful, sensual woman." And he wanted to bury himself so deep inside her that she would scream with pleasure.

"Thanks." She glanced over her shoulder at him. "But come on, you have to admit, I have reason to feel embarrassed."

"No, you don't." Hand behind his head, he stared at her, frustrated, wanting her to understand. He fucking would if he could. It wasn't her. It was totally and completely him. "See if you can get out of your lease," he said. "Stay here until you're ready to go home to Florida."

Sara didn't say anything, just stared at him, her mouth slightly open, tongue darting out to wet her bottom lip. "Why?" she asked finally.

"Because I want you to."

"Okay." Then she sighed again. "I want to sleep. Why won't it ever come to me?"

"Your mind is too busy, too crowded." Hell, he could see the wheels turning every time he looked at her. Unable to resist, he reached out and stroked the back of her hair. It was soft, springier than his, and his finger got caught in a curl.

"Do you sing?" she asked, shifting back slightly so she was closer to him.

The bed was getting warm and he was getting sleepy himself. "I love to sing. I'm just not all that good at it."

"But you're an artist, a musician. I bet you sing better than you think you do."

He wasn't being modest. He really couldn't sing. "No, I don't." No matter how hard he tried, his voice was flat. He could hear music, could coax the piano to provide the right sound, but his voice was incapable of hitting the notes.

"You have to sing for me sometime," she said, her words trailing off into a big yawn. "I want you to play 'Beth' by Kiss on the piano and sing it for me."

Gabriel laughed softly. "I can do that if we download the sheet music." She'd regret it, but it wouldn't be a bad regret, not like another could be if he gave her what they both really wanted. "Why Kiss?"

"Because it's the first song that popped into my head that has piano in it. My mom was a huge Kiss fan."

"I see."

"Gabriel?"

"Yes?" He forced himself to remove his hand from her head, though he snuck in one last stroke, pulling her blond strands out in front of him and letting them fall down onto her back.

"Nothing." Her words were mumbled.

Disappointed, wishing she had said whatever she'd been thinking, he waited. Then realized that Sara was in the first vestiges of sleep, little rushes of air coming from her mouth. Her body was tense still, shoulders tight, arms clasped in front of her, knees jutting out.

She wouldn't sleep long like that.

When he did a cursory sweep of her thoughts, sort of a surface scan, not wanting to violate her privacy, Gabriel saw and felt nothing but anxiety from her. She was worried. About Rafe. About him, Gabriel. About the kitten. About Rochelle. About herself. About her friend Jocelyn. About her mother's father. About her job. About Anne Donovan.

It was no wonder she couldn't sleep.

So Gabriel leaned over Sara and touched her forehead, her temple, caressing her cheek with his finger, quieting her worries, banishing her anxieties, filling her with warmth, with pleasant dreamy thoughts.

"I've fallen in love with you," he whispered, brushing his

lips across the bare skin of her shoulder where her tank top had slipped.

She gave a shuddery sigh in her sleep, and Gabriel reluctantly pulled back.

He'd given her what he could.

Now he just wanted to watch her sleep.

⁂

Sara slept for fourteen hours. She couldn't believe it. She'd been out cold from 5 p.m. to 7 the next morning. When she'd woken up, Gabriel had been sitting up in bed next to her reading the newspaper. Which meant not only had she slept, she had slept through his getting in and out of bed, possibly several times.

It felt like a major accomplishment. A triumph.

Then she and Gabriel had spent the day walking around the Quarter, playing tourist. The history he knew amazed her. He seemed to have a story, a thought, a reference for every street and nearly every building. He talked about the Pontalba, the Cabildo, the Creole ballroom on Orleans Street. But he never told the story she wanted to hear, which was that of his girlfriend.

She wouldn't pry, but she wanted to know. Wanted him to trust her with his hurt, his guilt. But he never said anything.

Instead he just occasionally smiled at her and told her anecdotes about people long dead, and while it was entertaining, intriguing, it struck Sara that everything she and Gabriel did and talked about was driven by the dead.

It was an eerie thought.

When they sat down on the steps in front of the Mississippi River, the sun beating down on their backs, Sara knew they needed to finish their business with the dead, and move forward as the living. There were no answers. There had never been answers. There never would be definitive answers. It only was speculation and isolated facts.

"What do you want to do about the case?" she asked, leaning forward onto her knees. "I can give you a DNA sample for comparison to Anne Donovan's. If we want rush results, I can overnight everything to my friend Jocelyn. She can do it in the lab after hours in a day or two."

Maybe she should even go back to Florida herself for a few days. She did want to see Rafe before he left for the West Coast.

Strangely enough, she wasn't feeling the fear anymore. The pictures, the newspaper article her mother had received, the absinthe bottle—it was all disturbing, and not her imagination. Someone was watching her. Someone who knew something. Possibly a murderer. Yet she felt like she had reached the bottom of the depths of her fear, had seen the worst, had lived with fear for so long that it no longer had the power to paralyze her.

Instead she felt a strange sort of calm, an acceptance.

Maybe it was getting a full night's sleep.

Maybe it was looking at the horrific possibilities of all that could happen and realizing she couldn't control the future, only her now.

Maybe it was the serenity of being with Gabriel, the magic of meeting someone who was a mirror, a reflection of all her pain and sorrow and yet hope. Sara glanced over at his profile, at his sharp nose, his beautiful cheekbones, his hair dancing in the small breeze.

Maybe it was falling in love.

Everything seemed easier to face when you had a man standing behind you with his hand on the small of your back.

She could be and was independent. Had been since the age of thirteen. But it was pleasant to have someone understand her, anticipate her, offer such a subtle support. Gabriel wasn't the type for overblown gestures like flowers or public displays of affection, but she liked his quiet style better.

It was sexier to have him sketch her in private than to have him hold her hand in public.

No question about it, she was in love with him, and she had the conviction that they would be together. They were together. Sex, some sort of permanency, would come later, when they were both ready for it. But they were together.

"I need to tell you something," he said, interrupting her dreamy sun-soaked musings.

"Yeah? What's that?" Wary of his tone, she glanced over at him. He looked uncomfortable with whatever he was about to say.

"Doing a comparison in your lab is a good idea. And the thing is, we can take it a step further. Because now we know you're Anne Donovan's descendent." He cleared his throat. "And I'm Jonathon Thiroux's. So if your DNA and my DNA don't have markers that match the blood found on the knife, then there was a third person in the room who nicked themselves when they stabbed Anne."

Sara sat up straighter and gaped at him. "You're Jonathon Thiroux's descendent?"

He nodded, staring straight ahead at the river, fingers drumming on his knees.

"Were you planning on telling me?" And how dare he express indignation the day before that she had kept her biology a secret when he had been withholding the same information and still had, even after her confession?

"Probably. Eventually. But I didn't want you to think I was biased. I actually don't think Jonathon Thiroux did it, but I suspect you do."

"I do think he did it. I think he was a psychopath." It was the only thing that made sense to her. There hadn't been anyone else in the vicinity that they could tell from the distance of a hundred and fifty years. The evidence was lousy, the facts all open for dispute. But no one had doubted that Jonathon Thiroux had been in the room. And it seemed the most logical explanation to Sara. In 1849 they hadn't known what a psychopath was, nor had they access to forensic analysis. But the whole point of Gabriel's book was that both were irrelevant when a conviction was at the mercy of a judge and jury influenced by the media.

Yet she thought he did it.

She added, "I think it's natural to be biased if he's an ancestor of yours. But I don't think you have any reason to conclude that anyone other than Thiroux did it." For some reason, she felt irritated with him. The whole case took on a different perspective knowing that he did in fact have some sort of personal stake in it. Not that she was any different. She'd withheld her own history from him too.

Yet she was still irritated, irrationally or not.

"And I think Rafe Marino killed your mother."

"*What?*" Sara went from irritated to furious. "Why would you even say that? I told you it's not Rafe."

"Why are you so sure? Is it because you have feelings for him?"

Sara's face went hot and her hand flew up. "Oh, you did *not* just say that."

That Gabriel of all people would accuse her of pining for her mother's lover made her furious. "Why can't a man and a woman like each other without people assuming that they're harboring secret love?"

"I don't mean that you had a relationship, I just mean that if you care about him, it would be really hard to accept that he could do something so horrible. You said yourself that you didn't want to believe he could be capable of that kind of violence because it called into question your judgment."

"He didn't do it." Maybe that was just her being stubborn. But damn it, she had seen the way Rafe had looked at her mom. "My mom wasn't easy to love, and he loved her."

"People kill those they claim to love."

"Like Jonathon Thiroux killed Anne Donovan?"

Gabriel's jaw tightened. "I don't believe he ever claimed to love her. Or she him. But he doesn't seem like a man capable of murder."

Sara threw up her hands in exasperation. "Neither does Rafe! You're not using the same argument, the same standard for both cases."

"Neither are you. You said Jonathon Thiroux was a sociopath, that he charmed everyone and fooled them into thinking he was just a quiet artist. So why can't Rafe Marino have done the same thing?"

He had a point, which was irritating in the extreme. "Well, why do you think he did it? The prosecutor couldn't prove it."

"Did you hear that Bible quote? There's something off about that."

"Maybe he was bored in prison and took to reading the Bible. I would think being accused of murder would make you search for a higher power."

"Or maybe he enjoys that his crime is known only to him and God."

Sara just stared at Gabriel. "I guess you're right. Only God and the murderer know irrefutably who killed my mother. The same for Anne Donovan. But I don't think it was Rafe and I'm going back to Florida to say good-bye to him and run the DNA." What had just been an idea five minutes earlier now suddenly seemed absolutely essential. "We can fly since it's faster."

"We?" Gabriel frowned at her. "I'm not going to Florida."

"Why not? I need your blood." And she wanted to be with him. On a consistent and regular basis. She wanted her and he to be a *we*.

"I'm not giving you my blood."

"Why not?" Now that just flat-out astonished her. "You just said you're Thiroux's descendent and that we could run the DNA. You and I are the key to isolating Anne and Jonathon from someone else."

"But there's no way I'm going to put in the book that either of us is a descendent of them, because neither one of us needs or wants that kind of notoriety or scrutiny, so really there's no point in running the data."

"But don't you want to know? Isn't that the whole point?"

"Maybe we're not meant to know."

She could only gape at him. It was like he'd done a complete one-eighty. And he was just staring out at the river, eyes narrowed, fingers tapping, tapping, tapping a restless rhythm on his knees.

"You're kidding."

"Nope."

"Okay." Not really. She wanted to smack some sense into him, but knew that wasn't the method of reasoning to use with Gabriel. He would only withdraw if she started shouting at him. "You can still come to Florida with me."

"I don't like to travel."

"It's just to Florida, not China. It's a two-hour flight." Maybe he was afraid of flying. That was a common enough fear. "We can drive if you want."

But he just shook his head. "No, I don't want to go."

Gabriel was well aware that Sara was staring at him like he had entirely lost his mind, but he didn't have a choice. He was bound to New Orleans and couldn't leave. There was no way around it. And he couldn't give her his blood because she would discover he wasn't Jonathon Thiroux's descendent, but the same man.

But he didn't like the way she reached for him, hooking her arm around his elbow, her chin resting on his shoulder. It made the ache in his heart all that much deeper.

"Gabriel," she said, her voice coaxing, close to his ear. "I'd really like you to go with me."

"No, I really can't." It felt terrible to say, and he knew he was hurting her, but he didn't have any other options. The truth wasn't possible and he didn't want to spin a lie.

She made a sound of frustration and pulled back. "You just told me you think Rafe killed my mother."

He turned, not sure where she was headed with that statement. "Yeah, and you said you don't believe me."

"But if you believe Rafe is capable of violence—murder— why would you let me go to Florida to meet with him alone? Aren't you at all worried that he might hurt me?" She twisted her hair on the side of face and held the coil on her shoulder. "Not that he would, but you seem to think he could. So don't you care about me at all?"

Her lip had started to quiver and he could see how that angered her. It was slicing him, the burning guilt and regret tearing through him, and he wanted to just pull her into his arms, to tell her that he loved her, that if he had his way, he would never let her leave him. But they were sitting in public, a dozen people around them, the lap of the water on the dock a reminder that this wasn't the time or the place for revelations. In fact, there would never be an appropriate time to tell her that he was a demon, immortal, bound to the city of his shame for an indefinite period of time.

He didn't want her to go to Florida because he didn't want to be without her. But he wasn't worried about her safety. Because Gabriel was 99 percent sure that Raphael, or Rafe as he called himself now, was back in New Orleans. He was the face in the window of the house on Dauphine that Sara had seen. He had dropped the bottle of absinthe off as a mocking gift.

"Of course I care about you, Sara. I care about you tremendously. But if you want to go to Florida, I can't stop you."

And truthfully, there was a benefit to her being gone. Gabriel had to confront Raphael, and that could get ugly. Because Gabriel was going to get a confession from him, for both murders, and maybe all the murders on down the line of

Sara's family, regardless of what it took. Gabriel was no longer an angel, but he could vanquish another fallen one if he had justification, and he did.

Anne hadn't deserved to die. And she had because of her association with Raphael, with him.

So he was going to punish Raphael, for what he had done to Anne, and to Sara. And possibly to all the other women in Sara's family who had suffered the same horrific fate.

"You can't stop me?" she said flatly.

"No. You're a grown woman. You can do what you want."

"You could say, 'I don't want you to go. It's dangerous.' You could say, 'I'll go with you to make sure you're safe.' You could say, 'Stay here and just overnight the lab work to your friend.' But you're not. You're just sitting there." Her voice was getting high and shrill and she was jerking on his arm to emphasize each point she made.

Gabriel almost wanted to tell her the truth. Almost wanted to blurt out who and what he was, what he'd seen, what he'd done, what he felt. Instead, he gathered his strength, his resolve, his determination. He had to do what was right for Sara, not what he wanted. So he looked her in the eye and said, "Stay here and just overnight the lab work to your friend."

He knew it would piss her off. And it did.

She gasped and dropped her hand from his arm. Tears in her eyes, she popped up on the steps. "I'm going back to pack."

"Okay, I'll walk with you." He stood up too, stretching out his arms as he turned to follow her up the stairs.

"Gee, thanks so much," she said sarcastically.

He could have said something. Knew she wanted him to.

But Gabriel kept his mouth shut.

Chapter Sixteen

JURY SET TO DELIBERATE
IN THIROUX TRIAL!

January 22, 1850—After instructions from the judge, the jury will go into seclusion to deliberate the verdict in the shocking and sometimes unbelievable trial of Mr. Jonathon Thiroux, accused of stabbing Anne Donovan seventeen times to her death. While it would seem the prosecution has a strong case, one can only speculate what a jury will decide. Mr. Thiroux is an attractive, quality member of our city's society, a true peer to those sitting in the box, who has never displayed any violence in a public setting. It is hard for the mind to wrap itself around the concept that such a gentle artist could lift a bowie knife and strike with such ferocity and ill intent, especially when one looks into the frequently confused and sad eyes of the defendant.

If Mr. Thiroux is found guilty, anticipate the temperance and vigilance movements to gather steam and push their opposition to spirits, for if a man such as Jonathon Thiroux can kill under the influence, they would ask you to imagine it in the hands of the less gently bred. The prosecutor maintains that the question of the connection of alcohol to crime will be debated another day, and not through this case, but the majority will recognize that this is naïve. It was public outcry that forced the initial arrest, not justice for Miss Donovan, and from the beginning the question of the influence of alcohol on behavior has been indelibly wrapped around this case just as the oppressive heat of summer tendrils about our city.

Sara hung up the phone after purchasing her airline ticket and went to pack her suitcase, the unmistakable and irritating feeling of tears in her eyes yet again. She didn't know why she felt like crying. She was angry, maybe irrationally so, given the length and depth of her relationship with Gabriel. She had no right to assume anything or to expect anything from him.

But she had. She did.

It made her angry at herself. She had wanted something from Gabriel, right from the beginning, without even being aware of it. She had thought he could provide it, only to discover that she really didn't know him as well as she'd thought she did.

Tossing her suitcase on his bed, she started shoving random clothes into it, pulling her things out of his drawers. That upset her even more. She had actually unpacked her clothes into his drawers. Yet they'd never even had sex. How weird was that? She had allowed herself to get carried away by that friendship, that sense of comfort she felt with him. She'd made assumptions.

Now she felt like a fool.

Gabriel was tapping his absinthe spoons in the other room. She could hear the frantic, agitated rhythm of two spoons hitting the desk simultaneously. Absinthe. God. Why had he let her drink it when he knew exactly what it did? He'd admitted it had been his drink of choice prior to his sobriety.

It didn't make sense. None of it made sense. Gabriel had

withheld important information from her, had accused Rafe of murder, yet was perfectly willing to let her go to lunch and pal around with Rafe.

Sara leaned over Gabriel's bed, which neither one of them had bothered to make after her marathon sleep session, to snag her pillow. She never traveled without her down pillow. Dragging it across the bed, she was irritated to see that one of Gabriel's long caramel-colored hairs was stuck to her white pillowcase. It was irrational, but seeing that made her absolutely furious. He wouldn't have sex with her, but he could shed on her linens, depositing his DNA all over the place.

The random thought made her pause in the act of picking the hair off the pillow, her original intention to fling it down onto *his* pillow. Wait a minute. Tossing it defiantly back at him made no sense. It was his DNA. In her possession. Glancing toward the door, reassuring herself that he couldn't see her, Sara took the hair and unzipped the makeup bag she had already slung into her suitcase. Wrapping the hair around a lipstick, she settled the tube and hair in the bottom of the bag, zipped the case back shut, and jammed it in her purse. She could head down to Royal Street and mail it overnight to Jocelyn with the other samples so she could have the results sooner. Maybe Gabriel wasn't curious to see what a comparison would show, but she was.

It wouldn't change the past or the future, but she wanted to know if Jonathon Thiroux was a killer.

From the Court Records of
the Willful Murder Trial of Anne Donovan,
State of Louisiana v. Jonathon Thiroux
January 23, 1850

FOREMAN: We the jury find the defendant,
    Jonathon Thiroux, not guilty of murder in
    the first degree.

From the Court Records of
the State of Florida v. Dr. Rafe Marino
July 31, 2007

FOREMAN: We the jury find the defendant, Rafe
Marino, not guilty of murder in the first
degree.

Gabriel pulled up to the terminal at the airport the next
morning and put his car into park. When he glanced over to
ask Sara what time her flight was supposed to arrive in
Naples, she was already opening the passenger door and
climbing out. Great. She was just going to grab her suitcase
and leave without saying a word.

Turning his car off, he jumped out and beat her to the trunk
of the car, pulling out her suitcase before she could. He set it
on the ground and pulled the handle up, facing her. It had been
a cold, quiet day and night, with her avoiding speaking to him
more than was absolutely necessary, and he was frustrated. He
missed her. Wanted to see her smile.

"Call me when you get in," he said.

She just nodded. "Thanks for watching Angel."

"Sure, no problem."

The longing to touch her, to reassure, to make everything
right again, was almost overwhelming. Gabriel clenched his
fists and studied her, wanting her to see in his eyes what he
couldn't say in words. Wanting her to know that there were a
million things he wanted to tell her but couldn't. That she had
stepped into his lonely life and made it better. Made him better. That he had met and known a lot of women, but that she
was the only one who had ever made him feel such an acute
longing, such true, deep love.

"You're coming back, aren't you?" he asked.

"Probably."

"Probably? No, you need to come back." He wanted a
commitment, a promise. Needed to hear that she would be
back, and soon. She wouldn't leave her kitten with him per-
manently, he was positive of that, but he wanted her to return
to be with him, not just to collect the cat.

"Why should I come back?" Her head tilted and she was
asking so much more. She was asking for all the answers, for
everything.

He gave her all he could. "Because I want you to."

Sara sighed.

Gabriel ground his teeth together, desire, frustration, love all spilling up and over and making him want to kick her suitcase. Or more accurately, to pull Sara into his arms and kiss her senseless.

Instead he settled for a watered down nothing of a kiss that he brushed over her forehead and a muttered "Be careful," before he turned and walked away, afraid of what else he might say or do.

Afraid that if she asked again, he would tell. Touch.

But when he got in the car and looked in the rearview mirror, she was already walking through the airport doors, without a single glance back, and he was regretful anyway.

Either way, he was going to lose, and he hated it.

⁂

Rafe wasn't home. In fact, it looked like he had moved out. Sara stood on the front walk of his condo and glanced around. Everything was quiet. The blinds were partially open and there was no furniture in his dining room.

He had left. Without telling her.

Stunned and hurt, Sara felt more tears pricking her eyes. Damn it, she hated to cry, and she'd been on the verge for twenty-four hours.

She wouldn't do it.

Taking a deep breath, she dialed Rafe on her cell phone, leaving a voice mail for him to call her back when he didn't pick up.

She had turned to head back to her rental car and to Jocelyn's apartment, where she was staying, when she almost collided with a woman with dark hair and big sunglasses. "Oh! Sorry."

"It's okay." The woman smiled. "You're Sara, aren't you?"

Anyone knowing her name made her wary now, so Sara said cautiously, "Do I know you?" She didn't recognize the woman, but the sunglasses make it harder to see her features. Sara estimated the woman was in her late twenties, and that she had money, given her sundress and expensive handbag. She had a firm, curvy figure, and her dress was flattering, her demeanor confident and sensual.

"No. I'm Rafe's girlfriend."

Sara took an instinctive step back and said, "What?" Since when the hell did Rafe have a girlfriend? Her mother was his girlfriend.

"I'm Marguerite." She stuck out her hand. "Rafe's told me a lot about you."

He'd told *her* jackshit about Marguerite. Sara took her hand and shook it lightly. "Where is he, by the way?" She couldn't force a nice-to-meet-you platitude because she really had no goddamn interest in meeting the woman who had replaced her mother in Rafe's life.

She was angry. It had been a year already, and she understood that eventually he would move on, but it seemed too soon. She hadn't moved on, not yet. How had he? Plus he'd been on trial for murder. When the hell had he been dating?

"He's moved in with me. I just stopped over to pick up his mail. It's not being forwarded correctly."

"Oh, I see. Well." Sara had no clue what the hell to say. "I just left him a voice mail, but tell him I said hello. I'll only be in town for two days if he wants to give me a call." She had wanted to see him, but now she wasn't sure she did.

"I'm sure he'll want to talk to you. Maybe we can go out to dinner."

So the three of them could discuss how he'd been tried for her mother's murder? Yeah, that sounded like good times. "Sure. Lovely." She was such a bad liar and she wanted away from whoever the hell her name was. "Nice meeting you. I have an appointment I have to run to."

Sara waved and started toward her car.

The woman called after her, "I'll see you soon. And say hi to Gabriel for me."

That brought Sara to a grinding halt. Heart pounding, she turned around, wondering if she could have possibly just heard that. The woman was already walking in the opposite direction across the parking lot, her back to Sara, too far away to question.

But she'd heard that name, coming from that strange woman's lips. No question about it.

The real question was how in the hell could Rafe's new girlfriend know Gabriel St. John?

Chapter Seventeen

Gabriel picked his way down the narrow alley next to the house on Dauphine Street, tromping through brush and over a random pile of bricks. Ending up behind the house, he assessed the windows and the door. Unlike some of the neighboring houses, this one still had the original wooden pane windows and no evidence of a deadbolt on the door. While not dilapidated, it was easily one of the shabbier houses on the block, paint peeling and various rusted-out pieces of furniture and car parts strewn across the small back courtyard.

Deciding the easiest approach was the door, Gabriel went up the brick step, turned the knob, and shoved, using his immortal strength. The lock gave and the door swung open with a slight squeak. Stepping in, Gabriel paused to get his bearings. This room was a kitchen now. Gabriel couldn't remember how it had been used in the House of Rest, but it looked like it had been modernized in the eighties. The cabinets were dark, the walls a ruddy yellow, a red fruit-themed wallpaper border hung above the cabinets.

The overall effect was tired and gloomy, the original charm of the transom over the door, the thick moldings, and the wood floor lost under the influence of the drop ceiling and the muted yellow countertops. But someone was obviously in residence, since there was a dirty coffee mug in the sink and a sticky spoon on the countertop.

Moving forward through the kitchen door into the next room, Gabriel saw that a half bathroom had been added in the corner, and the remaining room was being used as an office, a desk and bookcase prominent in it. The house was shotgun style, with the rooms leading off of each other, and no central hallways. When he moved into the front room, he recognized it as the original parlor, where he had entered from the street so many nights all those years ago. At some point it had been painted a mauve color, which offended his artistic sensibilities in the extreme, and the floor was carpeted in a periwinkle blue, but beyond that, the room was unchanged. The fireplace and moldings were intact, and the front windows still had traditional shutters.

He could see it, the way it had looked then, with its scarlet sofas and peeling wallpaper, smoke hanging in the air, the women spilling out of their gowns, perched on the laps of men as they watched them play cards, waiting for the moment when the wine and the winning would cease, and the gentlemen would seek comfort upstairs. Gabriel could still hear the random and sour notes being pounded out on an out-of-tune piano that Madame had won in a game of keno, and could only marvel now how the level of his tolerance for depravity and disgusting surroundings had increased in conjunction with his addiction.

While it wasn't as crass as it had been as a cheap bordello, it wasn't a well-loved house either. Most of the structure and decor looked like it hadn't been bothered with in a good twenty years. The stairs had also been carpeted in the offensive blue, and the railings a dirty white that begged for fresh paint. Gabriel jogged quickly up the stairs, knowing that what he was looking for was waiting for him.

The succession of little rooms seemed to have been consolidated into two larger bedrooms and a bathroom. But oddly enough, or maybe appropriately so, Anne's little room at the end of the hallway had been left untouched, serving as a minute guest room with a daybed.

"John, isn't my room just lovely?" Anne asked him, quite serious, a smile on her face as she spun around and fell backward
onto her bed. She gave a contented sigh, surveying her tiny domain.

He thought the room was a stuffy little hole in the wall, the
plaster crumbling, the sheets yellow with age, the dressing
table chipped and wobbly, the shutters missing slats. It had the
odor of damp and a thick layer of dust on the baseboards and
there was absolutely nothing lovely about it.

Madame was charging him too much for it, but he didn't
really care if he was being fleeced. Money was only money,
and Anne had his absinthe. It didn't matter where he drank it
and the room was enough to please Anne.

"Not as lovely as you," he said. *"Pour my drink then let me
sketch you."* He wanted to capture that smile, that satisfaction
on her face.

Maybe if he captured it, he could figure out how to create it
for himself.

⬦⬦⬦

Raphael was sitting on the daybed, cross-legged, a stack of
papers in his hand, more on the mattress next to him. "Hello,
Gabriel," he said without looking up. "I figured I would see
you sooner or later."

Gabriel stepped into the room, the floor creaking beneath
his boots. "Raphael. I assume you know why I'm here."

Setting his papers aside, Raphael sighed and looked up, his
expression calm. Gabriel had been expecting anger, disdain,
sarcasm, maybe a sick satisfaction. But he saw none of that on
the demon's face. "I think you are planning to tell me to stay
away from Sara Michaels."

"To start with." Gabriel had other thoughts as well, but first
he wanted to hear what Raphael had to say. "Are you going to
agree quietly or do I have to convince you?"

There was nothing but a shrug. Raphael's passivity was unnerving. Gabriel had arrived expecting, anticipating, a battle.
He had a sheath knife in his back pocket, prepared to kill
Raphael if he had to, knowing full well only an immortal
could kill another immortal.

But the man he had come to think of as his nemesis, the

one who had taken Anne's life, making him doubt his own innocence, his soul, his very self, and who by killing her mother had hurt Sara in ways that could never be repaired, just sat there hunched over in khaki cargo shorts and a red golf shirt.

"I'll stay away from Sara because I don't want her to get hurt," Raphael said. "I never wanted to hurt her, and I'm sorry that she has been affected by all of this . . . by me. I came here to watch her, to protect her. I admit I was surprised that she was with you . . . I didn't anticipate that, but I figured it was a good thing. With both of us watching out for her, she should be safe, right? She is safe, isn't she? Where is she?"

Confused, Gabriel just stared at Raphael. What the hell was he talking about? Safe from who? It didn't sound like the words of a man who had sent her pictures of her mother's crime scene, but Gabriel was wary of drawing any conclusions. "She's safe. Why do you care?"

Raphael propped his chin up with his hand. "I care about Sara. She's a wonderful person. Kind, giving, and she loved her mother even though Jessie had her fair share of problems. I should have stayed away from both of them."

"If you care about Sara so damn much, why did you kill her mother? That nearly destroyed her." And Raphael had clearly lost his mind. He was eerily calm, melancholy, unfocused.

But Gabriel's words made Raphael's head snap up. "I didn't kill Jessie. Gabriel, I swear by all that is holy, I didn't kill Jessie. I loved her. We had a good relationship. Together, we were helping each other be better, if that makes sense."

Gabriel did understand that. It was the very way he had thought of his relationship with Sara. But he couldn't wrap his mind around Raphael being innocent. All evidence pointed to his guilt. "Then who did? You were the last one with her. Your DNA was found on her. There was no forced entry."

Raphael waved his hand in dismissal. "And like my attorney said in court, we were in a relationship. There was reason for my DNA to be on her. But I don't want to run through all the forensic evidence. I can't stand the thought of it any longer. I can't stand what was done to her. I came here to kill myself, you know. To end it. Where it began." Raphael stacked up the pile of papers neatly and held them out. "My last will and testament, if you please."

Still unsure of what exactly was going on, Gabriel took the papers, feeling like the last piece to the puzzle was still missing. "Why did you kill Anne? She did nothing to you, and if it was to punish me in some way, why did you testify for the defense in my trial?"

But Raphael just shook his head. "I didn't kill Anne either. I was upset when she chose you over me because I was fond of her, but I was willing to recognize that you had more money than me, and a prettier face. I also realized that Anne didn't appreciate my love of the French ménage à trois. I couldn't resist one last visit to her though that night, but you arrived early and Madame sent me packing."

Not bothering to hide his disbelief, Gabriel crossed his arms over his chest, crumpling the papers in the process. "So you're telling me that you had nothing to do with any of these women's deaths? That you're just an innocent little lamb prancing around the fucking meadow?"

"I never said I was innocent, any more than you are innocent. We are fallen angels, you know. We've sinned, over and over, you and I. But yes, I am telling you that I did not kill those women. But clearly, I am responsible ultimately for their deaths, because in the last one hundred and fifty years, every woman I have had an intimate relationship with has been murdered." He gave a short laugh. "It rather ruins the ardor."

"You're a crazy mother fucker, Raphael. You're killing these women and you know it." Gabriel didn't understand who it could be if it wasn't Raphael and it wasn't him. No one else had ties to both Anne Donovan and Jessie Michaels, and it clearly had to be an immortal.

It couldn't just be a sick and weird coincidence. "Why did you send those pictures to Sara?"

"What pictures?"

"And the absinthe?"

"Absinthe? What are you talking about?" Raphael frowned. "I thought you stopped drinking that swill. Don't tell me you've fallen off the wagon. I thought you were better than that these days."

Gabriel stared at his fellow demon. Either Raphael had completely lost his grip on reality, or he was telling the truth.

Unfolding the stack of papers Raphael had handed him, Gabriel glanced at the will, a quote toward the bottom of the page leaping out at him.

I live in sin, to kill myself I live; no longer my life my own, but sin's; my good is given to me by heaven, my evil by myself, by my free will, of which I am deprived.—Michelangelo

"What's with this sudden obsession with Michelangelo?" he asked as he stuffed Raphael's will in his back pocket, angry that he couldn't make sense of what was going on.

Raphael gave a slight smile. "Michelangelo saw angels. 'I saw the angel in the marble and I carved until I set him free.' Don't you think it's odd that these women, the women I cared about, the women I loved, the women I wanted to help, Gabriel, were carved? Carved until set free . . . sent to heaven."

A cold sweat broke out over Gabriel's flesh. That was the most appalling visual, the most horrific metaphor, he'd ever heard, and he almost choked on his disgust. Raphael had done it, had killed those women, and he was sitting there in his suburban doctor clothes with a stupid smile on his face.

Gabriel reached for his knife without hesitation. "Raphael, stand up so I can send you back to our Maker."

Chapter Eighteen

✥

Jocelyn pulled the door to her apartment open immediately. "You're back early."

"Rafe's not home."

"Good. Well, not good, but I'm glad you're back, because I really want to talk to you about your samples, but I didn't want to hold you up when you got here earlier. You seemed really eager to see Rafe."

She had been. Not so much anymore. "So what did you find with the samples?"

"Well, your samples were tainted or mislabeled."

"What do you mean?" Sara was still unnerved from the encounter with Rafe's girlfriend, and the quasi-fight she'd had with Gabriel the night before when she'd left New Orleans. She wasn't sure she could wrap her mind around deciphering how she could have screwed up the samples.

They sat down on Jocelyn's sofa and Sara pulled her legs under her skirt. She was tired. Numb. Jocelyn, who was a six-foot-tall brunette with funky retro glasses and more energy in one minute than Sara had in an entire day, had a glass of red wine in her hand. "Do you want a drink? You look worn out, Sara."

"No, I'm fine, thanks. I just had a weird thing happen. I'll tell you about it after I hear the lab results. You've got me curious. I don't see how I could have mislabeled those samples." But then again, she had sent the samples overnight to Jocelyn when she had been distracted and irritated with Gabriel. She supposed anything was possible.

"Well, here's the thing. I found the markers matching your blood sample to the sample you said came from your ancestor. So that made sense. There wasn't a lot to work with, given the age and size of the sample, but I did a DNA comp to the first hair sample you gave me and there was no match. So whoever that hair belonged to, it wasn't his blood on that knife. Which again, makes sense since you said it was a woman's blood on the knife, the victim. But then I compared the two hair samples to each other, since you said the two men are related. Only they're not related."

"They're not related?" But then why the hell had Gabriel said he was a descendent of John Thiroux if he wasn't? Or did Gabriel just think he was, but he wasn't?

"No." Jocelyn gave her a shrug. "They're better than related. They're the same guy."

"*What?*" That made absolutely no sense whatsoever. "That's impossible."

"Nope. There's no doubt about it. Those two hairs came from the same dude, Sara."

Sara wished she'd said yes to the wine. She sat back against the couch cushions, mind racing. How could she have wound up with two samples from Gabriel? That was just impossible because she was sure there had only been one hair on her pillow, and the other hair had come from Gabriel's sample of John Thiroux. Unless the hair Gabriel had given her as John Thiroux's was really Gabriel's all along and he had known that. But why the hell would he lie about something like that?

"That's just so weird . . . I don't see how they could have gotten mixed up like that. Maybe he's just a close match to his relative." Even as she said the words, she knew that wasn't possible. Jocelyn knew what she was doing and she would be able to tell the difference between mere markers and a match.

"DNA doesn't lie, honey. For whatever reason, you wound up with two samples of the same guy. And I'm hoping after I'm done telling you the rest of my findings, you're going to illuminate me as to who all these samples belong to, and what exactly it all means. I thought you were in New Orleans on sabbatical."

That was a polite way to explain what she had been doing. "I'll tell you everything, I promise." God knew she needed to talk to someone. "But first tell me what else you found." Not that it was going to matter if she had screwed all the samples up. Which infuriated her. She didn't like to mess up, couldn't explain how she could have done that.

"That patent print you sent me? I entered it in AFIS and got a list of four possible matches. Patricia ran through them last night for me, which means you owe her big time for doing that on a Saturday night, but anyway, she made a conclusive match. Twelve points."

Sara narrowed her eyes at Jocelyn. "Wait a minute. I only sent you one fingerprint scan. How the hell could that match prints in AFIS?"

"Because it's the same person." Jocelyn looked at her blankly. "What do you mean? Why did you send it if you weren't looking for a match?"

What she meant was that the print she'd sent Jocelyn had been the bloody fingerprint on the sketch of Anne Donovan, left there in 1849. Almost a hundred and sixty years earlier. She'd sent it merely to ask Jocelyn if she thought there was any possibility of extracting DNA from the bloody fingerprint on the original sketch, but she'd never actually gotten around to asking that of Jocelyn, so her friend had obviously assumed she wanted to search for a match. Which hadn't occurred to her as even a possibility because of its age. "It's an old print. There's no way there should have been a match."

"How old?"

"It was from 1849." A chill went up Sara's spine. Something was very wrong, only she had no idea what it was.

"What? That's impossible. Patricia doesn't mess up like that. She's an expert fingerprint tech and she's been doing this for fifteen years. She found twelve fucking points of comp, Sara."

"That's why it doesn't make any sense!" Sara rubbed her temples. Nothing made sense. "Who did the match come up as? Just some random petty criminal?"

"No. It's a woman who was arrested in Louisiana in 2003 for running a prostitution ring. Her name is Marguerite Charles. Does that ring any bells?"

It did. Sara sat straight up. That's what the woman outside Rafe's had said her name was. Marguerite. But she hadn't told her a last name, so why did the whole name Marguerite Charles sound familiar?

"I don't know . . . maybe. I went over to Rafe's before I came here and some woman was there getting his mail. He had obviously moved out of his condo. This woman said she was his girlfriend . . . and that her name was Marguerite." She had also mentioned Gabriel. *Say hi to Gabriel.*

Oh my God. Sara suddenly remembered where she had seen the name Marguerite Charles. In the court records of the trial of Jonathon Thiroux. Marguerite was the congressman's wife who had posed nude for him.

"Since when does Rafe have a girlfriend?" Jocelyn looked as offended as Sara had felt. "It's a little soon to be moving in with another woman. It's been three weeks since his acquittal. God, that's tacky."

"*Thank* you." Sara couldn't agree more. "That is exactly what I thought, but I figured I was totally biased." She either had to be wrong or it was some kind of monstrous and weird coincidence that a woman arrested for prostitution in Louisiana could be the same woman Rafe was dating. And it was flat-out impossible that she could be the same Marguerite in the court records, or that she could have been physically present at the scene of Anne Donovan's death.

But now she was curious to know if Gabriel knew a Marguerite, and how.

"Well, I guess that's typical for a man," Jocelyn said. "But it's still rude."

"She invited me to dinner with the two of them."

"Eew." Jocelyn wrinkled her nose. "I hope you told her to go fuck herself."

Sara laughed. God, she loved Jocelyn, and she had missed her. "Not exactly, but I doubt she was serious. She was just trying to be territorial and prove a point." And in light of everything else, Sara no longer really gave a damn that Rafe had a girlfriend. What concerned her was who the girlfriend was, and what relevance she had to Gabriel or herself.

Everything was too strange, too circular, too oddly familiar and overlapping, and it was disturbing, unnerving.

"I think I'd like that glass of wine. And if you don't mind, I'd like to give Gabriel a quick call."

Jocelyn's eyebrows went up. "Who the hell is Gabriel and why did your eyes go soft when you said his name?"

"Oh. Didn't I mention him?" Sara felt a burn race up her neck to her cheeks. "Let me call him really quick and then I swear, I'll tell you everything."

But first she had to find out what he knew about a curvy and seemingly wealthy brunette named Marguerite.

❦

Raphael just shook his head at him. "I don't think so. If I'm going to die, it will be my own hand." He frowned. "Besides, I thought we were friends. We used to go to dinner at the club together. I did my best to steer the jury to a not guilty verdict in your trial. Why would you want to kill me?"

Gabriel couldn't imagine what was so hard to grasp about the concept. "You've killed what . . . four women? The first of whom was under my protection. It's my responsibility, fallen or not, to vanquish you."

"I told you, I didn't kill them." Raphael fell backward onto the bed and stared up at the ceiling. "Don't you understand what I'm saying? This has been my punishment . . . that if I care for a woman, if I have sexual intimacies with her, she is killed."

"But . . ." Gabriel lowered the knife in his hand. That didn't sound like a legitimate punishment. Death to a mortal wasn't something even a Grigori demon would condone. "Why so long into your relationship with them? And why wasn't there evidence of intercourse with either Anne or Jessie?" It was crude, but he felt like he had to ask.

Raphael stayed on his back, expression rueful. "I don't know why it happens when it happens. And there was no evidence of intercourse with Anne because I was the coroner. I lied, thinking it would help your case. I didn't want to see you rotting in prison. As for Jessie, the reason is because we didn't have sex that night. Doesn't mean we didn't plenty of times before that."

He put his hand out, not wanting details. "Okay, I got it. But if I believe you, which I'm not sure I do, then who killed them?"

"I don't know. I wish I knew."

Pacing back and forth in the narrow room, Gabriel felt the humid heat, the small space, the lack of answers, pressing in on him. The floors were the original wood planks, dusty and nicked, but there was no evidence of where Anne's blood had been in front of the bed. The stain had been sanded away. But Gabriel couldn't make it disappear as easily. He wanted, needed, to know who would have done such a thing. If it was punishment for him, for Raphael, or a horrible sick quest that had nothing to do with either of them.

His cell phone rang in his pocket and he pulled it out. It was Sara's number. He wanted to answer it, but if she was calling, then clearly she was okay and he needed to finish this conversation before he spoke to her.

"You can answer it," Raphael said. "I don't care."

"It's too late. She hung up." Phone in his left hand, knife in his right, Gabriel stared at the shutters. What the hell was he supposed to do? He knew he had to do something, knew there was a key, something he was supposed to accomplish before he would be free, but he had no idea what it was. He wanted to solve these murders but didn't know where to look next.

Raphael's cell phone started ringing, his ring tone an irritating hip-hop song.

Pulling it out of his pocket, Raphael glanced at the screen. "It's Sara. I'm going to answer it."

Feeling offended that Sara had called Raphael immediately after calling him, he glanced down at his own phone. She hadn't even left him a voice mail. She was clearly still angry with him. But it still made his blood pressure increase to know that the woman he loved was perfectly happy chatting with Raphael.

Raphael had sat up, and he said, "Hi, Sara, how are you?"

There was nothing as annoying as standing there only able to hear one half of a conversation. He should be talking to Sara, not feeling like a complete outsider, in that room of all places. He was ready to leave, wanted away from the bed, the dingy walls, the lingering smell of cigarettes and rot. He was standing right where Anne's little table and his chair used to rest, and it made him frustrated in ways he couldn't even describe or explain.

Raphael was frowning. "I told you I was moving out."

It sounded like Sara was angry with Raphael too, which gave him a petty satisfaction.

"What? Who? Sara, calm down . . . no, I didn't. I don't know what you're talking about. Hold on a second. Here's Gabriel." Raphael shoved his cell phone at him. "I think you should talk to her. She's really upset and I'm not sure why."

Great. Just great. They weren't even supposed to know each other and Raphael had just blurted out that he was standing right next to him. He hadn't given him any way to ease Sara into an explanation, but had just handed him a hand grenade.

"Sara? I'm sorry I just missed your call. Is everything okay? How are you?" Gabriel put his own phone in his front pants pocket and twirled the knife with his free hand. He had a bad feeling this wasn't going to be a good conversation.

"Why the hell are you with Rafe?" she said. "You said you weren't going to come to Florida! What the *hell* is going on?"

No. That wasn't a good start. "I'm not in Florida. I'm still in New Orleans."

"How can you be in New Orleans? Why is Rafe there? And how do you know each other?"

There was no easy way to explain their relationship or what was happening. So he stuck his hand in his hair and closed his eyes and said, "Um. It turns out we do know each other. I didn't realize that because he's using a different name now, but I just saw a picture of him and put two and two together. And I was pretty sure he was here in New Orleans, because I figured out he owns the house on Dauphine Street. Which is why I was okay with you going back to Florida, because I was almost positive he wouldn't be there, but here. Therefore, you wouldn't be in any danger from him."

Oh, God. That sounded absolutely all wrong. The more he spoke, the deeper the hole he was digging. From her perspective it wasn't going to make any sense.

"Okay, I cannot even figure out what is going on here . . . there was this woman at Rafe's condo and his stuff is all gone, and she said she's his girlfriend and that they've moved in together. She invited me to dinner with the two of them, but now you're telling me that Rafe is in New Orleans? And my friend Jocelyn ran the samples I gave her, and she did a fingerprint search on the print from the Anne Donovan sketch, because I forgot to tell her I didn't need a search, but here's the really bizarre thing—she found a match. That fingerprint on the sketch matches a woman named Marguerite Charles who was arrested for running a prostitution ring in Louisiana in 2003. Louisiana. Marguerite Charles. A match. And the woman who said she's Rafe's girlfriend also said her name was Marguerite. What kind of a freak-out coincidence is all of that?"

Marguerite. Gabriel's eyes shot open. He started pacing again, kicking Raphael's foot to get his attention. "Marguerite's prints match prints from the Donovan crime scene?"

"Yes."

Holy shit. Alex's daughter was a killer. Gabriel would have never suspected in a million years, had no reason to suspect. Raphael's eyes had gone wide in shock, but there was no skepticism. He looked like he believed Marguerite perfectly capable of murder.

"It's obviously some bizarre mistake," Sara said, "since it's not possible that a woman today could match the prints of someone from a hundred-and-fifty-some years ago, but the whole thing is just off . . . I don't understand any of it."

It was entirely too possible, and Gabriel felt the firm grip of fear when he realized what exactly Sara had said earlier. "Marguerite was at Rafe's condo? She's in Naples?"

Raphael jumped off the bed. "Gabriel. Sara's in danger."

That was exactly what he had just determined. And they were both a thousand miles away from her.

"Yes. Do you know Marguerite? Right as she was leaving she told me to say hi to you. I'm so completely confused, and I'm angry because I feel like you know what's going on and you're not telling me."

He wanted to, but there wasn't time. And you didn't tell someone about your immortality over the phone anyway. "Sara, listen to me, sweetheart. I'll explain everything as soon as I get to Naples. I'm going to catch the next flight. Stay with your friend until I get there, okay? And don't go anywhere near Rafe's condo or Marguerite."

"Why? What's going on?"

"I think Marguerite killed your mother. So does Rafe."

There was silence for a long second, and Gabriel stopped pacing. He wished he knew how to reassure her, comfort her, keep her safe until he could get to her.

"Gabriel, I'm scared."

He could hear it in her voice. She was frightened of what she knew was real—death—and what she didn't understand—how he, Raphael, and Marguerite were all connected. "It's going to be okay. I'm on my way."

Hand in his hair, he paused on his way to the door. "And Sara?"

"Yes?"

"I love you." Maybe that was too much, too soon, but he needed to say what he knew to be true. He had never spoken those words to a woman, had never understood the true joy of loving another person, but he did with Sara. It was a beautiful and amazing thing to feel at complete peace in another's presence, to look at someone and know you were better for being with them.

She didn't answer, but he didn't expect her to. She was too overwhelmed to offer him the same commitment at that moment, under the circumstances, but he had fallen in love with her, and he would give his life for her, and he needed her to know.

After a quick good-bye he hung up the phone and tossed it back to Raphael, who was following Gabriel out the door.

"How are you going to Florida?" Raphael asked. "I thought you were bound to New Orleans."

"I am." Gabriel strode down the hallway and took the steps two at a time.

"If you defy your binding, you'll never gain your freedom . . . you'll be stuck here forever."

"I know," he said grimly. It wasn't an attractive future, but he had no other choice. He wasn't going to sit there and let Sara be killed just to save his own worthless ass.

"I can go to Naples. I can bring Sara back here."

"No, I'll do it." There was no way he could wait, not knowing if Sara was safe.

Raphael's footsteps pounded behind him as they jogged across the front room, back through the office, and out the back door of the kitchen. "I'm going with you anyway, you know. Marguerite . . . she's my problem."

"She's a demon child. She's both of our problem." Gabriel crashed through the brush on the side of the house, jumping over the bricks, letting his demon legs make use of their full immortal speed.

"It's me, you know. She's doing it because of me. Marguerite's wanted me to marry her since, well, the beginning . . . but I had no idea, I swear, I had no clue she was doing this. I never thought she was capable of something so horrible."

Gabriel glanced back at Raphael, who was running at pace with him. Raphael was pasty white and looked like he was capable of throwing up at any given second. Like he was truly sickened by the realization of what Marguerite had done. Gabriel wanted to believe him.

"We can't change the past, Raphael. We can only change the present."

He finally understood that.

Chapter Nineteen

꧁⁕꧂

Sara wasn't sure if fear or frustration was winning. Gabriel had frightened her with the tone of his voice, the way he'd been so adamant that she needed to stay and wait for him. But she was also completely angry—boiling blood mad—that everyone seemed to know what the hell was going on but her.

She was a self-professed control freak, and not having all the information available to her was maddening. Especially when it appeared to exist, but no one saw fit to share it with her.

As far as she could tell, Gabriel had confessed three things to her. That he knew Rafe and Marguerite. That he thought Marguerite had killed her mother. And that he was in love with her.

She hadn't expected any of that, and she wasn't sure which had shocked her the most. She hadn't seen any of them coming, but his profession of love had sideswiped her, and she hadn't been able to process it in any way and give him a response before he had said good-bye and hung up. Which was probably for the best, because she didn't know what she would have said in return. She had thought she loved him. Still did. But it worried her that there were so many apparent secrets, so much he had withheld from her. And nothing about any of the murders, past or present, made sense. She was on emotional and intellectual overload, with no answers in sight.

"Do you love him?" Jocelyn asked, handing Sara a glass of wine.

Sara took it and swirled the liquid around and around in the glass. "Yes." Whether that was a mistake or not, she didn't know. But it was what it was and she couldn't change that. She loved him quietly, passionately, softly, wondrously.

"I've never seen you in love before. It was pretty obvious to me from the second you said his name."

Crossing her legs and pulling her skirt down over them on the sofa, Sara looked at Jocelyn. "I don't fall in love easily. Or I didn't think I did. You've known me, what, six years? I'm emotionally reserved. I know that. I try not to be, but I can't help it."

"I wouldn't say that about you at all. I think you're very emotionally giving . . . you're loyal and loving and incredibly generous. But I think that's why there are few people you really reach out to—you give so much, all of yourself, to relationships, that you can't have a crowd of friends and lovers. You're selective, with meaningful friendships instead of superficial ones, and I appreciate that about you."

Sara felt so raw, so scraped and banged and smacked that Jocelyn's words had her sucking in a huge breath to avoid tears, to hold it together. She would keep it together. "Thanks. That means a lot to me. And I do love Gabriel . . . I can't explain how or why it's happened so fast, but I met him and it seemed from that very first day, our paths were meant to cross. That we're connected . . . that we knew each other already because we're so similar." She took a sip of her wine. "God, that sounds weird, but it's true. I just *adore* him."

Sappy and pathetic as it was, she did. She had never understood, never realized how uplifting and exciting it would be, to feel the kind of emotion she did for Gabriel. She had thought she'd loved men before, but this was different, deeper, richer, more exciting, more enticing, more all-consuming.

"So what's going on? What's with all the DNA, and why are you here in Florida and he's in New Orleans?"

"I hope you don't have any plans tonight, because it might take awhile to explain this."

"I have no plans and I'm all ears." Jocelyn kicked her shoes off and pulled her legs up onto the sofa. "There is obviously a story here."

Sara didn't know where to start, exactly, but she figured the easiest place was to explain why she was really in New Orleans. So she told Jocelyn about Gabriel contacting her, the book concept, meeting and working with him. The strange evidence that seemed to dead-end, the parallels between the cases. Two hours later, she thought she had Jocelyn pretty well updated, leaving out personal details like Gabriel's unwillingness to have sex with her, and the absinthe encounter.

"So, that name you gave me—Marguerite Charles—was in the court records of the trial of Jonathon Thiroux. And Rafe's girlfriend is named Marguerite too. So it's all completely strange and doesn't make sense. The print matching is just crazy. Obviously it's not the same person."

"But that's where you're wrong."

Sara almost dropped her wine when she turned and saw Marguerite standing in the kitchen of Jocelyn's apartment, leaning against the column dividing the kitchen from the dining area.

"I am the same person. You would think you would have figured that out by now, but you're not as bright as Gabriel or Raphael gives you credit."

"How the hell did you get in here?" Sara asked.

"Demon trick. It's not hard, really." Marguerite was wearing a yellow sundress and heels and her shoes clicked on the tile floor as she moved forward.

"Demon . . . What are you talking about?" Sara was angry that everyone was talking in circles and riddles. Who was Raphael and what did demons have to do with anything?

"Oh, are you kidding me? Gabriel hasn't told you? That's interesting, very interesting. I would be pissed off about that if I were you." Marguerite was right in front of them now, and she reached out and snatched out of Jocelyn's hand the cell phone Sara's friend had picked up off the coffee table. "You don't need that."

Sara was sorry she had dragged Jocelyn into this mess, whatever it was exactly, and she turned to reassure her friend, only to find Jocelyn staring vacantly into space, features and body frozen. Sara let out a scream. "Oh, my God, what's the matter with her?" She touched Jocelyn, and she was warm to the touch, but completely still. "Jocelyn, are you okay?"

"She'll be fine. I just thought it would be better if she takes a little nap while we have our chat. This way she won't remember anything and you don't have to feel guilty about involving her."

"Involving her in what?"

"Involving her with demons. That's what we are, you know, Gabriel, Raphael, and I. We're immortal demons, though technically I'm only half-demon. But Gabriel and Raphael are full demons. They're fallen angels. How sexy is that?"

Sara was still holding Jocelyn's hand, and she was glad for the contact, even if Jocelyn seemed completely out of it. Gabriel had been right to warn her about Marguerite. The woman was totally insane. She was saying they were all demons.

"You don't look like you think that's sexy. And yet I know you have the hots for Gabriel. It took you about a minute to move in with him and start drinking his absinthe."

Sara felt an icy fear slide across her, her heart pounding and her breathing shallow and rapid. "You left the bottle outside the door, didn't you?"

Marguerite gave a small smile. "That was funny, wasn't it? Gabriel has always been so aloof, so untouchable, so sure of his superiority, of his talent, yet he has no reason to be. He can't function with other people for more than a minute, and he's a total drunk. It's fun to fuck with him. It's too bad he was acquitted for Anne's murder—that would have been the ultimate joke. But Raphael was too nice. He testified for Gabriel and got him off."

Marguerite was blending past and present, talking about the men as if they had been involved, alive, for the Anne Donovan case. It was making Sara's skin crawl and she wanted Marguerite gone. "What do you want?"

Sara was sorry she asked. Because Marguerite's smile grew wide and maniacal.

"I want you to stay away from my boyfriend. And to make sure that you do, I'm going to kill you."

Gabriel was exhausted and worried sick that he was too late. Sara wasn't answering her cell phone, and neither was her friend Jocelyn, whose number she had given him as a contact. It had taken longer than he had expected to secure a rental car at the airport, and the whole process of traveling had been unnerving. He'd never flown on a plane before, and it had felt claustrophobic, agitating. He had found he was actually grateful for Raphael's presence, guiding him through the whole check-in and security process. He didn't want his own ineptitude to delay getting to Sara.

At least he had good computer skills. He had found and mapped the route to Jocelyn's apartment, and with Raphael driving since he had lived in Naples, they made it to her complex with no problem. It was dark and they missed her building initially, but Raphael backed up and parked and they were out, Gabriel running.

Only Alex stepped in front of him on the walkway to the building. "Gabriel. Raphael."

Shit. Gabriel stopped running. "Alex. What the hell are you doing here?"

"You know, I'm starting to get the feeling you're not as fond of me as I am of you." Alex put his hands in the pocket of his dress pants. "I feel highly insulted."

"I think you'll get over it. Now I'm going to assume that Marguerite is in there with my girlfriend, so step to the side please." Before he lost complete control and ripped Alex's face off. He was completely out of patience, and his fear was choking him. He couldn't handle finding Sara like Anne had been. He wouldn't survive that.

"Oh, now she's your girlfriend? A week ago she was just someone you were working on a project with."

"Just drop it." He started to brush past Alex, but the demon grabbed his arm.

Alex had a gun in his hand, retrieved from his pocket. "One moment please. I need to talk to you and Raphael."

"What?" The barrel of the gun was in his face, but Gabriel stared it down. Alex wasn't going to intimidate him.

"Marguerite is unhappy and I can't stand to see my daughter

so upset. She's had a harder life than her sister Rosa, because she's always been insecure. And she's always had a thing for Raphael—I have no clue why, it's not like he's all that great of a catch—but there it is. She wants him." Alex turned to Raphael, who was behind Gabriel on the walkway. "So I guess this is what they would call a shotgun wedding. I want you to go in there and tell Marguerite you'll marry her finally, because I'm sick to death of riding the crazy train with her. I'm too old for this shit."

Gabriel couldn't believe Alex was so nonchalant about the whole thing. Didn't he realize his daughter was insane? That she had killed at least four women? And there was no way Raphael would agree to marry her.

But he did. Raphael just nodded. "Okay. I'll marry her."

"Raphael, have you lost your mind?" Gabriel asked, appalled at the idea of being saddled to Marguerite for eternity.

Raphael just shook his head. "It's what I need to do. To make it right." He headed for the front door.

Gabriel went to follow him, but Alex grabbed him again. "No. You stay here."

"Fuck you, Alex. I want to see Sara." Gabriel yanked his arm out of Alex's hold.

The gun was suddenly on his temple. "I said stay here."

Gabriel knocked the gun away. "And I said fuck you." He was so tired and angry. All of this, all the death and suffering and pain, for what? Because Marguerite hadn't been able to wrangle a ring from Raphael? It made him sick.

He started for the door again, but Alex moved. Gabriel instinctively ducked and avoided Alex's blow to the head. "What is your problem?" He turned and blocked another punch.

"They need a minute to work things out. Leave them alone."

"No." Gabriel was so frustrated, he threw a punch back.

Alex blocked, and the next thing Gabriel knew, they were locked in combat, exchanging vicious blows that made Gabriel's teeth rattle and blood burst from Alex's nose.

❧

Sara kept her mouth shut so that Marguerite wouldn't hear her teeth chattering. She was scared witless. Marguerite had al-

ready moved Jocelyn by taking her by the hand and leading
her down the hallway. Sara had watched Marguerite give Jocelyn a little push and her friend fall down on her bed, eyes
vacant and staring at the ceiling.

She had run for it then, realizing it was her chance to escape, grabbing her purse as she flew past the sofa, but suddenly Marguerite had been between her and the door. It
wasn't possible, but there she was, and she slapped Sara so
hard she saw stars and lost her balance, stumbling backward.
Marguerite had grabbed her arm and shoved her so that she
fell back onto the sofa.

Now she was sitting there, afraid to move, unsure what to
do, all too aware that something was very, very wrong. This
wasn't just a woman who was feeling possessive about her
man. This was crazy.

Marguerite was studying her manicure. "You know, I think
I'm going to have to find a new salon. I just had my nails done
yesterday and they're chipped already. I don't know this area
all that well. Can you recommend a salon?"

Sara just shook her head. Her mind was a complete blank,
her thoughts skittering left and right, trying to figure out how
she was going to contact someone for help. How she might escape.

Swinging one leg over the other as she sat in an oversized
chair across from Sara, Marguerite sighed. "No? That's a
damn shame. But I guess I'm not surprised. You look a little
on the earthy side. You really need to put more effort into your
appearance, hon. Your hair could use highlights to lift it, and
some quality concealer could really cover up those dark circles under your eyes. I realize Gabriel likes your helpless del-
icateness, but still, you don't want to look like a crackhead. Of
course, I guess it doesn't really matter since I'm going to kill
you."

"When were you planning on doing that exactly?" Sara
asked, annoyance slicing through her fear. She didn't like being toyed with, nor did she like being insulted. She had in-
somnia. She was entitled to dark circles under her eyes.

Marguerite glared at her. "Whenever I feel like it. And
maybe I won't be compassionate and put you in a trance like I
did with Anne Donovan and your mother. Maybe I'll just let

you struggle while I slice you open like a fish. You'll feel everything and you'll fight me, and you won't be able to stop me because I'm a hundred times stronger than you, and I'm the one with the big knife."

"I don't see any knife," Sara said, suddenly feeling defiant and infuriated. Was this bitch admitting she had killed her mother? Sara would be damned if she would just sit there and be murdered. If it hadn't been for Jocelyn in the bedroom, she would have made a rush for the door again, but she didn't want to leave her friend behind.

Marguerite pulled a knife out of her purse. "Right here. Isn't it pretty?"

They both heard the front door open at the same time and Sara didn't hesitate. She ran for it, wanting to make sure whoever was there would understand the danger, that they would go for help. She screamed for good measure, yelling and shrieking as she tore for the door, waving her arms. There was a tug on the back of her shirt and she was suddenly lying on the floor, the wind completely knocked out of her and pain exploding in the back of her head.

"Marguerite."

It was Rafe. Sara tried to suck in a breath, blinking back tears. She had no idea how Marguerite had grabbed her so quickly, but she had given her a brutal smackdown. Every inch of Sara's body hurt and she couldn't seem to speak, no matter how desperately she wanted to get Rafe's attention. She could see his legs as he moved into the room, closing the door behind him. That door closing bothered her. She wanted out. So she forced herself to press her hands to the floor and sit up. Everything spun for a second, but she swallowed back the nausea and tried to get her bearings. She was a good five feet from the door, but Rafe and Marguerite were behind her.

Rafe was talking in a low voice to Marguerite, and he was rubbing her arms in a soothing manner. She was shaking her head. Sara couldn't hear what Rafe was saying, but she really didn't care. She was just relieved for the distraction and whatever form of assistance Rafe could offer. Grabbing the leg of the end table, she heaved herself to her feet, shaky and nauseated, wondering how in the hell she was going to get Jocelyn out of the house. She was going for her purse with her cell phone inside it when the front door exploded, flying off the hinges.

Sara let out a yelp and jumped back, stumbling over the coffee table. A man fell backward onto the floor, skidding on top of the now horizontal front door. It was Alex, and the man who obviously had shoved him was Gabriel, out of breath, fists raised, blood all over his yellow T-shirt. What did Alex have to do with anything and why was Gabriel so angry with him? With no clue what was going on, Sara stepped onto the couch, away from the fray, intending to avoid contact with everyone and go quietly down the hallway to Jocelyn. She was going to force Jocelyn up and they were getting the hell out before she really stopped to think about what she was seeing and she absolutely and utterly lost it.

"Are you okay?" Gabriel asked her, glancing over, worry on his face even as he dodged a vicious kick aimed at his shin from Alex's left foot.

She nodded. It was startling to see Gabriel, who she thought of as such a quiet, artistic, non-confrontational man, in a brutal fistfight. Alex was back on his feet and they were exchanging blows, without any sort of regard for the rules of good sportsmanship. When Alex landed a hit to the kidney Gabriel winced in pain, but came right back at Alex with a punch that collided with Alex's skull with such force Sara actually heard the crack.

Jesus Christ. They were going to kill each other. Sara ran past Rafe and Marguerite, purse in her hand, her goal to get to Jocelyn and then call the police. They needed help, because while Gabriel looked like he was holding his own, she didn't like the ferocity of his fight with Alex. Someone was going to wind up with a concussion or in a coma and she sure in the hell didn't want it to be Gabriel.

The shadow rising on the wall in front of her as she stumbled down the hall had her instinctively turning to see what had caused it.

Then wishing she hadn't.

Because what she was seeing didn't make any sense. It was completely illogical. Insane. But there it was—Rafe and Marguerite embracing, his arms around her patting her back, her head on his shoulder. Three feet off the floor. They were hovering in space, in air, in nothingness, their feet flat like they were standing on solid ground, only they weren't.

Sara squeezed her eyes shut hard. Reopened them. They were still floating like human helium balloons. Beyond them, Gabriel and Alex continued to grapple with each other, and Gabriel rammed Alex into the wall so hard that when he pulled back there was a hole in the drywall from his elbow.

It wasn't right. None of it was right and she wasn't seeing what she was seeing.

Afraid that she was on the verge of going down, her head swimming, mouth hot, stomach churning, Sara whirled and went for the bedroom, slamming and locking the door behind her.

❧

Gabriel was glad Sara had finally left the room. She had lingered longer than he was comfortable with, given that Marguerite was a loose cannon and Alex hell-bent on beating the shit out of him. It made him feel better that she was in another room with the door closed.

Alex taunted him. "Your girlfriend doesn't know anything about you, does she? She doesn't know you're a drunk and a drug addict."

"Actually, she does." Gabriel ducked when Alex swung to him in the face. "So no need to run off and tell on me. She's perfectly aware of my flaws." He didn't bother to argue that he was no longer a drunk and a drug addict since he had been clean for seventy-five years. He didn't need to explain himself or justify anything to Alex.

They were both out of breath and seemed to have reached an unspoken agreement to pause in pummeling each other, because they were just circling, fists up. Gabriel flicked his hair out of his eyes and watched Alex warily.

"This is nothing personal, Gabriel."

"Then what the fuck is it?"

"I just want my daughter happy."

"Your daughter shouldn't have hurt those women."

"What women? I don't know anything about any of that. I just know she wants Raphael and I'm here to ensure she gets what makes her happy." He tilted his head to the side, where

Raphael was hugging Marguerite. "So now that they appear to have worked something out, I suppose you and I can cease this nonsense." Alex wiped at his bloody nose.

"You started this nonsense." Gabriel wasn't sure he could in good conscience just let Marguerite walk away, not after what she had done, even with Raphael willing to sacrifice himself to act as watchdog.

But then he heard the sound, the click of a lock once, twice, and he and Alex both turned to Raphael and Marguerite. Raphael had bound her hand and foot to him with the power of punishment, chains that usually only demons and angels could see, but a bond that couldn't be broken until the last days of the earth. It was more than Gabriel would have expected Raphael to do, condemning himself to an eternity as security guard.

Alex made a sound of rage in the back of his throat.

When he would have attacked Raphael, Gabriel stepped in front and stopped him, putting his hand on Alex's chest. "Don't. She looks pleased, and this will keep her from harming anyone. It's for the best."

Marguerite did look satisfied. She had gotten what she wanted—Raphael.

Now Gabriel was going to go and determine if it was at all possible for him to have what he wanted.

Chapter Twenty

❧

Gabriel found Sara in the bedroom on her cell phone talking to the police.

"I'm not sure what the address is, but I'm in the Harper's Landing apartment complex." She was biting her fingernail and staring at her friend, who Marguerite had clearly put into a sleep state.

Gabriel reached out and took the phone from Sara and pushed the End button to hang it up.

"What are you doing?" she asked, startled, glancing at the door in fear.

"We don't need the police. It's all under control."

Her eyes went wide. "What do you mean? She . . . I saw . . ."

Sara looked panicked, and her fear wasn't just for what she had seen in the living room. She was afraid of who and what he was. He could sense it, see the goose bumps on her arms.

"Raphael took care of Marguerite, and Alex left." With a warning from Gabriel to stay a hundred yards or more away from Sara or he would vanquish him. The demon version of a restraining order. "Everything's okay, I promise."

He reached for her, but she took a step back. "What do you mean, took care of Marguerite? Explain to me what is going on. They were floating in the air. That's not possible. And you and Alex . . . those punches should have knocked you both unconscious."

This wasn't how he wanted to have this particular conversation, but he didn't really have a choice. "Sara, I know this is going to seem crazy, impossible, but just listen to me and trust me. The truth is that Alex, Rafe, Marguerite, and I are all immortal and have known each other for hundreds of years. We don't age. Alex is Marguerite's father. Rafe is Dr. Raphael from the old court records."

She shook her head. "What? That's insane."

"No. It's true. And I am Jonathon Thiroux—the painter, the pianist, the addict."

Those three words summed up the entire length and breadth of his existence.

Her face drained of all color. "Oh God, the hair. The DNA . . . Jocelyn said the two hairs came from the same man, but I thought it was a mistake. That I had mixed up the samples somehow. Because it can't be possible."

"What hair?" He had intentionally refused to give her his DNA because he had known what she would find. But apparently she had found precisely that—that he was a match to John Thiroux—and she had chosen to believe it couldn't be true. She had chosen to accept the more logical explanation that there was a lab error, which he had to admit was probably what the majority of people would conclude. The truth really was unbelievable when you didn't come from his world.

"One of your hairs was stuck to my pillow so I took it. I had Jocelyn compare it to Thiroux's hair, and she said it was from the same man. A perfect match." She shook her head. "I thought I had goofed somehow, but now you're telling me it's true? That's crazy. Just crazy."

"It's not crazy. It's true, Sara, I swear to you." He had no idea how to convince her. He had never told anyone the truth of what he was. So what he did was instinctive, the only way he knew to show her so she could believe. He reached out and took her hands, opening his mind and projecting it onto her, letting her see his thoughts, feel his emotions, trace his life back to the beginning. Back to when he was Jonathon Thiroux and Dauphine Street was filled with brothels and drinking holes.

He opened himself and showed her the truth.

Sara felt it the second Gabriel's hands touched hers. It was a tingle, a static shock, the sensation of electricity rushing up her arms and vibrating in her shoulders. She would have jerked back, except that his grip on her was tight, and his deep brown eyes were drawing her in, holding her in place, mesmerizing. It should have frightened her, the intensity, the gleam, the depth in his eyes, but instead, she was reassured. This was Gabriel. This was the man she had fallen in love with.

And he was letting her into his thoughts. She could see and feel them, wrapping around her, whispering in her ear, his fear that she might have been hurt by Marguerite, his desperate relief that she wasn't. His powerful and honest love for her, the surprise he felt at the depth of his emotion. She felt the struggle it had been for him to not touch her, how much he had wanted to make love to her fully and completely, and how torturous his restraint had been.

She would have spoken, would have questioned why he couldn't touch her, share the pleasure of their bodies together, but he put his finger on her lips. The *shhh* reverberated in her brain, as clear as if he'd spoken it, but he hadn't. *Just watch,* he said into her consciousness, and she barely had time to register the wonderment of having him inside her mind, his thoughts blending with hers, when she saw it.

It was the years clicking backward, like pages in a calendar, until she saw Gabriel in the same apartment, wearing clothes with an odd seventies cut, quiet and alone, resigned but in control, the French Quarter outside him dirtier than what she had encountered. Lonely, both the man and the street, shabby and knocked around a bit, bleak, but calm. It shifted, blending and blurring until he was writing on a typewriter, and walking dark streets crowded with mid-twentieth-century cars, women in voluminous skirts and bright lipstick rushing by in pumps, Gabriel's demeanor cautious, brittle, a residual hardness lingering as he refused to make eye contact or speak with anyone. Then she saw him in a smoky bar, women with short capped hair and straight dresses laughing and dancing, the atmosphere secretive, seedy, seductive. Gabriel was watching the piano player croon to the crowd with a longing to touch the keys himself. But mostly he watched with loathing. There was a drink in Gabriel's hand, several empty glasses in front of him, and his mood was bitter, dark, desperate. He wanted to fling the glass at the piano and make the halfhearted, unimaginative music stop.

Then suddenly he was lying in the gutter, filthy and bruised, his hair caked and crusted with grime, sweat, an empty bottle clutched to his chest. People walked over him, sniffing in distaste, someone stealing his boots right off his feet while Gabriel sang quietly to himself off-key, his eyes closed, heart screaming with a pain so violent that Sara wanted to weep for him, for all he had been, all he had lost.

But the image shifted again, and she was there. In that tiny room. Seeing through Gabriel's eyes the loveliness of Anne's arm in the moonlight, his desire to capture her. She felt the fuzziness of his mind, understood the languor, the sharpness, the pleasure of the powerful absinthe-and-opium cocktail. Then the confusion, the sharp shock when he realized that Anne was dead, her blood on his fingertips. The shift from pleasure to horror in the minute it took his fog-filled brain to process what the smell, the wet feel on his fingers was. The smack of death, harsh and ugly, ripping into his daily stupor.

The vision cut off before she could see Anne's face, but it was enough to understand the horror of the moment, the self-hatred, the grief, the guilt.

Sara whispered, "Gabriel. I'm so sorry."

It wasn't possible that he was immortal, not by the standards of the reality she had always lived in, but she knew it was true. She had seen it, felt it. However it was possible, whatever it meant, he was the same man.

He squeezed her hands. "So it was me who found Anne Donovan dead. She was the girlfriend I told you about who was murdered, and for a hundred and fifty years I wondered if I could have done that, if I could have been hallucinating, blacked out, and taken a knife and killed her. I had to know. I had to find some way to deal with the answer—to make it right, for Anne."

"Why would Marguerite do that to Anne?" she asked, glancing back at Jocelyn. "And please tell me my friend is going to be okay."

"She'll be fine. When we're done talking, I can wake her up. She won't remember anything."

He was holding her hands so tightly her fingers hurt, but she couldn't bring herself to tell him to ease up. The solidity of his touch was comforting and she suspected he actually needed to hold on to her, to reassure himself that she was still there, standing with him.

"Marguerite did all of this because she was jealous. She was jealous of women Raphael was involved with. He had visited Anne earlier that night before I got there, and Marguerite must have seen them together. She seems to have concluded that her relationship with Raphael was more than it was, because I don't think they were ever actually dating."

"So she killed my mother because Rafe was in a relationship with her? That's appalling." And she didn't know what was worse—when she hadn't known why someone would do that, or now that she knew someone had for such a flimsy, selfish reason. But there was a soft, sad comfort in knowing that she had been right about Rafe, that his love had been genuine. It helped to know that her mother had enjoyed the last year of her life with him, and that it was legitimate emotion on his part.

"I'm sorry, Sara. I truly, truly am."

Sara looked up at him, her brain still processing everything, lingering sorrow from Gabriel's memories hanging over her. There was so much to ask, so much she needed and wanted to understand. "What happened to you, Gabriel? You were drinking *before* Anne . . . why?"

How could he explain who he was, what he'd been, how he had fallen so hard, so fast? He didn't understand it himself, and some days he found it hard to comprehend what exactly he had been thinking all those years ago. "Do you believe me when I tell you I'm immortal, that I was an angel once, now a demon?" he asked.

Her eyes were so wise, such a deep blue, so full of the knowledge of life that came from hard living, immense joy and agonizing pain. She nodded. "I believe you're something more than what I thought or can truly comprehend."

"I was sent to watch humans, to guide and protect them. But I wasn't prepared for the suffering, the sadness, the devastation of emotion that radiates from mortals. It was so hard to watch, so difficult not to be able to ease their pain, and it was overwhelming. When I drank, it was easier to handle. I could simply ignore all of it." That was his shame, but he wanted to face it, admit it, forgive himself for it, and move forward.

"I understand that. I do. I couldn't sleep you know, like I can't sleep now, and I would lie there and my mind would race with guilt and grief and fear and I just wanted it all to go away. I wanted oblivion. That's what the sleeping pills gave me."

"And now you still can't sleep." He touched her cheek, brushing his thumb across the deep bruises under her eyes, the stain of months and months of inadequate sleep.

"Yeah, but it's better this way. Better to not sleep and be in control. To face my grief, to deal with it." She turned her head, rubbing her lips over the inside of his wrist, her eyes drifting closed. "And do you notice," she whispered, "that I can sleep when I'm with you?"

"I'm glad that you sleep better with me." He wanted to repeat his earlier words, to tell her that he loved her, but it wasn't time yet. She needed more answers, and when he spoke his feelings, he wanted her ready to give him the same in return.

"And you know what is so very strange? You're telling me the most fantastical things . . . things I shouldn't believe. I should assume you're a lunatic and walk away, but I believe you. It's like I knew, in my gut, that coming to you would give me answers. And here they are. They're odd, and overwhelming, but for the first time in a year, I don't feel afraid. That fear isn't pressing on me. I feel sick that Marguerite would do this, and I'm worried that she'll do it again, but at the same time, I just feel relief. The bogeyman has a face, you know?"

"I understand. And I promise you that Raphael and I won't let Marguerite harm anyone else. Raphael bound her to him."

"What does that mean?"

Gabriel sighed. "There's a lot I need to tell you. A lot. Let's wake Jocelyn up and go somewhere and talk."

An hour later they had dropped Jocelyn at a hotel after securing her apartment door shut with plywood and feeding her a ridiculous story about rambunctious teenagers running wild through the apartment complex after too many beers. She seemed baffled that she had somehow missed it, but Sara had convinced her she'd had way more wine than she actually had. Now Gabriel and Sara were standing on the deck outside an ice cream shop overlooking the beach and the ocean and he was telling her about his punishment.

Sara leaned on the wooden railing and blinked at him, a strawberry smoothie in her hand that she wasn't drinking. "You're saying women become addicted to you? Like they crave you and have to have you?"

He nodded. "Yes. It happens when I touch women."

"Like Rochelle?"

"Yes."

Sara shivered. "Oh, God, that's awful."

"That's why I can't . . . why I've tried so hard to stay away from you." He frowned, realizing that he may have tried, but he hadn't completely succeeded. "I haven't done a great job of that."

"But you touch me. I'm assuming way more than you ever touched Rochelle, and I'm fine."

"That's true. I only touched Rochelle on the arm once. But it just means you're stronger—a lot stronger—than her. She has a weaker will. But eventually you'll succumb if I were to touch you as a lover."

"I'm not sure I believe you."

"Believe me." He was absolutely sure of it. "Don't you remember the letters from Jane Gallier? The court records of the women fighting? Think of Rochelle, her tears, that blood running down her wrists. I don't want you to end up like any of them." He wanted her to understand exactly what he was saying. "That would be my biggest regret, if I was what finally broke you. After all you've survived, if it was me that finally stripped away your strength, I couldn't stand that. I couldn't."

"I don't want to be without—"

Gabriel cut her off. He didn't want to hear whatever she was going to say. He couldn't hear it. Sara was ten times a greater temptation than alcohol had ever been and he needed to clamp down, hold together his emotions, build up his control until it was an impenetrable wall with barbed wire on top. He was going to do that, because he wanted to be with Sara, wasn't willing to give her up.

"I don't want to be without either. You know, in some ways it would be easier to walk away from you. But I've been doing the easy thing my entire existence." He was sorry for that. Wanted to stand firm and stop passively letting everything slide over and past him. He wanted to control his own destiny and stop hiding from it. "I want to be with you, spend time with you, love you. And while I can't touch you, I can share my life with you. I want to share my every day with you, do you understand?" It was a hell of a lot to ask, and he shouldn't, but he had to. He had to know that he had tried, offered her what he could.

Sara gripped the railing tighter, her hair blowing over her shoulders, the smoothie tipping so far over in her clenched hand he was expecting the lid to pop off. "Be together, but no touching?"

"No touching."

She didn't say anything, so Gabriel sighed, his heart aching for what he couldn't have as he looked across the beach. It was a quiet view, the heat of Florida different than New Orleans. There was humidity in the air, but somehow it wasn't as lush, as damp and smothering as southern Louisiana. The foliage on and around the deck was manicured, the houses in all directions new and crisply white and ivory, the retail buildings all soldiered along the main roads. It was very beautiful, he had to admit that. But it didn't touch his soul.

"I've never been out of New Orleans," he said. "I've only seen Florida on TV and in movies. It's pretty here. Peaceful."

"You've never been out of New Orleans? Why not?"

"I'm bound to New Orleans in exchange for a shorter punishment."

"Then how are you here?"

Love. That's how he was there. "I came to protect you."

"But . . ." She rested her smoothie on the top of the railing and tucked her hair behind her ears. "What does that mean for your punishment then?"

"It means it won't be shorter."

"I'm sorry," she whispered. "I didn't know when I came here . . . I was mad at you for not coming with me and I was being stubborn."

"And I didn't know about Marguerite or I never would have let you come by yourself. I thought you would be safe because I knew Raphael was in New Orleans. There's nothing for you to be sorry about. None of this was your doing, and I made my choice to defy my binding freely and clearly. Trust me, I don't regret it."

"So what do you do now?"

"I have to go back," Gabriel said, trying to keep his voice even. He didn't want her to feel guilty, didn't want to influence her choice in any way. "Will you come back with me?"

"I don't know if that's a good idea," Sara said, even as she knew she wanted to. Her heart was screaming that all she needed was a ticket and she was there. That it should be easy. He said he loved her. She knew she loved him.

Yet she needed to stay home in Florida, process everything she had learned, reflect, think about what she wanted to do. Decide if it was realistic to accept what he was offering, a platonic love affair. That in and of itself was an oxymoron. The idea of living with him, loving him, yet never able to have a sexual relationship sounded torturous, maddening.

But so did being apart from him.

What she wanted was to be with Gabriel.

What she needed to decide was how she could do that and retain her sanity.

He was immortal.

She was very much mortal.

At the moment, staring out at the water, watching wave after wave roll in, she didn't see how she could have everything. Yet wasn't sure that she could live with nothing.

"I won't push you," he said. "I know I'm asking a lot of you, and it's your decision, but know that I want you with me."

She glanced over at him, wanting to touch him, to lean against him, stroke his hair, feel his lips on her. How could she ache for that and never have it? How could she not know, just once, what it felt like to have him inside her, their bare skin touching everywhere, her ankles locked around his waist, the sweet scent of sweat and sex hovering between them, his dark eyes staring down at her?

"I love you," she said softly.

His eyes went wide and his jaw shifted, hands clasped together in a fist as he leaned over the railing. "I love you too."

She knew that, but it was lovely to hear him say it again, even if there were no easy options for them. "But I need time to think and I'm exhausted. Let's go get a room at the hotel. There are no flights to New Orleans until the morning anyway, I'm sure."

He nodded.

Sara had no idea what she would decide to do in the morning, but she knew how she wanted to spend the night.

And it wasn't sleeping.

Chapter Twenty-one

❦

Gabriel wanted to say something to Sara, anything, to convince her to go back to New Orleans with him, but he knew what he was suggesting was a huge sacrifice for Sara, more than it was for him. He was asking her to live with him without any hope of marriage or children or a normal sexual relationship, giving up the chance to date and meet a man who could give her all of those things.

It was more than he should ever expect her to have to live without.

So he bit his tongue and kept his damn mouth shut when he really wanted to coax and cajole and remind her of the love he felt.

And she was tired, overwhelmed, processing what she had learned about demons and the death of her mother. She didn't need his selfish whining, didn't need to make an impulsive decision based on emotion and wake up in two years, five years, regretting the choice, the time she had wasted.

So Gabriel didn't say a word, getting them a room at the hotel they had put Jocelyn in, a standard chain hotel with pleasant staff and lots of floral prints blanketing the lobby and the room itself. He didn't have any luggage, and Sara had left her bag at Jocelyn's apartment, so he secured toothbrushes and other necessaries at the front desk, and was putting them in the bathroom as Sara kicked off her sandals. When he walked back out, he was a little surprised to see her standing in her tank top and bikini panties, bent over the bed and systematically removing all the pillows but two, tossing the unwanted extras onto the other bed in a way that made her ass shake a little with each throw.

The view was one he certainly appreciated, and it created an immediate response from his own body, but it also confused him. Sara wasn't one to run around in her underwear. But then again, she was clearly just getting ready for bed and she had no pajamas with her, so it meant nothing more than that she wanted to be comfortable.

"I'm going to call the airline and see about getting a flight back tomorrow," he said. "Check times."

"Okay," she said, heading into the bathroom.

He heard the water running and her brushing her teeth. That wasn't the answer he had wanted. He had really been asking if he should get two tickets or one, but he didn't want to ask that straight-out. So he just called the airline on his cell phone and got flight times and asked about availability. Reassured that there were plenty of seats on the three o'clock afternoon flight for the next day, he left it at that and hung up. Sara had gotten into bed already and was lying with her eyes closed.

She was so quiet. Gabriel didn't like that. It made him nervous. He shucked off his T-shirt and used the other toothbrush. In the bathroom he debated leaving his jeans on or not, and decided they were dirty, he was tired, and he wanted to be completely comfortable. The jeans went and he got into bed in his boxer briefs.

He was already accustomed to sleeping with Sara beside him. He enjoyed her presence, her scent, her breathing, her soft sighs, her warmth. He would miss her if she didn't go back with him, in every part of his life. In a short amount of time, she had become a part of the fabric of every day, the voice he listened for, the person he shared his thoughts with. She was his balance, his temperance, his advocate, his champion.

Letting her stay, knowing he had to respect her decision, felt like the most difficult thing he'd ever done.

Sara rolled over and scooted in beside him, her hand sliding across his chest, her leg entwining with his. Gabriel froze, the embrace unexpected, his defenses not adequately in place. She was next to him, touching him, and it felt so damn good. His arm automatically went around her back and he wanted her nestled up against him, but it was a very dangerous place for them to wander.

"Are you okay?" he asked her, wondering if she was scared and just needed reassurance.

"I'm okay."

Her hand stroked across the waistband of his boxer briefs, making him grit his teeth at the kick of desire that nailed him in the groin. Maybe it was an absentminded touch on her part, but it was downright painful for him. An erection was already springing to life from her leg rubbing over his, and her fingers made the problem worse as they played along his abs, flipping his waistband down then back up. She obviously had no idea what she was doing to him.

"I want you, Gabriel," she said, and her hand went lower, cupping his erection and stroking him through his briefs.

Fuck. Gabriel sucked in a breath and closed his eyes for a second, enjoying the hot rush of pleasure, the rapid swelling of his cock beneath her fingers, before he forced himself to put his hand over hers and stop her. "Sara. Don't."

"Why not?"

"Because there's nowhere to go with this. I can't touch you. I won't risk it." He moved his hand away from hers now that she had stopped stroking him, and swallowed hard.

"Don't you want to know?" she asked, propping up on her elbow to look at him, her hair falling onto his shoulder. "Don't you want just one time between us to hold on to?"

"Of course I do." That wasn't the issue. "I want more than once. I want *every* night, with you beneath me. But we can't. I won't touch you, Sara. I won't turn you into Jane or Molly or Rochelle."

"Maybe I'm strong enough to be able to handle it."

She had no idea how tempting what she was offering was. Gabriel lay as motionless as he possibly could, afraid to brush against her, afraid to inspire her hand to start up stroking again, afraid to breathe and catch a whiff of her scent, her shampoo, her femininity. "No, Sara."

"You don't have to touch me," she said, a wicked smile spreading across her face. "I can do all the touching. Just one time, that's all I'm asking for."

And she brushed his hair off his face, her fingers trailing all the way down to the tips, her gaze following her touch. He shivered from the feel of her gentle and reverent caress as she pulled back and did it again, starting at his scalp and sliding her fingers down his overgrown hair.

"It's so soft," she whispered. "So beautiful." Her gaze shifted to his lips, to his face. "You're beautiful."

"Men shouldn't be beautiful." But it was a token protest. He enjoyed that she thought he was attractive, was proud and pleased by the look of adoration on her face. She loved him and he wanted to hold that, take it inside him.

"You are beautiful. And I want you."

"Take me." His resistance was gone. He couldn't deny her what they both wanted.

She pulled back slightly. "Do you mean it?"

He nodded, knowing what he had to do was damn near impossible, but unable to say no. "But I'm not going to touch any more than I have to. I want to protect you."

Her eyes were wide, her mouth open, tongue darting out to wet her lips. "Okay. I'll do all the work, I promise."

It almost made him laugh, but his amusement was cut short by her hands roaming across his chest, exploring and scratching lightly, before descending down to the waistband of his briefs. Her fingers lingered there, wandering back and forth again, while her lips pressed onto his shoulder. Her mouth was warm, and she brushed her lips across his collarbone on the right, then the left side, before sinking her teeth gently into the flesh of his shoulder. Gabriel closed his eyes and sighed. The scent of her filled his nostrils, the hot rush of her breath dancing over his flesh, the weight of her hip leaning against his, the smoothness of her leg massaging his calf.

She touched his arms, her index finger dipping into the bend of each of his elbows. Her mouth slid in alongside his cheek, perilously close to his lips, but she didn't touch them. She brushed the stubble on his chin, traced the line of each cheekbone, ran her lips over his eyelashes, and buried her mouth and nose in his hair, her chest pressing against his, while he lay with his hands clenched at his sides, heart racing, palms sweating. Her touch was sweet and delicate and sensual, and he felt the appreciation, the wonder of her feelings for him, and he was humbled, satisfied, even as his body ached for her. It was worth the torment to have the feel of her fingers and her soft lips on him, and he watched her, the light from the hotel lamp casting shadows over her smooth skin.

Sitting up, she took her tank top off and Gabriel saw her bare breasts for the first time, her nipples taut and mere inches from his mouth. Her breasts were small and high, proportioned for her petite frame, and her blond hair spilled over her shoulders. She had slight tan marks, but it looked like it was from her tanks instead of a bathing suit, and he wanted to run his finger over the white line of her skin, but he didn't. Nor did he encircle her waist, her back, bury his lips in her neck, when she leaned forward and pressed the warmth of her chest against his, her nipples brushing over him.

She sighed at impact, eyes momentarily fluttering shut. He groaned.

"I wish you weren't so damn noble," she said. "I wish you were cruel and heartless and were perfectly willing to risk my becoming enslaved . . . I wish you would touch me everywhere, with your fingers, your lips, your tongue."

"No, you don't," he said. "You don't really mean that."

Sara peeled down his briefs, on her knees in front of him, and she glanced up at him over the length of his erection. "Right at this moment, yes, I absolutely do. I want you to be a total bastard and fuck me."

Damn it. The vehemence of her words sent a burst of hot air from her lips straight onto his cock, and he gritted his teeth, dug his fingernails into his palms, released air slowly through his nostrils, fighting for control.

"But I would regret it long-term, I know that. You're right." Her hand closed around the head of his erection briefly before she pulled it away. "And I wouldn't love you if you were a total bastard. Which I do." She licked her fingers thoroughly, then returned to him, stroking lightly up and down, her saliva creating a smooth, slick motion. "I completely and utterly love you."

"I love you, too. It's the only thing keeping me in control."

He kicked his briefs off to have a distraction from what she was doing, and to feel the freedom of being totally naked with her.

Her hands ran over his thighs, nails lightly scraping, while she bent over and took him into her mouth. Gabriel let one moan escape at the unexpected rush of ecstasy before he squeezed his lips and eyes shut. There was numbness in his hands from the pressure of the fists he was making, and his abs, thighs, biceps were all clenched tight as he fought for control, her wet, warm mouth over him, sucking slowly and languorously. Fingers tickled his testicles and he clung to his control, concentrating on enjoying her attention, even as he was painfully conscious of what he couldn't offer her in return.

When her tongue flicked across the tip of his shaft, he managed to say, "Sara. That's enough." He couldn't take any more. It had been so long since he'd felt the touch of a woman, the slick warm sensation of a woman's mouth sliding over him again and again. The last time he had been with a woman he'd been drunk, like all the times before that, and now he was seventy-five years sober. Everything was also heightened with Sara, sharper, more intense, because of his feelings, his love for her.

It made a difference and he didn't want to stroll too close to the edge too soon.

Sara sat up, her eyes bright with desire, lips shiny and wet, and she pushed her panties down over her hips and legs and dropped them onto the bed. For a second, she rested there, her hands on her ankles, her knees raised in the air, her back arching forward, hair spilling over her shoulders and chest as she looked at him, wide blue eyes unblinking, filled with love for him. Her body was gorgeous, delicate and feminine, soft curves and smooth skin, a lovely façade for an even lovelier woman. The display of her backside against the bed and her breasts resting against her knees was tantalizing, delectable, and his mouth watered, his fingers twitched, his body ached to touch, to taste, to take.

Gabriel wanted to say something, was struggling for the words to describe how beautiful she was to him, when she turned and straddled him, a knee on either side of him, her warm inner thighs pressing down on his erection, and he lost his entire train of thought. Her hands touched the bed, to the right and left of his head, and he was covered by her, surrounded, the tips of her breasts brushing his chest, and he reached back in desperation, grabbing the headboard and gripping it hard to resist the urge to touch. Not that he thought they weren't at risk for her to become addicted to him anyway, given what she was doing, but he had to try, had to stop himself from contributing.

She was rubbing herself lightly over his cock, and her body was moist from want already, so that when she poised herself over him, he knew she would slide down easily. His mouth was hot from desire, his entire body clenched tightly, coiled in anticipation, more than ready for her.

Sara said, "Oh, I do love you," then spread her thighs and pushed, sending her body down over his in a hot, wet collision.

Gabriel closed his eyes and let the moan escape, let himself release the vocal burst of pleasure, and then just lay still in the moment of throbbing, intense ecstasy. He was inside her, and he never wanted to be anywhere else.

Sara's instinct was to close her eyes when she positioned herself over Gabriel and went down on him, her body giving, opening for him, everything hot and tight and sensitive as he filled her, but she wanted to see him. Forcing her eyes to stay open, she watched Gabriel lie still beneath her, his hands clenching the headboard of the hotel bed, knuckles white, his shoulders tense, dewy sweat sheen all over his skin, the hair at his temples damp with perspiration from his efforts to stay in control. She could feel him throbbing inside her, feel the strength and desire in him, knew he wanted to move his hips and thrust into her again and again. But he didn't. He stayed still and let her be in control, let her own the moment, and she took it slow, savoring the ripples of pleasure that each movement tripped off in her. Goose bumps rose on her skin as she gripped the bedsheet and rocked her hips, moving herself up and down on the length of him.

It was everything she had expected and more. She had never been the one completely in control, had never taken with such single-mindedness, never loved a man with the entirety of her body, heart, mind, soul, the way she did Gabriel.

Normally she liked to ride a man sitting straight up, but she wanted more of a connection with Gabriel, wanted her skin on his, wanted her breath intermingling with his, so she leaned forward, let their chests collide. She dropped her head by his chin and panted, the sensations acute and overwhelming and amazing. She loved the way her hair covered his, the blond and brown strands tangling together in a messy heap. Letting go of the sheet, she gripped a fistful of his hair instead, holding on as she moved faster, hips thrusting desperately as the tightness built inside her and the hard, slick slam of him into her body had her teeth tearing into her bottom lip.

It was good, so damn good, and she ground onto him, as her panting turned to moaning, which accelerated to yelling as she drowned in sensations, frantic and desperate, loving every second, but wanting more, harder. Then she paused, knew she was going over the edge, and gave one last thrust of her hips down onto him, and came with a soundless shudder.

Sara snapped her head back and rode out the waves of pleasure as she looked down at Gabriel. Something about the look on his face, the love she saw, the desperate clawing for control, the edgy darkness in his eyes, made her instinctively pull almost all the way off of him, then push down, as far as she could, and she saw and felt his own orgasm trigger. Together, it went on, and she gripped his hair and fought for breath, relaxing onto his shoulder.

They lay there, panting, her legs around him, bodies intimately connected, skin hot and flushed, her heart pounding, mind blissfully blank.

"You have no idea what you do to me," he said, his voice low and rough, his words punctuated by his heavy breathing.

Sara couldn't move, limp and satiated on his chest. "Oh, actually, I have a pretty good idea."

❧

Gabriel knew that she wasn't going back to New Orleans with him. He felt it in the way she clung to him, the softness of her eyes, the anxiety that slowly crawled up and overtook her languid post-sex contentment.

When she said, "I don't know how to say this . . . ," Gabriel put his finger on her lip.

"You don't have to say anything. I know."

"Know what?" She had pulled off of him and slid in alongside him on the bed, her arm across his chest as she stroked his skin lightly.

"That you have to stay. I can feel your thoughts."

"Feel my thoughts?"

"Yes, it's kind of like an aura. I understand why you need time to think. It's okay. I don't want you to do anything impulsively or that you aren't comfortable with. Take all the time you need to think about us." He wanted to kiss her, but didn't dare. "I know I'm asking a lot of you."

She propped herself up on her elbow and stared down at him, frowning. "Look at me."

"I am."

"Tell me what you are."

Gabriel brushed his fingers over the tips of her hair and swallowed. "I'm a demon." It hurt to say that, but he had to own the truth.

She nodded. "Yes, I do need time to think. Go ahead and buy your ticket and head back tomorrow and I'll call you in a few days."

Only she wouldn't. He knew it as surely as he knew he was fallen.

Her decision was already made whether she even knew it or not, and her future didn't include him.

It was something he had to accept.

And he owed her a huge debt for showing him how to love again, for facing who he was and what he needed to do.

So he cupped her cheek with his hand and let her eyes lock with his, let her inside the remnants of his palace, let her see the color and shine and strength of his love.

Her eyes went wide and lost focus as she embraced his gift, and fell into a sleep that would be filled with dreams of everything that made her happy, where there was no murder, no suffering or pain or hatred.

Tomorrow she would wake up and start her life over again, and he would be gone.

Chapter Twenty-two

❧

Walking hadn't helped. Gabriel had paced down Dumaine to Chartres, across the square, down by the river, walking on and on trying to shake off his feelings, trying to exhaust his body and quiet his thoughts, but it hadn't worked. He couldn't stop thinking about Sara, couldn't stop missing her, wanting her.

The past, his mistakes, were struggling to hold him, and he was fighting to forgive himself, to look ahead to a future that was no longer isolating and self-deprecating. Tired of the anxiety, of the restless wandering, Gabriel stepped into a bar on Conti Street and made his way to the back, where it was dark and quiet.

He ordered a whiskey without hesitation. He smelled it, breathing the sting and tang deeply into his nostrils. He stared at it in his hand, then he set it back on the bar. He watched the ice gradually melt into the amber liquid and he studied the signs on the dingy walls that advertised liquor and beer. He glanced at a waitress moving around the room collecting empties.

Gabriel was amazed at how much he hurt, how he ached and burned, how the thought of Sara made everything in him convulse and squeeze in agony.

But he also knew that if there were no pain, there would never have been pleasure.

That was what living with mortals had taught him. To appreciate the beautiful moments, the joy, the love, the now.

The bartender was wiping down the counter, her thick brown hair falling across her face. She tucked it behind her ear and Gabriel saw a scar on her cheek, running from the right ear to her chin, a jagged white line that was shiny and bright against the rich end-of-summer tan glowing on the rest of her face. She must have sensed his stare because she glanced up at him and smiled, even as her fingertips brushed her scar, like she was conscious of the fact that she had exposed it, that he might be looking at it.

"You going to drink that or just look at it? You've been here an hour and you haven't even taken a sip." She pulled her hair forward again, covering her imperfection.

He had no intention of drinking his whiskey. It was sitting there to remind him of who he had been and what he was now. To show him that he was a man, master of his own destiny, owner of his actions, and unworthy of pity. He had been granted gifts that he intended to use again.

"I'm here for the company, not the alcohol."

Her brown eyes went wide. "Are you kidding? Here? Nobody's good company here, sweetie."

It was true the clientele was a bit tired and eccentric. Most of the people in the bar seemed to be propped up against the counter, with little conversation or interaction other than that with their glass.

"Do you have a pen and paper?" he asked.

"Here's a pen." She tossed one his way, then reached under the counter. "And here's a paper bag. That's the best I can do."

"Thanks. That will work." While she got someone a beer and emptied ashtrays, Gabriel sketched her, capturing the lushness of her lips, the thickness of her hair, the wide eyes and high cheekbones.

When he was done, he gestured to her.

"You want another one?" she asked, raising an eyebrow at his still-full glass. "Or how about a soft drink or something?"

"I just wanted to show you." He pushed the bag over to her, wanting her to see her the way he did, as a work of art, a thing of beauty, a woman with a lovely smile, and a cheerful approach to a thankless job.

Her curious gaze turned to shock, then pleasure. "It's me," she said in wonder. "I think."

"Of course it's you."

"You made me look . . . sort of pretty." Her fingers touched the paper.

"That's how I see you," he told her.

Her mouth rounded into an O shape. "Wow. Thanks. Can I keep this?"

"Sure." Gabriel lifted the glass of whiskey and drew in a deep breath, smelling its rich aroma again.

He set it back down. He didn't need it. Didn't crave it. Didn't want it.

He was free.

⁂

Sara was alone again. Gabriel had left, which he'd had to do. Which she had told him to do, because it was necessary. She had encouraged him to leave without her.

He wasn't human, wasn't mortal, or a man in the sense of what she had always understood. He was from another world, with different rules, and he had to go back.

She knew that.

Yet she was conscious of the fact that she was alone yet again.

It seemed her path in life, no matter which way it weaved and turned, was to be walked in solitude.

Sara drove to her mother's house and parked in front in the dark. There were lights on all over the house, and she could see two small girls running around in the family room since the blinds hadn't been drawn. She had sold the house to a young couple who had needed the reasonable price for their growing family, and were willing to overlook the fact that someone had been murdered there. It was nice to see the hustle and bustle of a family moving around the rooms, a plastic play set in the backyard.

Getting out of the car, Sara stood in the dark, leaning against her door, listening to the sounds of the neighborhood. She had grown up on this street, had a few fond memories, but was surprised to recognize, admit to herself for really the first time, that she hadn't had a traditional childhood, that she'd seen too much too fast, and had spent far too much time alone, taking care of herself. She could forgive her mother for that now. But she didn't feel any pangs of regret for selling the house either.

She was proud of herself for standing in the silence, for not letting fear of the shadows, potential dangers, force her back into her car. Tears trickled down her face, though she didn't cry for her mother, but finally, for the first time, she cried for herself. For Gabriel. For what they had both endured. For their mistakes. For the future together that seemed daunting and insurmountable.

For a person who liked definites, the logic of science, the hardest lesson Sara had to learn over and over was that there were no answers. No such thing as black and white. She needed to trust herself to understand what was right for her.

Gabriel was Gabriel, demon or fallen angel or whatever it was he really should be called. He was still just Gabriel, the man she had fallen in love with.

On impulse she pulled out her cell phone and sent him a text message. *Are you the Gabriel who came to Mary?* It was a weird question, but one that had been gnawing at her. She didn't know what she believed exactly, or why it mattered, but she needed to know what he would say.

Her phone chimed two minutes later. He had replied already. *No. I was a lesser angel.*

Relief seemed a strange emotion, but it was there, intense and immediate. That would have been too much, too difficult to accept, too unnatural to think of what she felt for him in such an extreme context. Manners dictated she answer, so she just typed, *Thanks,* and left it at that. He wouldn't question her or respond back. She knew that about him. He would let her have the time and space she needed, and she appreciated that.

The scene in front of her tantalized, beckoned her. The lure of hearth and home and children. If she went to Gabriel, she would never have a family, never have babies to raise.

But who was to say she would if she didn't go to him? Who was to say that she would ever find a man she loved enough to share her life with, children with?

No answers.

Except she did know that she wasn't afraid of being alone anymore.

She wasn't afraid of anything.

Chapter Twenty-three

✤

Foreword to *The Stain of Crime* by Gabriel St. John

When a murder occurs and a suspect is in custody, media attention quickly shifts to the accused. What kind of person are they? Why did they do it? Most people are incapable of understanding what motivates a criminal, yet that is always our focus. We want details, explanations, answers. They don't exist. They kill because they are murderers. It isn't our responsibility to evaluate individuals or their motivations, but to ensure that they are punished for their crimes, and that the focus remains on the victims.

I have tried to do that in the cases of Anne Donovan and Jessie Michaels, but ultimately, their deaths are overshadowed by the investigations that failed to guarantee justice for these women.

The dead speak, but the living are louder.

"Are you sure this is a good idea?" Jocelyn eyeballed her with a great deal of doubt as they stood on the curb at the airport.

"I'm sure." Well, not necessarily that it was a good idea, but Sara was sure she had to do it.

Jocelyn gave her a hug, bending at the knees so she could be at eye level from her nearly foot advantage over Sara. "Call me if you need anything. And don't hesitate to bail if things get weird. You can stay with me as long as you need to."

"Thanks, you know that means a lot to me." Sara hugged her back. "But it's going to be fine. Good."

Grabbing her suitcase handle, she walked into the airport, giving Jocelyn a smile and a wave over her shoulder. It *was* fine, and all good. It felt right to be going back to New Orleans. Like returning home. It wasn't logical since she had only lived there for a few weeks, and considering that sometimes the city had made her downright uncomfortable. It was eclectic and odd and intriguing and occasionally it had felt unsafe, but she missed it. Missed the smells, the rough sidewalk, the friendly smiles, the clip-clop of the horses rushing past with their carriages carrying tourists, the drip of water from freshly hosed balcony ferns.

She had fallen in love with New Orleans. And she had fallen in love in New Orleans. The pull of both was too strong to ignore.

It had been five weeks since Gabriel had left, and she hadn't spoken to him other than the text message the day after he'd left. She hadn't been able to pick up the phone and call. Being with Gabriel, understanding who and what he was, making love to him while he had struggled to hold back, keep his hands and mouth off of her, had been overwhelming, lovely and intense, heartbreaking. She had needed distance afterward.

Now she knew she didn't want any space between them at all. She wanted to go back to him, on her terms, in control of her emotions, knowing she could get a job in New Orleans in a forensics lab, knowing that if her conversation with Gabriel went well, she could move her possessions, her life, to him and it wouldn't be a sacrifice. They could make it work, despite their obvious obstacles.

It had taken four weeks to make her decision, but in the seven days since she had, she'd slept a solid six hours every night. She felt healthy, well rested, vibrant, full of energy and confidence.

She had even called her grandfather. He had been so pleased to hear from her, he had choked up on the phone, and

Sara couldn't wait to meet him in person. He had lost both his wife and his daughter, and she a mother. Together maybe they could forge a relationship, take comfort in getting to know each other. Healing past the hurt.

She wasn't afraid to be alone, but she could choose not to be.

Sara was looking forward to seeing her kitten again too. She had missed Angel and had wanted to send for her, but somehow calling Gabriel and asking him to ship Angel to Florida had seemed like she would be saying something she didn't really intend to. She hadn't wanted him to think she was never coming back.

Yet why would he think anything else given that she hadn't spoken to him in five weeks? She wasn't sure. But he was the one who had left without saying good-bye. And she had understood why he had done that, and she was certain he would understand why she hadn't called. They had never been demanding of each other, and that was part of what made her relationship with him so comfortable.

It was all good. She was going to talk to him, express the concerns she still had about the murders, ask him all her many questions about who and what he was, and make him an offer.

Hopefully it would be one he couldn't refuse.

❧

Gabriel lay on his living room floor staring at the ceiling. There was a vicious crack up there he'd never noticed. Interesting that he and the building, this apartment, had existed together in New Orleans through a hundred and fifty years. Through addiction, murder, hurricanes, they had survived, and they had both changed so very little. There was a defiance to them now, a stubbornness to stand stronger and sturdier in the face of such small expectations from the world, to be exactly as they pleased. Or maybe that was just him.

Or more likely still that he needed to stop working sixteen-hour days and roaming around the Quarter for hours on end. It wasn't really all that normal to be lying on the floor, but it felt good. He felt good. He had just wanted to stretch out while he edited the first three chapters of his manuscript, so he had printed them out and read them above his head, enjoying the hardwood pressing into his spine, forcing his muscles to relax.

Eventually he had stopped reading and had taken to just staring at the ceiling, just thinking.

He was pleased with his progress on the book. The first draft was written. Since it was going to be his last true crime book, he wanted it to be solid, something he and Sara could both be satisfied with. And the sooner he was done, the sooner he would have a legitimate reason to contact Sara, which he really wanted to do. He wanted desperately to hear her voice, just to talk, but he had to give her the space she needed.

Even if it sucked.

There was a knock on his door. Probably his landlord. He had been hanging around the building for two days overseeing some repairs.

"Come in," Gabriel called, no intention of getting up. He was extremely comfortable on the floor.

The door opened and he heard, "Gabriel?"

It was Sara. He whipped his head to the side and saw her standing in his doorway, smiling tentatively. It was really her, Sara, standing in his doorway and wearing jeans. He'd never seen her wear jeans before, and he liked the way the denim showed off her legs. Her hair was up in a bouncy ponytail, her skin fresh and clear, the shadows under her eyes lighter. She seemed to have gained about five pounds, and overall she looked very healthy. The best he'd ever seen her. She looked amazing.

"Sara," he said, unable to prevent a smile from breaking out on his face. Damn, it was so good to see her. He had missed her intensely.

Yet her smile was fading as she looked at him, glanced around the room. "Are you okay? Why are you lying on the floor?" She stepped over an empty pizza box. "And it looks like you've stopped cleaning since I left."

That was probably true. He sat upright and drew his knees up, surveying the room with its many piles of papers, laundry, and food wrappers. "I'm a disgusting pig when I'm writing a book. It's just part of my process."

"Part of your process is to stop taking out the trash?" She picked up the pizza box and three soft drink cans and walked into the kitchen.

"Yep." He stood up and shook his hair off his face.

She reappeared empty-handed and gave him a smile, gazing up at him from under her eyelashes. Pointing to his shirt, she said, "And you stop doing laundry?"

Glancing down, he realized there was chocolate on his T-shirt. "Yep." Then because chocolate and pizza boxes and papers didn't matter when he was faced with her in front of him, in the flesh, he reached out and touched her arm with just one finger, sliding it down her warm, smooth skin. "I'm so glad you're here. I missed you, babe, a lot."

The softness in her eyes and the wide, genuine smile were both reassuring. "I missed you, too."

It wasn't enough, to say those words, it didn't even begin to encompass what he meant. How could he explain that while he had been doing so well, working so hard, and reaching outside of himself for the first time in years, he had missed her? That he thought about her every day, that he longed to hear her voice, smell her cinnamon scent, touch her soft skin and hair. That he ached with want and loneliness to just see her, be with her, feel her. Words weren't enough, would never be specific or emotional enough to convey the depth of his love, his passion, his yearning for her.

She stepped in closer to him, dropping her purse onto the floor. Gabriel stood still, wondering how close she would get, aching to touch her, to take her in his arms and feel her body, her skin, her hair, her very existence. He wanted to own the right to hold her, to know that when she walked into a room, her connection was to him, that no matter who she was with or what she did, her relationship with him was the most important in her life.

Moving in alongside of him, she brushed his hair off his shoulder and murmured in his ear. "Don't worry, I know you can't touch me." Her lips ran along his jaw, a gentle caress. "I just want to be near you. I want to love you. I want to be with you."

Longing, intense and worse than any need for absinthe had ever been, arose in him, and he couldn't prevent himself from leaning his head back, moving away, needing space before he grabbed and took, and through his weakness ruined the beauty of who Sara was and what they shared. "I love you too, Sara, in ways that I can't even describe. I look at you and I can't believe that I can feel this much for someone."

He wanted to say more, needed to remind her that what he

wanted and what he had to do were two separate things, but Sara stopped him.

"You don't have to say it," she said. "I know. I'm here knowing it. It's okay, for now. I want to be with you and see where it takes us."

An unpleasant thought suddenly flooded over him. Maybe she was back because she had made love to him in Florida. Maybe she had returned because she *had* to have him, because compulsion had demanded she be with him. "Was this a choice? Or were you driven to be here?" He didn't know how else to ask without insulting her.

Her eyes narrowed. "If you're asking if I'm going to beg like Rochelle or those other women, the answer is a big fat no. I won't beg to be with you. I love you, I want to move in with you, but you're never going to hear pleading coming from my lips. If you don't want me or this, I'll go back to Florida and I'll move on. I'll be perfectly fine."

Apparently he had insulted her anyway. The longer she spoke, the feistier her words became, and Gabriel tried not to grin at her. It was a relief to hear her getting offended at the very idea of begging him for anything. And he knew she would go on without him. She was a survivor.

"Sorry. Just checking."

Giving a huff of exasperation, she whacked his arm, which startled him. Sara had never been playful with him, and he liked it. So he laughed, his pleasure that she was standing next to him, that she loved him, full and rich and overflowing.

Sara watched Gabriel laugh as a grin spread huge and wide across his face, the deep timbre of his voice loud in the quiet room, and she was overwhelmed. She didn't think she had ever actually heard him laugh before, and God, it was a sexy thing. Not pretty, and maybe even mildly obnoxious, but sexy as hell because there was joy on his face. A happiness that she had never seen there before, and she realized she hadn't been aware of its absence until she saw and heard it. She burst out with her own laugh.

"It's not funny," she told him, and it wasn't. Yet somehow it was. And it felt amazing to laugh with him. "Now clean this apartment up. I'm not moving into this filth."

"Yes, ma'am," he said, reaching for the nearest empty soft

drink can, but then ruining the effect by sticking his tongue out at her.

Which was so casual, so free, so out of character yet somehow so Gabriel that she laughed even harder. It was right, it was good, it was so hopeful, the sound of their laughter intermingling, that the questions didn't matter. The ambiguity, the mysteries, the unknown, didn't really matter as much as it did to just be together, to share this moment, this day, this life with each other.

Sara spotted Angel lying in the sun spot on the floor, and went to greet her kitten. The cat purred as she scooped her up, and with Angel in her arms, she stepped back out into the hall and pulled in the suitcase she'd left outside the door. Rolling it inside the apartment, she let go of the cat and the handle and picked up another empty pizza box. It boggled the mind to consider how many pizzas he could have possibly consumed in five weeks, and she grabbed a napkin stuck to the box and wiped at the grease spot it had left on the table. It was then she saw the sketchbook shoved to the back of the table, opened to a drawing in pencil of her chewing her lip, studying a paper in her hand. Sara flipped the page and found another of her lying in bed on her side, back visible, wearing a T-shirt, the sheet up to her waist. Then another of her dancing in her miniskirt, legs bent, arms out, a sassy smile on her face. And one of her naked, sitting with her knees to her chest, her eyes shiny and filled with love, lust.

Sara glanced over at Gabriel, unable to speak.

He was watching her. With a small smile and a shrug, he said, "I told you I've been busy."

She could definitely live like this.

❧

"I thought the same thing," Gabriel said to Sara later, over Cajun food he had snagged from a restaurant up the street. He suspected he was talking a lot, frequently with food in his mouth, which wasn't classy or attractive, but he was so damn glad she was back that the words were tripping over each other to get out of his mouth. He had the sense that he needed to say everything as quickly as possible in case she disappeared and he never had another chance.

They had spent the afternoon companionably shoveling out his mess, and now while they ate they were dissecting the questions that still remained in the murder cases.

Sara shook her head and picked up her water, sitting on the sofa with her legs crossed. "I just can't see why Marguerite would murder four generations of women without a more concrete reason. I mean, I sincerely doubt my grandmother was having an affair with Rafe."

"Here are my concerns," Gabriel said. He had given a lot of thought to the conclusion of Marguerite as murderer as he'd written the book during the last few weeks and there were still some seriously loose threads dangling. "Why would Raphael buy the house on Dauphine? That seems incredibly random for a man who never admitted he was aware of Jessie's relationship to Anne. Nor did I ever consider Raphael at all emotionally involved with Anne. Secondly, you said there was a Bible verse on that absinthe bottle. Given what Raphael was quoted during the trial as saying, that seems like too large of a coincidence. Why would both Marguerite and Raphael be using Bible quotes?"

"I don't know. That's been the problem the whole time. Too many questions. And I want to know what happened to Rafe's stuff in his condo. If he wasn't involved with Marguerite, how did she know he moved out? And was he planning to take his stuff to the house on Dauphine Street? Why would he do that? And who sent the crime scene pics?"

"I don't know either." Gabriel abandoned his plate of food and went to his office. Bringing his laptop back into the living room and sitting on the couch next to Sara, he opened his pictures file and clicked on the folder that contained all the shots he'd taken for the book. He wanted a look at the house on Dauphine Street for some reason. Wanted to see if he could see Raphael in the top window. He cropped and enlarged the photo of the front of the house, but he didn't see anything.

"You think it was Raphael in the window?" Sara asked.

"I don't see who else it would have been. Did it look like him?"

"I don't know. It was so quick, so out of context . . . I wouldn't have expected to see him."

Since Gabriel was already in the folder, he started ran-

domly clicking through all the pictures he'd taken that day—
of the street sign, the house, Sara on the street, Anne's tomb—
looking for something, anything he hadn't noticed before.

"What's that?" Sara touched the screen, right on the upper
left of Anne's tomb.

"It's graffiti." Which he didn't remember being there when
they had visited the tomb. He had thought the tomb was
freshly painted. But there was clearly writing on it.

"What does it say?" Sara was squinting at the screen.

Gabriel clicked Edit and enlarged the photo. It was a little
grainy, but they could read the words.

" 'In Him we have redemption,' " Sara read.

"Where have I heard that before?" Gabriel stared hard at it.
"And do you remember that being on the tomb? I could have
sworn there was no writing on the tomb when we were there.
We would have noticed this . . . it's not normal graffiti."

Sara grabbed his wrist. "Gabriel. Where are the crime
scene photos of my mother?"

"In my office. Why?"

"I have a terrible feeling . . . Will you go get them?"

"Sure." He stood up, handing her his laptop. He had no
idea what they would see in those pictures, but he agreed with
her. He had a bad feeling too. None of this was right and none
of it was a coincidence. There was an answer, he just had to
find it. The envelope was in his desk drawer, and he undid the
clasp, pulling out the graphic pictures. Flipping through them
as he walked, he scanned them carefully, hoping to avoid
showing Sara the horrific images if at all possible.

He didn't see anything he hadn't noticed before. It was
true, the one shot looked like it had been taken from the window, which was odd, but he supposed possible for the police
to have done.

Sara was holding her hand out. "Let me see them."

Wanting to delay the inevitable and hopefully preserve her
feelings, Gabriel turned the stack over and shuffled through
them looking at their backs. There was writing on the backside of the one picture. "Hold on."

Lifting it up, he looked closely. The writing was small, in
the upper left-hand corner. " 'Through His blood, the forgiveness of sins.' "

Holy shit. Gabriel gripped the picture, glancing over at Sara. "These go together. The words on the tomb and this. That's all one quote. 'In Him we have redemption through His blood, the forgiveness of sins.' It's Ephesians."

Her face had gone completely white. She dropped his laptop on the couch and jumped up. "Where's that bottle?"

"What bottle?" Gabriel jammed the pictures back into the envelope. "I've seen that quote before, Sara."

"So have I. On the absinthe bottle. Where is that bottle? The one I found on the doorstep."

"I don't know. I think I put it in the kitchen." He couldn't even remember what he had done with it, and his mind was distracted, shocked by the knowledge of where he had seen that same quote. He should have known. He should have pursued it.

She was already in the kitchen, opening cabinets. A second later she reemerged with the green bottle in her hand. Yanking the label off the neck, she handed it to him. "See? It's the same damn quote."

Gabriel read the paper tag, obviously printed on a computer. He couldn't believe he had shoved the bottle into a cabinet without even looking at the stupid label. "Sara, I saw this quote too. On Raphael's will."

Raphael had done it after all. The fucking bastard. Gabriel took deep breaths, trying to control the swell of anger, the disgust, the recrimination.

Sara shook her head, face pale, eyes wide. "Oh no . . . you're not saying . . ."

Nodding his head once, he said quietly, "That's exactly what I'm saying. I'm sorry. I'm so sorry."

"Why? Why would he do that?"

The pain, the betrayal in her voice sliced through his heart. "I don't know, babe, I just don't know." Gabriel wanted to soften the blow, wanted to take her suffering away, wanted to make everything okay for Sara forever and always, but he couldn't do that. Sara surprised him though. She reached out, touched his arm briefly, and nodded.

"I know you don't know. It was a rhetorical question, really. I'm sure we'll never know, or understand, and that's okay. Well, not exactly okay, but we'll deal with it."

Gabriel was impressed all over again. Sara had been dealt a bad hand most of her life, and yet she was an amazing, strong, and giving woman, and he loved her all the more for it.

"I still have that will." He had shoved it in his back pocket, then tossed it in the backseat of his car. "It's in my car."

She followed him as he jogged down the steps, two at a time. He should have known not to trust Raphael, should have known that a killer was capable of lying.

He yanked open the back door to his car and found the papers on the floor. What he saw made his heart nearly stop. "Holy shit."

"What?"

"He told me this was his will . . . It's not his, it's yours." It had Sara's name on the top, and it glared up at him, taunting and macabre.

"What?" She tried to yank it away from him, but he held on to it. "Gabriel . . . I didn't make this will."

"I know." And he was going to kill Raphael for being sick enough to do such a thing.

"So what do we do now?" she asked, still gripping the neck of the absinthe bottle, her eyes wide.

He was going to track down Raphael, but he didn't want to scare her. "First I want to go to Anne's tomb. I don't remember that writing being there, yet it showed in the picture. Which means there's no doubt that Raphael wrote it. Only a demon could pull that trick. You don't have to go with me. I'll be fast. I just need to see for myself."

He wanted absolute confirmation of the truth, wanted to know that for a hundred and fifty years the answer had never had anything to do with him. He wanted to know beyond a shadow of a doubt that Raphael had killed Anne and Jessie and all those other women. Then he was going to find the bastard and figure out why. And punish him.

"No, I'll go with you." She took his hand. "We're in this together. We're together."

Yes, they were. He crumpled up the papers into a ball and nodded. "Okay, let's go."

Chapter Twenty-four

❦

Sara followed Gabriel into the cemetery in the dark, realizing suddenly why it was so easy for him to break a lock and gain entrance. He had strength, powers she didn't understand. She also now knew that he didn't have to fear mortals the way she did, that he could protect himself, and her, from common criminals like muggers. It was reassuring at the same time it was unnerving. She didn't, couldn't, comprehend the full scope of who and what he was.

"Walk next to me," he said, slowing down and gesturing for her to fall in beside him. "I don't sense anything, but I want you close to me."

No complaints from her. She wasn't afraid, but she wasn't entirely comfortable either. The cemetery was quiet, the tombs rising stark and cold against the darkness, the crunch of the shells beneath her feet loud and obvious.

She was sure that if the writing had been on Anne's tomb that day they had visited, when Gabriel had taken the shots, they would have noticed it. In her mind, she could picture the day perfectly, the tomb crisp and clean, bright white, freshly painted, the heat crushing her as she leaned on the fleur-de-lis fence, staring at the blank spot where the nameplate had fallen off. She would have noticed graffiti.

Gabriel had a flashlight, and when they stopped at Anne's tomb, he shone it all over the front surface. Sara didn't see anything at all. No writing.

There was no explanation why, but it was obvious that Rafe, who she needed to think of as Raphael, had been involved in the murders, involved with Marguerite far beyond what Sara had understood. It made her angry, because enough was enough, damn it. She didn't want to feel the sorrow, didn't want to suffocate yet again under its crushing hopelessness, didn't want to feel the sting of betrayal. But she surprised herself. The wash of pain when she had discovered the truth had been short and shallow, and as she stood staring into the darkness, at the tomb of a woman who had lost her life to the violence and insanity of a demon, Sara felt intact, whole, safe, strong.

Nothing could destroy her.

Suddenly Gabriel was in front of her, pushing her, his hand over her mouth. In the dark, she couldn't see his face, just his outline and the beam of the flashlight bouncing around the ground as his hand moved erratically, pushing her up against the fence. Then before she could process, focus in the dark, gain her balance, he had her completely around the side of the tomb.

"Stay still," he whispered in her ear. "Don't move until I come back for you. I don't want you getting lost in the cemetery."

She wanted to ask what the hell was the matter with him, but his hand was so tight over her mouth, she couldn't speak. So she closed her eyes and concentrated on projecting the words into his head. She had no idea if it worked like that, or if only he could enter her mind, but it was worth a shot. It was dark and she didn't hear anything other than the sound of their breathing, and she hated not knowing what was going on.

Then she heard Gabriel whispering in her head, like he had before. *He's here,* he said. *Don't worry, I'll take care of him.*

Cool air rushed over her as he disappeared, leaving her feeling bereft without his presence, missing the warmth of his hard body against hers, his towering masculinity hovering over her. Peering around the corner of the tomb, Sara wiped her hands on her jeans and tried to see in the dark. She could see Gabriel's back and the light from the flashlight cutting through the inky blackness, shining straight down the walkway and hitting Raphael in the face.

Even in the dark and from ten feet away, his expression made her shiver. That didn't look anything like the man she had known. This man was cruel, amused, manic, flat-out crazy.

"Have you figured it out?" he asked, his voice excited, hands in his pockets.

"That you killed Anne and Jessie?" Gabriel asked, holding the flashlight steady on Raphael's face. "Yes. Or did you make Marguerite do your dirty work for you?"

"Oh, we did it together. Marguerite finds it sexually exciting, which is crude, but there it is."

Sara clung to the side of the tomb, heart racing, eyes straining to see in the dark, knowing that Gabriel was pointing the beam on Raphael for her benefit, for her protection. She felt a little sick to her stomach and she wondered if she really wanted to hear everything Raphael might say. Up until an hour earlier, she had thought of him as Rafe, her mother's devoted boyfriend. Even knowing he was immortal, a fallen angel, hadn't altered the essence of her opinion of him. She had thought he was a nice guy. Now he was standing there and blithely saying that his real girlfriend found it exciting to slice women to pieces with him.

She felt a disgust, a hatred so profound that it overwhelmed her, kept her frozen to the wall she was leaning against, unable to look away.

Gabriel's beam shifted to the left, and suddenly Sara realized Marguerite was standing there, beside Raphael. "Hello, Marguerite," Gabriel said, his voice deceptively calm, but with a tightness Sara knew revealed his controlled anger. "It's been awhile."

"Hi, Gabriel," Marguerite replied, with a sly smile and a wave. "I just want you to know it wasn't anything personal with you—you know, Anne, and the trial. I did it for Raphael, that's all."

"Feeling guilty?" Gabriel asked.

Marguerite blinked. "No, not really. Of course not. Why would I?"

"Aren't you going to ask why I did it?" Raphael asked, stepping in front of Marguerite and shoving her behind him so that she stumbled. She gave a cry of protest, but he silenced her with a look.

It was a look that sent chills down Sara's spine. She didn't know this man at all, had never seen that kind of patronizing dominance on his face, and it was disturbing, paralyzing.

"No, I'm not going to ask why," Gabriel said. "You can't possibly have any reason worth listening to."

Sara didn't want to hear it either. But obviously Raphael wanted to talk, because he spoke as if Gabriel had enthusiastically inquired.

"I know you'll understand, Gabriel. I did it because these women were stuck here in this hell of mortality. Those women were whores and drunks and strippers, and I elevated them because they showed potential, a good heart. I took them out of this world, out of their frail, weak human bodies, and have kept them with me, in a better place. I've given them immortality, and doesn't everyone want that? And I'll admit it, I was angry. You were such a mess, a sloppy drunk, wandering around in an opium haze feeling sorry for mortals and yourself, and yet you managed to steal my mistress. It was a perversion, and poor pathetic Anne needed to be saved. It hasn't been easy to do this, you know, to maintain the focus, to keep Marguerite in line, for all these years. But I couldn't be selfish."

Wondering if the ringing in her ears meant she was actually going to faint, Sara took deep breaths and struggled to stay standing, to not make a sound that would let them know she was there. Then again, maybe they were already fully aware of her. She had no real understanding of what demons could and couldn't do. But she didn't want to go down, no matter how sick and twisted and disgusting Raphael's words were. She needed to hear the truth, wanted to take it in and let it go, wanted to show him and herself that she could stand strong.

"So you put them under a demon sleep so they wouldn't be aware, wouldn't fight back, and killed them?"

"Yes. And you have me to thank for getting you acquitted for Anne's murder. I put my neck out for you."

"Marguerite defamed my character."

Marguerite spoke over Raphael's shoulder. "That's because I was worried they would pin something on Raphael. Sorry. If it was you or him that had to hang, I had to choose you."

"Why the same family?" Gabriel asked Raphael.

Raphael smiled, the corners of his mouth turning up fully in the light of the flashlight. "Because it's like the same woman over and over . . . I keep waiting, expecting improvement, and they always disappoint me. They're all the same. I thought Jessie's mother might be worth leaving here, but then I discovered she was hooked on pain meds. They're all the same . . . such a shame. Again, I thought maybe Sara was different. But then came the sleeping pills, the absinthe, having sex with a man she hardly knows . . ."

And then Raphael turned right toward her. Even in the dark, Sara could feel the weight of his stare, the sting of his malice, and she knew he was speaking directly to her. Knew in that moment that it had been him in the window on Dauphine Street, him watching her from the strip club. She felt the same shock, the same skin-crawling invasion of privacy as he locked eyes with her. "Now it's Sara's turn."

The sudden intensity of her fear crawled up her throat, choking her. His eyes were boring into her, his smile maniacal and amused, and he wanted to hurt her. Kill her. Slash her to bits with a big knife and enjoy it. Her first instinct was to run, but she knew that was a bad idea. The cemetery was dark, the paths were gravel, tombs rising in all directions, creating a maze that was easy to get lost in. And Raphael was immortal, with powers she didn't understand.

She would have to stand her ground, because despite the unnerving feeling of Raphael's eyes on her, she knew that Gabriel was between the two of them. He would protect her.

He already was.

With a speed that made an involuntary yelp leave her mouth, Gabriel was on Raphael in a dark blur. The flashlight hit the ground, plunging her into darkness, but she could hear the sounds of combat, fists landing, grunts of pain, heavy breathing. Then Gabriel must have shoved Raphael backward, because she saw him bounce off a tomb fence in the light from a street lamp. Raphael landed on the ground and rolled onto his side, swearing.

Sara, stay back, she heard in that insidious whisper Gabriel used, that erotic and comforting display of connectedness. He was in her heart, he'd been in her body, now he was in her mind.

"Okay," she said out loud, because it felt more natural to whisper the words than to think them. As soon as she spoke, she realized why he had urged her to stay away.

A beam of light shot forth from Gabriel, pinning a groaning Raphael on the ground.

"Oh, Jesus Christ," she whispered, shocked and awed in spite of what she had already known. The white translucent light illuminated the entire pathway, leaving Gabriel through his fingertips in a straight line and smoldering as it hit Raphael. Marguerite was visible again in the vivid light, cowering away from Raphael on the ground, tucking herself into a one-sided fetal position, one arm and one leg stretched out toward Raphael. Sara squinted, wondering why Marguerite was leaning like that, and realized there were transparent shackles connecting Marguerite to Raphael. Her left leg and wrist were bound to his right.

That was probably the most disturbing thing Sara had seen yet, and she eased back, clinging to the tomb next to her, wanting more space between her and Raphael. More space between her and what she didn't, couldn't, understand.

Raphael writhed in pain under the assault of Gabriel's light, but suddenly he shot straight up into the air vertically, Marguerite screaming and dangling below him, one of her sandals dropping off and hitting the fence of the tomb beneath them. She quickly righted herself and hovered next to Raphael, her arms crossed, head tucked in, shoulders slumped.

Raphael yelled in anger, "Gabriel, this has nothing to do with you. Leave and we'll call it even."

Sara watched Gabriel rise straight up in the air to stand in front of Raphael, graceful and masculine, his body tight with tension, hands in fists, voice strong and steady and confident. "It's not a matter of anything being even. It's a matter of doing what's right. You know what can be done to a fallen one."

"Yes, but if you do that to me, you have to do it to Marguerite, and you won't. I know you won't."

Sara thought Raphael was wrong. Gabriel would do what was right, what was necessary. She felt it radiating from him, like the light from his fingers, a moral strength, a conviction of character, a decision. It awed and overwhelmed her to see him as he truly was, in his element, freed from the worry and torment of thinking he might have killed Anne.

He had forgiven himself and was prepared to do the right thing.

Sara's fear eased, and she moved from behind the tomb to get a better view, to stand under the light of fallen angels.

Gabriel saw his advantage at Raphael's words. Raphael thought he could hide behind Marguerite's skirts, that Gabriel wouldn't be able to punish her. But Gabriel saw no reason to protect Marguerite. She had chosen her path, she had killed innocent women, brutally and incomprehensibly, alongside Raphael. They had acted as a serial killing team. The violence and senselessness of their perversion of their power disgusted him so thoroughly that he had no qualms about vanquishing both of them. It was his responsibility to protect humans, to protect Sara, and he would do whatever was necessary.

So he used his power, allowing himself to unleash it entirely, to feel the true scope of all that he was for the first time in one hundred and fifty years. It channeled and flowed through him, all his energy, all his strength, all the goodness he had ever owned, and it rose up strong and right and sure and turned on Raphael. The impact was like a spontaneous combustion. The second Gabriel's energy hit Raphael, the sky exploded with light, rippling out from the demon in glaring white rings, sending Gabriel's own power rushing back over him, warm and intense.

With twin screams of shock and rage, Raphael and Marguerite fell to the ground, their bodies hitting hard, a cloud of air, dust, and light unfurling in all directions.

Gabriel dropped himself lower to get a closer look and he felt it then—the wave of sorrow, of human suffering, the release of the souls of Anne and Jessie and the other women Marguerite and Raphael had killed. It flowed over him like a humid rush of air, wrapping around him and immersing him in the pain, the grief, the tears, the magnitude of human agony.

Instead of trying to close himself off, or stagger under the weight the way he had always done, Gabriel stood straight as he hovered in the air, hands out, and accepted it, took the pain, took the pleas, and absorbed them into himself. Death was the beginning, not the end, and his responsibility, his guardianship, was to comfort, reassure, steer mortals in the direction of beauty and pleasure and contentment, to ease their human suffering.

He wanted to do that again.

Watch. Guide. Protect.

Sara was standing directly behind him, having abandoned her hiding place behind the tomb. She stared at him in wonder, eyes wide, cheeks pale, mouth open.

"What happened?" she asked.

"They're dead," he said, hoping that she could handle that reality. It had been necessary.

"Dead?" she whispered, her voice a little shaky, and she glanced down at the bodies. "How? And where's the flashlight? I can't really see anything."

"Oh. Sorry." Gabriel searched around on the ground and found the flashlight where he had dropped it, the beam pointing in the opposite direction of Sara. He went to her and put it in her hand, squeezing her gently. "I'm sorry you had to see that."

"How do you know they're dead?" she asked, pointing the light directly onto Raphael and Marguerite.

How could he ever explain what he was and what he could do? There were no answers, no explanations, no human words. Gabriel just knew. "Their mortal bodies are dead. But their souls still exist inside these bodies . . . it's an imprisonment, which is exactly what they deserve."

"So what do we do now?"

"I have to dispose of them. Maybe you should leave. I don't have time to take you home though. I have to do this before the cops get here." He was surprised the police hadn't already shown up, given the lights and the noise they had been making. But the cemetery butted up to housing projects, the residents of which probably had no interest in getting involved in any potential crime and hadn't bothered to call the police.

Gabriel turned and opened the gate to Anne's tomb without waiting for Sara's answer. He didn't want to scare her, but he didn't want to get caught with dead bodies either. It was highly doubtful he'd be acquitted this time around. Stepping inside, he removed the front of Anne's tomb and opened the drawer.

"What the hell are you doing?" Sara asked, coming up behind him.

"I have to hide them, and this is actually a perfect place." Reaching into the darkness, Gabriel extracted the bag that held Anne's ashes and set it carefully on the path outside the gate.

Sara just stood there as he went over and lifted both Marguerite and Raphael up and carried them to the tomb. Gabriel felt terrible that she was watching, and he said, "Sara, close your eyes, babe. This isn't going to be pretty."

But she just shook her head. "No, I have to see. And did you know—though I'm sure you know—that when the Watchers fell, God sent the four archangels to retrieve them? Raphael bound one of them hand and foot. Gabriel destroyed some of the fallen ones by inciting them to civil war. And Michael put others in a dark cave for seventy generations. A dark cave . . . like this tomb."

Gabriel shoved Raphael into the dark opening, sweat rolling down the back of his T-shirt even as he felt a chill at Sara's words. "I'm not an archangel. I'm a fallen one."

"But you're righting a wrong . . . destroying fallen ones who were well and truly evil. And I don't think it's any sort of coincidence that you and Raphael were named after two of the archangels. And that my last name is the name of the third."

"I don't think it's a coincidence either," he conceded, crossing Raphael's legs at the ankles. It would have been a hell of a lot easier getting him in the tomb in a casket, but he had to make do, and as quickly as possible. Gabriel got the body fully into the hole and did the same with Marguerite.

Out of breath, he turned back to Sara. She was standing there, the flashlight slack in her hand, the beam bouncing around the ground, her face pale, eyes wide. "Gabriel. I have to close it with you. It's you and I. We're the ones who have to end this . . . Gabriel St. John and Sara Michaels."

"I don't think . . . ," he started, not wanting her to be a part of what he was doing. Not wanting to burden her or give her further grief, or any sort of guilt. But then he trailed off when she stepped through the gate and looked up at him. She was tenacious, determined.

She was right. They needed to do this together. It made sense, brought the past to the present full circle and ended what had started all those years ago in that nasty room on Dauphine.

He nodded. "Okay."

Her hand went over his, and they both closed the door, pushing hard. Then Gabriel sealed it shut.

The explosion sent him hurtling through the gate and crashing onto the path, flat on his back. It knocked the wind out of him and he blinked, startled, not sure what exactly had happened. His head spun as he tried to sit up, and he quickly descended again, searching in the dark for Sara. "Sara? Are you okay?"

"Gabriel!" Sara knelt down beside him, hands brushing his hair off his face. "I'm fine. Nothing happened to me. You got hit with . . . something, and it sent you flying. Are you okay?"

"Yeah, I'm fine." Though he felt strange. Weak. Gabriel sat up quickly and almost threw up, intense nausea rolling over him.

"Sara . . ." He looked at her, looked around him, moved his legs, tested his fingers. He was fine, but he felt different. Mortal. Jesus Christ, he felt mortal. That's exactly what he felt like. "Oh my God . . ."

"What?" She was groping all over his shoulders and pushing his hair back, checking his temples and sliding her hands over his chest. "What hurts? You're not bleeding."

"There's nothing wrong with me. I'm fine." He was better than fine. He was mortal, a human, like everyone else. Like Sara. Freed from his punishment, freed from eternity. He looked over at her, excited, relieved, stunned. "It's over. I'm free."

She just blinked at him. "What do you mean?"

Gabriel stood up and dusted off his jeans, feeling a huge

sense of wonder, of clarity, of hope, of awe. "I mean that I'm no longer fallen. Nor am I an angel. I'm mortal."

Her mouth dropped open. "How do you know?"

"I know." How could he explain the difference? It was like the world around him had dimmed, his limbs had gotten heavier, the visual chaos had cleared, the sound of humanity quiet, less deafening. And at the same time, without all the sensory overload, his mind felt clearer, stronger, acute, and he was conscious suddenly of ticking time and the finiteness of life and love and talent. He had a focus he didn't remember ever really having before.

She put her hands up to her face. "Are you sure?" There was a tremble in her voice.

"Yes. I'm positive." He leaned over, brushed his lips over her forehead, wanting to linger, to savor the feeling, her, but knowing they couldn't. "We have to leave now."

She just nodded as he walked over to Anne's tomb and pulled the gate shut. Then he picked up the bag of ashes and secured it under his arm.

"Gabriel, look at the angel," Sara said, her voice low and in awe.

Turning, he followed her gaze, looking up and over his shoulder. The weeping angel statue on top of Anne's tomb had two red streaks trailing down her cheeks. Blood tears. It should have looked gruesome, but he didn't sense that was its intent.

"In Him we have redemption, through His blood, the forgiveness of sins," he murmured, as he felt the weight of guilt lift, the light of forgiveness wash over him.

Chapter Twenty-five

❦

Sara stood in Gabriel's living room as he closed the door behind them. He said he was mortal. How was that possible? How was it possible that he had ever been anything but? She felt the tightness of tears in her eyes, not of sadness or of happiness, but of emotional confusion, of uncertainty.

Where did they go from here?

But then he set Anne's ashes down on the piano and turned to her.

The look on his face made her forget any questions she had, any fears or worries she had been about to voice. He was staring at her, intensely, but with a peace, a calm, a relief, that she had never seen from him.

She stood still as he walked up to her, sensing that he was going to touch her.

He did.

His hands touched her shoulders, his thumbs brushing her hair back, before he slid up her neck, to her jaw, her chin, then cupped her cheeks in both of his hands. Sara closed her eyes, sighing at the pleasure of his warmth so close to her, his long fingers and masculine hands holding her so gently, as if she were precious.

"I'm going to make love to you," he whispered in her ear, his breath tickling her. "As a man."

Sara shivered, her arousal immediate and powerful. He was going to touch her. Something she'd thought she would never have. Her knees actually trembled, and she reached out to wrap her arms around him, to mold their bodies together, but he pushed her hands down by her side.

"Just let me feel you for a minute," he said, his nose brushing over her cheek, his lips tasting the corner of her mouth.

Her eyes drifted closed again and she stood still, overwhelmed by the simple pleasure of his exploratory kiss, his hands caressing her hair, her neck, her clavicle. His legs surrounded hers, and his waist, erection, brushed against her but shifted and moved, never coming in full contact, a soft whisper of what to expect, but a reminder that this needed to happen slowly.

Then his mouth was on hers, in a slow, devotional kiss that took her breath away. Sara sighed, her fingers reaching out and grasping the belt loops of his jeans so she wouldn't stumble. It felt so good, so pure, so warm and lovely and sensual, to finally feel his mouth again, to taste his lips and know that he was hers. He kissed her again and again, with no hurry, with no destination in mind, but with slow and easy and worshipful presses that had her breath catching, her body aching.

"Gabriel," she whispered.

His eyes were bright and shiny, a rich chocolate brown, as they trailed all over her face, as if he were memorizing her features. His fingers followed his gaze, chin to jaw to cheekbone, lingering on her bottom lip, slipping into the divot above her top lip. He tucked her unruly hair behind her ears, even touching the lobes briefly before brushing the backs of his thumbs over her eyelashes.

The warmth of his breath, the feel of his chest just barely touching hers, his fingers exploring, left her trembling, wanting more, all of him, yet at the same time ultimately satisfied. She was getting more than she had ever expected Gabriel would be able to give, and she felt it, understood it. Knew that connection people talked about, that feeling she had waited for and had never experienced until him, that conviction that the two of them were destined to be together, their feelings strong and amazing and deep.

That they had seen each other's soul and found where they belonged.

"You feel so good," he murmured. "Sara."

She had never thought her name was anything particularly special, but when he said it, when his deep voice washed over her with such devotion, such respect, such longing, she thought she would never get tired of hearing it.

And when his forehead rested briefly on hers, his hand cupping the back of her neck, she sighed again. Her body was impatient, wanting more, but at the same time she wanted the moment to stretch and last, to make up for all the weeks of being without him.

Gabriel kissed her, a press, then a pull back, again and again, quick but passionate touches that tossed over her earlier conviction. She did want more. The kisses were so intense, so teasing, so fleeting, so filled with intensity, and she tried to hold them, tried to take more, but he pulled back over and over. Her breathing hitched, her inner thighs ached, her nipples tightened painfully against her T-shirt. She clung to his jeans, her grip tightening, and she gave up trying to follow his mouth.

His hands went everywhere, lingering briefly with the barest of touches on her neck, her head, her back, her waist, while he took her mouth so fully, so completely, that she lost track of time, lost track of anything but the possession of her lips by his. Her eyes couldn't stay open, her head couldn't stay up, as she gave herself up to being taken by him, slowly and tauntingly. Worshipfully.

When his tongue finally invaded her mouth and touched hers, she squeezed his waist, rocking back involuntarily at the pleasure. But again, he didn't take hard and fast, but he explored with a control that amazed her, that left her weak, clinging to him, body humming, heart full. She could feel his erection pressing against her, but he ignored it, never attempting to grind against her, his hands staying above her waist. His tongue took hers, mimicking sex until she thought she couldn't take another second, not one more kiss or slide or suck.

He pulled entirely back, his eyes hot and dark. "You taste

so good I want to eat you," he said, and leaned forward and nipped at her bottom lip with his teeth.

Sara sucked in a breath as the bite shot an ache of desire through her. "So eat me."

"Oh, I will. But I'm going to take my time." He ran his finger along the neckline of her T-shirt, then across her bottom lip. "I never thought I would have this, never thought I would have you. I want to enjoy you."

She wanted to be enjoyed.

Sara reached out and buried her fingers in his soft hair and kissed him the way he had been kissing her, with love and longing and wonder, before pulling back.

He gave her a Gabriel smile, the kind where only the corner of his mouth tilted up, while his lips stayed together, like he had a private thought that amused and pleased him. "I love you," he said, his mouth forming the words, but no sound coming out.

Sara felt the tears again, and she wondered why she fought them. There was no shame in her emotions, no reason to apologize for the intensity of what she felt, for the feeling that this was forever, that this man, this moment, had changed her life. That she was in love. Deeply and joyfully in love, and that was worth a tear or two.

So she let a drop slide down each cheek unencumbered as she studied Gabriel, the straight line of his jaw, the whiskers that had snuck up onto his chin in the last few hours. She couldn't resist touching him, running her fingers over and down his cheekbones and his lips, before cupping his cheeks the way he had with her.

Gabriel kissed her, and Sara opened up for him, let him have everything she had to offer, let him taste her, let him feel and know that she was his.

His hands slipped lower, caressing her back as he tasted her, as their tongues tangled and she felt a hope, a happiness she had never expected to know. Because not only had she never loved any man like she did Gabriel, she had never been loved this way. Had never felt such adoration, such devotion, such true and pure love as she did from him, and the fact that he had lived for so many years only made it all that much sexier. It was like he had been waiting for her and she for him.

And just when she thought he intended to do nothing but kiss her indefinitely, he took the bottom of her T-shirt, pulled it up and over her head, and tossed it on the floor. Sara shivered from the sudden movement of air over her bare skin and from the immediate tickle of his fingertips over her shoulders and down to her elbows as he stroked her. He did that everywhere, just touching lightly, all over her arms, her stomach, her cleavage, acquainting himself with her feel, and Sara swallowed hard, pleased by his interest, his intensity, but tortured by it. Her body was tight and tense, impatient, wanting more, wanting to take him inside her. She gripped the hem of his shirt for balance and let her head fall back as Gabriel slid her bra straps over her shoulders, kissing her along the path he bared.

"You feel so good. You smell so good. Like cinnamon." He licked her flesh, the tip of his tongue tripping off goose bumps on her shoulder.

"Body oil," she said, though he probably didn't need or want an answer. His tongue slid down, down, until he was tracing the swell of her breast above her bra.

"I've wanted to touch you since the moment I met you," he said, his hair tickling her arm as he peeled down the front of her bra.

"What a coincidence. I've been wanting you to touch me since the moment I met you." Sara sucked in her breath when his finger brushed her taut nipple. She was so tight, so eager, so ready for him.

He glanced up at her, his expression serious. "But you came back knowing I couldn't."

She nodded. "Yes, I did." And she would have stayed even if the outcome had been different.

His head dipped in acknowledgment. "Thank you."

"For what?" Sara moved her hands across his chest, enjoying the firm feel of him so close to her.

"For loving me like that."

As if she deserved gratitude for that. "My pleasure."

Her bra disappeared. And his answer was to cover her nipple with his mouth, to suck it and lick and pluck at it with his teeth. Sara moaned, feeling that tug all the way down to her toes. Then she didn't even have the ability to make sound, because Gabriel was touching and kissing her everywhere. He moved from nipple to nipple, to neck, to mouth, plunging his tongue inside her and kissing her hard and fast, then soft and sweet. He kissed her chin, her nose, her eyelids, the insides of her elbows.

"I can't get enough of you," he murmured. "I want to touch you everywhere."

That worked for her. Sara buried her hands in his hair and held on, overwhelmed with desire, by his attention, his intensity. His fingers popped the snap on her jeans, and slid inside to cup her. She knew what he felt. Her panties were wet already, obviously so, and the way he pressed his finger into her softness confirmed that he knew exactly that little fact.

It was his fault for being so damn sexy, and she moved her legs a little further apart, encouraging him to touch her. She craved that moment when he took her, when he was the force behind the thrust, when he took and possessed her body with his for what was truly the first time. She had taken him last time and he had let her.

Now she wanted him to make her his.

Gabriel had been enjoying taking his time, exploring and touching Sara everywhere. He felt like he had been granted a gift so amazing and beautiful and huge he needed to reassure himself that it was real. That she was real. That he was entitled to such happiness, such pleasure.

But when she thrust her hips forward toward him, the front of her panties damp with desire, Gabriel felt the urge to take what she was offering, to finally and truly have Sara the way he had wanted to from the beginning. There was no reason to hold back this time and he knew it. He felt the lust rising hot and fast, driving him to shove down her jeans as he dominated her mouth with his tongue.

Sara gasped, her head falling back, her neck tantalizing. Gabriel licked her soft flesh and bent to make sure her jeans had cleared her knees. Then he pulled the waistband of her panties and slid his finger inside, straight down her clitoris and right inside her. Her moan, and the hot, wet feel of her eager body, made him ache with a pain so intense he knew he couldn't wait another minute. Maybe not even thirty seconds.

She was his. He loved her. And now they were both going to enjoy the fact that he could fully and freely fuck her.

Taking her by the shoulders, Gabriel demanded, "Step out of your jeans."

She did, kicking them to the side, her eyes wide and glassy with lust and love and excitement.

Gabriel turned her impatiently and pushed her against the wall. Sara's breasts jumped, her breath caught, her hands came up to spread across the plaster. He could see her ribs, the curve of her abdomen, the disarray of her hair as she waited, so beautiful and eager. Moving in closer to her, Gabriel stripped off his own shirt and jeans, reached forward, and kissed her hard, biting her, wanting that taste of her on his tongue.

He slid her panties down and melded his hard body against the warmth and softness of her, holding her right hand captive under his. Then with his free hand, he spread her legs, nice and wide, opened her, and thrust his erection fully into her.

Sara whimpered, and her hand jumped beneath his. Gabriel closed his eyes, letting himself throb inside her for a second, savoring, enjoying. Then his body demanded he move, and he did, hard, fast, furious, taking what he had waited for so long. Her body held on to his, gripping him, accepting him. Gabriel clenched her hand with one hand, her waist with the other, and buried his face in her neck, no words to express what he felt, how much he loved her, how amazing it felt to be fully and deeply inside her.

He knew when she came, her head snapping up, her eyes wide and stunned, her fingernails digging into the palm of his hand, her inner muscles convulsing around his cock, her mouth open in a silent scream.

It was more than enough to send him over the edge, letting go completely, pounding his relief, his pleasure, into her, allowing his body to do what it wanted without guilt or recrimination or personal censure. This was right, this was his future.

His happiness.

⚜

Sara woke up slowly and languorously, feeling like she never wanted to move from Gabriel's bed. Ever. The sheet had slipped at some point during the night but she wasn't cold, and her nakedness actually pleased her. She knew Gabriel wasn't in bed with her because he was what had woken her from a sound sleep. The best sleep she'd had in a year or more. It was clearly morning, given the sun streaming in the bedroom window, and while she hadn't been aware of Gabriel climbing out of bed, she knew he was in the other room because she could hear the piano.

He was playing his piano.

It was a soft song, delicate, lovely, beautiful. The sound drifted over her like the light touch of a feather, like the gentle shift of Gabriel's fingers through her hair, like the kisses he dropped on the corners of her mouth.

Sara lay still and listened, letting it wrap around her, knowing what it must mean to him to have music back in his life, his soul. When she couldn't stay away any longer, when the need to see him, touch him, surpassed her desire to give him privacy, she climbed out of bed and got one of his T-shirts out of the drawer and pulled it on. Her panties were still in the living room, left behind when Gabriel had dragged her to bed for round two.

Knowing she was smiling, knowing she was embarrassingly in love, she walked into the living room. And was devastated by him all over again. He was gorgeous. Unbelievably so. Gabriel was sitting at the piano shirtless, his jeans low on his hips, his feet bare. His hair slid over his shoulders and his eyes were closed as he played. She shifted so she could see his fingers, watch them trail over the keys, long and powerful and talented, confident in their movements.

It was mesmerizing, the way he coaxed such a beauty of sound from the piano, and she knew she could watch him for a lifetime.

But he sensed her presence and opened his eyes. Gabriel smiled at her, his hair falling forward as he kept playing. "Good morning."

"Good morning. The song is beautiful."

"It's your song."

"My song?" She didn't recognize it, but then she wasn't at all familiar with classical music. Whatever it was, she liked it.

"Yep. I wrote it for you."

Sara stared at him as he kept playing, his mastery effortless, his focus on her instead of his fingers. "What? What do you mean?" Surely he wasn't saying what she thought he was saying.

"I mean I wrote it. It's your song. It's how I hear you."

Oh, God. Sara sucked in a shaky breath, overwhelmed with love, with joy, with gratitude. "It's lovely," she whispered.

"Like you."

Sara buried her eyes behind her hand, feeling the tears demanding release. Sniffling, she let them trail down each cheek. "I'm glad to see that losing your immortality didn't take away your talent. It's incomparable."

His smile was satisfied. "It's a gift. As are you."

Sara went over to him, needing to touch him, wanting to feel his mouth on hers. She leaned over and kissed him, a lingering embrace that had her sighing. "I love you."

"I love you too," he said, sliding his hand under the T-shirt to cup her bare backside. "Now let's go get some coffee."

Sara laughed. He was as random as always. "Okay. Let me put pants on."

"Probably a good idea."

⁂

Five minutes later, Gabriel pushed open the courtyard gate and stepped out onto the sidewalk, Sara holding on to the crook of his elbow. The bag of Anne's ashes was in his other hand.

"It's just beautiful out," Sara said, pausing to breathe in deeply. "It's not too hot."

"What should we do today?" he asked her, unable to stop himself from kissing the top of her head. Twice. And a third time for good measure.

"I want to look for a job. It's time for me to go back to work in a lab."

She spoke with an easy conviction and Gabriel was pleased to hear it.

"And arrange to ship my stuff here."

He looked at her in amusement as they started to head down toward Chartres Street. "Are we going to need a bigger apartment?"

"No. I like this apartment."

"We'll have more room if I sell my absinthe spoon collection." Not that it took up any space really, but it was the segue he'd been looking for, a way to reassure her his addictions were a thing of the past.

She glanced up at him. "Only if you want to."

He nodded. "It's time." That was the past, and he wanted to embrace the power and beauty of living in the now.

They walked in the warmth, Sara's sandals shuffling on the sidewalk, her sky blue skirt billowing around her legs, crossing through Jackson Square. He could leave New Orleans now, but he wouldn't. It was home.

As they climbed up the hill to cross the tracks and reach the river, an old man approached them with a smile.

He held out a vibrant pink flower to Sara. "Have a wonderful day, precious," he said, with a nod of his head and a hand flourish.

"Thank you," she said and accepted the offering with a bright, warm smile.

Gabriel tried to tip the man, but he waved him off. When Gabriel turned to say something to Sara, tears were in her eyes. "What's wrong?"

"It's a hot pink carnation," she said. "My mother's favorite flower."

"I'm sorry." He didn't know what else to say, but she shook her head.

"Don't be sorry. It's good. It's a sign. She's telling me she's okay."

Sara stopped in front of the river, not on the observation steps that were crowded with tourists, but fifty feet away. They were above the river, not in direct contact with the water, but the privacy worth the distance.

Removing the tie to the bag, Gabriel tipped it over and watched as Anne's remains drifted down through the air. Sara tossed the carnation after, and its weight pulled it faster so that it caught up with the ashes and intermingled among them, until they collectively descended into the water.

Fallen.

Gabriel took Sara's hand into his and walked away from the river.

Turn the page for a look at

THE TAKING

the next paranormal romance
by Erin McCarthy.
Coming soon from Jove Books.

NEW ORLEANS, 1878

The latest yellow fever epidemic held the city in its iron grip for nine days and nights, the bodies piling up like corded wood in the cemeteries, in the hospitals, and in the streets themselves, as ordinary business and cheerful living bowed in deference to death. With nary a streak of sun in the sky, the shrouded city was quiet save for the constant clatter of carriages carrying corpses and the roar of cannons in the square to clear the putrid air. The tally of dead raised daily—dozens each hour—and the endless opening of doors to bring out a parade of victims to the carts and wheelbarrows waiting on the streets contributed to a weary denizen of despair, of darkness, of numb drudgery.

No stores, businesses, or banks were open, as those who could fled to the country, and all other conveyances were pressed into service as hearses, while the cloud of the smoke from burning bodies created a stinging mist that lingered for days. The agony of melancholy and the silence of profound grief crept into every corner, every house, as the disease swept mercilessly from block to block, taking the young, the old,

*the rich, and the poor with equal enthusiasm—the sick,
the dying, and the dead all intermingling.*

*I performed innumerable Last Rites from morning
to night each endless day as the plague raged on, both
on those I knew and victims I had never before laid
eyes on. Children I had only recently baptized, adults
seeking absolution for their final sins on earth, those
with no one to grieve them, and whole families who left
this earth together, all received my prayer.*

*Specific tales of tragedy abound everywhere, from
the death of a young bride on her wedding night, to the
unfortunate end of the wealthy and proud Comeaux
family that dominated Louisiana business and politics
for decades. Seven members of the Comeaux family sat
down to dine, hearty and hale and confident in their
place of power in our city, on the second day of the in-
festation, and twenty-four hours later all save one were
dead. Camille, the Comeaux's youngest and unmarried
daughter, is left at the tender age of twenty void of her
entire family. One can only ask what such a loss would
do to the state of one's mind and heart, and how many
will be forced to confront such a future in the epidemic's aftermath.*

—From the diary of Father John Henri, Catholic priest

Camille Comeaux lit the candles on either side of the
French doors to the gallery, igniting taper after taper, and
watching with pleasure as the flames cast dancing shadows on
the wall behind, framing the doors with a moving, undulating
arch of darkness.

"Don't light too many," Felix said from behind her, his
hands coming to rest on her shoulders. "You'll risk a fire."

Enjoying the press of his strong fingers on her bare shoulders, Camille lit another candle and still one more, pleased
with the effect, excited by the danger. If the draperies caught
on fire, it would only be fitting. Conjuring the dead deserved
drama.

"I want to be sure it works," she told him. She wanted that
more than anything.

She knew that Felix didn't understand her drive, her need,

but then she knew he was using her, the same as she was using him. He wanted her wealth, and perhaps her body, while she wanted—needed—his power. His magic.

"It will work," he said, leaning around her and snuffing the last two candles she had lit by squeezing the flames between the tips of his thumb and forefinger. "I don't perform any ritual that isn't successful."

It was easy to believe such confidence, and Camille studied his profile, pleased with her choice of hoodoo practitioner. Daring, bold, and successful, Felix was also singularly beautiful, with the thick dark hair and rich skin tone that revealed the African heritage of his mother's family, along with the narrow, aquiline nose of his French father.

At some point soon he would take her virginity, along with the vast amounts of her money he had already acquired. She knew that. Perhaps even tonight. Regardless of when it happened, it was inevitable, given the course she had set them upon, and she could not regret it. The future had been altered irrevocably when her entire family had perished in the fever four months earlier, and every day, every decision had led her here to this moment.

This was the night she would call forth her mother and father and sisters from the grave.

Felix stared at her, and she stared back, a smile playing about her lips. There was a question in his brilliant blue eyes, a doubt that she could see the ritual through to the end, and it made her laugh out loud. She had no doubts, none whatsoever, and she would do whatever was necessary to speak to them, to express her love, her loneliness, her grief and desperation.

"Are you sure?"

"Yes." Perhaps he thought she was mad. Perhaps she was. Certainly twelve months earlier she would never have imagined that she would be standing in her parent's bedroom *en chemise* with a man such as Felix, the expensive chest of drawers from France converted to an altar for his implements to aid in the ritual. A year ago, Camille had been a pleasant, content young woman of wealthy means, her days busy with embroidery, playing her instrument, receiving callers with her mother, and doing acts of charity in the hospitals of less salubrious neighborhoods.

But she was no longer that girl. She was a woman now, a manic, angry woman with no one to love her, and no one to live for. Camille grabbed the open wine bottle off the altar and drank straight from it, the sweetness sliding down her throat. "I am absolutely certain."

Felix didn't hesitate. He closed the distance between them and kissed her, a hot, skillful taking of her mouth that had Camille's head spinning and her body igniting as the candles had. He gripped the back of her head, his tongue tasting and teasing, his thumbs brushing over the front of her chemise, finding her nipples and stroking them.

Camille was always surprised at how good it felt when Felix touched her, how wonderfully free and alive it made her feel. She ran her fingers over his bare chest, excited by the hard muscles, by the power his body contained. Whether it was the wine, or the excitement, or the sexual desire stirring to life, she didn't know and didn't care, but she could see through half-closed eyes that the room was in motion, the shadows pressing in and back out again, the furniture crisp and sharp, the candles appearing pliant and alive.

Everything was dark and warm, the yellow glow of the tapers plunging the altar into light, yet leaving the corners of the room black and secretive. Felix slid his tongue across her bottom lip and she shivered, her body aching deep inside, between her thighs. He stepped away and turned his back to her, leaving her breathing hard and reaching up into her hair to pull the pins away, to let the brown tresses tumble over her shoulders. Her bare feet dug into the rug and she licked her moist lips, the heat from the sultry September night, from the candles, from her own pleasure and excitement, creating a deep flush on her face along with a dewy sheen between her breasts.

When Felix turned around to face her again, he had a snake in his hand, its long brown body wriggling in an attempt to escape. But his captor brandished him high in the air, chanting lowly. Camille hadn't known about the snake, had never guessed one of the baskets was holding a living reptile, and she gasped. Not from fear, but from excitement. This was right. This was magic.

Felix's hand moved the snake so skillfully that it looked as if it were dancing, its body moving to a rhythm his master created, a decadent, primitive form of expression. A glance down the length of Felix's hard chest and past his trousers showed that his bare foot tapped out a beat, and with his free hand he pulled a stick from his pocket and hit the chest of drawers, the sharp rap of the rhythm loud in the closed room. The hand tapped out time, the snake did his dance, Felix's foot went up and down, but the rest of him held still—a hard, lean body of control.

"Dance for me, Camille," Felix commanded, his eyes trained upward.

She did, first swaying softly, hands in her loose hair, then she closed her eyes and let her body feel the rhythm. It started in her feet and worked its way up to her hips, to her shoulders, until she was careening to the staccato beat, feeling it from inside her, springing to life, wanting out, needing air to fan the flames.

"You have the power," he told her. "The magic comes from you. Reach for it."

It did. She could feel it boiling up in her body, and she would have it. Camille opened her eyes as she moved, dancing in a pounding circle, her arms reaching up and out, sweat trickling down her back, and she loosened her chemise in a sharp tug at the ribbons, wanting the air, wanting the brush against her bare skin, wanting Felix to see her, wanting to connect with her very essence, the heart of who she was.

Felix brought the snake to her, and where she would normally have recoiled, Camille didn't flinch or retreat, but instead danced for Felix while the reptile twisted and turned in front of her. They moved together, and she tore at her chemise with trembling, excited hands until she was completely naked, writhing like the snake, her fingers in her hair.

"You *are* ready," Felix said.

She was. She was ready for whatever this night would bring.

My life…
My love…

My Immortal

By *USA Today* Bestselling Author
ERIN McCARTHY

In the late eighteenth century, plantation owner Damien du Bourg struck an unholy bargain with a fallen angel: an eternity of inspiring lust in others in exchange for the gift of immortality. However, when Marley Turner stumbles upon Damien's plantation while searching for her missing sister, for the first time in two hundred years it's Damien who can't resist the lure of a woman. But his past sins aren't so easily forgotten—or forgiven…

"*My Immortal* is truly a passionately written piece of art." —*Night Owl Romance*

penguin.com

M174T1107